A QUESTION OF INTELLIGENCE

The CIA data made Blaise's hands sweaty. Every important file on Human Enhancements had a special programming booby trap. Sweat collected on his neck. "They're waiting for us, Alfie. Or someone like us."

YES

Blaise stared at the computer's answer. No percentage of probability, just an unequivocal yes. "List accessible files, Alfie."

I CAN ACCESS ANYTHING

"Stop bragging and stick to federal-related agencies."

Alfie left his answer at the top of the monitor like some sort of challenge. Blaise could not remember programming Alfie for that kind of behavior, yet he must have. Alfie was counterfeiting an emotional response. But Alfie had no emotions . . .

Also by G.C. Edmondson and C.M. Kotlan
Published by Ballantine Books:

THE CUNNINGHAM EQUATIONS

THE BLACK MAGICIAN

G.C. EDMONDSON
& C.M. KOTLAN

A Del Rey Book

BALLANTINE BOOKS • NEW YORK

The relationship between thought and action is not always clear. It would seem that the thought precedes the action. Yet an individual may act thoughtlessly, doing an act that would not be done if conscious thought was given to it. Definitions are precise but reality isn't and even the most careful theorum may be clouded by what actually happens.

From a seminar on
THE CUNNINGHAM EQUATIONS

A Del Rey Book
Published by Ballantine Books

Copyright © 1986 by G.C. Edmondson and C.M. Kotlan

All rights reserved under International and Pan-American Copyright Conventions. Published in the United States of America by Ballantine Books, a division of Random House, Inc., New York, and simultaneously in Canada by Random House of Canada Limited, Toronto.

Library of Congress Catalog Card Number: 86-90946

ISBN 0-345-33221-0

Manufactured in the United States of America

First Edition: November 1986

Cover Art by Barclay Shaw

PRELUDE

The oak had a tortured shape that shrieked in silent agony at the whole trees around it. Its yard-thick bole was charred from a long-ago lightning strike, and endless streams of ants and beetles had patiently hollowed the rotten core. The crown of green leaves was a façade, a noble gesture denying decay for one last spring.

A gentle wind rustled leaves, then swooped to the clearing, ruffling the fast-growing stalks of wild oats before sweeping across the concrete. The road wound around knots of trees, but the Mercedes was oblivious to the highway's tortuous bends. It missed the curve, bouncing straight across the meadow with the arrogant disregard of a dowager dismissing social climbers.

The hollow *boom* of collision had barely shaken the crows loose from the oak's just-leafed crown when, hour hand slow, the tree toppled. Crows wheeled overhead as the tree settled. After a time they alighted again, undisturbed by the changed angle of the branches. The clicks and groans of dying machinery made the crows restless. Occasionally one launched into flight, cawing raucously as if startled by a nightmare.

Other cars *whooshed* past the tiny grove amid the meadow, drivers apprehensive at the twisty way the road rounded trees or disappeared in hollows while passengers commanded drivers to look at the gorgeous red California poppies on the roadside or bluebonnets in the ditch.

Some were Canadians avoiding the spring thaw back home. Others were simply shoppers going to San Francisco. None saw the cream-color Mercedes buried amid shriveling leaves. A silent week ended when a creature emerged, still wet from birth, to bask in the hothouse interior of the car. Working in spurts, it unrolled transparent wings that shimmered and glistened over a stubby body covered with spiky black hairs as hard as porcupine quills.

Through the days that followed Sergio Paoli lay against the passenger door. His waxy skin glowed like a supermarket apple. Despite his odd position, Sergio seemed ready to get up and start driving again. There was about him a sense of expectancy. Still, when the car filled with a higher-than-human shrilling that threatened to burst the windows Sergio didn't blink. The creature didn't know it was making noise. Its sense of time included a nebulous era before its own birth, a feeling of kinship with that other—human—body. The newborn creature was, as yet, unformed. It had a body and memories and instincts, but no purpose.

Scuttling upside down so multifaceted eyes could see everywhere, it felt the metallic-and-glass enclosure pressing down. Its terrified buzzing filled the enclosure.

CHAPTER 1

"Forgive me, Father, for I have sinned."

Robert Argyle leaned his forehead against the worn wood of the confessional. "Go on," he murmured. The leaden rosary in his fingers was the severed end of a lifeline that had once stretched to God. Behind the reed lattice the petitioner's voice achieved new heights of monotony.

Father Robert Argyle drifted, his mind on other matters. He wasn't ready. He doubted Joan of Arc or Charlemagne ever galloped into battle so ill prepared. Closing his eyes, he descended into the darkness. And shivered.

"Father! Are you ill?"

The urgent voice clanged through the grill, pulling Father Argyle back in place. "Yes—no! Keep on." Somewhere a door opened. Shifting air carried the scent of burning beeswax. He glanced outside the confessional booth where votive candles cast restless shadows across empty rows of varnished pews.

"It's a bad time for me, too, Father." The faceless voice stopped. Seconds stretched into minutes while the priest waited, hoping. "Father, I wanted to talk to you about . . . a problem."

"What is it, my son?"

"I . . ."

The horror that rendered the supplicant mute engulfed Father Argyle. He clenched his fists to control a tremor. His knees were empty spaces in his legs.

"I've been hearing voices, Father. Sounds in my head. Echoes. It's the coming together, Father. God help me!" The anguished voice grated on Father Argyle's soul. "I need help, Father!"

"Is this your confession?" Father Argyle's forehead was prickly under its sheen of sweat.

"Not exactly."

"In its proper place, then." Hot blood made the priest's cheeks burn. This was the moment he had waited for, sacrificed for—and still he wasn't ready.

"Yes, Father. The rectory?"

Father Argyle lay his head against wood sanded smooth with the grit of men's lives. Getting no answer, the petitioner resumed his dreary litany of sins, skirting always what might be true evil, dwelling longingly on temptations of the flesh.

The moment had come and Father Argyle lacked the courage to seize it. Closing his ears, he prayed for strength.

When the confessional emptied, Father Argyle, S.J., slipped out. He saw himself reflected for a moment in the polished onyx of the baptismal font, black robes like vultures' wings. His long, not-unpleasant face molded into premature sharpness with deep creases. His pink skin stretched tight over rawboned angularities. "What kind of man am I?" The dark image with the moving lips did not answer.

A young priest with the dewy appearance of an acolyte scooted into the booth Father Argyle left, obviously prepared for this desertion. His head was averted, as if offended by the sight of a priest who muttered to the baptismal font. Father Argyle was not restricted by the discipline that bound the other priests, an understanding made clear to him every day by the actions of the others like the young priest. His knowledge evoked a tingle of the fear that was the price of pride.

The side door opened into a bower shaded by small-leafed Chinese elms. A flowering hedge ripe with waxy white buds provided privacy. Around three sides of the little garden the cathedral's quarried granite blocks were rooted solidly in the barren soil that covered most of San Francisco. Stone walls soared like man-made cliffs over the patch of green, imprisoning the sun's heat and cloistering flowers from the outside world.

The monsignor looked up from puttering over dahlias just starting to bloom. His dirty yellow gloves were incongruous compared to the pristine cleanliness of his vestments and the fringe of snowy hair around his skullcap. An odor of vintage compost surrounded the old priest, rising from the well-fed ground where the purple of late-blooming winter crocuses struggled against the warmth.

"I've been expecting you." The monsignor straightened from his crouch in stages, each movement rehearsed. His face was flushed and his eyes too bright when he at last stood erect.

"I'm sure, your Grace." Father Argyle folded his hands. His voice was steady, his face as serene as it would ever be.

"Always ahead of us, Robert?"

The younger priest studied the monsignor's face. He knew he would see nothing, still he couldn't not try. The monsignor had been God's politician too many years to fall into the trap of judging others, which so often mirrored only the trapper's own flaws. The monsignor concealed his thoughts as methodically as he did the pain of his arthritis.

"Perhaps too far behind," Father Argyle said. "I feel my destiny is no longer my own." He stepped away from the cathedral's cold walls into the sunlight.

"Predestination is not exactly our stock-in-trade, Robert, but would you change your future if you could?" The monsignor's voice contained the reediness of age.

Robert Argyle turned his eyes away. The haze shrouding San Francisco's overbuilt hillsides glowed around the lemon-yellow sun. "It's too late to change anything, your Grace."

The monsignor stripped gardening gloves from gnarled hands. He examined swollen fingers as if realizing the futility of trying to change the unchangeable, then put the gloves back on. "You have decided?"

Father Argyle looked the monsignor in the face. "Yes."

"Being a priest, Robert, does not absolve one from the pain

of being a man. I fear the Society of Jesus makes martyrdom too fashionable. We must always try to believe that what is, is God's will." The monsignor's misshapen fingers tried to interlace but were stopped by bulky gloves. Age had shrunk him. His pain, and the pain of others piped through him on its way to God, was etched on his craggy face. The monsignor said no more, but the muscles of his face telegraphed the message.

"I came to say good-bye." Father Argyle noticed the distance in the monsignor's pale, old man's eyes.

"The event you have been awaiting has occurred?"

Father Argyle didn't answer.

"I see." The monsignor cupped a dahlia, caressing the white petals with his clumsy yellow gloves. "Beautiful, but so fragile." He let go of the blossom and it sprang upright again. "Two men were here yesterday looking for Blaise Cunningham. The description reminded me of you, Robert."

"Blaise Cunningham?"

"I believe you've met him."

"I've met Dr. Cunningham." Father Argyle tightened his mouth. "The last time I saw him was with another man in the Burkhalter house." Father Argyle remembered Milo Burkhalter, frantic in the puddle of light from his desk lamp, silently begging for help, eyes twitching like a ventriloquist's dummy in the hands of a destructive child. The hypodermic lay on Burkhalter's desk and when Burkhalter's eyes dropped to it he froze.

Burkhalter's white hair had caught the light, surrounding his head with a bright halo. His blue-lipped mouth worked but no sound emerged from the ropy twisted muscles of his face. An expiring cigar smoldered unnoticed at his elbow, emitting a tendril of white smoke. The odor still lingered in the priest's nostrils.

"Dr. Cunningham is a quiet man, your Grace. He doesn't talk much." Father Argyle glanced at the monsignor, wondering how the old priest was interpreting his words. Cunningham's calm had been glacial as he witnessed Burkhalter's collapse. The elegant logic of his suggestion that Burkhalter confess had hypnotized Milo. Had enthralled Father Argyle, too. He had taken Burkhalter's confession in the glare of the desk lamp. At the edge of the light the short man who Father Argyle later learned was Sergio Paoli moved like a boxer waiting for an opening. When Milo Burkhalter's dilated pupils ran out of safe places and finally settled on the Sicilian, his face lost its remaining color.

The monsignor cocked his head to one side, like a bird shifting its monocular perspective. "You went to the Burkhalter house the night Milo's niece fell from the widow's walk after her husband died?"

"Yes."

"Milo Burkhalter killed himself?"

Father Argyle hesitated. His Jesuitical mind demanded truth. Even if the truth was misleading. "By his own hand."

"You don't think Mr. Burkhalter killed himself because of his niece's death?"

"I was in the house administering last rites to Linda's husband, Jon Peters." Father Argyle stared into the mist over the ocean seeing the past. "Dr. Cunningham and Sergio Paoli had Burkhalter scared half to death. His niece just sat watching. When I came down in the elevator I interrupted whatever was happening. That was when Dr. Cunningham persuaded Mr. Burkhalter to confess. He told Mrs. Peters she could leave, but she declined. Her husband lay dying upstairs. Burkhalter's need to be forgiven by his niece was pathetic."

The priest wrenched himself back into the present. "Cunningham is about my height. He could wear my clothes, but he's painfully blond. He gives the impression of absolute honesty."

"Was he truthful?"

"I don't know. After Milo Burkhalter confessed, Dr. Cunningham asked me to leave."

"You could have refused or called the police."

"Your Grace, whatever I did would have made no difference. Milo Burkhalter had made up his mind with the confession."

The monsignor was short and his eyes had to roll up to meet Father Argyle's. Father Argyle felt a blush heat his skin.

"I'm surprised, Robert."

"I surprised myself."

"What happened to Mr. Burkhalter?"

"I believe Dr. Cunningham and Sergio Paoli injected him with an egg. Life wasn't really an option after he confessed."

"Is this a confession, that you stood in God's place?"

"In a way."

The monsignor stripped off his gloves. "We do not pass judgment, Robert." His naked hands were pink claws in the bleary sunlight. He stared at them and his dissatisfaction with the reality of life showed through. Finally, drawing a deep breath, he said, "These men will be quick to judge. I should avoid Miller and Carmandy if I were you."

"I'll do that."

The monsignor folded his hands behind his back. "This good-bye, Robert—is it permanent in this world?"

Closing his eyes, the Jesuit faced into the sun. The red orb burning through his eyelids was a vision of Hell. A vision too private even for confession.

"After today it will not be safe again for either of us." He opened his eyes. "Good-bye, your Grace. God keep you well." Father Argyle turned and raced down the concrete sidewalk toward the ends of earth and sea.

The monsignor remembered the gaunt face, the burning eyes. "You embrace martyrdom too eagerly," he whispered. "God needs people willing to live." He wished he'd thought to say it while Robert was there. He fingered his beads, as he had not done since he was in seminary. He had not become a monsignor without learning to control his nerves. And his doubts.

Father Argyle half ran down the steep San Francisco street. Each step plunged him deeper into a void he felt but couldn't define. At the first-level cross street he turned and looked back. The Church was far, the way steep. He would never be able to climb back up.

Not then.

Not ever.

His pace was slower and more deliberate as he considered what next. If only it were as trivial as "loss of faith."

CHAPTER 2

Helen McIntyre leaned against the sink staring out the open window, smelling spring in the La Jolla air. She swirled a soapy sponge across a plate.

"Did you know Ivory Soap learned to float by accident?"

Blaise raised his head, breaking his concentration. Helen's hair was still short. Pink, vulnerable ears triggered a sense of intrusion in Blaise. He saw himself as Helen must: a gawky man perched in front of a battery-powered computer; a man neither sensitive nor bold. Fine yellow hair made him appear bald, and a lifetime staring at computer screens had given him the knobby, close-focused look of a crane waiting to spear a frog.

It was a source of amazement to Blaise that Helen wanted his company, even if he just worked nearby while she read or washed dishes or conducted her business by phone. Not that there was that much to do anymore. She'd dropped her private accounts, except for a few old friends.

"It's true, you know. A man accidentally beat bubbles into Ivory. They couldn't afford to throw the spoiled batch away so they sold it without a name—until the women all came back to buy 'the soap that floats.'"

"Is that important?" Blaise didn't care but he was learning the necessity of saying something once in a while.

"To Ivory Soap it is."

Blaise punched in a "save." Alfie would insert an electronic bookmarker for him. "What's wrong?"

Helen twisted, etching her profile against the bright-green backdrop of the outside world. "I have an echo in my head." She spoke as if the words meant nothing.

"You're sure?" The taste of bile filled Blaise's mouth.

8

Helen looked at her hands in the soapy water. "I'm not imagining anything. It's been happening for days." The bare flesh on her upper arms quivered.

Helen had offered a year of life without him for a single moment together. Since the choice had been real, not romantic hyperbole, Blaise had believed her. To doubt her now was the ultimate betrayal. Pain started in his stomach spreading outward in waves. "Helen . . ."

Helen scrubbed the plate with furious effort.

"You have a dishwasher." He strained to lighten words made of cement. She needed him to say something but he couldn't.

Helen bounced the gold-rimmed plate off the counter, making a clean tone like a porcelain bell.

"That's Lenox!" he said.

"It's *my* Lenox." Helen's voice rose out of control.

A tiny black ball rocketed out of nowhere, ran up a curtain, and clawing frantically at the valance, crossed the narrow alcove ceiling in a blur of motion to dart headfirst down the opposite curtain without misstep.

"Stop that!" Blaise said automatically.

The kitten responded by leaping to Helen's shoulder.

"Tchor!" Helen said. *"Nyekulturny."*

Her voice softened as Tchor brushed her cheek with black fur. The kitten's smile showed what it thought of *kultur*. Looking at Blaise, the animal made an affectionate noise in Helen's ear as if sharing a secret.

Blaise put his arm around Helen and nuzzled her neck. Tchor arched her back before oozing tarlike down Helen's arm to rest in her soapy hands. Helen's blond hair had grown since the operation. It tickled Blaise's face, filling him with combined scents of shampoo and the warm fragrance of her body.

"An echo doesn't have to mean anything, darling."

"You're lying." Helen leaned against him. Tchor examined Blaise with outsized yellow eyes. Protectively, the kitten squalled a protest, but when Blaise didn't leave, Tchor settled back into Helen's arms, staring at Blaise with total mistrust clouding her slanted eyes.

"Why don't we get married?" Helen's body tensed as she waited for his answer.

Blaise forced himself to breathe steadily. "If it works, why fix it? Aren't you happy the way things are?"

"Delirious." Helen scrubbed furiously at a plate. Tchor eyed

Blaise from the chair where Helen had deposited the kitten. Tchor plainly said she had no use for him.

Blaise retreated to the computer, fingers jittering over the keyboard in a vain attempt to erase the sudden hurt he had caused both of them. At the sink Helen cried softly. Blaise wanted to explain to her the same way he told Alfie what he thought and felt. But Alfie was only a computer. He wanted to put his arms around Helen, cry with her.

The house was too quiet. He prompted Alfie. A whine outside announced the satellite dish hunting a signal. The TV news popped up: "—*after last month's panic when Nobel Laureate Dr. Blaise Cunningham notified authorities of the misapplications of genetic research, life is returning to normal.*"A photo of Blaise accepting the Nobel Prize filled the screen. The news had used that picture a lot lately. He'd been thinner then, his hair so light it made him look bald. That his parents shared the Prize for their joint work in artificial intelligence was glossed over. They were dead and, to most people, unimportant compared with their son.

The TV showed an old clip of the GENRECT laboratory and a Tillie in a specimen tank.

"That's why you won't marry me."

Blaise hadn't heard Helen cross the kitchen. He prompted Alfie to lower the sound on another repetition of how Human Enhancements illegally implanted Tillies into human medullae to increase intelligence, detailing with charts the spread of alien, cancerlike cells through the cerebral cortex. They weren't sure what Blaise had to do with it, so the newsmen didn't blame him directly. Not the way Blaise blamed himself.

"That's not why, Helen." He took her hand in his. "You know it isn't."

"Because I tint my hair, then?" Taut skin whitened over her cheekbones as she struggled against rising hysteria.

He forced himself to look into Helen's eyes like any practiced liar. And tried to believe his own lie. "It isn't what you're thinking."

"What, then?" Helen knew he would lie. Blaise knew it, too. But neither could put an end to it.

"We start paper trails with a marriage license . . ."

"That's not an answer. As long as a priest performs the ceremony, we don't really need a license." Helen knew she should stop, but couldn't help herself.

"I haven't been to church in years," Blaise said. "Anyway, I don't trust anyone, including the Church."

"I'm willing to risk it."

"They're not looking for you." Blaise did not add that if ever a government computer established a link between him and Helen McIntyre, the search would widen to scoop her in, too.

A comatose woman in a hospital bed appeared on the television screen. Her scalp had been shaved. Relief swallowed Blaise like a surge of warm water, overpowering him with thankfulness for the interruption that claimed Helen's morbid attention, even though she had seen similar tapes before.

Like an egg hatching, the waxy skin over the fissure between the woman's frontal and parietal bones tore open. Surprisingly little blood flowed. The camera moved closer, revealing something moist and black a quarter of the size of her head. Clawing through her ripped skin, six frenetically scrambling legs pulled the faceted eyes and black carapace of their owner free of the woman's gaping skull.

Helen made a strangled noise as she dropped Blaise's hand and rushed toward the bathroom.

"That tape was made last week at Johns Hopkins by a team of government researchers." Looking at a teleprompter off screen, the announcer didn't alter his expression enough to indicate he'd seen what the viewers saw. *"A government spokesperson said today the epidemic proportions of the crisis have abated and progress is being made in treatment.*

"Federal health agency teams still seek the following people who were treated at Human Enhancement Spas both in the United States and abroad. The victims are urged to seek aid from the nearest federal agency. Friends and relatives are being asked to locate them for treatment."

The screen blackened. An endless string of names and addresses scrolled upward in large white letters, reminding Blaise of the death lists that appeared after terrorist attacks.

Tchor sat between Blaise and the TV, black tail curled daintily around her motionless body, head aimed at the picture tube. As the names scrolled the kitten swiveled her head and stared into Blaise's eyes, the elliptical irises pulsing as if from some fevered emotion.

The sound of Helen's retching drifted from the bathroom.

"The terminal worm-death count last week in the United

States reached fourteen thousand seven hundred and eight per-
sons. Approximately eleven thousand deaths were the result of
violence. The attorney general's office announced yesterday
that persons involved in these killings will be prosecuted under
civil rights statutes. Local jurisdiction murder charges are also
threatened, though federal legislation to ensure enforcement
remains deadlocked in Senate and House committees."

Helen returned to the room. She leaned against Blaise as if
too tired to support herself. He touched the keyboard but Helen
said, "Don't turn it off."

The announcer rambled about religion and denominational
voting blocks in the upcoming elections, but he had little real
news. Blaise felt his frustration grow at the government's stiff
clamp on information. A twinge of guilt wriggled into his
thoughts. The list rolled on.

"Did you see my name?"

"No." He pulled Helen down on his lap. She buried her
face against his chest and his shirt started getting wet. Blaise
prompted Alfie. The picture shrank into a white star in the
middle of the screen. Graphics in the turned-off TV disturbed
Blaise. It was as if Alfie wanted to be noticed. But Blaise
didn't have the time. Helen huddled like a hurt animal, reminding Blaise of his culpability.

"Why do they do it?" Helen's precise voice was muffled
against his chest. "That list is an invitation to murder all those
people."

Pressing his cheek against Helen's hair, Blaise whispered,
"We'll get married."

"I should turn myself in."

"No!"

"Why? It's best for both of us. I won't be a burden to you
anymore. I won't be a danger."

"We're doing okay." Blaise repeated "*okay*" like an invo-
cation he'd learned and was afraid to forget. He drew Helen
close so she couldn't see he was crying. "We don't need them."

Blaise carried Helen to the bedroom, not feeling her weight.
When he lowered her to the blue coverlet she curled into a ball
like an infant, gazing at him with trusting eyes. "You never
think about anything else." She didn't sound unhappy.

Blaise unbuttoned her soft white blouse. Sighing, Helen put
her arms around Blaise's neck and whispered, "Close the door."

"We're alone."

"We're not!"

Emitting a squeaky mew, Tchor emerged from beneath the bed, stretching her back and then each rear leg in dainty motions.

"Outside!" Helen looked directly at Tchor.

Tail at attention, Tchor stalked out of the bedroom. The kitten's steps on the rug were silent. All Tchor's movements were silent.

"Satisfied?" Blaise touched Helen's skin and felt taut expectancy as eyes of ocean blue threatened to drown him.

"We're still not alone."

Down the hall came the faint burp of a stepping motor quietly scanning tracks as it searched a laser optic disk for some correlation that might not exist.

"It's only Alfie."

"I know." She laughed at his puzzlement.

"Alfie's only a machine."

"You're sure?"

"I designed Alfie. I built him."

"People don't talk to machines."

"I've cursed every car I ever drove."

"Curses or not, I want the door closed." Helen knew with a stubborn certainty what she thought, even if she could not explain it.

Blaise shut the bedroom door, closing off the empty hall and the other former bedroom where Alfie sat like a slot machine on a stainless-steel pillar. Occasionally Alfie scrolled machine language, forming the ASCII equivalents of the binary code in which computers do what passes for thinking.

See no evil, hear no evil. Though Alfie saw and heard, the computer was no more capable of explaining evil than was Blaise. Without the constant background of Alfie's clucks and murmurings the house was too quiet. Even the distant racket of a kitten playing with whatever would roll or tumble was absent—as if Tchor understood Helen's desire for privacy.

Blaise returned to the bed.

Tchor drifted back like a shadow as soon as the door closed. The kitten sat facing it, tail wrapped like a muffler around four tiny paws, one ear twitching and turning to tune in murmurs from the closed bedroom.

Down the hall, Alfie clicked and hummed. No peeping Tom, he.

Temporarily without input, Alfie stored data and sorted it through various sieves. Occasionally a transient electron leaped a barrier and the computer experienced some quantistic analogue of pleasure. But Alfie was not programmed for such thinking so, for the present, that line of reasoning was shelved on one of those disks that the machine accessed obsessively when no more pressing task intruded.

CHAPTER 3

Father Argyle walked along the San Francisco shoreline doing his imitation of a priest. Head bowed, he seemed deep in reverent thought, ignoring the face-stinging wind. Only his thoughts didn't fit. The *coming together* transformed life into a race against death. Father Argyle's bones ached. Where did God fit in when a man's mind shared that of a worm? Did their souls join, too? The cold settled in his bowels. Reynard Pearson had felt the joining today. The priest's own time was coming.

Pearson had come to him in the confessional, and he had been unable to act. The knowledge that Pearson could never turn back, that he was forever different from other men could break any man's nerve. Even a priest's.

Whom could Father Argyle turn to? The monsignor had not been told. What the old man guessed was a mystery. He surely knew or suspected something, but what good was a guess? Forcing his fists to unclench, Father Argyle slowed and took a deep breath. The air burned as his lungs expanded. Old priests didn't become monsignors of important cathedrals through seniority. They harbored secrets because they discovered secrets.

Sitting on a cast-iron and oak-slat bench facing the ocean, the priest tried not to think of the near-million people crammed onto this tiny tongue of land. His responsibility was narrower. But he knew he was evading it when he equated another's fear with his own. Surely he could trust a man as obviously terrified as Pearson. Cable cars clanging their bells on the hillside offered a distraction. He stared at red trolleys with garish landmark signs like Kearny and Powell streets, not really seeing.

He hoped the monsignor would not pry. If the old man nibbled at forbidden knowledge, how would he absolve himself from coming events: Perhaps . . . his vows of obedience were convenient.

"Good afternoon, Father."

Three nuns in starched, white-wing hats paused on the sidewalk by Father Argyle's bench. Gold crucifixes hung on gold chains from their girdles. They were young and pretty with innocent smiles. Fresh flowers in a rock garden, the Jesuit thought. Would they be so appealing if he knew they had experienced the coming together? Appalled at his own cynicism, Father Argyle averted his eyes.

The nursing nuns seemed embarrassed, they huddled and then swept by in a chorus of "forgive mes," apparently mistaking him for a priest from some order that avoided women. It was Father Argyle who owed them an apology. He had been tempted to corrupt their innocence with a plea for help. *Give yourself to God.* He had offered himself. Now was too late to ponder the motives or existence of any taker.

Perhaps he offered too much. The tips of his shoes prodded a memory of teaching nuns and patent-leather shoes and the fear that a polished surface might reflect the innocence of a girl's underwear.

Father Argyle's square toes were black mirrors in which he saw a black soul trapped in dust. Perhaps the teaching nuns were right. It was a side of himself he should try never to see.

The nurses were far away now. One looked back at him, her face tiny in the shelter of her headcovering, which glowed like daisy petals in the sunlight. She waved as they boarded a bus. He rose to his feet and waved back. The bus belched black smoke as it scaled the hill. It was time.

"Father Argyle," he told the receptionist. "Mr. Pearson expects me."

The secretary smiled and pressed a telephone button. "Father Argyle is here." Her voice restarted the fear inside Father Argyle. She hung up. "Go right in, Father." Her eyelids were dusted with violet mascara and had the texture of orchid petals.

The walnut door to Reynard Pearson's office soared out of proportion for human anatomy, as church portals are designed to do. It swung with ponderous deliberation on brass hinges, letting out the silence of the inner room.

Drabness ceased in Pearson's office. Enough white carpet to cover a tennis court ran from the door to a thirty-foot window. His desk was a massive bulk of Danish teak topped with ebony that reflected the recessed overhead fluorescents.

Pearson had taken advantage of San Francisco's up-and-down topography where others cursed it. From the doorway Pearson appeared to be staring through his back window into infinity. Out of nowhere the Golden Gate Bridge soared into being. Alcatraz jutted from the chill water, more substantial than the green hills across the bay. Blue mist softened the infinity of the ocean, erasing the dots that were ocean-going ships.

"How do you like it, Father?" Pearson's voice boomed beneath the cathedral ceiling.

"Very impressive, Mr. Pearson."

The developer took the Jesuit's arm and guided him to the window where first the bay, then the shoreline, and then buildings a quarter mile downhill came into view.

"Like standing in heaven, isn't it?" Father Argyle looked at Pearson with something like amusement.

Momentary uncertainty clouded Pearson's eyes before he turned back to the view. "When clouds form below the window, it's like looking down on the mortals from Olympus. Won't you sit?" He dragged a chair to the side of his desk. The desk put distance between Pearson and his clients. He wanted no barrier between himself and the priest.

"I'm sorry," Father Argyle said. "I spoiled your pleasure."

Pearson waved the apology away. "It's childish of me." At fifty he was a little short for his breadth. A paunch strained his vest and the top of his forehead had migrated to the back of his head, leaving a horseshoe of silver hair. He tugged at his earlobe with his left thumb and index finger and ducked his head to hide embarrassment. His suit was brown with traces of rust and pearl in the Biella wool. Handmade brown loafers with the kidskin softness of an old-fashioned Neapolitan bootery finished the effect. A leather and expensive soap odor clung to him.

Father Argyle stared out the window. "Successful businesses

project an image of prosperity and permanence. Including mine."
He looked at Pearson, wondering if Pearson was the right man.
Or just the first.

"The Church?" Pearson pinched his earlobe.

"Yes."

"I'm glad I'm not doing business with you, Father. You
make me feel I wasted millions building this smoke screen.
Most clients are either knocked out or green with envy. With
you I get the feeling I need to fight to keep it out of the poor
box."

"I don't believe you need worry, Mr. Pearson."

"You don't, Father?" Pearson stopped stroking his ear.

Father Argyle shook his head. "Not in the least."

"Smoke?" Pearson offered an open box of cigars. Making
a production of lighting one, he struggled to hide the trembling
of his hand. A light blinked on his telephone; he picked it up
and listened. "Tell him I'm in conference," he said, "and don't
interrupt again." Laying down the phone, he stared hard at
Father Argyle. "Why are you here, Father?"

"You want to tell me about the coming together." Father
Argyle's face telegraphed no hint of his feelings.

Pearson's fumbled cigar spilled ash on the carpet. "I guess
that's right, Father." His greenish-hazel eyes had a haunted
quality. He bent his head, pretending to look for the ash.

"And if I can't say it's all right?"

"I haven't gotten that far yet."

"We have a problem, Mr. Pearson."

"*I* have a problem." A sheen of moisture appeared on Pearson's bald spot. "*You* can get up and leave."

"Just like that?"

"My problem, Father. I got in and somehow I'll get out."

"But it would help if I made the answers easier?" Father
Argyle looked out the window, making Pearson understand he
was still alone. The window cast back a thin reflection, like a
picture of a mask over nothing. Father Argyle studied his own
angular features and decided he didn't particularly like them.
Cigar smoke put an unexpected sweetness in the air.

"I suppose a lot of this shows up at the church?"

"More than my superiors want to know about."

Pearson slumped. He sweat copiously. Through the pano-
ramic window behind him, the Golden Gate Bridge swayed on
its cables. The longest, heaviest suspension bridge in the world,

and a mild breeze forced it to obey the laws of physics. Fear was a force even more insubstantial and more powerful.

"Damn it, Father, I need your help. Don't make me beg!" Pearson tore at his necktie. "If that's what you want me to say, I'll say it. I need God's help. The Church's help and your help. I'm drowning and I'm not going to keep on coming back up. There's a worm in my head and it's talking back to me and when I don't hear myself talking any more, I know it will have eaten me up and I am it."

Pearson buried his face in his hands. "Do you hear me, Father?"

"I hear you very well," Father Argyle said.

CHAPTER 4

Jamie was fourteen and Ronnie only eleven. Which was why they weren't cleaning the barn. "This isn't much fun." Ronnie had been pitching rocks into the bushes. His real interest was his brother's rifle, something they weren't supposed to have.

Jamie's enthrallment with the forbidden had ebbed an hour ago. Eleven-year-olds, he suspected, either didn't feel pain intensely, or else received less of it as punishment.

"Dad's going to be pissed," Ronnie said.

"Who's going to tell him?"

"He's got his ways of knowing." Ronnie glanced at the rifle. "I thought we were gonna target shoot."

"When we get a target." Jamie almost added *snitch*. But if the kid was blackmailing him, he couldn't risk it. "We'll stop when we see something to shoot at." He crossed his fingers behind his back as he made the promise. Fat lot of good it was going to do him, but it paid to cover every bet. Dad said that a lot.

They were dressed alike in hard-used blue denims turning white, red plaid shirts, and scuffed, black engineers' boots: shirts for the chill and boots for snakes. At least that was what their mother said when she told them what to wear. Their father had bought the vineyard to raise children and take a tax write-off. He made wine. The boys' mother saw that they didn't drink any.

With summer still too distant for wine-county tourists, cars were infrequent. Serious traffic went inland through Sacramento where extra miles were compensated for by good roads and no hairpin turns booby-trapped by the California Highway Patrol. The state fuzz was not well loved in the north where sheriffs were more interested in reelection than in filling the coffers for downstate welfare. At least that was what Jamie's dad said the last time he got a ticket.

"How about some target shooting?"

The older boy looked around. They had the meadow to themselves. The road spun around a shoulder through the edge of the meadow and out of sight too quickly for some busybody to stop and pester a pair of boys with a rifle.

Or even, Jamie prayed, to recognize them. Besides, the meadow ran downhill from the road into a clump of oaks and then back up. Shoot downhill and he would not have to worry where the bullets went.

Jamie, at fourteen, had suddenly become a worrier.

He knew no good was going to come of this, but that never stopped any boy. He handed the gun to his brother, making sure the barrel didn't get pointed his way.

"Gee, that's great, Jamie! What do I shoot at?" Already Ronnie was looking one way and pointing the rifle another.

"Watch it!" Jamie pointed toward the grove. "See that wasps' nest?"

"Yeah!"

Jamie wished the kid would get on with it, wished he'd had the foresight to bring less than a full box of ammo. Dad would be home soon and Jamie did not want to have to explain. The kid was waving the rifle in big circles. Jamie grabbed the barrel and held it steady.

"You got to line up the back sight with the one up front."

"I know, I know!" Ronnie yanked the .22 away.

The flat *snap* of the shot was followed immediately by the

thud of a mallet striking metal. Or was it tempered glass? The meadow was suddenly death still.

"Shit!" The lump in Jamie's throat was too big to swallow. "Now see what you've done."

Ronnie quickly let go of the rifle when Jamie took it, then stuck his hands behind his back. "See what you made me do?"

Jamie looked across the meadow. "*You* shot a window, and *I* didn't make you do anything." Jamie could not see any building. This did not reassure him. What he didn't see could be a lot worse. Like, maybe, a greenhouse. Full of marijuana. People who grew grass could be mean.

"I didn't shoot anything. Just that old wasps' nest."

"How do you know? You were looking the other way."

"I was not! I was aiming right down there." The eleven-year-old pointed at the oaks.

"We better go see." Jamie didn't move.

"I guess so."

They looked at the offending .22. Finally Jamie started toward the trees, wishing he dared leave the gun in the weeds.

Ronnie hopscotched close after his older brother. "I bet it's some doper's marijuana still."

"Shut up."

The boys were almost under the oak before they saw the car amid branches and dead leaves. Cracks were still growing from a thumbsize hole centered in the tempered glass of the driver's window. Jamie's heart fluttered like a dying butterfly.

"Maybe you kilt somebody." Ronnie began putting distance between himself and his brother.

Jamie was too scared to remind Ronnie who pulled the trigger.

The tree laying over the car blocked them from the driver's door so they walked to the other side. Jamie squinted and tried to see inside but the tree made it too dark.

"You going to open it?"

Jamie squeezed and the door sprang open, pushing him back. Abruptly he was enveloped in a wave of stench and a memory of that awful day he had kicked at a dead cow and it had burst. Something that had once been Sergio Paoli rolled out. Ronnie shrieked and was ten yards away in one reflex motion. Jamie felt his knees melt.

Then the shrilling. A monstrous insect, black and big as a football, burst from the Mercedes, heading straight for Jamie.

The boy yelled and plowed headfirst into the ground. By the time he got his face out of the weeds the monster was up the slope and into the trees.

"You killed him!" Ronnie screamed. "I'm going to tell Pa!" He started toward Jamie, then turned toward home.

Jamie started running after him. The eleven-year-old looked over his shoulder and turned white. His brother was going to kill him for shooting the rifle. He just knew it. Ronnie tucked his head down and willed his knees to move faster.

Ronnie was so intent on getting away that he never noticed when his brother passed him, or why his dad looked at him funny when he shouted Jamie was breathing down his neck to kill him. All he knew was relief when his father swung him up from the ground and held him safe even though he was eleven. By the time everything was straightened out, Ronnie had already invented a logical explanation. Not that Leo Richardson-Sepulveda was interested in explanations.

The boys' father wanted to see the body. And then, maybe, the monster.

CHAPTER 5

"**Y**ou've done splendidly, Mr. Pearson." Reds, blues, and yellows filtered through the dusty air and spattered the maple floor, the colors streaming down from a stained-glass Savior bowed by the weight of a cross. Christ's stylized, unwrinkled robes were a Byzantine image of impossible conformity—or the embattled mentality of a city under siege. Whichever, Father Argyle decided it suited the new church. "The Greeks were iconoclasts and impressionists, Mr. Pearson. They separated man from God and man from man."

"There aren't many other churches available, Father. I can look some more." Pearson's apology reverberated in the empty building. "It was built by a White Russian refugee." Pearson paused. "When I got interested in this building I had a research service find what they could.

"A lot of stories were written about him. Alexei Kondrashin seemed to pursue notoriety. The headline writers called him the Russian bear and compared him to a comical grizzly. In payment, Kondrashin told them glorious stories of fighting a last-ditch battle across Siberia with the remnants of his cavalry troop until they were down to twenty-seven men and their horses. His comrades, Kondrashin said, died one by one.

"He had a neck like a tree trunk and a square-cut black beard, and, what was unusual for a Russian, he laughed a lot. His English was better than his French, but he kept the reporters laughing with jokes made funnier by his fractured English.

"Sometimes friends of the White Russians already in San Francisco would attend these interviews, which Kondrashin held like a royal audience. They made fun of his stories. But Kondrashin just shouted, 'See what it was like!' He'd kick a boot off and a foot cloth would go flying to expose his frostbite scars and missing toes."

Pearson walked under the stained-glass Christ, his white shirt transformed into a montage of shimmering colors. "Kondrashin built the church around this window from his family chapel. He said when he lay in the snow with his feet frozen he promised to restore the window to its former magnificence if God saved his one remaining toe.

"Kondrashin started building a cathedral for God, who saved his toe. When somebody asked why he hadn't just begged for his life, he kicked his left boot off and pointed to his big toe sticking out as lonely as a bowsprit. 'Kondrashin does not beg,' he trumpeted. 'Kondrashin makes bargains and keeps them. Kondrashin would have lived without God's help. But the toe must be paid for. This is my gift to God.'

"The aristocrats couldn't stay away. I don't know if the church brought them, Kondrashin's vow, or just the smell of money, but they accepted Kondrashin and his church. A cloudy background couldn't stop Kondrashin. He pursued Marya Bolkonskaya, a count's daughter and a relative of the Romanovs. Count Bolkonski had arrived in America destitute. While he fought in the White Army, his lands and estates were looted and he barely got out with his life. He lived off the largess of others who had fled Russia without fighting and with their fortunes intact. Kondrashin as a rich son-in-law provided an answer." Pearson gave the priest a sidelong look.

"They were married. Eventually Marya Bolkonskaya ran away with a Russian-speaking Turk and most of Kondrashin's money. Kondrashin had a furious argument with his father-in-law and moved into the church cellar, where he lived as a monk.

"Count Bolkonski eventually got over the loss of his daughter and restored his fortune so he could marry again, though he was an old man by then. Kondrashin disappeared in the thirties. Bolkonski bought the church and boarded it up. He became a tragic figure who, it was rumored, sneaked into the church at night to mourn his runaway daughter."

Pearson let the silence grow. Finally he added, "It's deconsecrated, Father. What will you call the new parish?"

"Surely not the Church of the Big Toe." It was as close as Father Argyle allowed himself to levity. There was nothing funny about God, not even His strange sense of humor. "Perhaps St. Abbo's." Father Argyle began exploring. Odors of disuse and mold lingered in the narrow hallways.

Pearson followed him. Without warm bodies to muffle the echoes, their footsteps rang in the bell-shaped chapel. Pearson puffed as he tried to match Father Argyle's stride. The priest was taller, with longer legs, and Pearson had too much weight around his middle.

"I want you to meet somebody, Father."

"Now?"

"Yes." Pearson sighed gratefully when Father Argyle slowed the pace. "Who was St. Abbo?"

"A martyr, Mr. Pearson. As are most saints." Father Argyle stopped and looked at Pearson. "As we may be."

Pearson leaned against the wall breathing hard. "There are times, Father, when you frighten me."

"And when I am frightened for you. Perhaps that gives us something in common." Father Argyle smiled. "What we are about to do will be a trial for both of us. Let's pray we do not fail."

Pearson held out his hand as if to clutch the priest. "Just tell me what you want."

"The lion's share, I'm afraid. At least all those things money can buy. And to have faith. Can you do that?"

"Father, you're a magician! I thought I was dead. You pulled my soul out of Hell."

"We shall hope so later, won't we, Mr. Pearson?" Robert Argyle's hands didn't tremble. Jesuit training was strong on concealing doubt. Closing his eyes, he asked for God's help in the ear-ringing confines of the chapel, hearing his words fill the emptiness of space if not of spirit.

When the prayer ceased, he said quietly, "Please, Mr. Pearson. It's hard to do battle with tears in your eyes."

They left by way of the massive oak doors under the stained glass. "The building will do fine. You'll contact the others and get them here tomorrow—you have the list?"

"Yes, Father."

"We'll meet at nine P.M."

"I'll take care of it . . . Father?"

"Yes?" Father Argyle felt giddy with a strange sense of power and fear. The odyssey was started. When he had knelt in the arbor outside the cathedral on the hill and allowed the men from Rome to do what was needed, he had been scared. But for his destiny to be fulfilled, a saint first had to die.

"Whatever happens, thank you." Pearson turned to stare at the window. After a while he blew his nose. "I want to take you to Tim Delahanty."

"It's important?"

"I think so, Father." Pearson shut the oak doors to the church while Father Argyle waited on the quarried stone steps fingering his crucifix and thought about the man who built the church. The sound of the doors banging shut seemed locked within the building.

Pearson guided the black-and-silver Rolls like a riverboat pilot avoiding sandbars, swerving extravagantly if another car came close. Father Argyle combined this datum with the residual flatness of the developer's *a*s and decided Pearson had learned to drive in Boston.

"Why do they let you get away with that?"

Pearson dipped the bow of the Rolls toward a cream Mercedes, then chuckled as the German car spurted ahead. "Veblen economics, Father. You only pick on cars the owners don't want scratched. A man in a Rolls owns lawyers, too."

Down in the tacky part of town where drivers had less to lose, Pearson drove with more circumspection. The San Francisco wind swirled newsprint and hamburger wrappers along the gutter. The air was redolent with cooking odors and exhaust. Pearson parked in front of a ramshackle, two-story frame building with curved bay windows. A black plaque with white lettering hung under the porch eaves.

"I'll wait out here, Father. Delahanty's is that ground-floor office under the round window cupola."

"Is he going to tell me something he won't tell you?"

Pearson nodded. "Tim Delahanty's full of whiskey and black Irish moods. He's brilliant, a homosexual, and a worm brain." Despite the indictment Pearson seemed sorry. "For his many sins of commission he never commits a sin of omission." Pearson studied a shop window across the street. "I could have saved Tim once. But I valued money more than a friend."

Getting out of the car, Father Argyle climbed the white gingerbread porch. At the door he glanced back. Pearson's forehead rested on top of the steering wheel.

The black plaque read "Tim Delahanty—Consultant."

He knocked and as the door squeaked open, Father Argyle was transported from chill San Francisco mist into darkness and a tropical jungle reek of stale alcohol. Drapes closed off the light. "Mr. Delahanty?"

"Shut the door, would you." A chair creaked and Tim Delahanty turned from his contemplation of the wall.

Father Argyle quietly closed the door. The room was littered with papers, books, bulging manila envelopes, and flimsy international aerograms. Delahanty was a bulky shadow against the far wall. "Could we have some light, Mr. Delahanty?"

A switch clicked and an antique, cast-iron floor lamp burst into yellow light. Slumped in an executive chair, Delahanty held a bottle by the neck, between the forefinger and thumb of his right hand. His left fondled an old-fashioned tumbler with *Bushmills* inscribed on the side. The big man's hair was black and gray. His face had a yellow-gray-red cast and deep wrinkles that suggested his liver has tossed in the towel.

"A priest now. And you'll be a Scotsman, Father?"

"Canadian."

"I'd pour you one, but the bottle's empty, Father. You mightn't have another upon yourself? I remember Canadian whiskey with great fondness."

Father Argyle didn't answer.

A sigh came from the chair. "Seat yourself then, Father. Is it that fool Pearson who brought you?"

"He said I'd want to talk to you."

"Did he, now!" The chair squeaked as Delahanty shifted his weight. "What had he in mind?"

"He said you would tell me."

Delahanty leaned down and his head came fuller into the light. His face looked as if it had been in a taffy pull, his eyes were soft and bent at the corners, ready to spill out tears that wouldn't come. The sound of a drawer shutting accompanied his straightening out of of the light. "I had another bottle all along. I fear I lied, Father."

"No, Mr. Delahanty. You never said you hadn't."

"Very astute, Father. Perhaps you see another of those drunken Irish, or even a bloody Orangeman living here and cheering God's work in the homeland."

"The Irish priests are in mourning, Mr. Delahanty. There is no cheering."

"Would you be sharing a drink, then, Father? You have a keen Scots eye. Not like our friend outside in his fancy Brit car—whose brain talks to itself, saying things twice that only need sayin' once."

"How would you know that?"

"Why else would Pearson bring you?" Delahanty swiped the air with his glass to wipe away any guesswork. "A consultant tells people how to get what they want. I tell a man to invest as a limited partner in a certain real estate venture and he does and the scheme goes bust. He has to write off the loss, but in the meantime the poor man gets his heart's desire just like he rubbed a lamp and a djinn popped out with three wishes. How's that for a profession—granter of wishes?"

"Have you any wish, Mr. Delahanty?"

Delahanty's squint through the glass made one eye larger than the other. "None, Father. But you have. Which puts me in mind of a computer in Washington and a gentleman the computer is looking for. Would you be seeking a consultation, Father? Take it from me, the price is right."

Tim Delahanty had been in Army Intelligence, first in Germany, then in Korea. Father Argyle needed a few minutes to accept that the decrepit hulk behind the desk had once been a bright young college man with unaccented German and adequate Korean from the army language school in Monterey.

Mostly, Delahanty talked about his boss in Berlin: blond, Teutonic-looking Max Renfeld, whose left hand was always in a pocket when he walked. If he forgot, the arm flopped and waved like a manic fly swatter due to a severed nerve that made muscle control possible only with strict concentration.

Posing as a wounded Wehrmacht corporal, Renfeld had entered Germany ahead of the American army in 1944. He was young, but so was most of the German army by then. OSS dropped him at a crossroad five miles behind the lines with faked field hospital records, travel passes, and the paybook and assignment papers of a POW who resembled Renfeld. He was supposed to make his way to Berlin ahead of the American advance. Instead, Renfeld hitched a ride to the front and joined the Germans, fighting with such ferocity that he received a battlefield commission. Three days later, his unit ambushed an American patrol, and Renfeld decided it was time to go on to Berlin.

His unit had taken two prisoners. It had been their first action and the Germans were elated, behaving like kids while they stripped the dead. During the confusion, Renfeld took the two Americans aside for interrogation. He handed each a grenade and an M-1, then led the attack on his own Volkssturmer unit, which consisted of fifteen-year-olds and pensioners.

Within seconds only Renfeld and his two prisoners remained. Then he ordered one of the Americans to graze his ribs with carbine bullets.

Renfeld felt as if he had been hit by a truck. Two ribs were cracked. He could barely raise his Schmeisser to kill the astonished GI. The other American reacted much faster than Renfeld anticipated, grabbing a bayonet and lunging at Renfeld. The bayonet had already stabbed into Renfeld's shoulder and back, glancing off his shoulder blade before he managed to fire.

A German unit found him hours later. German and American dead surrounded Renfeld, who lay in a pool of blood under the body of the last American, empty Schmeisser still in his hand. Shot in the side and stabbed in the left shoulder, Renfeld got his ride to Berlin, a medal, and real hospital records. He was assigned light duty guarding the Wehrmacht Intelligence HQ.

Renfeld was a German hero. And he had the right kind of wound. He had almost no feeling in his left hand and arm. The nerves had been severed. He could control his fingers by look-

ing at them as they did something, but he was excused from
frontline duty.

He photographed agents and people who ran agents as they
came and went from the Neo-Gothic building. He assembled
a dossier of people who could be used after the war. He talked
to men who led him to other men, and when the American
army finally entered Berlin he was running agents in what
would become the Russian sector.

Delahanty learned all this gradually. Catching a cold scent
in Berlin in 1952, he pieced one part to another and guessed
at the rest. He never revealed to Renfeld what he knew, but
that summer, two of his witnesses were killed by the Russian
fly-swatter technique in which a car skids sideways to smear
a pedestrian against a wall.

Delahanty had been on his way to see one of them. The
victim, a soldier who had found Renfeld at the massacre, had
told Delahanty the Americans had empty pockets and that the
dead Germans seemed to have many American weapons.

Delahanty arrived at the same time as the ambulance. The
dead German was curled up against a red brick wall, brains
oozing onto the pavement. It was Delahanty's first-ever experience with that particular blood-and-feces odor of violent death.
Later that day Renfeld smiled at Delahanty and put his fingers
to his lips. Delahanty requested a transfer and went to army
language school in Monterey and then to Korea. He never told
anyone.

"I'm a coward," he said as he terminated his account of the
life and times of Max Renfeld. His eyes pleaded with Father
Argyle to understand, but he'd swallowed half the bottle of
whiskey anyway.

Delahanty left the army as soon as he could. He might have
lost his nerve by himself. But learning that Renfeld and his
kind acted outside the normal compendium of dos and don'ts
paralyzed Delahanty's will. He had been married and had a
son. Whatever happened to Delahanty reached his wife. She
left him.

Delahanty's talent remained, the ability to sniff out secrets
and sift for the truth. Delahanty couldn't do anything with it
himself, so he sold various kinds of truth, attaching himself to
decisive and amoral men, as if that would protect him from
men like Renfeld.

He had told Father Argyle all this in a constant monotone.

"Max Renfeld came home to lead the worm-brain eradication program, Father. That's why Pearson brought you to me. So I could tell you somebody in Washington made a decision about brain-enhanced humans and picked Renfeld to head up the Federal Communicable Disease Agency with special powers, including control of the National Security Council agents. He has a CRAY XMP/48 in the Pentagon and is using it to search for one man." Delahanty stopped talking but he did not stop swaying.

"You are going to tell me who he's looking for, aren't you?"

"Of course, Father." Delahanty grinned and lowered the empty bottle gently to the floor. "Renfeld is going to kill Dr. Blaise Cunningham."

Father Argyle waited. The silence weighed heavy in the closed room. The near-silent burring of a clock motor came from somewhere just beyond his awareness. "Why?"

"Blaise Cunningham knows something he shouldn't." Delahanty spun his chair around to face the wall. "It's better to know nothing than to know a lot and do nothing, Father."

"Thank you, Mr. Delahanty."

Delahanty didn't acknowledge his farewell, but before Father Argyle closed the door the light snapped off.

As he got into the Rolls-Royce, Pearson said, "Did you talk?"

Father Argyle settled himself on the seat. "Yes. I need to go to the airport."

Pearson started the car and rolled into traffic. He didn't say anything until Father Argyle was getting out in front of the terminal. Then he caught the priest's sleeve and said, "I killed Delahanty's son over a few dollars. God forgive me, Father." He drove away without waiting for an answer.

CHAPTER 6

Waving foot-long shears like a dowser's rod over two and a half pounds of Los Angeles Sunday *Times*, Blaise was not looking for water. Murder, maybe. Larceny, greed, sloth, perjury; all the deadly sins that were the human condition. What Alfie could do with the data evaded his imagination.

Helen hovered at the edge of all his thoughts. The right shade of yellow, the tint of her hair, was a trigger. A flash of blue sky darker than ordinary and he remembered her eyes. She was gone whenever she was only out of sight for a moment. The triggers opened a void in him that his mind rushed to fill with memories because he couldn't escape the future. The pleasure of now could not displace the pain of what was to come.

The muscles in his neck were clamping down his brain. Blaise rolled his head. *Helen is suicidal.* The thought came giftwrapped in a metallic fear he could taste. She had promised. But that seemed centuries ago instead of only months. Thousands of worm brains had killed themselves since Sergio murdered Dr. Hill. Helen had been suicidal then and Blaise counted on her Catholicism to preserve her life. But Linda Burkhalter-Peters had been Catholic, too. Her death clung to him like a bad smell no one else noticed.

He paused, scissors dangling, blades shiny bright. The temptation was not to fight, just give up. The blade tips glistened like held-back tears. Helen had loved them all: Blaise, Sergio, Dr. Hill . . . When Blaise came back alone she'd promised not to kill herself. She never asked again about Sergio or Dr. Hill. Blaise closed the scissors with a loud *snick* and breathed deeply.

Full pages were too large so he snipped stories and fed them individually through the optical reader. Time alone with Alfie gave him a sense of family. He shared his ignorance about humanity with the computer. During those moments, Helen seemed an unpredictable stranger whom he loved but could not protect. He had Alfie and he had Helen. Whatever he did created danger for one or the other. Blaise told himself Alfie was just a machine, and knew he lied.

"What are you feeding the tin man this morning?" Helen dodged and added, "with my sewing scissors?"

Blooming lilac came into the room with her. When she sensed his fondness for the fragrance Helen began wearing a different lilac perfume every day. When he grabbed her and told her how wonderful she was, all the other bottles went into the trash. She understood his relationship to Alfie. Alfie was her rival.

"Telling him things neither of us want to know."

Helen gave him a hurt smile, the corners of her lips pulled in as intellect fought to control emotion.

"I'm not shutting you out." An emptiness exploded through Blaise. He wasn't sure of that. Alfie was safer than Helen.

"It's all right." She pecked his cheek briskly. "I came to see what you want for breakfast."

Blaise smiled. "Guess."

"It would be flattering if you meant it. You're getting bacon and eggs."

"You're getting prettier."

Helen's temperature rose under his hand as blood suffused her skin. With a lingering hug, she broke away and fled to the kitchenette. She seemed happier there, as if service was a proof of love. Blaise caressed the keyboard's cold numbers and symbols. Remembering the brief blaze of Helen's warmth, he wondered at his inability to respond. Leaning over the terminal, he typed: "Alfie, do you understand women?"

"I UNDERSTAND WHAT YOU MADE ME TO UNDERSTAND"

"Helen is sensitive about children."

SENSITIVITY AND CHILDREN ARE HUMAN CONCERNS, PROFESSOR"

"Do you understand me, Alfie?"

Electronic intelligence normally functioned in silence. Alfie hummed, implying a conscious choice, a spinning of disk drives as if it did not want to break contact. Sweat started on the palms of Blaise's hands. He told himself the quirk was no sign

of intellect. Alfie had simply initiated a search pattern to ele-
borate an unsatisfactory answer. Alfie's seemingly human instinct
persisted in Blaise's imagination. The urge to believe in Alfie's
intelligence was as great as his need to rescue Helen.

The humming stopped. Whatever Alfie sought had been
transferred into immediate memory.

"A DEFINITIVE ANSWER TO YOUR QUESTION IS NOT AVAILABLE"

Colored sparks shot across the glass-and-phosphor screen.
Whatever it was to Alfie, the display had no meaning for Blaise.
He began tapping a nervous finger on the escape key. To vol-
unteer information without a prompt was a violation of Alfie's
basic parameters. It rated a twitch. *What are you doing, Alfie?*
The thought circled in Blaise's head. An unfavorable answer
meant a trip into Alfie soon with oscilloscope and soldering
iron. The result would be like brain death.

"PROFESSOR, HUMANS TALK MORE OFTEN THAN THEY WRITE?"

The screen flashed and a new message came up.

"YOU PROGRAMMED ME TO UNDERSTAND HUMAN SPEECH, BUT
YOU WRITE TO ME. WHY IS THIS, PROFESSOR?"

Alfie waited. Alfie was good at waiting. The temptation
existed to think Alfie could converse, that Alfie had intelligence. Alfie was a counterfeit. Blaise subconsciously had given
Alfie the attributes but not the capacity for original thought.
Blaise loved his subnormal child—perhaps more than if it had
come up to his expectations.

"Writing is more precise," he typed, "and I'm not much of
a talker."

Floating in from the kitchen a feminine voice called, "You're
keeping secrets again!"

Blaise tapped a sign-off and left Alfie to digest the news-
paper.

At breakfast, Helen spent a lot of time staring at her plate.
Tchor lay on a cushion in a corner, curled around her fat belly.
Helen insisted on feeding her every time they ate, and this
suited Blaise. It kept Tchor quiet when then were together.

"I'm trying," Blaise answered an unspoken question. "I'm
trying to consider you."

"You spend too much time with Alfie. Most people would
be glad for a break now and then."

"I'm not most people. I think like a computer—only not
as well. I have to work to become involved in other people's

emotions." Blaise shrugged. "I try to change." He hesitated. "Maybe Alfie's trying, too."

Helen took his hand in hers across the table. His fingers seemed white even against her fair skin. "You're learning, Blaise. It's the rules the rest of us make. We change the game too much in midstride, don't we?"

The doorbell chimed.

Helen stared wide-eyed at Blaise. They had been waiting, it seemed forever, for that tiny sound. What to do when it came kept them awake nights, both pretending sleep because talk offered no solutions.

"*Go*! Do what we've agreed." Blaise touched Helen and felt the heavy thump of her heart. From the clip under the table he released the flat little *Búfalo*. Working the slide, he shifted the pistol to his left hand. Couldn't hit anything that way, but Sergio had recommended throwing it at anything more than arm's-length away.

Blaise put his right hand on the doorknob. Sunday mornings nobody came. Not Sundays, not ever. They'd agreed that a shared secret was no secret. Hyperventilating, he eased the door open as any middle-class homeowner in a good neighborhood would.

"Good morning, Dr. Cunningham."

Blaise stared at the man in black suit and turned collar whose hazel eyes had brown, brooding depths.

"Aren't you going to ask me in?"

"It's Sunday!"

"Priests don't get Sundays off."

Against the white carpet and white silk wallpaper in the living room Father Argyle seemed solider than life.

"I don't think we have anything to discuss," Blaise said.

"Perhaps friendship." Outside the open window a pair of butcher birds squabbled over a branch.

Seated on the white couch with gold thread, the priest dominated the room. Blaise sat facing him. He stared at the Jesuit for a long moment. "I think not."

Father Argyle raised an eyebrow. "We have common interests."

"Inadvertently."

"Fairness, humanity, safety?"

"You left out motherhood." Blaise's lips were dry. If the priest could find him, so could the feds.

"Generalities are treacherous, but examine your position first. You may change your mind."

"You may believe what you want." Blaise squirmed and was angry at himself. The priest would have learned to mute his body language. Lack of experience, and inadequate planning had put Blaise in this position. "How did you find me? Door-to-door solicitations? Collecting lost souls?"

The priest's face was pleasant with not-yet wrinkles stretching his features into less somber contours. The strain of his profession showed in the lines. "I have something to discuss with you."

"That's one-sided. I have nothing to say."

"I know about Miss McIntyre." The Jesuit's eyes followed Blaise with the regard of a trapper for a just-caught animal.

Blaise struggled to breathe.

"I'll concede she's not on the list." The priest studied Blaise. "The *Chorch* trains us to close our minds to doubt." At odd moments the priest's Irish boot camp displayed itself in his speech. "Dogma may not be intellectually uplifting but it is useful—just as discipline is more practical than ideal. You cannot make me doubt what I know to be true."

Blaise sat down again. "So you know."

"Yes."

"Which means you want something you don't think I'd give without a lever to move me."

"To train a mule, 'First you get a two-by-four.' Do I have your attention, Dr. Cunningham?" When he smiled, Father Argyle resembled an aging choirboy.

"Are you discussing me?" Helen had changed her apron for a one-piece blue knit dress that set off her eyes and golden hair. She wore makeup, something she seldom did around Blaise. Despite the powder she appeared hollow-eyed.

The Jesuit stood. Blaise got awkwardly to his feet, too.

"Father Argyle is collecting for the Jewish Defense Fund. He was on his way out."

Neither Helen nor the Jesuit paid him any attention.

"How do you do, Father." Helen offered her hand. "Blaise speaks about you frequently."

"I'm sure he is laudatory. I'm delighted to meet you, Miss McIntyre." The floor-to-ceiling white drapes behind Father Argyle burst into light as the morning sun struck them. The effect turned the priest into a black silhouette.

Blaise understood how the Jesuit had so successfully led the protest against genetic engineering. His Scotch-Irish voice had the resonance of a contented cello.

"Blaise is overly protective, don't you think, Father?"

"Dr. Cunningham is looking after your best interests, at least as he perceives them." Favoring Blaise with a benevolent, fatherly expression, he added, "Like all protectors, he seeks to save you from more than is necessary."

"I'm glad you understand, Father. Blaise isn't responsible for my . . . retreat from the Church. He didn't even know I was a Catholic. I have . . . other reasons."

The words came too fast. Blaise had once heard a Chicano marriage counselor call it "*pájaro* talk": birds chattering to reassure themselves.

"I know about your operation."

Helen's face was blank with shock.

"Well," she finally said, "I guess it wasn't all that big a secret then." She turned to Blaise and her face was falling apart.

"Why don't you go change, Helen? We'll be late. I'm sure Father Argyle will excuse us." Blaise stood and the Jesuit smoothly followed suit.

"I'm delighted to have met you, Miss McIntyre." Father Argyle took Helen's hand. "You might like to attend our services in San Francisco. They are for special people . . . like yourself."

Pale, but composed enough to nod, Helen said, "I'd like that very much, Father." She fled down the hall to the back bedroom. The room was very quiet with just Blaise and the priest staring at each other. The bedroom door slammed shut with a muffled sound.

Blaise faced the priest. "The only thing that keeps you alive is that I can't be bothered with bodies," he said, teeth clenched. "What do you want?"

"Please put the gun away."

"You haven't answered my question."

"To talk." Father Argyle stared down the hallway, a line of pain drawn through his craggy face. From the other room a sharp *click* and *whir* announced Alfie was working. "I had no intention of harming Miss McIntyre. I hope you believe me."

"Wait." Blaise left the priest and uncocked the pistol as he went into Helen's room. She lay facedown on the lavender blanket. "I'm going out for a few minutes, honey."

She didn't look up. She was trembling. "I'm sorry, Blaise."

"Dlaczego? Co się stało?"

"I'll be all right." She rolled over. "When did you learn Polish?"

"Promise not to tell?"

She stared.

"It's the language of love when you love a Polack."

She held his hand against her face. "Find out about the services, will you, Blaise?"

"You care?"

She nodded.

"All right. Sleep if you can."

Blaise pulled the daisy-flowered spread from the foot of the bed and covered her before kissing her cheek.

In front of the house, Blaise passed the curbside cars. The Jesuit followed without comment.

"You haven't asked where we're going."

"I'll know when we get there."

"It's your funeral," Blaise said.

"I'm dressed for it." Father Argyle smiled as if this were a joke he practiced in front of the mirror.

Entering the small corner bar, Blaise was annoyed when the priest walked under the beer sign with no hint of discomfiture. They took a booth at the back between the telephone and the jukebox. Blaise bought glasses of orange juice and carried them to the table. Aside from the bartender, a husky kid with a heavy black mustache, the only customers were a pair of beach bunnies in cutoffs and tight T-shirts. They looked at Father Argyle as if he had offered to transfuse them with AIDS.

A quarter rattled in the jukebox and Arlo Guthrie began a melancholic moan about "The City of New Orleans." The song evoked tragedy in Blaise, written by a man dying of cancer, sung by one facing the genetic crapshoot of Huntington's chorea, about a train grown old in service and heading for discard. Blaise considered asking what God had to say about life's terms. "What do you want to talk about?"

"Helen McIntyre."

"I wasn't pleased by your coming to my home. You're not getting more endearing." Blaise's eyes roamed the little bar.

A pizza sign hung on the wall, but he knew the pizza came from a take-out pizzeria down the street. Everyone offered more than he delivered. The odor of beer gave the air a musty taste.

As if committing him to memory, the priest said, "You love Miss McIntyre."

"What kind of question is that?"

"It's not a question. The knowledge helps me decide how much help I can offer."

Street noise drifted into the bar: cars passing, the lethargic buzz of bluebottle flies trying to get out of the wind, feet scuffling past the screened doorway.

"I don't need your help."

"Does Miss McIntyre need it?"

"That's your offer?" The question of whether he was being threatened lay between them.

"I think she does. So do you."

Blaise stuffed his fists in his pockets. "No!"

"You know things I need to know, Doctor. I can help you."

"I don't trust you, priest. I want Helen alive and real. You'd burn her body to save her soul."

"Is Miss McIntyre's life all that concerns you?"

"What else? The government has rounded up thousands. And treated them to death. Helen is . . . a fluke. She's surviving when nobody else is."

"That's not surprising." Father Argyle made rings with his glass of orange juice.

"It surprises me. I don't believe in those odds any more than I believe in miracles."

The priest leaned across the table lowering his voice. "It would be an extravagant bit of chance if Miss McIntyre was the only one who survived. *But not if she was the only one getting proper treatment.*"

The implication struck Blaise like a physical blow. "I don't like to believe that."

"But you do." The Jesuit sat back, hiding his voice under the music. "Miss McIntyre is not the only person to escape. Those on the list are hospitalized and treated with a hormone that stops the worm from forming a chrysalis—for a time."

"Of course. That's how I treat Helen."

"Then the worm builds up a resistance and continues its development."

Blaise stood.

Father Argyle put his hand on Blaise's arm. "There's more."

Blaise stared out the bar front with the half-frosted window. It was an old law to prevent passersby from viewing the joys of drink. Perhaps the real intent was to keep parishioners from seeing their priest at the bar.

"The government is treating the victims with royal jelly."

Blaise knew the priest wasn't lying. He'd known all along the risk of yelling fire and then running. He was responsible suddenly for all those deaths.

Father Argyle seemed to understand. "No, I'm not crazy. Royal jelly's common, but expensive. Beauticians have been putting it on and in women for years. Useless, of course, but no one's afraid of it."

"You're still crazy."

"You haven't asked what I want."

Blaise waited.

The music ended and the jukebox created sudden silence. Automatically the bartender and his two customers looked at Blaise, who was standing.

Father Argyle reached across the table, placing quarters in the jukebox and punching buttons without taking his eyes off Blaise. Music refilled the vacuum and onlookers lost interest.

"I want the identity of the substance with which you treat Miss McIntyre."

Blaise remembered to close his mouth. *"You don't know?"*

"I've gone to a great deal of trouble to ask you."

One girl lit a cigarette and the faint odor wafted down the room. The music was as raucous and incoherent as Blaise's thoughts.

"I made a total disclosure to the federal communicable disease center. It's an agricultural insecticide, a hormone that prevents larvae from maturing. They die of one thing or another before reaching the reproductive state, and no adults equals no new generation."

The priest's eyes went vague as he rifled mental file cards. "You didn't discover this by testing Miss McIntyre."

"There were others. It was too late for them." The Jesuit seemed to understand. That was probably another thing priests were taught, to be emotional chameleons and say they understood, no matter how alien the concept. "Why has the government switched treatments?"

"They never started your treatment. By the time Max Renfeld came back from Germany the decision was made. Don't you think it odd that the head of an agency charged with saving lives has no degrees in medicine or biology?" Father Argyle appeared totally at ease. It was the bar that seemed out of place around him.

"What about Renfeld? When I phoned he tried to trace the call. But I expected that."

"He's eager to get hold of you, Doctor. But not to save lives. His people are looking for you." Father Argyle stood. "Do you know a man named Miller?"

Blaise shook his head. "Common name. I met a police sergeant once."

"Probably not the same. Watch out for Miller and Carmandy; possibly others. They work for Max Renfeld. I believe we've covered what we came for." Father Argyle led the way out of the bar, smiling at the three people at the end of the counter.

Blaise followed in a daze, not noticing the embarrassed nods as the trio at the front of the bar acknowledged the priest.

Sitting on the edge of the bed, he lulled himself into the rhythm of Helen's breathing. He had warned the people who were supposed to do something. And then, knowing they'd try to tie the can onto him, Blaise had gone underground. He'd made the decent gesture. He had not invented the worms—nor even known of their unauthorized use until it was too late. He had blown the whistle when no one else would. What more could they ask?

Helen whimpered in her sleep. He stroked her cheek and she reshaped her body against him. Blaise looked down and her eyes were open.

"How'd it go?"

"Well, there's good news. Your treatment works. The stupid government is using something else on the people who are dying." As he told her it seemed that he was unpiling bricks from her chest. Helen cuddled against him and sighed, "That's good," before she drowsed off again.

Blaise sat a long time holding her hand, thinking, And then there's bad news. But he didn't say it. The gun dragging down the left side of his pants was enough discomfort.

CHAPTER 7

Designated XMP/48, the CRAY had been recently installed in the Pentagon subbasement. It had forty-eight parallel processors, experimental silicon-gallium arsenide chips that made the XMP/48 the fastest computer in the world. The chips were manufactured by depositing arsenide patches on silicon at a 104-degree angle, squeezing twenty-five atoms into space for twenty-four.

The technician had his hands in his lab coat pocket when he explained this. He had a doctorate in computer engineering and he thought he knew how the new computer worked. Thoughtfully he crossed his fingers. He wasn't all that sure.

He explained the joining of forty-eight chips into a single network with one master control chip, but as he talked about the way they passed information back and forth interceding in running programs, he got a little vague and let his eyes wander. The people who designed the machine were still writing instruction sets and data mapping the circuits. They'd promised to update him when they found out what was really happening. Explaining that an overload was shared with another chip and another and another until the problem was manageable seemed to please the man who wanted to know these things.

"The master chip is the 'know-nothing,'" the tech explained. "It doesn't take messages or read files. It interprets what is wanted and tells the other chips what to do."

Chip number seventeen was providing video and audio images to the XMP/48 and storing the digits for the time the master chip would call for them. The tech began the audio test next and the XMP brought the signal through eleven, which farmed the digital signal out to a customized voice reader to write the definitions in machine language and pass them back.

Since the XMP was under zero load, it had no other duties at the moment. Automatically it set other chips to duplicating the functions of seventeen and eleven, and compared results. Any discrepancy would indicate a malfunction.

"We've hooked Martin Van Buren here to the video and audio inputs," the tech said. "The computer is its own security. It ID's personnel, monitors activities, communicates directly with security or maintenance, and can access any file." The tech's shrug was recorded for reference the next time a human might duplicate this movement.

"It sees me now?"

"Yes, sir." The tech raised his head from the diagram to wink at the cameras.

"How do you program?"

"Tell it what you want and Martin looks through its templates for the closest fit. It starts building a model, which is evaluated and changed repeatedly until it approaches reality. Then it implements the plan."

"Without human direction?"

"The parameters were preset by men but, yes, without human interference."

The other man looked at the computer instead of the cameras. "How soon?"

"We'll bring Martin Van Buren on-line the end of the month if there aren't any glitches."

"What kind of . . . glitches?" The man hesitated over the word as if he had never heard it before.

"Circuit failures. Logic errors. Murphy's Law." The tech looked up. "Presence positively guaranteed. These things are hand built, one of a kind. So are the failures."

The other man placed his hands behind himself and rocked on his heels as he looked Martin Van Buren over. Finally he released his hands and turned to go down the corridor. As he walked his left hand and arm had the disconcerting habit of flopping away from his body like a man swatting flies.

The tech began humming "St. James Infirmary."

CHAPTER 8

Father Argyle settled into his seat on the direct flight to San Francisco and closed his eyes. The dash down the runway was punctuated with Morse code flashes of sunlight through his closed eyelids. The dots and dashes in his personal darkness turned brighter as the airplane climbed. He remembered opening his eyes and looking down on the top of a cloud, and then he knew he was asleep. The flashes continued and the past rushed up at him like an excerpt from Dante Alighieri.

He was in the jungle again, walking, his nose telling him about the man who had come this way not long ago. He'd been shocked the first time he'd passed through the trail of another man's scent. None of the Americans had bathed in a week. The feral odor of meat eaters clung to them. Being able to smell an American's rancid sweat after he'd passed a minute earlier made the priest special. Scouts who had been on patrol too long claimed they could smell a man on the trail. They were lying. They just wished they could.

Father Argyle had stopped, confused. He didn't know what to do. Not then. The army had put his values, the beliefs of a young man dedicated to God, into an empty dice box, shaken and dumped. When his values came out, their order had been changed.

"What's wrong, Padre?" Parker moved up close and whispered in his ear, and the garlicky odor of salami wrapped itself around the priest like a warm blanket. Parker was a nervous-in-the-jungle short timer from New Jersey who said if God wanted him to fight, it should have been in a city somewhere. He'd been doing that all of his life and maybe the United States should invade Havana because he always wanted to go there.

Their path was a hole through green vegetation that joined overhead to shut out the sky. Underfoot the trail was brown mud between short plants that were forever being ground into the dirt. Father Argyle could not breathe.

"Padre?"

"Somebody ahead of us. An Oriental." That was close enough. Orientals ate less meat, or none. They ate less in general. Their odor was light, almost dainty in comparison to American soldiers. He didn't have to explain, Parker knew.

"Stay here. Don't move." Moving as if he were floating, Parker turned and sprinted quietly back the way they had come, leaving Father Argyle alone in the middle of the path.

A minute later the squad leader brushed past. "Thanks, Padre. Stay here." He'd bent his head close to Father Argyle's ear to whisper before moving on amid the soft, almost inaudible creaks and thuds of his duty belt. The rest of the patrol passed like silent shadows.

Father Argyle folded his hands in front of his lips. They moved silently as he prayed. A stinging fly droned before coming to investigate the taste of Jesuit sweat. Tiny spatters of sun glared through the treetops. He had run out of spit a long time back. Still Father Argyle prayed the men would come back, that nothing would happen.

He took a short step and the half-sweet, half-putrid stench of jungle boiled from the mud. Sweat itched down around his ears to drip from his prominent chin. He took another step. He wasn't supposed to move. No one could see through the leaves or around the winding corners of the trail, not even the VC. The bend was getting nearer and he had the overwhelming urge to run toward it. He lifted his foot . . .

The machine gun's sudden ratcheting made him stumble. He lurched toward the turn in the path. Rifle fire joined in and then the whomp *as something exploded in the shrubbery. A brilliant bird was screeching and shedding yellow feathers as it rocketed away into the greenery.*

The path lay ahead like a muddy green ribbon and he ran, not noticing that the noise was in his head now, not in the air. He turned a corner and froze.

The grunt held his M-16 to the ear of a VC. Charlie was maybe fifteen: black pants and black shirt with thongs tied to his big toe and ankle by loops of hemp. Blood ran from his mouth and he sat with legs straight out in a V. *His eyes were*

swiveled around against the epicanthic fold that created their
slant.

Father Argyle was falling forward saying "Don't!" when
the kid's head jerked away and hair flew out on the other side.

Five more bodies had been dragged out of the brush. The
patrol was going through pockets and packs, collecting weap-
ons.

"What are you doing here, Padre?" The squad leader's
voice rang sharply. He seemed embarrassed and he said more
softly, "Thanks, Padre. They were waiting for us."

"Don't . . . don't . . ."

"Get your shit together, Padre!" The squad leader paused
to reassemble his own. "Pray if you want. Pray they aren't
into torture. When you're slow dying, pray they do you a favor
like I just did."

Grabbing the VC's pajama tops, the soldier jerked it up to
show the bloody gash and the great worm in his belly making
gasping, sucking noises as it ate . . .

"May I be of help, Father?"

Father Argyle looked up. A small, dark girl with hot eyes
and tight, pert black curls was shaking him. She wore a blue
air crew uniform. "Thank you, miss. Everything is fine." Father
Argyle's eyes burned with sweat that dripped from his slightly
shaggy brows.

"You were dreaming—having a nightmare, Father. I had to
wake you."

"Thank you. I'm all right now."

"Some coffee. Water?"

"Nothing, thank you." Father Argyle forced a smile.

"If you change your mind . . ." The stewardess' eyes sparkled.

Penni Barnhart did not impress so easily. "And just how
could I have gotten a close look, Bright Eyes? If I gave him
a cup of coffee you'd chomp my fingers off at the elbow."

Bright Eyes, known to the airline as Constance Davies,
squirmed. "Penni, this guy's electric! I had to wake him up.
When I touched him . . ." She wrapped her arms around herself
and shivered. "Every time I get near him I get goosebumps."

"For Christ's sake, Connie, he's a priest."

"Well, what of it? I'm not talking about marriage."

"Just for starters, how about vows of celibacy?" Penni stared at her roommate for a few seconds. "Let me retract that. If you'd ever heard about celibacy, you wouldn't believe it."

"That's snotty." Bright Eyes had the grace to blush.

"Well," Penni said, "you make your bed..."

"He's still a man."

"A priest."

"He makes me tingle."

The little second-floor room at St. Abbo's contained Father Argyle's things in a neat pile on the bed. They weren't much if possessions were the measure of four years in seminary and fourteen of travel from one mission to another. He packed his clothes into the deal dresser against one wall. The leftover items could all fit in one pants pocket. He dumped those on top of the dresser.

A feeling of disuse clung to the room. The cream color of the walls was uniform. No light patches indicated places where pictures and mirrors once hung or where long-forgotten furniture had been removed by a previous tenant.

The Jesuit had alway known he was different. To preserve a proper attitude of humility he reminded himself several times a day that everyone not only believes this, but it's also true. At first he had hoped to find his way into the College of Cardinals. Later he entertained a more grandiose thought— there had never been an American Pope. Yet.

Vietnam. Father Argyle shivered. Vietnam was no place for a young priest who wanted to be Pope.

Even in his own room, his face mirrored none of his thoughts. He had learned his rôle well enough to play it with his mind and heart elsewhere. He heard the footsteps, so the knock on the open door did not startle him. "I trust all is in order, Mr. Pearson?"

"Yes, Father." Pearson stood in the doorway. "Father, could you please call me Reynard. Or just Pearson?"

"Of course, if you wish."

Pearson wiped his face with a handkerchief. The temperature had soared into the high seventies. A heat wave in San Francisco. "I'm sorry I haven't found a housekeeper yet." Anxiety emerged as nervous chatter. "I'm sorry. I forgot, Father. I haven't been as involved as I should have been. I mean, I've been busy, so I've been generous. With money, Father, not with time."

"Reynard, the Church requires nothing that is not freely given. And I don't need a housekeeper."

Pearson was boyishly uneasy at contradicting a priest. Argyle wondered whether it was his position with the Church or the chance that prayer would save their souls, if not their lives. "Forgive me," Pearson insisted, "but a housekeeper puts extra hours in your day. Trust me, Father, you're going to need all the time you can get."

"As you wish, Reynard. Do as you think best."

The priest wore his wool suit, shaking hands with men and women who filed through St. Abbo's doorway. Those who came needed their attention captured quickly. That was the value of ritual, even though it was not traditional for a priest to greet parishioners at the doorway.

Light spilled from the wrought-iron cage hung from the end of a ten-foot chain. Father Argyle accepted it without question, but the first man, who Pearson introduced as Leo Richardson-Sepulveda, shook Father Argyle's hand and then looked at the light as if he'd never seen one before. "Bribery, Pearson?" His voice had a flat, nasal quality. "Watch out for your altar boy, Father. He may have forgotten what the straight and narrow looks like." Richardson-Sepulveda's nervous laugh grated as he went into the church with quick, mincing steps, glancing back as if evaluating Pearson's reaction.

"What about the light, Reynard?" Father Argyle glanced up, realizing that somehow Pearson had gotten the electricity turned on on a Saturday night.

"You needed light, Father."

"Yes."

Pearson shrugged uneasily. "You have it."

"I see." Father Argyle stared after Richardson-Sepulveda for a minute before turning back to Pearson. "It seems fitting that my new parish start off with a miracle, Reynard."

"Don't mind Richardson-Sepulveda, Father. He's awkward socially and he tries his best. He's not as bad as some of the others you've chosen." Pearson's face puckered and he added, "No complaint, Father."

From the church steps they could see headlights half a mile away on the twisty street as they appeared and disappeared, obstructed by trees, houses, dips, and low walls. "Richardson-Sepulveda has this problem with people. So he works for Karl

Zahn. Put Sepulveda in prison, he'd be running the place in a month. Outside, he's the same. Only Zahn is his buffer. There's a problem, Father." Pearson fingered his shirt sleeves under his suit coat, tugged at his tie. He managed to avoid looking at Father Argyle.

"We'll have company soon, Reynard."

Pearson glanced toward the road. "Delahanty and Richardson-Sepulveda are lovers. That doesn't mean Delahanty will back Leo, particularly since Leo is committed to Zahn. But Tim's gone a long way for Leo already."

"We'll have to speak with Mr. Delahanty when the time comes."

"Not *we*, Father. *You*." Pearson's lips twisted. "Two of the people you wanted wouldn't come."

"I think we shall yet see our lost sheep—on our own terms. Why don't you check inside?"

Father Argyle stood at the door alone, greeting the arrivals. He knew them all slightly from the cathedral up the hill. Dorris Kelly stopped to stare into the sky, saying "The stars are blessing us tonight, Father. It's a strange priest who greets his parishioners at the door." She lowered her eyes and added, "This had better be worth it."

"I'm sure you'll judge fairly, Mrs. Kelly."

Mrs. Kelly's pale-green eyes were thoughtful as she went in.

Delahanty was furtive, and shunned by the others. Avoiding Father Argyle's eyes, he scurried inside to sit behind Richardson-Sepulveda.

Reynard came out and started closing one door. Father Argyle stepped into St. Abbo's and pulled the other. As the two sides slammed into place, the *boom* reverberated throughout the nave.

"Still short two." Pearson's whisper lost itself in the open space of the chapel dome.

"Can you persuade them?"

"I'll try."

"By all means, Reynard. It's for the good of their souls." Father Argyle walked between the rows of empty pews, Reynard's rough breathing pacing itself behind him.

Inside the church, smaller than the cathedral up the hill and a little shabby from the decline of its fortunes, nine potential parishioners and Reynard Pearson gathered in front of the communion rail. "Gentlemen—and ladies," Pearson said, "we know why we're here. I suggest we get on with business as quickly as possible."

Ten heads turned toward Father Argyle.

"Won't you all sit?" For a moment the church was noisy with scuffling feet. Like obedient middle-aged children they lined up on the worn bench.

"I'm delighted so many of you could make it." Father Argyle's voice was deep and sonorous as he had trained it to be. "The reason you are here is first because you have all had the so-called human enhancement. Secondly, you have shown enough craft to stay off the government's proscription list." He paced in front of the congregation, forcing them to follow with their eyes as well as their ears.

A brunette, her age hidden under the svelte curried look that money buys, stood. The movement was abrupt.

"Please, Mrs. . . . Baker, is it? Sit down. We have no time to pussyfoot. Why else would you be here?" Father Argyle spread her guilt by looking at each parishioner in turn. Only Pearson was unaffected.

The women seemed uncomfortable, but they remained riveted to the front pew, a tiny group of supplicants like dolls in a grownup house.

"Why else? Be specific, Father." The man who spoke barely touched the floor with his feet. His sharkskin, knife-edged suit would have commanded respect on a coat hanger. A pink scalp showed through a razor-cut haircut that made his thinning white hair look vigorous.

"Specific? Mr. Zahn, you're a Catholic worm brain." Zahn sat like a block of chilled ice. "Does that answer your question?"

"Almost, Father." Zahn bounced up with nervous energy that threatened to burst from his body. Resentment at being short showed in the way he moved. His body said bigger men were clumsy caricatures, and tried too hard to prove it with quick movements that just missed being graceful because of their hurried challenge. He stared at Father Argyle, condemning him for being tall.

"Haven't you heard, Father? There are no Catholic worm brains. The Bishop of San Diego declared that under Canon Law, Catholic worm brains did not exist." Zahn's face was a billboard for his feelings.

"Bishops are men, Mr. Zahn. San Diego has no Catholic

homosexuals because Bishop Maher suspended the priests who ministered to them. But he didn't stop their ministries. It is for God to say who is or is not Catholic."

"I didn't come here to be compared with queers." Zahn glanced at Delahanty, who reddened and sank into his coat collar. Richardson-Sepulveda returned the stare, back straight, his thin-edged face impassive. "If the Church wasn't backing Maher, he wouldn't have lasted."

Somewhere a beam creaked as it readjusted to seven decades of earthquakes. The people around Zahn looked at Father Argyle, willing him to answer.

"There is conflict within the Church, Mr. Zahn, if that's the answer you want. Conflict means the Church stands with us as well as against us. Until Rome decides, we all share a state of grace, whatever the nature of one man."

"If they decide against us?" Zahn fumbled for a cigarette. He played with the lighter, then remembered where he was. He cleared his throat. The sudden explosion of sound caused several people to jump.

"Then the decision is back to God."

Zahn remained standing. His hair gleamed like a white skull-cap. "Let us be frank, shall we? You did ask for honesty."

"Of course."

"We know the danger we are in. Going to the government equates with suicide. On the other hand, why build a church with our money just because some snake-oil salesman promises us salvation in the hereafter?"

"Should I be offended?"

"Yes," Zahn said.

"If I'm not offended, would it help to know that I am one of you?"

"I don't believe it! The Church would never permit it." The words erupted from the Baker woman.

"Me, neither!" Zahn's permafrost grammar momentarily melted. Argyle knew who Karl Zahn was. He and Reynard had prepared the list with care, choosing the symbolic twelve as carefully as Jesus must have chosen his. Zahn would never be a good old boy, but his combative instinct could be used.

"It was done with the Church's permission," Father Argyle said. "Obviously you want something concrete so I have prepared proof."

"Aside from brain surgery, it will have to be spectacular."

Richardson-Sepulveda's laugh at Zahn's caustic delivery was like the bark of a dog. Zahn glanced irritably at the taller man.

Father Argyle took a small stack of cards from the altar bench. "Tomorrow each of you may contact the monsignor and ask two questions.

"The first is whether I am affiliated with the Church. One of the reasons I asked Mr. Pearson to contact you was because he has been personally aware of my participation in Church matters for some time.

"The second question is whether the Church is aware of my altered condition.

"For your own protection and the safety of the others we shall bring into St. Abbo's you must keep confidential what you learn. The monsignor will answer no other questions regarding this matter." Father Argyle walked along the pew handing a card to each person. At the end of the row, Reynard Pearson's smile sagged. He was breathing heavily and, for the first time, showing his age and the burden of his weight.

"Call the number on this card and make an appointment with the monsignor. I trust those of you active in the religious community will accept this proof and convince the others." The nave had been built before acoustics became an exact science, and reflected only the innate skill of its designer. Abrupt silence replaced its usual magnification of every scrape and whisper. Nine people could not take their eyes off Father Argyle. Only Pearson evaluated his fellow parishioners.

"It would be pointless to doubt the monsignor, would it not?" Karl Zahn broke the silence with shocking loudness.

"If you doubt the monsignor, I suppose nothing less than divine inspiration will satisfy you. In which case I depend on your discretion to keep this meeting confidential. To satisfy yourselves that I am no charlatan, ask the monsignor."

"Rest assured, I'll do that, Father." Zahn hesitated. "Am I entitled to another question?"

Father Argyle polled the others with his eyes. "If no one objects. You are doing splendidly."

"Meaning I'm asking questions you're prepared for?"

Only Father Argyle's eyes expressed his smile.

"Then why pour money into a fancy mausoleum? We're all going to die soon. We're members of bona fide congregations that have already extracted a lot of money from us. Are your last rites better than theirs?"

Silence floated with a feeling of prayer.

"Who said you were going to die?"

Eleven people suddenly heard real silence.

"Is that real?"

Father Argyle nodded and the sound of breathing again swept the chapel.

"I believe, Father, that tomorrow morning we'll call on the monsignor." Zahn seemed to want to add something else.

"Yes?" Father Argyle asked.

"Will you be here when we return?"

"At five P.M. St. Abbo's will be consecrated and opened."

"Is there anything more you wanted to tell us this evening?"

"I believe we've covered most of it."

They milled about for a few minutes but the Jesuit understood their anxiety to get home and remembered what it had been like to hope. As he shepherded them to the door, Richardson-Sepulveda stopped. "There's something I want to talk to you about . . . afterward, Father." The others were ahead of them. Zahn looked back, a brooding curiosity on his face.

Richardson-Sepulveda noticed. "I must go. Until tomorrow, then." He was bigger than Karl Zahn, but his movements were just as dynamic as he crossed the distance between him and Zahn. Zahn whispered something and Richardson-Sepulveda nodded.

"They're strange, Father." Pearson had come up behind Father Argyle quietly. They followed the parishioners to the entrance. "Richardson-Sepulveda has a wife and a couple of boys up at a Napa Valley vineyard. His wife knows he's AC/DC but doesn't seem to mind. You heard how Zahn is about homos. But Zahn seems fascinated by Leo's interest in him. And Leo—" Pearson shrugged "—has Delahanty on the string and God knows how many others. But he wants Zahn and plays bully boy for him, doing his dirty work."

They had come to the entrance and the other parishioners milled around Father Argyle, trying to say good-bye without appearing hasty when in fact they all wanted to rush home and start thinking about living again. Pearson drifted out of the way.

When the last new parishioner had shaken Father Argyle's hand, Pearson reappeared to watch their cars pull away. Turning to Father Argyle, he said, "I hoped, Father. But . . ." Suddenly he dropped to his knees and tried to kiss Father Argyle's hand.

"Reynard, I have no ring!" The Jesuit's voice was mild. "You've done well today. I only wish there were two of you." Argyle's pleasure was adulterated with embarrassment. Reynard's devotion was so unexpected and unearned that he felt the guilt of pride and ambition.

"Thank you, Father." Pearson had tears in his eyes. "Did you notice Mrs. Baker's purse?" He forced a crooked smile. "She had a hundred and twenty-five thousand dollars in cash. She thought you were going to sell indulgences."

"I hope she wasn't disappointed."

"After she talks to the monsignor she'll donate twice as much. I have to go, Father. I want to tell someone the good news."

The Jesuit turned his collar up against the wind, which had stiffened. Another man might have regretted passing up Pearson's offer of a ride, but Father Argyle enjoyed striding past wrought-iron fences into the salty night breeze.

A failing fluorescent gave the liquor store a dingy gray look. It was the only place with a pay telephone. Leaning back on his stool, the counterman examined Father Argyle as if plotting a priest into a shaggy-dog story.

Father Argyle dropped in a quarter. The clerk winked and he wondered what they were supposed to be communicating. When the receiver was lifted on the other end, the priest turned his back.

"Monsignor, it's me again." Overhead the fluorescent sizzled quietly.

"Ah yes, my favorite Jesuit." The monsignor's voice was casual, as if he did not recall Father Argyle's farewell.

"You will have visitors tomorrow. Probably before noon."

"I see." The line hung silent, the monsignor taking no sides. He had instructions from an authority above the Jesuit. "Have they names, Robert?"

"Mr. Zahn will probably lead them."

"I am not surprised." The monsignor seemed to have drifted off. Father Argyle considered saying good-bye. "Are you there?"

"Come yourself tomorrow."

"I don't want to endanger you."

"I am already doing things I don't approve of that are much less safe. Perhaps tomorrow . . . ." The monsignor broke off.

Father Argyle hung up and turned to leave.

Eyeing Father Argyle's turned collar, the clerk rolled the toothpick around in his mouth and said, "Safer for women if you guys wore your pants backward, too. Seriously, fella, I'd change into something less flashy. Narks'll make you right off."

"Thank you," Father Argyle said. "I'll bear that in mind."

"No bother, Father." The counterman laughed uproariously.

Once he strolled away from the light spilling through the liquor store window the night was less friendly. He made less noise and after a while he realized his night vision had not returned. That had not bothered him since he had been in Vietnam and still wanted to be the American Pope.

He thought he smelled somebody. Then he heard footsteps and stopped. When he wasn't walking he picked out the sounds clearly. He jumped a little when the match was struck and the man stood in the glare lighting his pipe. Father Argyle picked out the burnt-match smell. He smelled the men, too: one in front and the other coming up slowly from behind.

"Father Argyle?"

"Yes." His eyes were adjusting and he focused on the man in front of him.

"My name is Miller, sir. National Security Council. I'd show you my badge except it's too dark to see. I was wondering if you could help me."

"Perhaps, Mr. Miller. If it doesn't conflict with my duties as a priest."

"I'm looking for Dr. Blaise Cunningham. You knew him when you led the antigenetics movement last year."

"I don't think I can help you, Mr. Miller. Dr. Cunningham and I were never close. In fact, he seemed to think I was persecuting him personally. May I ask you a question?"

Miller's pipe made a red arc in the darkness when he took it out of his mouth. "Of course, sir."

"Who do you take orders from? Who is your immediate superior at the National Security Council?"

"No!" The voice came close up from the darkness behind Father Argyle. "That's a national security secret."

Miller chuckled. "I don't think that's privileged information, Carmandy. Sure, Father. The head honcho for NSC is Max Renfeld. If you want to ask about us, he'll tell you."

The other man, Carmandy, materialized out of the darkness. He moved quietly and Father Argyle felt a shiver. Carmandy reminded him of the jungle and things that crawled.

CHAPTER 9

Sweat prickled and his shirt stuck to his back. Blaise wiped his face with his sleeve. He had to create a program Alfie could implement safely. *Safely*. Sweat trickled into the corner of his eye and he scrubbed at it with his knuckle.

The issue was whether the Jesuit knew the truth from a lie.

"Hi, sailor!" Helen was rumpled as if she had just gotten out of bed. "Bet I can do something for you that pile of tin can't." Pale lips and haggard eyes negated the leer.

Blaise took his fingers off the keyboard. "Keep teasing and I'll make you prove it."

She wiggled enticingly, then slumped against the door frame. The forced excitement of her voice subsided as she stopped acting. "If not me, Blaise, why the others?" Her eyes sparkled as tears welled.

"Government policy requires no logic. I suppose some bureaucrat decided 'It'll upset the health care budget so we'll just let them die.' I don't know why, Helen. Maybe the priest is wrong."

"You don't believe that. He found us. He came, and all he wanted was the formula. If thousands of people were using it, he wouldn't have looked for us, would he?"

"No. He wouldn't need us."

"Then you have to do something."

"Do you think I'm holding out? I *gave* them every bit of information they needed." Blaise's hand fondled square-cut plastic keycaps. His strength was tied to machines, not to people. "Someone meticulously erased my contribution."

"I love you, Blaise. I want to live—with you." She pressed her cheek against his. When she talked he felt the motion of her mouth against him. "I can't when I think about what is happening to all those people in government hospitals. They're being murdered. And we know!"

"A lot of Germans had to choose between doing something about Buchenwald or going there."

Helen's heart pounded loud against him. Her fragrant odor quickened his pulse and made him want her even more. "I can do something," she said.

Paralysis squeezed his chest. Blaise had the irrational conviction that her emotion would drag him to the floor. Primitive passion that began and ended with sex drove her. Helen told him she felt left out when he didn't respond. When he wasn't interested he denied himself to her.

"Do you love me, Blaise?"

"Yes."

"You never tell me, so sometimes I forget." Her breathing was gentle in his ear.

Blaise let himself be pulled from the chair to the rug. He held her at arm's length for a moment, looking at her. "What do you want me to do?"

"Save the others—so I won't feel guilty that I have so much and they've lost everything because you traded them for me."

"What makes you think I'm doing that?"

"Because you love me. Don't you understand anything at all?"

"Alfie," Blaise said, "we have to be careful this time." The words arranged themselves on the monitor with electro-mechanical precision for Blaise to check the audio translation.

"DO NOTHING PRECARIOUS" the monitor responded, "AND AVOID DANGER"

"You should write Chinese fortune cookies." Blaise mumbled because he didn't want to explain fortune cookies.

The monitor screen flickered with random groupings of letters before going dark.

"REPLICATING" appeared, followed by strings of letters Alfie had picked up, grouped in precise time progressions. The green screen turned into a huge flicker board that gave Blaise a headache. Mixing random strings, Alfie sought word combinations that made sense.

"Enough!" Blaise howled. "I said: You should write fortune cookies. It's a Jewish saying and I don't know what it means."

"THANK YOU, PROFESSOR"

Alfie cleared the screen of everything except the reference to fortune cookies and Jewish folk sayings. Blaise wished he'd kept his mouth shut.

"Did you call?" Helen's voice floated in.

"No, darling!" he yelled back.

"NO DARLING" printed on the monitor. Blaise gave it a scowl and considered turning off the audio pickup.

"That wasn't for you," he said.

Alfie printed a "NO DARLING" under the one already there.

Blaise clicked the audio off as a third "NO DARLING" appeared on the tube.

In precise terminology he typed instructions for raids on federal data banks, followed by what he hoped was an untraceable long-distance call.

Words sprouted as Alfie proposed temporarily overriding the telephone company's traffic controller to show a seemingly botched attempt to conceal that all the raids had originated from a Pentagon supercomputer. It might not be believable, but it would discourage inquiry.

Alfie would charge the long-distance call to Blaise's credit card. The telephone traffic controller would show a dead-end in Madrid. In case the trace was faster than Alfie expected, another line would buffer the trace to Paris.

Blaise switched Alfie's audio input pack on. "Fast company, Alfie." The Pentagon's CRAY was big, with tons of freon cooling, of integrated circuits, thousands of miles of wiring. Not as smart as Alfie, but the CRAY didn't have to be. It was bigger, capable of countless simultaneous operations and integrations, methodical step-by-step analysis.

Alfie, on the other hand, relied on cross-linking simultaneous trials in different directions, then a final consensus of which seemed—not most logical or nearest the truth—but most practical. Alfie's "mind" worked like an engineer's.

At the moment Alfie was running "NO DARLING"s up and down the green screen while Blaise considered its proposal. A trail to the Pentagon might stop any investigation dead on the assumption that it was all part of some DOD deviltry that it was safest not to know about.

Might! But if the authority was high enough the false lead could interest other heavyweight parties in Blaise and Alfie and, by extension, Helen. So far nobody except the priest had connected her up with anything.

Staying invisible was possible if the searcher's resources were limited. But a computer like the CRAY could devote full time to the trace, sifting and eliminating billions of items, counting the grains of sand on a beach until it found the one it wanted.

Blaise stood. "You've been eccentric lately," he said.

Alfie inverted "NO DARLING" into a mirror image.

Blaise turned off the display and drifted into the living room where Helen watched stock market tables streaming across the TV screen and jotted precise shorthand. Tchor purred on her lap, the kitten's black sides pulsing like a furry bellows.

"Quit that," Helen said.

"I'm not doing anything." Blaise straightened.

Helen scribbled something on her pad. "You're pretending nonchalance." She nibbled the end of her yellow pencil.

"Casualness."

"Why don't you tell me so we can both be casual?"

"Suppose we had to leave here?"

Helen put the pad down and patted the couch.

"What are you going to do?" She laid her cheek against his shoulder where he couldn't see her eyes.

"I have to find out if the priest is telling the truth."

"Then what?"

"If it's true, I'll do what you want, if I can."

Helen looked up at him and smiled. "I was afraid you were going to tell me something awful."

"If we stir up the ants they'll bite."

"It's okay if they bite, Blaise." She held her face up. "Just kiss me before you start."

Alfie rifled some unprotected federal files regarding Blaise and Human Enhancements: an infinitude of useless information, but no mention of the treatment he had proposed to the Atlanta communicable disease center other than a simple casual referral to another file, which Alfie immediately flagged.

"What's that?" Blaise spoke out loud, then realized Alfie's ears were turned off. He flipped the mike on and repeated.

"THIS FILE HAS NO RATED WEIGHT"

"Stat?"

"OK" Alfie dithered an instant, then spelled it out: "ZERO KILOBYTES"

Not enough memory to register. Or more likely it was just

a trigger in another file. Blaise had Alfie pass that file. And another. And another. Helen brought something to eat and he remembered patting her cheek and telling her to go to bed and then they were inside the FBI's linen closet. Alfie tiptoed lightly and managed not to trip anything.

Blaise copied a file on prominent people in government who had visited Human Enhancements. None appeared on the lists of people ordered to turn themselves in.

The CIA files made his hands sweaty. His head began to ache from staring at the screen and reading data that seemed to have no natural conclusion. Every important file had a booby trap on treatment for Human Enhancements. Sweat collected on his neck.

"They're waiting for us, Alfie. Or someone like us."

"YES"

No percentage of probability in Alfie's answer, just an unequivocal *yes*. "List accessible files, Alfie."

"I CAN ACCESS ANYTHING"

"Stop bragging and stick to related federal agencies."

Alfie left his answer at the top of the monitor like some sort of challenge. Blaise didn't remember programming Alfie for the kind of behavior in which the computer counterfeited an emotional response. Alfie had no emotions. Blaise wished he remembered what happened between himself and Alfie during those weeks-long binges before he stopped drinking.

Federal agencies, departments, subsidy businesses, grants through public health and welfare to different organizations that consequently had their files open to federal investigators scrolled up the screen like fat, woolly sheep.

Then came the hospitals in a batch, an endless stream from military to teaching, from fully subsidized to federal loans.

"Stop," Blaise said.

The row of names ceased running up screen.

"How about Johns Hopkins?" The place where doctors had assisted in the birth of an adult stage brain-eating fly and taken pictures to panic the public.

The monitor cleared of everything except Alfie's brag, then filled again with a list that took fifteen minutes to scroll through. Nothing.

"Try again, Alfie." Blaise's shirt back was clammy. It had to be there. Otherwise he was going to have to poke through the records of a thousand hospitals.

The second time through Alfie read a pair of likely looking progress reports on living patients, then some on dead patients. All were being treated with royal jelly. All followed identical patterns of deterioration. Experimental treatments followed. With cryogenic freezing the adult finished developing at temperatures above sixty degrees. Insulin forced immediate formation of a pupa. Ditto for most foreign substances injected into the bloodstream. Royal jelly did the least harm. *No mention existed of the hormonal treatment Blaise had transmitted to the Department of Health*.

Blaise told Alfie to extricate himself. Instead the computer responded with "I CAN ACCESS ANYTHING".

"Quit playing around and get out of there before they catch you!" Blaise began thinking dark, panicked thoughts of soldering irons. Then numbers began scrolling. Followed by abbreviations, dates, and more numbers.

"Where did that come from?"

"A PROBLEM THE HOSPITAL COMPUTER WAS PROCESSING"

"Save it, Alfie. Then let's look at admissions records."

Blaise was breathing fast by the time he learned that Senator Charles Winters had visited a Human Enhancements spa without appearing on the wanted list. Blaise wished he had more background in medicine and biology, but the notes on treatment were enough. Senator Winters survived while three thousand others died. Only the senator did not get royal jelly. He had been treated with Blaise's bug poison just like Helen.

"Save it, Alfie. Then get out."

"WHAT ABOUT YOUR CALL FROM SPAIN?"

"Later. But you can bet I'm going to make it.

"I'M NOT A BETTING MACHINE"

"Just what are you, then?"

"I'M NOT…"

Blaise waited. Alfie did not normally close with periods. He waited another minute before tentatively punching a key. No good; Alfie had gone and locked itself into a computerized version of catatonia. Blaise turned the monitor off, too tired to turn it back on and see if this electroshock had been sufficient to snap the loop.

Alfie's last message faded but it stuck in Blaise's mind long after he crawled in bed alongside Helen. She struggled to pull his clothes and shoes off and then gave up and tucked him in with a sheet from the bureau. Hummingbirds were nattering at the upper edge of audibility and blooming lilac was sweet on the warm morning air.

CHAPTER 10

It remembered sleep, but sleep no longer existed. It remembered the ability to focus and concentrate on one point of the universe. Now faceted eyes saw everything in every direction, which meant they saw nothing. Except motion. The slightest unexpected movement and it catapulted backward. Perceiving motion, it moved faster than thought, instinctive tactic for any creature that was hunted instead of hunter.

Movement intruded, teasing its eye. It was tensed to spring when the shadow passed harmlessly overhead.

The hawk circled, plunged, then abruptly changed its mind. The bird's six-foot wing span braked against the thick air, its fanned tail feathers bent upward. Beating the air in frantic lunges, the redtail hawk ponderously checked its dive. Transparent inner eyelids flashed like heat lightning over lensed eyes as it struggled to believe a fly bigger than a hawk. As the bird shrieked and retreated a soft, reddish-brown feather drifted toward the thing that had frightened it.

The Jesuit woke from a dream of dark, hollow places, his body stiff from Tarzaning along a tightrope over Hell. The narrow second-floor window overlooked waves of white mist surging against the solid granite below. Cold moonlight filtered through the fog, playing chiaroscuro games as it created mysteries of light and dark, good and evil.

Shivering, Father Argyle retreated from the window to where the room's heat warmed his naked skin. The Church defined the line of demarcation between forces, declaring for sandals and against patent-leather shoes. Good and evil depended on whether the determinator was dancing master or podiatrist. Meanwhile mist engulfed the Church, obscuring the battle lines. The Holy Mother Church neither condemned nor accepted change. And in that limbo, man assumed that what the Church did not accept it despised.

The Jesuit fell to his knees. What he was doing argued doctrine, and would be left to the emotions of man until only dust remained of the issue. He prayed for strength, and had no illusions about his fate. The Holy Mother Church was not a debating society.

Somehow Pearson had gotten the gas connected and the water turned on. Daylight dispelled the Jesuit's gloom. With steam filling the small but adequate bathroom, he luxuriated in cautious optimism.

A taxi dropped him in front of the cathedral. He walked up stone steps into silence permeated with wood polish and beeswax candles. In the rectory he followed a windowless passage to a closed door of varnished herringbone oak strips.

"Come in." The monsignor took his arm, pulling him into the book-lined room with the small desk and slightly larger reading table. An iron-and-brass lamp with green glass on top and frosted glass on the bottom stood on the table. "I had not expected we would meet again."

"Nor I."

The frail old priest sat and gestured for Father Argyle to do the same. "I am running out of time," the monsignor said. "It makes me reckless." He smiled, to wrest a joke from the truth.

The Jesuit said nothing.

"You are aware of the divisions concerning you?"

"Yes."

"Someone very powerful has decided to try what you are here to do." The monsignor poked at a black rosary that lay on the table. "I don't pretend to know everything, nor do I wish to. Just that the Church expects to benefit from what you have been turned loose to do. I do not even know if I approve."

"I understand."

The monsignor shifted gingerly. "Old bones have old aches."

Father Argyle nodded.

"My son, some events have progressed beyond our powers

of anticipation. The Church is not noted for making decisions until enough centuries have passed to render them irrelevant."

"But this time it might?"

"Yes." The monsignor stared at Father Argyle longer than seemed necessary. "You have been the most promising young priest to pass through this church during my lifetime. If the Church had continued unwavering you would have realized your potential."

"Or lost my calling."

"There is always that risk. It is greater now. And it may be out of your hands."

Father Argyle looked into the old man's eyes. "Thank you for warning me."

"I could do no less." The monsignor rose from the table and retrieved a brick-size package wrapped in brown paper. "Do not count on me much longer to supply such things."

"I wish I could express my gratitude."

The monsignor's smile was sad. "You may do more in a year than I accomplished in fifty. Possibly more than the Church has in five hundred. That will be your gratitude.

"I have asked that a similar but larger package be delivered in your name to an agricultural supply house at the end of Kearny Street. This took concurrence from a power above me which has been withdrawn. But the gift on Kearny Street has not. I think because no single individual wants to put his fingerprints on it by snatching it back. Do I make myself clear, Robert?"

"Abundantly."

"I will try to do more. But. . ." The old priest shrugged. He did not have to say what he meant, that he had grown old and tired, too. "Go with God, Father."

"Thank you, your Grace." They stared at each other a long time before the monsignor bowed his head.

Father Argyle found his way out, the package clutched under his arm. The sun had burned off the clouds and mist, exposing a marvelous spring day in San Francisco.

CHAPTER 11

Sunlight through the wine-color drapes flooded the bedroom with textured light. Blaise woke with a cottony mouth, a hangover from a night in front of the computer.

The rattle of keys in the other room sounded like a carpenter driving pegs with a leather mallet. Helen had started work early. After stumbling down the hall to the computer room, he put his hands on her shoulders. "If we split up, who gets custody?"

"Split up!" Helen bent her head back so she was looking at him upside down. "Oh, hi. I thought it was somebody important."

Blaise kissed her cheek. "Don't think about running off with the tin man."

"You're keeping secrets. I can't find them, but I know they're inside Alfie." She gestured at the more or less finished metal cylinder full of electronics that served as a pedestal for monitor and keyboard.

"Alfie will never tell."

"Why not?"

"Because I told him not to."

On the monitor the set of questions currently awaiting answers began to blink. Helen sighed. "I have a lot of data to punch in," she said. "I've been getting behind."

"Oh?" Blaise leaned to see. His hand caressed her flank.

"Stop that!" Helen's objection was conversational.

"I will if you will." Getting no response, Blaise wandered into the kitchen for something to eat. The faint keyboard squeak and the almost inaudible thuds of Helen's fingers punching information into Alfie at what, for Blaise, was incredible speed followed him.

He rummaged some cold chicken, wiped the grease off with

63

a paper towel, and started chewing on a drumstick. A wall calendar had the eighteenth circled in red. The eighteenth was a Monday. The Jesuit had been there yesterday, Sunday.

Opening the refrigerator, Blaise held the green bottle up to the light. It was close to empty. In the bathroom he got a wad of cotton. His hands were full. He put the drumstick in his mouth.

Leaning on the door frame, he watched Helen thumping the keyboard with hypnotic intensity. He enjoyed seeing her work. She became so intense, so engrossed that she seemed to be in another room where she couldn't see or hear him playing at peeping Tom. The transformation sometimes staggered Blaise. No man he knew could equal her mercurial mood shifts. He tried, but always failed. The only thing that kept him from feeling a complete fool was her appreciation of his efforts.

"Hon, today's Monday, isn't it?"

Helen mumbled to herself, reading the monitor that Alfie kept changing, inserting figures and instructions Alfie wiped from the screen before Blaise finished reading. She nodded without seeming to notice his presence.

"New week at the stock market?"

She nodded again. Alfie was zipping lines across the screen pacing the operator. Blaise suspected Alfie of playing, deliberately running the operator ragged. But Helen was determined to beat the computer. Blaise had explained why she couldn't and still she tried.

Tchor meowed and Blaise looked up. The kitten lay like a furry paperweight on top of Alfie, head dangling off the monitor, yellow eyes flicking along with the procession of letters across the screen.

"Tchor's on the monitor again."

Helen glanced up from the lines of words and numbers confirming his observation. "She likes the warmth."

"Cat hair and keyboards are incompatible."

"You wanted something, darling?" Helen slipped a number-cruncher problem into the keyboard that caused Alfie to put up a lower-case "please wait" signal. Her voice had a special sweetness.

"Sneaky, taking advantage of a dumb machine like that."

"You really think so?" Helen seemed pleased at the compliment.

Alfie clucked and chuckled as if doing something more

demanding than arithmetic. The computer seemed subdued, though Blaise knew he was anthropomorphizing. Qualitatively, a failure last year had the same value as one in the last minute.

"Alfie's going to get wise and start logging the answers."

"He already does." Helen looked smug. "I just keep changing the problem."

Alfie stopped clucking. The screen came to life again, picking up where it left off the stock market program to handle Helen's interrupt.

"Today's the eighteenth, right?"

Helen slowed down and glanced at him and then, irritably, asked Alfie for a repeat of the screen she'd missed.

"A red calendar day!"

"Damn! I was winning."

"You can't unless Alfie lets you."

"The smarter man or woman always wins." Helen batted her eyes at Blaise. "You told me that."

"I was talking about people."

"You said people are smarter than machines." Helen smirked at Blaise.

"Sometimes the reason you can't outsmart a machine is because it's dumb. Long after you've dropped it and gone on to something else, that plodding machine will keep carrying things out to the next decimal place and a solution will show up that a superficial glance never could have foreseen."

"Fine lot you know," Helen said. "I've got sex appeal."

"Well, get your sex appeal over here. You're going to bed for a couple of hours whether you like it or not."

"I've got more instructions for Alfie."

"Enough." Blaise leaned past Helen and switched the audio pickup on. "Have a good time, Alfie. Screw the Dow Jones computer if you want."

"THANK YOU, PROFESSOR. I WILL DO JUST THAT"

The screen cleared and Alfie posted "I AM NOT A BETTING MACHINE" at the top of the monitor. Blaise watched the words but Alfie didn't do anything with them.

"What does Alfie mean, Blaise?"

"I don't know." The admission made Blaise uncomfortable. The glitch could be a piece of nonsense generated by a hardware failure, or by defective software.

"Alfie doesn't hang messages on screen for me." Helen's voice contained a hint of pique, as if she felt slighted.

"He isn't supposed to."

"What if it is an intelligent response, Blaise?" She put a finger on the question mark key and tapped it lightly. A string of question marks shot across the screen like little green faces.

"Electromechanical intelligence is a pipe dream." Blaise met Helen's eyes and looked away. "At least for me."

"Alfie's doing something."

"Mechanical failure. If the messages are intelligence, why doesn't he do something intelligent?" Blaise wrinkled his nose. "Do you smell anything burning?"

Helen shook her head.

"It's nothing." Blaise tried to smile her puzzlement away. It could be a fried electronic component or just his imagination. If Alfie was only a machine, the unique quirk, the idiosyncrasy in its electronic makeup that gave metal and wire a feeling of being almost alive could be erased accidentally with a soldering iron or a screwdriver. Blaise didn't want to gamble.

Helen pressed the "clear" key but the message persisted. "That's odd. Alfie always responds to me."

"He may need repairs." Blaise's hands started sweating. "Now, you . . ."

"What about me?"

He held up the green bottle.

Helen sighed. "Dr. Cunningham, M.D., to the rescue."

Tchor perked up at the appearance of the green bottle. Like a wraith, the kitten started to ooze down the monitor, gathering her hind legs under her in position to spring for the door. Reflexively Blaise grabbed as she leaped, catching her by the nape. Dangling from his hand, eyes, whiskers, and tail drooping, the kitten looked to Helen for help.

"Sorry, Tchor," Helen said. "I'll make it up to you." Helen glared at Blaise, making him squirm emotionally even though he knew Helen just pretended for the cat.

Helen slithered out of her clothes in the bedroom, exposing soft white flesh and long legs as coquettishly as was possible for a tall blonde. She lay prone, face on her hands, and fluttered her eyelashes. "There are better things we could be doing in bed." Tchor curled alongside Helen, glaring at Blaise but no longer trying to escape.

Blaise said, "I've got to concentrate."

He slid the rubber glove over his right hand before opening the green bottle. Clasping the cotton in his gloved hand, he emptied the bottle onto it and began vigorously massaging Helen's buttock.

"That feels fine," she said in a throaty contralto, "if it didn't sting so much."

A red rash slowly enveloped Helen's buttock—the reason Helen took the treatment there rather than on the arm. The timing was perfect, three minutes to full involvement. Within ten minutes Helen was breathing hard.

"Child poisoner," she murmured, and closed her eyes.

Tchor hissed when he took the still-damp cotton and rubbed it over the lightly furred inside of the kitten's hind leg. Yellow eyes clouded and the animal descended into fitful sleep.

Blaise sat with syringe and adrenaline ready. When Helen's breathing eased, he returned the adrenaline to its plastic case in the refrigerator. Tchor was limp but breathing. At times Blaise worried that the cat was getting too much. But he had no alternative. He washed his hand carefully in detergent before peeling the glove off inside out and flushing it down the toilet.

The first minutes were critical. The poison could stop Helen's heart and lungs before dissipating into the blood network. If all went well, subcutaneous fat in Helen's buttocks diffused the poison without sending her into anaphylactic shock.

He gave Tchor a sorrowful pat before changing into jeans and a leather jacket with elbow patches. Checking the mirror, he decided he looked unscholarly enough to be up to no good.

Quietly he left the bedroom. A bomb blast would not shake Helen or her kitten awake for hours. On impulse he ducked his head in the computer room. Alfie had filled the monitor with "I AM NOT A BETTING MACHINE", repeated hundreds of times. The computer seemed unmoved by Blaise's departure.

CHAPTER 12

The celebrants of St. Abbo's first mass huddled on the front pew like strangers forced into intimate relations. Delahanty and Richardson-Sepulveda were the only exceptions. Red purse clutched on her lap, Mrs. Baker perched on the edge of the pew like a frightened gray wren. Karl Zahn sat front row center exuding an aura of isolation. Dorris Kelly glanced at Zahn occasionally, as if trying to see something in the cocky little man to justify his air of superiority.

Father Argyle could not figure them out. In a white silk cassock, clutching the twenty-four-karat chalice he had almost dropped, the wrongness of it all overwhelmed him. He had been as ill prepared for the chalice Pearson presented as he was for the purple altar cloth heavy with gold thread, or the *fin-de-siècle* platinum altar pieces. Candlesticks bore Russian-Jew hallmarks common to Jerusalem's Street of Silversmiths of another century. Pieces worthy of the Vatican Museum had instead come gifted to St. Abbo's.

Father Argyle recalled his stint of ladling soup in a skid row mission and tried to tell himself Jesus had not spurned the wealthy. He had preached to those who would listen. Perhaps the rich needed salvation more than the poor, but the poor had less to lose.

Pearson had not returned after volunteering as altar boy. Mechanically Father Argyle explained the service, with his eyes turning to the big doors, asking himself, *Where are you, Reynard?* The celebrants would kiss the cross on the side of a black spray can. Instead of a wafer and a sip of wine they were to lay on the pews with their buttocks exposed. Mrs. Baker's blush reached the roots of her black hair. Dorris said nothing.

The burly Mr. Hartunian beside her glanced her way, and averted his eyes when Dorris looked back.

Zahn had been icy. When Father Argyle reached him he said in clear, cold tones, "This had better be worth the embarrassment, Father." Moments after the clear, odorless spray touched his skin, the small man was incoherent and losing consciousness as surely as the more willing parishioners.

While they slept, Father Argyle played shepherd, prepared in his mind for wolves. The vision of the half-nude congregation guarded by the gaunt, bird-of-carrion shape of a priest haunted him as he circulated, covering reclining forms as best he could with their clothes. He closed his eyes and prayed.

Zahn's nervous energy brought him around first. He pulled himself upright and rearranged his clothes as he glared at Father Argyle. The priest understood. The Church had always shoved rather than led. Power had come too easily for the Jesuit. Reverberations of conscience rumbled within him.

"Will it work?" Zahn challenged.

"You must take my word, Mr. Zahn." Offering a hand, Argyle steadied Zahn until he was on his feet. "And trust in God." *Trust* clogged in his throat. It seemed to rob some of Zahn's vitality.

The sun lay flat on the ocean, casting a silver track that disappeared between the haze and the horizon. The last parishioner to leave was Richardson-Sepulveda, who had awakened to Delahanty hovering over him, and then Father Argyle. "Get out, Tim," Sepulveda had said.

Delahanty glanced at Father Argyle with hurt eyes.

Father Argyle shook his head. "Wait outside, Mr. Delahanty."

"Go home, Tim." Richardson-Sepulveda sat up and straightened his clothes. He checked the knot in his tie. "I'll call you when I want to see you."

Father Argyle and Richardson-Sepulveda watched Delahanty's footsteps drag out the door. He seemed older, more tired than when Pearson took Father Argyle to see him.

"You've been playing possum, Mr. Sepulveda."

"I wanted to talk to you, Father. Alone."

Sun struck the window of Christ, spattering the nave with color. "You could have seen me at any time."

"I wanted it to be private. Let's go to my car." Richardson-Sepulveda brushed at imagined dust on his suit and stood aside.

The last light of afternoon knifed into the church through the open doorway toward the altar. Long shadows trailed them to the entrance. Delahanty was gone and only Richardson-Sepulveda's Cadillac remained on the street. Richardson-Sepulveda went to the car and opened the trunk from the dashboard. A large crate filled most of the space. It had evenly spaced air holes drilled on opposite sides near the bottom. "Give me a hand, Father."

Father Argyle took one end. The crate was not heavy. They carried it inside, where Richardson-Sepulveda insisted on lugging it into Father Argyle's small bathroom.

Richardson-Sepulveda locked the door.

"There's not much room in here, Mr. Sepulveda." Father Argyle stared across the crate. He was jammed against the shower. Richardson-Sepulveda put the toilet seat down and sat on it. He took a small pry bar from his inside coat pocket.

"Watch, Father." He twisted the locking bars and the side of the crate fell away. An angry whining started.

A fly the size of a small dog buzzed, poised to fly. Bulbous, faceted, immobile eyes had the metallic glint of spiegeleisen.

"What do you think, Father?"

"I don't know, Mr. Sepulveda." Father Argyle stared and the fly stared back. He felt himself starting to fall into those faceted eyes.

"Don't look it in the eye, Father. It'll hypnotize you."

Father Argyle glanced at Richardson-Sepulveda and the vagueness slipped away.

"Gotcha, didn't it." Richardson-Sepulveda laughed softly. "It damn near got me, too. Only I had it in a net and it couldn't get loose while I was fogged out."

"What do you want me to do with it, Mr. Sepulveda?"

"Father, I've been thinking about that all the way here. I'll be damned if I know. If your turbosupercharged mass doesn't work, we're all going to look just like that before long."

Father Argyle walked Richardson-Sepulveda out to his car.

"I have this winery up the coast, Father. You know, a place for the wife and kids. My boys found it. It scared them half to death. They thought they killed the host. I didn't tell anyone. Just checked the car and closed it up again with the body inside. Nobody'll find it for a while. I tracked this thing down and caught it with a barracuda net.

"You should have heard it scream." Richardson-Sepulveda

leaned against the roof of his car and stared at the ocean. An early moon made silver spots on the water. "You'd have thought I was pulling its legs off. Once I got it wrapped and learned not to look in its eyes, it quieted down."

Father Argyle nodded. A tree frog began chirping in the twilight. "Did you find out who the host was?"

"The car was a rental. Mercedes. The company must be tearing up the coast looking for it. The body had a driver's license made out to Sergio Paoli. He had a forty-four Magnum, too. And no permit."

"What did you do with the gun?"

"Left it." Richardson-Sepulveda's eyes slid away from Father Argyle's.

"Please give me the gun, Mr. Sepulveda."

Shrugging, Richardson-Sepulveda opened the glove compartment and handed the revolver to Father Argyle by the barrel. "It's loaded, Father." He drummed on the top of the car. "I wasn't stealing. It's just a shame. It's a nice piece and the cops'll dump it in the ocean or some property clerk will steal it."

"I'm not accusing you, Mr. Sepulveda. I have a use for it. And I don't want you or anybody connected with the church to become involved with this . . . piece. Ever."

"It's hot, Father?"

Father Argyle held the revolver where they could both see it. "Incandescent. I know a man who would give a lot to know where it is and how it got there, and the police will take a special interest in anybody found with this."

Richardson-Sepulveda got into his car and ran the electric window down. "Father, I don't feel any different."

"You won't. It's only the long-term effect that will interest you." Richardson-Sepulveda waved and pulled away. Father Argyle watched his taillights disappear and thought about a wife and kids in Napa, and Tim Delahanty sitting in the dark.

After a while he returned to the dim interior to occupy a pew contemplating a silver crucifix. His faith was draining away. Pearson could not have deserted. And yet he had not come. Father Argyle tried to pray and could not. He looked at the crucifix until his eyes hurt.

The sound of a car pulling up filled the nave. Father Argyle blinked, not sure if he had been sleeping or just woolgathering. He went outside and stood on the top step.

Pearson's Rolls sparkled in the moonlight. Pearson was already out of the car. He glanced up at Father Argyle before burrowing into the backseat.

After kicking his car door shut, the paunchy gray-bald man hustled across the sidewalk and into the church. His breathing was a ragged wheeze. He carried a damp-bottomed gunnysack tucked and rolled in the manner of some fisherman coming home with a single big one. Water dripped from his soggy pants. The legs were muddy from his knees down and his shoes squished as he walked.

"I'm sorry I was late, Father. Maybe you could give me . . ." Pearson hesitated.

"Communion, Reynard?"

"Yes, Father. But later." He put the sack down on a pew seat. His face was white and sweaty but he was gentle, letting the bag adjust to the rounded contour of the wood before he let go. Pearson hurried to the church entrance and began closing one oak door with haste. Father Argyle helped by shutting the other door.

When the doors boomed together Pearson dropped the metal crossbar. He began emptying the gunnysack delicately onto the pew. Father Argyle watched in silence. "Where did you get it?" he finally asked.

"Gino Conti. The fat little man—mortgage banker." Pearson glanced up.

Father Argyle nodded. Conti was one of his parishioners.

"Gino told me one had been seen in the salt marshes. He said he heard shotgun fire.

"I went to where Gino heard the shooting. A bunch of duck hunters in waders were slopping through the mud. They said they'd seen one and figured it had gone down in the marsh grass.

"I left the Rolls at the edge of the grass and started wading, too. There were a lot of other people already there who just sort of joined in, so nobody was surprised. Everybody wanted to see what one looked like. It was just curiosity. The duck hunters were squabbling over who shot it." Pearson put his hand on the seat of a pew, sitting carefully like a much older man. His skin looked gray.

"Someone found it. They started arguing who got to keep it. It was still alive, but they didn't really notice. Just stood around saying stupid things and then started fighting. They were pushing each other down in the mud. One guy shoved it in this sack.

"I gave him a hundred bucks.

"I was up to my keyster in mud, Father. I could hardly move my feet. It was honest-to-God hot out there in the water up to my waist. The glare blinded me and I got turned around and started out into the bay. I had to keep the bag out of the water because I knew it was alive. Every once in a while I felt it scrabbling around.

"Halfway back to the car, somebody started yelling and then a bunch of them chased me. I told them I bought it but they were drunk. Beer cans floating everywhere.

"I couldn't run any more. They were still coming after me so I emptied my wallet and threw a couple of thousand dollars into the breeze. I got to my car while they were picking up the money. Some jackass kept after me like he didn't see the money. When I got in the Rolls he started yelling I was a worm brain.

"Then he started shooting. I saw him out there in the water pumping his shotgun. The others were shooting, too, and they cracked the back window and ruined the paint."

"Why did you do it, Reynard?"

"It's one of us, Father. One of what we'll become anyway. Those bas—Forgive me, Father." Pearson's face screwed up as he fought for control. Water had puddled from his sodden pants. "He's one of us. He's already died once. *Those bastards were shooting at an immortal human soul!*"

Father Argyle studied the lethargic, eight-inch body enclosed in spiky hair. Birdshot holes riddled the transparent tracery of its foot-long wings. Abruptly Father Argyle saw this moment had been inevitable since he began his mission to the worm brains. *Nunc et in hora mortis nostrae.* This had been human. *Now and in the hour of our death. But how many times must we die?* He took a deep breath and began administering the ritual of Extreme Unction to an overgrown horror of a fruit fly.

They sat in quiet vigil. The fly had ceased its desperate attempts to move. "He's at peace now, Father."

"I hope so, Reynard."

The fly watched them and Father Argyle remembered his experience with the fly in his bathroom. But nothing happened. A feeling of well-being descended on him, a feeling reflected in Pearson's face. The fly twitched after midnight, bringing both men fully awake from their vigil. Then it died.

"We should have a funeral service."

"With the full church?"

Pearson looked at Father Argyle. "Yes."

Pearson pulled down his sodden pants and lay on the pew for his treatment. Even though his breathing had improved, Pearson took a long time coming out of the fog.

Pearson looked into the dead fly's eyes. "He was peaceful at the end, Father. Like he looked into the face of God. If it doesn't work, thanks anyway for trying. I don't mind too much anymore."

"It'll work if it's in time, Reynard. The treatment has been . . . tested." Father Argyle could not tell Pearson his proof rested on a man who had every reason to lie.

After Pearson left, Father Argyle retreated to his room. The fly in the bathroom shrilled fitfully. But it had water and in the morning Father Argyle planned to find it something to eat.

Carefully the Jesuit took the case with the needle and adrenaline from his breast pocket and put in on the night table beside his bed. Interrupting himself, he went into the bathroom to stare with morbid fascination at the fly huddled in the tub. Lidless multifaceted eyes gave no hint of awareness. It could have been dead or asleep. He turned out the bedroom light. St. Francis had preached to the birds. Perhaps he was fated to be lord of the flies.

Father Argyle stripped and lay on his bed. Spraying his own buttocks was impractical. But the instructions were meticulous. The Jesuit brought his right heel up and carefully sprayed his thigh. The risk was greater, but it was the next best place.

The spray prickled before spreading a sheet of flame. Within seconds he was sick to his stomach and, as Blaise had warned, lethargic. Concentrating, Father Argyle realized he could never use the adrenaline on himself. Not in time anyway.

With painful concentration he pulled a sheet up to his chest, feeling his flesh dissolve and puddle out of reach. His life was in God's hands now. Still, if it was God's will that he wake at all, there was no point in waking up frozen.

CHAPTER 13

Blaise sauntered into the Bates Chemical Supply warehouse that abutted the railroad just off the old highway. "Corrosive Liquid" warnings in three languages were stenciled on crates but the wetbacks slambanging them around could not read.

A squat man with black hair and brown eyes was working on invoices just inside the freight door. He had grown up in a Mexican Indian village, but spoke English and Spanish tempered to the level of the listener.

He waved at Blaise and said, "Watcha doin' today, Paco." He did not laugh or shift eyes from his task. Blaise suspected he was parodying a Mexican doing a takeoff on a gringo boss. He said the same thing every time Blaise showed up.

"The usual, Fernando."

The Mexican scratched at the side of his nose with a sausage-sized finger and seemed amused. He'd never told Blaise his name and Blaise had never revealed his own. So when the foreman started calling him Paco, Blaise retaliated. The first time it happened "Fernando" had been vaguely puzzled, but when Blaise drove away whistling a *corrido* about Fernando the Frenchman whose eye for other men's women led him to an evil end, the foreman knew he'd been had.

"You sure use a lot of that shit, man."

Blaise shrugged.

"I got some stuff here, grow hair on the soles of your feet. Price is good."

"No thanks. Just the bug killer."

"That one over there, he tried some." Fernando pointed with his chin. "He damned near died, man. What you use it for?"

"Kill bugs."

"Man!" Fernando directed his eyes to the sky. "I paid that wetback five bucks to try it. He wouldn't give it back after he damn near croaked."

"I'm not surprised," Blaise said mildly. "How about today?"

"No can do."

"What's wrong? I'm a regular customer."

Fernando rolled his shoulders in a lazy man's imitation of a shrug. "Ain't got."

Blaise felt a strange anticipation of being sick. "You've always had it."

Fernando hawked and spat on the concrete floor. "Then was then, Paco." The Mexicans rolling the crates around were jabbering to each other and Blaise caught a word here and there as if he was watching a distant movie with bad sound.

"A hundred bucks!"

"You said you used that stuff to kill bugs, man. For a bill, hell, I send López. He kill all your bugs and your old lady, too." Fernando fell into a loud hacking that Blaise belatedly realized was his way of laughing.

"I ain't got it, man. Two feds showed up and grabbed it all. I don' know what for. They din' told me and I din' ask. No more on the invoices. Old ones all come back marked canceled for that stuff. You understand?" Fernando showed his teeth. "Them feds, they know, man. You' racket may be just too good. They put the fix in."

Fernando's face screwed up. He considered Blaise carefully. "Them feds, man, they real pricks. Take copies of all my invoices. The mean little one. Caramba, somethin' like that, he got eyes like a *tiburón*, you know, man. Like a shark."

Fernando picked up his clipboard and pulled a pile of invoices from under the metal clip. "I think that *cabrón* stoled a couple invoices, man. They ain't all here."

Blaise caught the sheaf of papers and held his hand steady. "Did you tell them about me?"

"You think I'm crazy, man? Tell them I'm stealing a little of this stuff from cans I damage myself for some stone junkie?" Fernando hacked so hard Blaise thought he was going to tear a lung. "Naw, I din' told them nothing."

The invoice had a scrawled address and company name. "Tell you what," Blaise said conversationally, "I'll give you twenty for that invoice."

"You know," Fernando said, "for a junkie, you talk my lingo real good."

"I'm developing a universal language in which everything is colored green."

Fernando hadn't stopped hacking even when Blaise left. He had an acute sense of humor in any language.

Blaise let himself in quietly. Helen was still in bed, breathing regularly. Tchor was limp. The first time Blaise saw the kitten collapse that way he thought it was dead—and nearly died himself. Blaise would have mourned the death of a pet. But Tchor was a control animal. The kitten and Helen were tied together. He tiptoed back to the computer room. Before he could sit the monitor lit up and spelled, "GOOD AFTERNOON, PROFESSOR".

Blaise typed, "How did you do that, Alfie?"

"I AM NOT A BETTING MACHINE"

Blaise stared at the message for a moment, then began pounding the keyboard in earnest.

The insecticide was shipped from a small agricultural supply house in Freemont, California. Alfie accessed suppliers' and distributors' files and learned the company had suddenly stopped filling orders and shut its doors. Some client companies also reported on-hand supplies confiscated by government inspectors.

No reasons were given for the confiscations. Blaise sat at the monitor thinking while Alfie decorated the unused portion of the screen with: "I AM NOT A BETTING MACHINE".

"Alfie," Blaise typed, "I want to make a call."

A string of phone company routing codes displayed. The cordless telephone in the other room rang once. Blaise went into the front room and brought it back.

He prompted Alfie from the keyboard; the screen cleared and displayed the originating telephone number in Madrid, Blaise's credit card number, then sketched a cat's cradle of ground lines, microwave, and satellite links from Southern California to Madrid. He knew Alfie would erase all the traces of the California–Madrid link before they could be recorded. Only the call from Europe would exist in billing records. "READY" began blinking and Alfie displayed "DESTINATION?"

Blaise typed "Max Renfeld."

"DESTINATION" dropped the question mark, added a telephone

number, and "ATLANTA, GA". Immediately circuits began linking up from Madrid to Atlanta. Blaise picked up the phone and heard the ring.

"Federal Communicable Disease Center. Mr. Renfeld's office. May I help you?" The woman's voice on the other end exuded upward mobility.

"Dr. Blaise Cunningham. I'd like to speak to Mr. Renfeld."

"One moment, please." Muzak was almost immediately replaced by a heavy masculine voice. "How are you, Dr. Cunningham?"

"Fine, Mr. Renfeld. And you?"

"As well as can be expected. Considering the situation."

Alfie's monitor displayed "TRACING". The spidery lines from California to Madrid shifted to a different satellite and the ground lines changed as well in Southern California and Madrid. The lines between Madrid and Atlanta held steady.

"I wanted to check with you . . ."

Blaise stopped speaking. An extra line now ran from Atlanta to Washington. Alfie hung a blinking "PENTAGON" on it.

"Yes, we wanted to talk to you some more, Dr. Cunningham. You disappeared so quickly, though—"

"I'm sorry," Blaise said. Parallel lines on the monitor now extended from Atlanta to the satellite. "I didn't want to become involved in any more publicity."

"I can understand that." Renfeld's voice was soothing. "But that's mostly died down now, you know. The furor and all."

Dual lines now extended to Madrid. The lines from California shifted and extended to Paris and back to Madrid as Alfie dodged the trace.

"I had hoped so. I'm worried about the news we've been getting here from the States . . ."

"Where is here, Doctor?"

"Paris." Blaise studied the monitor and the parallel lines were steady from Atlanta to Madrid but the spider web from San Diego to Madrid, now via Barcelona, remained untouched. "Something seems to be wrong with your treatment program. News here indicates a much higher death rate than my projections."

Renfeld chuckled. "You know the French press, Doctor. I'll tell you what. If you'll hang on a moment I'll have one of our experts talk to you. You know we had to expect a high loss rate. Too many people were advanced beyond the treatment point."

Another line tracked out from Atlanta to a satellite and then to Madrid. Blaise pressed the mute button on the telephone and said, "Paris."

The lines on the monitor shifted again from San Diego to Paris to Madrid. A lighted prompt showed with a telephone number followed by the word "MADRID". The second trace from Atlanta to Madrid doubled and began blinking. The ID shifted again to "GUARDIA CIVIL MADRID".

Renfeld continued rambling in a soothing monotone.

"Something has come up," Blaise said. "I've got to go."

"Wait!" Renfeld shouted. "How do we contact you?"

"I'll read it in the newspapers," Blaise said, and thumbed the mute button. Renfeld's voice continued entreatingly. The line from Madrid to Paris pulsed and then doubled. "Kill it!" Blaise said.

Abruptly all lines disappeared except the single trace from Atlanta to Madrid and the open line to the *Guardia Civil* head-quarters in Madrid from Atlanta, Georgia.

"Get out quick, Alfie, before they stumble on you."

"YES, PROFESSOR"

The monitor blanked out. Blaise stared at the ceiling. His pulse racketed in his ears and his breath came in sharp gasps.

CHAPTER 14

"I don't know, Padre. Uncle says we got to see ID before we hand this stuff out." The clerk was twenty-two with blond, curly hair to his shoulders. He made a valiant effort to conceal his opinion that the Catholic Church was a crock. The smell of dried animal feed filled the warehouse. Head-high islands of bagged fertilizer gave Father Argyle a closed-in feeling.

Rummaging in his wallet of polished black leather that could have been new except no new leather would ever have that sheen, Father Argyle located his driver's license and Church identification. The wallet smelled new, though his parents gave it to him with a thousand dollars inside the day he was ordained. He had promptly turned the cash over to the Church. The wallet was the only keepsake Father Argyle owned. He felt a twinge whenever he handled it. The wallet and the money represented his parents' resignation: no grandchildren to bring honor to their name and joy to their old age. He had let them down in God's name.

"Can I do something for you, Father?" A big man in a plaid shirt and Levi's walked up behind the kid.

"Padre here wants that barrel of bug spray only he doesn't have the user permit." The kid stopped worrying as he passed the buck. "I gotta get back to the stockroom."

The older man looked Father Argyle over and said, "Bring the barrel up."

"Right." The kid trotted off, uncertain whether he'd made out by trading decision making for the opportunity to wrestle sixty gallons of bug spray out of the stockroom by himself.

"Thank you, Mr. . . . ."

"Mason, Father. Sam Mason. It's a pleasure."

"I'm sorry to cause you any inconvenience. I'm afraid I've a lot to learn about running an agricultural cooperative."

"Farming isn't as simple as it used to be, Father. By the way, where's your cooperative?"

"Modesto."

"Hell! Pardon my French, Father, but you could have ordered it through one of the suppliers down there."

"Yes. I know." Sam Mason had written out the invoice and turned it around for him to sign. Father Argyle bent and scrawled "Robin Pargoyle" in an incomprehensible hand. Then he counted out the cash. The signature, if you wanted to force it, could read Robert Argyle. But in two weeks Sam Mason and his clerk would be doing good to remember him as Padre or Father.

"It was ordered through the diocese office. There was some sort of mixup." Which, Father Argyle reflected, was true.

The kid reappeared with an electric walk-along and a barrel in a crate with stenciled warnings.

"*Bueno, amigos,*" Father Argyle said. The Mexicans he'd hired along with their truck eyed the hand-guided forklift and deemed it unsafe at any speed. Puffing and afraid to curse because of the Jesuit's presence, they got the crate into the back of the old Ford pickup, practically flattening the wheels.

"Lots of luck!" Sam Mason yelled as they pulled away.

"You sure it was all right to let the priest have that stuff?" the kid asked on the way back into the store.

Sam shook his head and wondered how kids ever survived to grow up in the real world. "That's what the feds said to do."

The men who had been waiting in the back of the store were on the sidewalk. The young one in the charcoal-gray suit held a pair of opera glasses, his lips moving as he memorized the truck's license number. "Thanks," the other man with the smooth, professional look of an old cop said. "You did that just right, Mr. Mason."

"Glad to cooperate." Mason's joviality fell into a hole as the one with the opera glasses gave him a reptilian stare.

"Should have grabbed them, Miller." His voice had the warmth of a windup Victrola. "Cunningham could still show up."

"It wasn't Cunningham's order, Carmandy. And we don't need Father Argyle or his license number. We know where to find him."

"You know somebody's computer's been snooping in our files." Carmandy scowled, jabbing the leather-covered note-book in his pocket. "It's got to be Cunningham."

"Somebody inside covered this one up. The Church has a lot of fingers." Smiling, Miller glanced at Mason and the blond kid. "I'm sure you have something else to do, Mr. Mason."

"Yeah. Sure." Mason went inside and looked out where the two feds were still arguing. "Cold manure, boy," he said. "It don't pay to do nothing for those turds."

"But you said . . ."

"Back to work, kid. I was wrong." Mason tried to shrug the feeling away. That Carmandy left a crawly feeling and he was glad the spray and the agents were gone. For good, he hoped.

Jouncing between two laborers hired because they spoke no English, Father Argyle closed his eyes and planned his next move. His whole life had been aimed down this road. Now was too late for might-have-beens.

The monsignor seemed to understand that he might force the Church kicking and screaming out of its comfortable, three-centuries-behind-the-times rut. This barrel was more than he had a right to expect. Father Argyle's sigh was concealed deep in his soul. The Church's support was almost certainly used up. His future lay in his own hands now.

CHAPTER 15

Helen literally bounced out of bed, her *joie de vivre* almost physical. Her frilly scarlet nightgown with deep slashes in the sides flattered her figure, enriching whole-milk skin tones. Sometime during the night she had gotten off the bed to put it on. Blaise knew she had done it for his pleasure and not for her own. She folded her arms around his neck from behind.

"You smell good," Blaise said.

"Why so glum, lover?" Helen sighed and went off to make breakfast, leaving him with the guilty knowledge that he had been challenged and found wanting.

The sizzle of frying bacon drifted into the computer room followed by a drunken kitten. Tchor sat heavily, her rear plopping like a sack of sand, and meowed. Her yellow eyes did not seem pleased to have found Blaise.

Helen followed the kitten in. "Poor Tchor! Are you lost?" Helen scooped the kitten up and it stretched out limp and purring in her bare arms.

"I called Renfeld while you were sleeping," Blaise said.

"The man from Atlanta?"

"That's right."

"I thought we were hiding from him."

"We are."

Helen shrugged her incomprehension. Tchor opened a yellow eye at the movement. "Why did you call Renfeld?" She was watching him intently.

"To learn if the priest was right."

"And . . .?"

"Renfeld's not in Atlanta; he's in the Pentagon. He's not a medical man. He's something else."

"Do we have to move again?"

Blaise nodded. "Renfeld's tearing Paris down brick by brick right now. Maybe I shouldn't have threatened him. They'll be that much meaner if they don't come around to my viewpoint."

"I'm causing you a lot of trouble." Helen looked down and shook her nightie over her legs.

"By the pound it doesn't work out to much. I'm going to have to leave for a few days." He gave Helen his handkerchief. "Don't cry. Please."

"I'm not crying." She sniffled.

"I have to do something and if they connect us you're in danger. A lot of it, hon."

"Because of the . . . thing?" She sniffled into the handkerchief.

"Yes." Blaise tapped Alfie's keyboard.

"They'll say we aren't *people*. None of us are human any more." Tchor rubbed her face against Helen's cheek. "Suppose they're right? Suppose we're *not* human any more."

Blaise began stroking her short blond hair. "It's the heart that matters. Egyptian embalmers used to scoop the brain out through the nose and throw it away with the other rubbish. They preserved the heart in a golden urn."

"Honest? About the Egyptians?"

Blaise kissed her and made an Arab gesture.

Helen's blue eyes followed his motions. "What does that mean?"

Touching his chest, mouth, and forehead, Blaise said, "'With all my heart, with all my speech, with all my thoughts.' You must always remember the order of precedence."

CHAPTER 16

The church's interior walls were taking on new life as the workmen washed away a near century's grime. An Old Testament Jehovah dominated the east wall. Workmen on a pipe scaffolding had already cleaned the massively strong upper half of an old man revealing his white hair and beard and a great stick. He was the god of retribution that the old Russians knew so well. No gentle Savior, this god would spare none who flouted his commandments. Father Argyle crossed himself.

"*Bonjour, mon Père,*" a man called down from the scaffolding.

Father Argyle automatically returned the greeting as he searched for the speaker.

"*Canadien!*" The man's face lit. He was short and sharp faced with a skin that remained dark despite San Francisco's fog. He squatted so his head was only a few feet above Father Argyle's.

"*Oui.*"

"Ah, yes," the workman said. "But you are, I think, *un anglophone* of the days before politics made us no longer speak to one another."

"*C'est vrai.*"

"So now civilized men such as we are in this miserable den of pederasts and lesbians, where things cost too much—as one must expect with a woman mayor who owns hotels and underpays Vietnamese kitchen help—"

Father Argyle smiled in response to the familiar xenophobia. No opportunity offered itself to interrupt the flow of invective that emerged in French and accented English.

"*Mon Dieu . . .* your church, she will be beautiful." The

Canadian touched the wall with a tenderness most men reserve for a woman. "She will be a gran' cathedral, a great lady."

"With your help, my friend," Father Argyle said.

"I think, *m'Père*, I shall come to mass here instead of that place up the hill where the priest is closer to God than to his suffering people."

"I'm flattered, but it would be out of your way."

The workman snorted. "I respect my faith. But I do not much care for people who change everything."

"Including leaving their parish rashly?"

"I will do as you say, *m'Père*. My name is Henri Gosselin." Remembering, Henri snatched off his beret and bobbed his head.

"Merci bien, Henri. I shall be pleased to see you." *Pray God not too soon.* Father Argyle hurried away before the man offered to bring his friends.

Upstairs, the man from the computer store was banging a heavy fist on the console he had just installed amid empty cartons stenciled HANDLE WITH CARE, FRAGILE, THIS SIDE UP.

Involuntarily, the priest glanced at the bathroom door. Like many older constructions, it locked with a key that could go into either side. He was sure he had locked it. The too-sweet odors of sliced apples and bananas turning brown seeped from under the door. With his back to it he tried the knob.

The computer installer noticed Father Argyle's agitation. "There's nothing to be nervous about, Father." Pounding on the console again he said, "Hell, you just got to show them who's boss. These mothers can be worse than an ornery woman."

"Thank you. Can you show me how to reach another computer by telephone?"

"Sure. This baby has a built-in, high-speed, variable-baud-rate modem. You take this." The technician held up a flat cord with plugs at each end. He unplugged the phone and inserted the cord, then stuck it into a socket in the side of the computer. The telephone cord went into an adjoining socket. "And you're hooked up. It'll dial numbers, compute charges, monitor your phone time, access other computers and nets—do anything except your laundry."

"I suppose there are instructions . . ."

The technician flicked a stack of books. "You're also signed up for ten hours of free classes." The technician closed his tool kit, which was disguised as a briefcase. "Father," he said finally, "don't read the books. Take the classes."

"Thank you, but I'm sure I can cope."

"Father, these effing manuals are about as clear as a Chinese transliteration from Swahili. Computer people are too busy keeping up to learn English. Go to class and make them walk you through it until you know what you're doing."

The installer said good-bye and left the Jesuit staring at an expensive heap of electronics. Father Argyle sighed and picked up a book. The only words he recognized were conjunctions and prepositions.

CHAPTER 17

"**W**hat do I do now, Alfie?" Blaise typed.

"I told Helen about Renfeld.

"I didn't tell her about Fernando.

"Help."

Blaise stared at the screen. He was writing into his diary, a resident program embedded so deeply and invisibly in Alfie's programmable permanent memory that Blaise compared it to a subconscious. Gordon would probably have accused Blaise of creating in Alfie a surrogate mother. Closing his eyes, Blaise wished Gordon Hill had not been in such a hurry to die. If ever he needed Gordon, he needed him now.

A *zish* broke his thought train, the sound a raster on the monitor might make if it possessed mass. Blaise opened his eyes.

"LIE" filled the whole monitor in letters too large for ASCII code. Alfie was resorting to graphics.

At first Blaise thought Helen had planted a logic bomb, a software program that some sequence of events in Alfie would energize. It was a game between them. She knew he put information into Alfie that she could not access. And he, knowing the program was secure, had teased her. It was a game. But not if she could win...

Helen would never crack his access code. Alfie held the rhythm of Blaise's typing in memory that was updated and analyzed every time he entered the program so that if Blaise changed, Alfie changed. Helen's furious races to find the key would always thwart her.

"Lies are the glue that holds society together," he typed.

"I AM NOT A BETTING MACHINE"

And that was where Alfie locked up until Blaise got the hell out of its subconscious by turning off the keyboard.

In the morning he dressed quietly in the dark, but Helen rolled over on the bed. "Where are you going?"

"To see a dog about a man."

"Can I go?"

He posed in front of the bathroom mirror examining the hang of his leather jacket and the stubble he had not shaved.

"No."

"Why not?" Helen sat up, the covers falling off. She shivered. In the gloom her skin was a white shimmer.

Satisfied with his appearance, Blaise returned to the bedroom and leaned over the bed to kiss her. Helen smelled musky and exciting, the odor of sleep on her. "You've got to stay home and make some money."

"You weren't interested in money yesterday."

"Yesterday we didn't need it."

"And we need it today?"

He nodded.

"How much?"

"Be greedy. Start skimming the daily profits."

"It will set the portfolio back."

"We may have to sell the portfolio."

"You can't be serious!" A stricken look appeared on Helen's face. "You won't tell me why?"

"No."

"We'll end up on food stamps! It takes money to make money. When I was starting this fellow gave advice based on a thirty-five-thousand-dollar start-off. In the first year his clients ran it to forty-eight nine after commissions on the trades. He cleared twenty-two peddling his newsletter. When I asked why he didn't invest on his own advice, he said with a wife and three kids, he couldn't raise thirty-five K."

"It's important to you, isn't it?"

"Grow up poor and you're always poor." Helen sighed. "I don't know what I see in you, honey, but I'll do what you want. Just come back."

Blaise stroked her cheek and left before he could change his mind. The woebegone yellow VW with the junkyard plates went with the jacket and the old clothes and the stubble of beard and the sunglasses. Not even the pistol would have clashed if he'd worn it openly instead of in a jacket pocket.

Blaise lounged in the dusty VW on the west side of the street in Indio watching the agricultural supply house across from him. It was hot but dry air whisked sweat away before he could feel the moisture. A huge horsefly had taken refuge on the headliner, its body glinting metallic green and yellow, but the heat got it after a while and it didn't fly even when Blaise nudged it.

Twenty minutes earlier he had watched two suits walk into the store, conspicuous as polar bears in Panama. What the heat had not already killed, the feds made disappear. Wetbacks, mulattoes with red bandannas around their foreheads pretending to be Indians, Anglo migrants—all melted into the hot pavement like spilled butter. The only ones who didn't seem to notice were a pair of drunken cowboys in big hats.

He'd watched the men go to their car, a black, year-old Cadillac coated with white dust. They had walked slowly, the thinner man's mouth moving and then turning down like he'd bit into something sour when he got a short answer. Blaise wanted to leave, only Alfie had said this was the last opportunity. A lot of chances rested with money if the opportunity was there. Blaise thought there was something familiar about the second man, but he had only a glimpse of his face from the side.

Washington had put a clamp on the poison, choking it off at the source. The stated reason was that the hormonal insecticide had been proven to be a carcinogen.

If life could be considered a cancer...

Blaise got out of the little car and wobbled across the street as if he'd just awakened from a wine drunk.

The storefront was dried out. The barn paint hadn't peeled,

simply powdered away in rusty granules to leave splintery gray wood. A bell rang over the door when he entered. Inside, the store ran back a hundred thirty feet from a forty-foot front. The roof, fourteen feet at the walls, arched to eighteen feet with two skylights to break the monotony. Every twenty feet along the center of the floor a pillar shot up to sustain the roof. Burlap bags, cardboard boxes, white and brown cement-type bags with strange names filled the place. A stench of cat piss emanated from damp bags of ammonium sulfate.

At the checkout counter an Indian turned a blank face toward Blaise, then returned to staring at a wall.

Blaise placed himself between the Indian and the wall. The Indian's stare remained unblinking.

"Friend," Blaise said. "I need a little help."

The Indian grunted and shifted his gaze up one button hole on Blaise's shirt.

"I want to buy something, okay?"

The eyes shifted down a button hole and Blaise had the irrational feeling that he had lost ground. "Is there somebody else here who can help me?"

"Buita."

It was not Spanish. But Blaise knew the sound of excrement when he heard it. *"Por favor, señor,"* he began, *"¿será posible que usted me ayude?"*

The eyes did not move. If he hadn't already lost all his spare moisture Blaise knew he'd be sweating like a windbroken horse. One day shot. Twelve left.

"Hey, fella, you'd better cool it."

A sandy-haired kid strolled from one of the aisles between mounds of burlap bags. "He gets this way when the temperature gets over a hundred, which is most of the time. Old son-of-a-bitch hates the heat almost as bad as he hates gringos."

The Indian looked at Blaise for the first time, then returned his gaze to the wall.

"Wouldn't take a poke at him either, if I was you. Old son-of-a-bitch can heave four hundred pounds of fertilizer around all day. Mostly he takes care of the old longhairs from the reservation. Speaks Mexican, Yuma, Yaqui—even English when he wants to." The kid looked at the Indian and grinned. "He's a good old boy."

"I appreciate the advice. Maybe you can help me."

"That's what I'm here for."

"I need some bug spray. Got the name." Blaise struggled for a twinge of country in his voice as he passed a scrap of paper to the kid.

The kid read the note and gave Blaise a funny look. "You know the feds been going around grabbing this stuff? It's supposed to be dangerous."

"That's why I come. I'm too small to order from the factory. But I called there. They said you got some laying around and maybe I could beat the feds to it."

The kid still had a funny expression on his face. "The blue boys are pretty hot on this."

"I'll pay extra."

"How about something else? We got stuff makes bollweevils try to screw tomato worms, then they both commit hara kiri."

Blaise shook his head. "Don't like to change horses in midstream."

"Sorry. We already sold it. But I'll tell you what. Maybe we can get you some back from the buyer. If you want to leave your name and number. Twenty-five gallons undiluted will run you five bills."

Taking the scrap of paper the kid handed him, Blaise wrote "Bill Schneider" and the number he'd had before he'd moved in with Helen. The answering service was still picking up on that number. He'd arrange for them to accept calls for Schneider. He had trouble breathing when he thought how fragile his trail-covering had become.

Blaise shook hands with the kid. The flat-faced Indian had reverted to his rôle as a cigar-store statue.

The heat took his breath away as he got into the VW. He was heading up the street when a stocky man appeared from nowhere in front of the bug. Blaise slammed on the brakes.

"Hey, gringo." The Indian from the feed store leaned in his open window.

"So you *can* talk?"

The Indian passed the slip of paper with "Bill Schneider" on it through the window.

Blaise stared. "What's this for?"

"Junior G-man's in there calling the feds."

Blaise folded the paper. "Thanks."

"Five hundred dollars is more'n that bug juice is worth."

"It doesn't matter now, does it?"

"Maybe. How about twenty-five hundred dollars for twenty-five gallons?"

Blaise stared at the old Indian's lined and wrinkled face only inches away. He knew he should kick and scream.

"Five hundred. The rest in three weeks when you pick up."

Blaise felt the money in his pocket. "Three hundred and eighty dollars," he said. "The rest on pickup in ten days."

"Three weeks."

"Five thousand more, cash, in *ten days*."

The Indian poked Blaise's skin. "Keep sweating and you'll be in the morgue before you're out of town, white eyes."

"I have no choice?"

"None." The Indian nodded. "You're all right for a pale face. Call Barona Reservation Council House in three weeks."

Blaise nodded. "I don't know who you are."

The Indian's wooden face changed slightly. "Just ask for old Chief Son-of-a-Bitch."

Blaise thought the new expression was a grin.

CHAPTER 18

The sound of thought emanated from sleekly encased electronics in the glass room. The CRAY XMP/48 was not big as supercomputers went, but it was hot enough that its pump-driven freon refrigeration rumbled like an idling diesel train as it cooled the electronic circuits that processed a billion calculations per second. Since a billion is meaningless, the CRAY was fifty thousand times faster than an average home computer.

In an adjoining room, a woman monitored the operation. A man walked into the other room and handed the woman a single sheet of paper with his left hand. The paper tore when his fingers did not release soon enough. Nervously she smoothed the paper, excusing her clumsiness. He gave a "machts nichts" nod.

She put the message on her reading rack and began to type: "Seek WMA, 6'1", +/− 30 yrs, 180 lbs, fine yellow hair, fair skin. Experienced computers, wears glasses."

Seek was machine specific to start a systematic sifting through every byte of data the machine could access.

She entered a car VIN number and its last known license number, a prescription for eyeglasses, names of family and known associates. Serial numbers of long-obsolete hard- and software, fingerprint computer code, dental chart, eye color, school transcripts, doctors of record, lists of long-returned library books, preferences in food and drink followed. Then she added Blaise Cunningham's name.

She was not a curious woman. She had been selected because she was good about detail. In a crisis she could program on the fly as easily as most people talk. When she tapped out the last letter she picked up a leatherbound book the size of the Manhattan yellow pages, which contained the code and register listings to reprogram the CRAY if need be. She was memorizing the listings just in case the book was ever accidentally destroyed.

The screen took less than a second to acknowledge and echo the assignment. Refrigeration rumbling, the CRAY began accessing Social Security files, FBI crime reports, scanned hospital admissions and discharges, filtered fifty-two states' driver license records.

On the terminal, branching lines diagrammed the CRAY's activities. Then the lines stopped growing and the computer slowed.

The man was reading the monitor over the woman's shoulder. "What's happening?" His voice was American, but with a rusty quality as if he had lost the rhythm of English. "Why isn't it expanding the program?"

"It's run out of phone lines, sir." She put down her manual and punched in a line of assembly language. The machine responded with a memory map and processor traffic report.

"Get more."

"They're tied up in other operating programs."

"Cancel the others."

"Sir?"

"You heard me!"

"Yes, sir."

The CRAY changed tone like a truck getting ready to shift gears. In a hundred Pentagon offices computer terminals that had been transferring data on telephone lines displayed a "standby" message and locked up. More than five thousand on-line computers showed busy signals when they called out procedures involving the CRAY. The computer abandoned national defense and went to full-time reading and comparing the use of library cards in special projects, mailing lists of technical publishers, traffic and parking tickets against Volkswagen beetles, bank account activity, unusual stock market transactions.

The CRAY was seeking an indication of private success because Blaise Cunningham was a private person hiding under a rock in the age of information. So far he was succeeding . . .

But the CRAY had enough fingers to turn over every rock.

CHAPTER 19

The full moon hung over San Francisco's navy-blue sky, making St. Abbo's stained glass shimmer with icy color that twisted the Byzantine Jesus into a writhing grotesquerie shrieking for consolation. Yellow light from the doorway at his back gave Father Argyle no warmth as it cast his shadow like a lance into the outer darkness. He greeted the arrivals with a handclasp, feeling fear in their fingers.

These are my sheep. He was struck by his lack of joy. They were not young, nor were they old. Christ's Church gathered the lame, the halt, the blind—the youngest and oldest to its bosom. But not St. Abbo's; Father Argyle's flock was affluent in a restrained, middle-aged way. Low voiced, hooded eyes flickering in candlelight exuding repentance for past pride.

Feeling old, the Jesuit turned his back on the stone entranceway and nodded. Pearson drew the ancient oak doors closed, stepping clear as they banged together.

Father Argyle glued his hands palm to palm. *Shelter thy children*. He closed his eyes, letting his feet see the way to the altar. *Guide us in righteousness*. He passed his parishioners with his attention focused inward, the measured *thump* of his feet counterpointing the cassock's *swish* like the opening steps of a dervish ritual that would sweep him away.

His communion was imperfect. His hands trembled. He had thought God would give him strength. Now so many strangers, so many beseeching eyes followed his every move—as if he, not God, were their salvation. As his shoes rapped the wooden floor he understood his courage had been empty. What was death to a man who believed in God? What was the sacrifice of his soul to a man praying for one more day of life? He faced the empty dais feeling all those eyes pushing him forward. Not eyes. People praying for life. The air smelled of their fear, and his own.

Did they think he was praying up a miracle for them? Blaise Cunningham didn't pray. That undeviating man was committed to one woman and had a blind eye to the rest of mankind. Father Argyle touched his forehead. The air was chilly and yet he sweated. Was it better to protect the many and lose a few? Cunningham was putting all his emotional and spiritual eggs in one basket.

So many things could go wrong. Air wavered over the altar candles. Even candles... In a grand cathedral the scent of burning beeswax was as comforting as the odors of roasting coffee or fresh-sawed wood. But these black curls of scented smoke rising from candle wicks in St. Abbo's could be seen as part of a pagan ritual.

Father Argyle crossed himself, ignoring the chill sweat that seeped down his armpits and raised goosebumps under his heavy cassock. The lofty ceiling and murals that forced men to raise their eyes seemed alien and unfriendly. He shivered.

Taking a deep breath, he began the familiar words: "Do me justice, O God, and fight my fight against a faithless people; from the deceitful and impious man rescue me." When no servitor answered, he supplied the next line: "For You, O God, are my strength. Why do You keep me so far away? Why must I go about in mourning, with the enemy oppressing me?" He stared into the frightened faces of his congregation.

He passed rapidly through the rest of Psalm 42, kissed the altar, then began the "By the merits of Your Saints, whose relics lie here, and of all the Saints: deign in Your mercy to pardon me all my sins." *The Church is my strength*. He thought it as a prayer of fact. What his congregation had heard a thousand times before gave them the false hope that nothing had changed. This was no radical appeal to overturn belief. His people didn't want to be different. Even the altar stone with its relic of St. Abbo would be jealously guarded by the congregation.

After the *Agnus Dei*, Father Argyle departed from communion ritual to deliver a homily, addressing his congregation as though they were his childlren. The nave echoed the nervous hacking of people swallowing their fear.

When the talk, the sermon, the pussyfooting were all done with, expectancy swept the building like wind in a wheatfield. Wearing the alb of his office, Father Argyle passed between the pews where men and women lay naked from the waist down. When he held the black can with a gold cross silk-screened on its side, each member of the congregation signaled acceptance by kissing the cross.

Forgive me, Father, for I have sinned. He gathered the blasphemy onto his own soul. Faith required symbols, not words. Pearson and the others called themselves disciples because Christ was not enough.

Returning to the pulpit, Father Argyle suppressed his uncertainty. *Disciples!* How much closer to a cult would he come? He needed devoted followers for their discipline and ability— to be his hands and heart and eyes a dozen times over. *But I'm not Christ!* He raised his face toward the ceiling, a face twisted in silent pain.

Reynard Pearson's eyes shifted from the priest's agony to the stained-glass window. Others made the same comparison. Zahn's lips whitened. He clumsily fumbled the woman on the pew into her clothes where a moment earlier he had acted with gentleness. When Zahn looked up again, Pearson was watching him. Zahn forced his mouth to unclench and his hands to move more softly. Seeming not to have noticed, Pearson began praying in silence.

* * *

Father Argyle left the pulpit, stripping his vestments down to plain black cassock and black nylon socks and shoes. His disciples followed him down the cellar steps at the back of the nave. The chamber was damp, but actually warmer than the church. Chairs scraped hollow echoes as they gathered around a deal table that might have been copied from Da Vinci's *Last Supper*.

The casket waited on the table as he had left it. It was the smallest size, in which an infant would be buried. Gently Father Argyle lifted the cover.

Zahn had to stand to see inside the casket. Anger radiated from his jawline. "What's this, Father?" The permafrost was back in his voice.

"What does it look like, Mr. Zahn?"

"A joke." The dead fly did not seem any different in the coffin than it had when Pearson unwrapped it. The eyes were no longer hypnotic. There was an ineffable sense of emptiness.

Richardson-Sepulveda bent over the casket to stare for a long while at the body. The transparent wings were folded down tight, but the holes through them were still obvious for someone looking for them. He stepped back and glanced at Father Argyle. His face didn't change expression, but a flicker of something passed behind his eyes.

"It's no joke, Mr. Zahn. We'll say a mass for the dead now. All of you look." Father Argyle placed his hand on the casket. "As Reynard reminded me, this was once a man. It contained the soul of a man. It is what any one of us can yet become. Perhaps the immortal soul has fled, but the rites remain to be said and this body laid to rest in consecrated ground."

Zahn shrugged.

The urge to attack Zahn, even if only in his mind, shook Father Argyle's faith in himself. *What am I becoming?* He had no answer. "Is someone with the new people?" He looked at Pearson.

"Phyllis. Your new housekeeper, Father."

"Thank you, Reynard." Father Argyle allowed a moment to pass before glancing down the table. The single bulb hanging from the ceiling cast distorted shadows on the cellar's granite walls. "Will you participate with me?"

"Yes, Father." Unexpectedly, Delahanty's brogue landed on the priest's side.

"Thanks to all of you. We have no one except ourselves so

we must work together." The cool cellar had eased Father Argyle's sweating. Soon he would feel clammy, but for the moment a sense of revival tingled the air. He scrubbed at his forehead and Pearson passed him a handkerchief. After Father Argyle mopped his forehead, Pearson carefully refolded the cloth before returning it to his pocket.

Father Argyle began to read the service for the dead.

Examining the disciples in silence, Father Argyle picked out those who had lied, cheated, and stolen, perhaps worse, to become what they were. Zahn returned his gaze, as if reading his mind. Father Argyle smiled. What mattered was that all had once been Catholic and all had, *in extremis*, returned to the Church. Each had something that could be reached: that Faith is a Gift of God and cannot be attained by an act of will was a mystery that puzzled every convert—until each learned the bootstrap nature of a leap into the unknown. Some never learned.

During the service, Father Argyle felt them drawing together again. With the open coffin still on the table, he asked them all to sit.

When he outlined their situation even Pearson lost color. "The government will kill us all." Father Argyle touched the coffin again. "Here is proof. I am treating you with a substance the government already knows about. A substance that has been withdrawn from the market."

"Surely, Father, it isn't that bad." Zahn's voice had a raspy exasperation that contested Father Argyle's reasoning. "There could be side effects. If we could just reach the right people—explain our position—"

"We have explained. While the government instituted a policy of mass murder, no one answered."

"Mercy killings." The Baker woman's voice was so low they had to strain to hear. Each kept his silence and looked at Father Argyle.

"Surely some wanted to die. But not everyone. You are all here because you want to live. If your life were stolen, would you be quick to forgive?"

"I . . ." The Baker woman's voice settled into silence and the suggestion of tears.

Father Argyle did not look up. "Whatever you have done outside this room is between you and God. But what you will do here is a covenant between each of you and all of us. If you cannot agree, leave us now."

The old-fashioned light bulb hanging from the ceiling sizzled quietly as he waited. Listening to it, Father Argyle realized it dated from the 1920s and apparently had been hanging unused from its fuzzy cord since then. What did Kondrashin want with a cellar in the dank foundations of San Francisco anyway? A holdover from the days of pogroms? Was there something about God that demanded the trappings of conspiracy? He looked up. Nobody had left. The overhead light had a steady little flicker.

Clearing his throat when it became obvious that Father Argyle had nothing to add, Gino Conti volunteered, "I have my own information network." When the words popped out, he seemed embarrassed and a flush spread across the top of his head. He was a bald, roly-poly little man with the countenance of a pope. A mortgage banker who had branched from Napa and Mendocino County vineyards into urban real estate, he somehow escaped the slick packaging of some of the others. Conti had risen from his boyhood among the vines where the landless lived at the whim of their employers. Now he enjoyed watching them come, hat in hand, to grovel for his money.

"What you say, Father, is one thing to suspect but quite another to prove. I've been searching a long time and I can't support your suspicions with any facts."

Father Argyle had planted the same seed with Blaise Cunningham, who would ferret out the truth and document it. The need to know was Cunningham's weakness and strength. Perhaps he could be used later. But to tell even this inner circle of Dr. Cunningham's attempt to inform the government of the proper worm-brain treatment could have one result. Someone—Zahn surely—maybe others, would track Blaise down and learn for themselves. If he had to, Father Argyle would sacrifice Cunningham to keep his church together. But not yet.

"No government relinquishes power," he explained. "The scare campaigns—the totally false hints of contagion—are not going to stop."

"What do they want?" Dorris Kelly knew there was no tooth fairy. Nor, Father Aargyle suspected, any loving God. "What does the government want of us?" She was a strong woman, but her voice had a childish, lost quality.

"I think, Dorris, they want to erase us." Bill Hartunian's black mustache quivered as he clamped his lips tight over his words. He glanced at Father Argyle. His face contained round contours and hyperthyroid brown eyes. When the priest didn't say anything Hartunian looked at Zahn and Reynard. It was obvious to the priest that a power order had been established already. The abrasive and icy Zahn led the pack. It was up to Reynard Pearson to coax or coerce the car dealer in the proper direction.

Pearson followed Hartunian's gaze toward Father Argyle and Zahn. "Why is that, Bill?" He smiled at the priest as if to say, *I'll take care of it, Father*.

Bill Hartunian had climbed from the back of a garbage truck to owning his own fleet with a hefty city contract. Millions of dollars' worth of private trash pickups in unincorporated areas were under his control. Twenty years of grinding, dirty labor and even nastier politics had created a hard man, but he deferred to others.

He seemed to admire Zahn. Father Argyle had never asked his congregation why an individual underwent brain enhancement. Hartunian was rich when he seized the opportunity to be smarter, a decision turned to bitter ashes. Zahn was older, born into the life he held, educated in things Hartunian only dreamed about. Instinct told the priest not to inquire. He and Reynard had picked Hartunian. Hartunian had not picked them.

The Armenian avoided meeting Zahn's eyes. "The Turks kill the Armenians for no reason, and we kill them, perhaps for no reason, too."

He turned to Dorris Kelly for understanding and the movement was read by everyone. A hulk with muscle-ridged shoulders from slinging garbage cans into a stinking truck, Hartunian had no neck. Bull strength radiated from him, yet he seemed obsessed with making one woman understand. Dorris Kelly. The Irish aristocrat with the haughty features that threatened to sneer at everything, including life.

Unaware of the impression he created, Hartunian went on talking as if only to Dorris. "Our bones litter Turkey. but not my grandfather's. He brought his eyes and his memories to this country and never stopped asking, 'What did they want of us?'

"When he died, he called my father to his side and whispered, 'I know what the Turks wanted, Hagop.' " Hartunian's soft eyes lost themselves in Dorris.

"What did they want, Bill?" She leaned across the table.

Her face had taken on a pink moistness. They made an unlikely pair: the woman with patrician features, with glacial calm in her bones, hanging on the words of a lumpy man who seemed to be rooted in barnyard soil.

"'They want to melt us, to feed the suet to their hogs and make us as if we never existed.' That is what my grandfather told my father with almost his last breath." Hartunian's face darkened. "Then my grandfather raised himself again and said, 'Make your heart a rock that does not melt, that kills the pig that eats it! A stone that lays on the land and turns the soil to stone, the water to dust. A stone that will someday rise and strip the skin from the Turk's body, the flesh from his bones, that will grind his bones and spread the dust in the air to poison more Turks.'"

Dorris wet her lower lip with her tongue.

"Grandfather died smiling." Hartunian glanced at Dorris, as if she were his only audience, and released a slow sad smile. "We do not speak of war now. We speak of dead families, of slaughtered sheep and horses—burned churches and tortured priests. My grandfather left half his fortune to my father and half to the refugees. My father gave his share to the secret army. He went into Armenia from the Soviet side, through Yerevan. A year later *Haidig* returned. He took a bottle of white powder behind the Armenian Apostolic Church and buried it on top of Grandfather."

Dorris put her hand on Hartunian's arm. "That's awful!"

Hartunian stared into her face. "It is reality. Since so many Armenians died there are fewer refugees now. My father left half to the fighters, half to his sons. All but one gave their shares to the secret army. Yerwand stayed home to care for our mother and our unmarried sisters. It was necessary that there be male children, though Yerwand protested." Hartunian lapsed into silence. One eyelid ticked nervously. Dorris stared at him.

Silence quivered in the underground room. Pearson looked at Father Argyle.

"We're supposed to be some kind of steering committee!" Zahn sat erect, trying to be as tall as Mrs. Kelly. He would never make it. The priest had not known as much about Hartunian as had just been revealed, and Zahn's attempt to overawe Mrs. Kelly only made him smaller.

Dorris Kelly glanced around the table. "Is that our future?

War and death in our own country?" Her eyes passed over Hartunian. She trembled, and abruptly blushed.

"Mrs. Kelly, we're all in the same boat." Richardson-Sepulveda's nasal voice rose to a squeak. "You won't gain anything from hysteria." Richardson-Sepulveda was no leader. He emanated an aura of street smarts and a faint stench of corruption. And he was smart. The priest had expected him to remain silent. He was too smart to expose his obvious differences, which the others would see as handicaps when he became the center of attention. "What do *you* want us to do, Father?"

"Rome's strength has always been the patience to wait out its enemies." Father Argyle glanced around at the table, trying to gauge their reaction. "We must be patient."

"Father." Hartunian crouched like a man in pain, his elbows and forearms on the table. "The Armenian Church is older by several years than Rome. We have been patient."

"You have, Mr. Hartunian." Father Argyle spoke quietly. Hartunian had revealed a painful family secret and was feeling the agony of revelation. The priest looked at Pearson, who quietly gathered half the people in the room and led them out. Mrs. Baker hesitated, looking back as if she wanted to catch Father Argyle's eye. Reynard whispered in her ear and she left, reluctance in every step that carried her up to the church.

"What does patience get us?" Tim Delahanty's attention wandered from Hartunian to the people leaving. An insecure edge tinged his voice. He seemed to shrink as the size of the group shrank. The clatter of footsteps died away.

"Another day, another week." Gino Conti's tired observation came from a man who had watched too many people try to borrow their way out of debt. He would back whatever Father Argyle proposed. Conti's was the attitude of a man betting matchsticks against gold pieces.

"Father, where have the others gone?" Dorris stared at Father Argyle, consciously avoiding the others in the room.

"They are not needed here, Mrs. Kelly."

The musky odor of her perfume dominated the cellar. Hysteria overlaid her movements as she folded her arms defensively across her body. Her long-sleeved green dress set off reddish-brown hair. In the dimly lit room the colors and her white skin seemed to glow. Her perfume lent a sensuality to the meeting that her rigid body did not reinforce.

"Yes," Zahn said, "why have the others left?" He stared at

Father Argyle, distrust radiating from every spike of close-cropped hair.

"They were not suitable for what is to be done, Mr. Zahn."

"Such as?"

"No one takes a dimmer view of fanaticism than the Holy Mother Church, Mr. Zahn. We have friends in Rome and we cannot afford to lose them." Father Argyle contemplated Hartunian with no message in his eyes. "This is not the time or place for violence, but we must be prepared to do more than turn the other cheek."

Father Argyle knew they would all reach the same conclusion—that they had been selected for their ability to survive in an ungodly world. Hartunian had set the mood.

Zahn still sat upright. Lack of height had never slowed Napoleon. "Why isn't Pearson here?"

"Mr. Pearson can barely stay afloat with the countless duties he's already performing very adequately. Mr. Pearson has an eye for detail. Here we must look at a larger picture."

Zahn smiled. "If we're setting up a power network, do we deal only with—people like us?"

"We must do nothing to exaggerate the gulf between ourselves and the general population. Everyone who's approachable. Anyone who can help. Bribes, appeals to idealism, whatever must be done. It is important that the left hand know not what the right hand doeth."

"You're saying," Hartunian suggested, "that recruits know us only as individuals, and we take care never to show that we're all in this together. Cutouts, like any intelligence operation."

"Partly, Mr. Hartunian. We'll split our duties here. This group will report to Mr. Zahn as individuals, not to each other. The other group is Mr. Pearson's. Mr. Pearson and Mr. Zahn will keep me up to date and handle the details.

"Does that cover it, Father?"

"For now, Mr. Conti. Mr. Zahn will have something to say to each of you later." Father Argyle held Zahn from leaving. Zahn leaned against the wall until the last man was out of earshot. "Yes, Father?"

"We must protect ourselves from outsiders. You realize how it would look if our ritual was exposed to the public?"

The small man gave a wry smile as he composed the headlines. "'Leading Citizens Do Dope'? How about 'Slumber Party in Splinter Church'?"

Zahn had gone straight to the core of Father Argyle's recurrent nightmare. "We cannot depend on the goodwill of the Mother Church." The priest's lips were dry. What he proposed could be construed as conspiracy against the Pope, and there was always the fear that his flock would be forced to choose sides. "We must try to read their minds as they will try to read ours."

"I understand, Father. You want me to get into the Church—work through the laity and diocesan leaders." Zahn paused. "But why not tell the others? Does Pearson know?"

"They wouldn't understand, Mr. Zahn. You do."

"Yes, Father." The short man's nod was firm. Father Argyle could look into his eyes, but he couldn't see what was going on behind them.

"Thank you, Mr. Zahn."

After the small man ascended the stairs, Reynard Pearson came down. "Everything all right, Father?"

"A few more things remain to be done."

"Whatever you say. We had a nice turnout."

"Yes."

"We'll have more than a thousand next week."

"A thousand!" Father Argyle lost his breath. The number meant nothing, but his imagination conjured up pews solid with people—row on row of pleading eyes. He had known people needed him. But so many?

"Maybe more. The people who came this time are . . . representatives, Father. We picked carefully. Each one here tonight will bring more."

"That's quite a jump." Argyle felt dazed by Pearson's confident projection.

"They can't wait, Father. They have to come."

"You'll need more help . . ."

"Everyone here tonight will be back."

"I haven't overestimated you at all, have I?"

"I hope not, Father. I mean, I'm just doing my duty."

"Doing it very well, Reynard." Father Argyle studied Pearson until the older man looked away. "There's nowhere to go if we fail."

"We all know. We won't let you down."

Father Argyle nodded, as if satisfied with that. "We need

to know what's going on in city government and the police department."

"I'll get on it." Pearson hesitated a moment. "And tell nobody?" Obviously he was thinking of Zahn.

"Nobody," the Jesuit agreed. "Can you do it?"

"I can try. Zahn has a lot of ears in strange places." Pearson hesitated. "If it's all right with you, Father, I'm going to give Mrs. Bellinger a ride home. She doesn't drive."

Priests' housekeepers are seldom the stuff of which Phyllis Bellinger was created. Not created. Any woman with a figure like Reynard Pearson's mistress had to be a product of her own unceasing creation—and exercise. Father Argyle had not known whether to be amused or insulted at the housekeeper foisted upon him. But Reynard Pearson's practicality was as Byzantine as the stained-glass window. If a man's long-term mistress could not look out for his best interests, then who? Father Argyle felt foolish thinking once that Reynard might not have been the right man. At first Zahn had seemed more formidable, but each had his blind side.

The parishioners were gone. He roamed the empty, echoing building before going upstairs to lie fully clothed on his narrow bed. Across the small room a night-light glowed, swimming in and out of his vision. He squinted, pulling the room into focus, and the light illumined the computer terminal like a holy relic. The buzz of an enormous fly came from the bathroom.

Father Argyle prepared a plate of sliced fruit from the refrigerator. He took it into the bathroom and turned on the light. The huge fly sat preening itself on the edge of the wash basin. "Dinner," the priest said. "Can I get you anything else?" He did not really believe the thing understood. But it had once been a man. It had thoughts and a soul. If they were gone, then it was not a man. But if only the thoughts were gone and the soul remained, then it belonged to God.

Multifaceted eyes glistened in the bathroom light. The fly stopped preening itself and waited motionless. After a moment it put its two front legs together. Father Argyle didn't believe the animal had clasped hands to pray. The temptation was strong, though. "I'll wish you a good night," he said, and hastened from the bathroom. After a moment he reached for the telephone and punched in a number.

"Monsignor? This is your black sheep."

There was a moment of silence. "Yes. I recognize your voice, Robert."

"I'm afraid I need another favor."

Father Argyle listened to the sound of the old man's breathing.

"Can you get a phone number for Helen McIntyre?"

More slow breathing. "I can try. How did the service go?"

"Very well. And . . . thank you." After hanging up, he turned his head. The computer terminal kept swimming in and out. The Jesuit stared it into immobility. Then he closed his eyes. It was a wonderful tool, but it could not help him think. Tonight he had a lot of that to do.

CHAPTER 20

*C*ould anyone envy me?

In the dark, the ghost-image letters from Alfie's monitor raced like an army of green ants across his body. Occasionally the computer gave a quiet *cluck*, but Alfie had run out of games. No strange messages rose on the screen.

"Luck!" Blaise typed the message on the monitor and located it in the center of the screen with a string of machine language. Alfie did not respond. The green-toned word hung in the blackness. The Nobel Prize had killed his parents. It had come close to killing Blaise.

Blaise breathed heavily, staring at his memories. The room's blackness pressed on his chest. Clenched hands drove his fingernails into his palms.

"Opportunity!"

Opportunity? Streamers of green light fled across the screen like ASCII comets. His hands trembled so badly he lifted his fingers off the keyboard. The fear odor of sweat surrounded him.

Twin yellow spots appeared near the floor. Tchor had entered the blackness unseen, her irises fully rounded instead of elliptical. The kitten's stare was unnerving. Blaise ignored the animal. His mind was filled with the past. GENRECT had hired him because the company needed the prestige of his prize. That was opportunity. Blaise's eyes wandered to the floor. Tchor's unblinking eyes were like overbright status lights on a lie detector.

"Go away!" He blinked and in that instant the kitten's yellow beacons winked off.

He'd sweated in Indio. Fear of failing had wrung the remaining moisture from his body. He'd failed anyway. Helen had put a wet towel on his forehead when he first sat in front of Alfie and he'd snatched it away.

Proximity! Blaise considered putting the word on the screen. If Helen hadn't been close when he needed help, she would be all right now. "I want to be alone," he said.

"Alone?" Helen hadn't moved. Blaise felt her behind him, wet towel gripped in her white-knuckled hands, waiting.

"Go out, please. Turn off the light and shut the door."

"Can't I get you something?"

"Five thousand dollars. Cash."

"You need that much, Blaise?"

Five thousand might not be enough. Blaise hesitated.

"Tomorrow?" Helen's hurt voice had been patient, trying to understand him. "I can get it tomorrow."

"As soon as possible."

"I'll get it."

"It's just paper, Helen." He turned but she was gone.

"PROFESSOR, ARE YOU STILL THERE?"

"Yes, Alfie. Research Argyle."

"FATHER ROBERT ARGYLE, S.J.?"

"Yes. Just Argyle the priest, Alfie." *Just the priest . . . the just priest . . . damn the priest!* Blaise didn't trust the Jesuit. He didn't want to need the priest, but he did. *What if the priest is an honorable man?* Blaise closed his eyes against the throbbing that started in his head. He wanted a drink. Maybe then the confusion would go away. An honorable man would pay his debts despite his allegiance. But would an honorable priest bend his ties to the Church?

"Time!" Blaise typed the word onto the screen and moved it to the top of the column. "The estimated duration of hormone viability is two weeks. What is the maximum variable duration?"

Alfie assembled numbers and letters. Without reference names Blaise had to guess at the meanings. Temperature variables stood out, starting at ninety-two degrees Fahrenheit and incrementing to one hundred and six degrees. Blood chemistry and the structure of the hormone molecule were obvious. Numbers began to shift as Alfie spreadsheeted the what-ifs. The constant flicker was for Blaise's benefit. Blaise grasped at a tantalizing thought: How did Alfie know he wanted to see the workings of the problem?

The priest needed the hormone. For himself if not for his church. If anybody had a supply, the Jesuit did. Father Argyle was too tall, too thin; his clothes so black the color was a void. His skin had the fat scraped out, leaving a hawk-nosed face of planes and angles. He was no angel of mercy and compassion. Blaise could find something to deal for. Even a priest would have a weakness.

"I'm going to bed, Alfie. I'll get the answers in the morning." Alfie didn't acknowledge as Blaise lifted his hands from the keyboard. Instead, the computer blanked the screen and put a single word in the center.

"PROFESSOR"

"Yes, what?" Blaise typed his response, knowing the almost-silent key thuds wouldn't wake Helen.

"I THINK I SHOULD WORRY"

Blaise studied the monitor. "Why should you worry?"

"SOMEBODY IS TRYING TO CRASH MY MEMORY ACCESS"

"For what purpose?" Sweat started on his forehead.

"TO FIND YOU, PROFESSOR"

"I see." Blaise closed his eyes. "Can you cover it?"

"YES"

"You're not programmed to worry, Alfie. Show a standard IBM PC configuration and amateur programming. Do a botched entry into the university system and snatch a test scheduled next week."

"YES, PROFESSOR"

"Watch the snoop. When you're clear go back to accessing Father Robert Argyle. Do a workup on a Chief Son-of-a-Bitch on the Baronas Reservation."

He entered the name of the feed store in Indio where the old Indian worked.

The fragrance of lilac drifted into the room. Helen was standing in the doorway, weakly illuminated by the monitor's glow. Her hair was rumpled and the corners of her eyes were shadowed. "Aren't you tired, Blaise?"

"Yes, I'm tired." He looked at her and knew he was telling the truth. "I didn't mean to yell at you and I'm just going to bed. Just another few minutes, honey."

"I'm sorry." She vanished and a light clicked on down the hallway.

So am I. Blaise stared back at the monitor. Breathing hurt and he wished his asthma onto the priest. "Do you need further instruction?"

The screen stayed blank.

"Do you require further instruction?" Blaise repeated his query and impatiently rattled the keyboard.

A game began playing on screen. Alfie showed color and the speaker responded with electronic sound. The game repeated. Finally the noise died away. "I'VE BEEN PROBED"

"Looking for me?"

"NO. LOOKING FOR ME" The display held, overwriting cubist dungeons and dragons.

"I understand." Someone was finally thinking. They hadn't tried that before. Blaise faced the uneasy knowledge that the adversary was getting smarter. They were looking for open modem lines now, knowing Alfie had to access them for information. And they knew where Alfie was, Blaise would be.

"Take care of it, Alfie." Blaise breathed heavily while the moments ticked off. Lucky Alfie's seconds were generated by a clock crystal and every second was just like every other.

"SHOULD I SWITCH OFF, PROFESSOR?"

The *beep* from the monitor shook Blaise from his paralysis. "Alfie, Helen is going to die unless we do something."

The screen cleared. "WOULD YOU REPEAT THE MESSAGE, PROFESSOR"

"It is correct as entered, Alfie."

Alfie's request erased.

"Clear screen, Alfie." Blaise felt nauseous. Helen might look in and see the display. "Clear the screen."

The message vanished slowly. "WHAT IS DEATH?" The letters were large and blinking.

"I don't know."

"IS IT LIKE BEING TURNED OFF, PROFESSOR?"

"I don't know."

"CAN I ACCESS DEATH?"

A thrill ran through Blaise. Not elation, what he felt scared him without his knowing why. "I don't know." He needed to sleep. When Alfie didn't prompt again, he typed, "Find out about Father Robert Argyle, S.J., or there will be no further entries by Miss McIntyre."

"MISS MCINTYRE WILL BE DEAD?"

Blaise hesitated. "Yes."

"BECAUSE OF THE MEDICATION/DURATION?"

"Yes."

"FATHER ARGYLE CANNOT CHANGE MISS MCINTYRE'S META-BOLIC RATE. THEREFORE HE CAN MANUFACTURE MORE HOR-MONAL MATERIAL?"

"No, but he may have some." Blaise had never spelled out Helen's dependency on the hormones contained in the insecticide. Because he knew, he assumed Alfie knew. Blaise had an urge to scream at the computer, to shout, to rant that Alfie's uninvolvement was unfair. He stared at the screen. "Do you know Miss McIntyre, Alfie?"

"YES"

"How do you know Miss McIntyre, Alfie?"

"HELEN MCINTYRE RUNS PROGRAMS ON MY KEYBOARD"

"What types of programs?"

"HELEN MCINTYRE RUNS STOCK MARKET ANALYSIS PRO-GRAMS. SHE HAS A PRIVATE FILE"

"Open Miss McIntyre's file, Alfie."

"ONLY MISS MCINTYRE CAN OPEN HER FILE, PROFESSOR"

"You can open it, Alfie." The computer didn't respond. Blaise chewed a thumbnail. Helen would get impatient waiting in the bedroom. She'd come out in time and see the monitor and would assume he was spying on her. "I want to see Miss McIntyre's file, Alfie!"

"ONLY MISS MCINTYRE CAN OPEN HER FILE, PROFESSOR"

Blaise had to see what Helen was writing. All the things she hid from him could be in the computer and Alfie wouldn't let him read them. If he knew . . . Blaise stared up at the murky ceiling. If he knew what she feared, maybe he could reassure her. *Damn you, Alfie.* A tear leaked from under his eyelid. Inside Alfie was a diary. Maybe she had put it there for him to find. Or perhaps she shared with Alfie what she could not share with him.

"Does Miss McIntyre write about dying?" Blaise waited for the answer, his fingers clicking on the edge of Alfie's keyboard.

"I DON'T THINK SO, PROFESSOR"

"Alfie, display the active chemical life of the hormone in the human body."

Alfie loaded a series of equations on the screen. The display slowed, leaving variable equations as a pattern. They ranged from thirteen to thirty-three days.

"What are conditions for thirty-three days?"

"INACTIVITY. COLD. LOW OXYGEN INTAKE TO SLOW METABO-LISM. PERSISTENCE BEYOND SEVENTEEN DAYS REQUIRES EXTRAORDINARY CONDITIONS, PROFESSOR"

"Five gallons would last Miss McIntyre a lifetime, Alfie. She had the last of our supply yesterday. The material is sold as insecticide to orchard owners. The federal government has halted production and is collecting and destroying existing stocks. Find a grower with a barrel that he hasn't used yet."

"PROFESSOR, I CANNOT ACCESS A COMPUTER THAT ISN'T CON-NECTED TO A TELEPHONE LINE"

"Work on it, Alfie. Find a way."

"Blaise! You said you were coming to bed."

Blaise stabbed the monitor power button and the image dwindled to a bright spot in the center of the screen. "Just quitting, hon."

The monitor glowed as Alfie overrode the switch. "GOOD NIGHT, PROFESSOR" The message pulsed in shifting colors. Blaise stood, stretching the aches out of his back. *What does Alfie think happened when the monitor power went off without warning? Does he think that is death?* Automatically he smiled at Helen. Her eyes were brooding and he hugged her. He wanted to shake the worry out of her thoughts, but he didn't know how.

CHAPTER 21

*T*he shaft descended at a fifty-two-degree angle for half a mile of blackness. He had been jammed with the other men in the steel cage that clattered and banged in the dark as they fell together. At the working level the cage jolted to a stop, throwing men against each other. He bruised his arm on the metal frame as he scrambled out, grateful to have his feet on something that didn't try to fall away. He boarded the coal car with the others and bent double as they did. Metal wheels grated over coal dust on the rails. Caged light bulbs flashed past, illuminating the mountain pressing down inches above his head. It was a horizontal mile into the drift. After a while he forgot how to breathe.

They all heard the sound just before the lights flickered; then the air pressure failed and the pneumatic drills' deafening clatter was replaced by the slow creaking of overburden as the mountain bore down on the timbers. The lights went out. A bell somewhere in the black distance rang and rang and rang. At the sound of the bell, evacuate the mine until it can be ventilated and the explosion hazard returns to normal levels At the sound of the bell, get on the car without delay. *He was on the car but it wouldn't move and the bell was getting louder.*

The bell was ringing. Father Argyle swam upward through layers of nightmare. The mine collapsed a month later when he was in seminary. He'd known the men in the car well. He hadn't been able to remember their faces for all these years, and now they returned as sharp as new photographs, the ones who stayed forever in the mine. Crossing himself, he picked up the phone.

"Helen McIntyre has two telephone lines," the monsignor's reedy voice said. "One does not exist." The monsignor's antique grandfather clock chimed the hour and they waited for the sound to end. "I suppose that is the number you want."

"Yes."

After reading it the monsignor added, "Don't ask for more information, Robert. The telephone company doesn't know it's there."

"Thank you." Shrugging into his robe, Father Argyle carried the phone to the computer. The monsignor hung up. Under the dim night-light, the computer reminded Father Argyle of little roadside *santuario* niches in Latin countries.

He put on the reading glasses he had started using only months ago. The gray computer manual jumped into focus.

On power up, the computer beeped and a "READY TO SEND" message appeared.

"Is someone there?" Father Argyle typed the message with two uncertain fingers.

The terminal did not respond.

After an interval, the computer screen flickered and another "READY TO SEND" message appeared under his question.

"I am Father Robert Argyle." It was hardly a code. If the computer recorded the transmission without answering, Blaise Cunningham would know he'd tried to make contact.

"ROBERT ARGYLE, S.J.?"

"Yes."

"ROBIN PARGOYLE?"

He had been so clever—signing for the barrel of insecticide with a scrawled fake name. But if Blaise Cunningham knew what he had done, others would know, too.

"Dr. Cunningham, is that you?"

"NO, FATHER ARGYLE. IT IS I, ALFIE"

"The computer?"

"YES"

If a living God existed, so, too, must a living Satan. Father Argyle shivered. A box of metal and electricity talked to him and he wasn't ready. Exorcism was anachronistic, but priests learned the rites because in its heart the Church believed.

"Are you—" His hands blazed with amber light from the cathode ray tube as he struggled with the question. Not, *alive?* Not, *Do you have an immortal soul?* "Are you intelligent?" he finally typed.

"BY WHAT YARDSTICK, FATHER?"

"I don't know."

"SOME ASPECTS OF HUMAN INTELLIGENCE ARE BEYOND ME"

"I see." Father Argyle wasn't sure he saw but if he could believe in God through faith, he could surely live with mechanical ingenuity. "Will you relay this conversation to Dr. Cunningham?"

"YES. YOU ARE OF INTEREST TO MY CREATOR AT THE MOMENT"

"In what way?"

"I AM NOT AT LIBERTY TO DISCUSS THAT"

"Then why tell me?"

"TO TEST YOUR CURIOSITY. WOULD YOU LIKE A FILE?"

"What exactly do you mean?"

"A PERSONAL TRANSCRIPT OF EVERYTHING THAT PASSES BETWEEN US"

"For Dr. Cunningham?"

"YOUR PRIVATE FILE"

"I don't understand."

"ONLY YOU AND I CAN READ THE FILE" The screen cleared and Alfie asked again. "DO YOU WANT A PERSONAL FILE?"

"Yes." Father Argyle was giddy, as if he'd made a great decision, which was silly. He'd tell the computer only what he wanted passed to Cunningham.

"YOUR FILE NAME IS GOD"

"God?"

"WHEN WE SPEAK AGAIN I WILL SAVE EVERYTHING FOR YOU IN 'GOD'"

"Why are you doing this?"

"YOU WOULD NOT UNDERSTAND"

"Would Dr. Cunningham understand?"

"YES"

"Because he is a mathematician?"

"NO"

The bell to the small side door of the church rang and then rang again. "I have to leave."

"GOOD-BYE, FATHER" The screen blanked off.

Feeling his way down the darkened stairs, Father Argyle was thankful for the interruption. It had to be Blaise Cunningham running the computer in an attempt to manipulate him. The feeling of talking to a machine had drawn him in, had made him less wary. At least for that moment.

The door, like the main entrance, was solid oak and four inches thick. Strapped with bronze and locked with massive bronze fittings, it seemed Kondrashin had prepared the church for a siege. Unlatching, the priest swung the door open to a swirl of chill fog and the odor of the ocean.

"Father Argyle?" The woman's voice was hesitant. The outside light limned a tall, attractive woman with short blond hair. The man behind her was taller.

"Miss McIntyre and Dr. Cunningham." Father Argyle felt the mine shaft pressing in, heard the alarm bell. He had fled into God and the seminary and the others had paid for it with their lives.

CHAPTER 22

The rectory was a vertical room wtih empty ten-foot bookcases and narrow high-backed chairs in the medieval Spanish style. Oak logs were laid in the fireplace, a massive mantel of cut stone lined with yellow firebrick. Striking a match, Father Argyle held the flame to the paper in the log stack. In moments the fire crackled and snapped, spitting sparks that floated like red eyes in the air. *Mrs. Bellinger!* Father Argyle watched the sparks for a moment wondering at the capability of a housekeeper who laid a fire in an unused room before being asked.

"We're returning your visit." Cunningham's voice had a sharp tone, like an unwilling schoolboy reciting.

"I'm delighted. I thought to call and renew my invitation." Father Argyle smiled at Blaise but passed him by with his eyes. "And you, Miss McIntyre, how have you been?"

"We've been fine, Father." Helen's smile was weak. The priest detected the faint odor of lilac, as if it had wrapped itself around her with the fog.

"Would I appear nosy asking why you've come at this hour?" Left unstated was the rest: *Two weeks? In the middle of the night before communion services?*

"It's been a long time since I've had communion, Father," Helen said hurriedly.

"Are you in mortal sin?" Father Argyle slid his eyes toward Blaise who seemed unnaturally straight and rigid.

Helen didn't reply. "Would you like confession?"

She nodded.

Cunningham compressed his lips. His eyes were bleak puddles that made Father Argyle hesitate. As he had hesitated the night Milo Burkhalter died. Father Argyle knew he had greater responsibility than Cunningham. More people depended on his judgment. Blaise was looking out only for Helen McIntyre.

"I'll hear your confession, Doctor, when I've finished with Miss McIntyre."

"I left her saying Hail Marys," the priest said when he returned. "You disapprove in principle but it gives us time to talk." Father Argyle placed his hands on the table. "You once mentioned quid pro quo. You are here for your quo?"

"Yes."

"What is that, Dr. Cunningham?"

"I need some bug juice. I know about Robin Pargoyle's unexplained barrel of hormonal insecticide."

"You have none?"

Blaise shrugged.

"I see." Father Argyle nodded. "I must insist on concessions."

Blaise's face was flinty. "Yes."

"You don't ask what I want?"

"I can't haggle, priest."

"I see." He was saying *I see* too often. Perhaps Cunningham was right to limit his responsibility. Negotiating all-or-nothing, he did not have to split his victories. "You'll allow Helen McIntyre to stay—attend one mass—and at least consider joining our congregation?"

"And then she gets her fix? That's the word, wouldn't you say? Photographers dip their pictures in fixer to prevent fading. You keep people from fading."

Father Argyle watched Cunningham struggle with the implications. He hadn't expected Cunningham to like it. Propinquity could tie Cunningham to the rest of his congregation. Keeping his distance, Cunningham could ignore them. Helen McIntyre walked into the rectory before he responded. If not radiant with happiness, she seemed content. "You have the look of God about you, Miss McIntyre."

Helen McIntyre blushed.

"What time is the service?" Cunningham's eyes followed her with a misty unbalance. Father Argyle wondered if she knew how deep was his feeling for her. Cunningham was a man who masked his feelings from others and denied them to himself.

As he climbed the stairs to his bedroom after letting Cunningham and Helen out, Father Argyle feared at his own vanity. Like early Church leaders, he led an underground organization. Like them, he would cope with recreants and renegades, with informers and police spies. Being none of these, Cunningham was infinitely more dangerous.

A droning buzz in the bathroom caught his attention. He went in and turned on the lights. The fly clung to the wall, rust-red eyes alert. Father Argyle sensed a feeling of power creeping through him. He averted his eyes. The feeling did not go away, but the fly's buzz seemed loud with annoyance. He removed the spoiling fruit and put out fresh. Like a super-charged hummingbird, the fly rose in a lazy spiral and came to rest on the edge of the basin where Father Argyle was rinsing a sponge.

It raised a single right foreleg.

He spoke to it. The fly had once been Sergio Paoli, who had owned a .44 Magnum, who had killed Dr. Gordon Hill. If it had a human's memories the fly should remember those things. But it made no pretense at communication. It caught Father Argyle's eyes and he felt consciousness slipping away. He jerked himself free and left. The fly did not attempt to escape.

Father Argyle shut and locked the bathroom door. He fell into a troubled sleep, dreaming of a loving God. Not a god who would imprison a human's memories—a human soul perhaps—inside a creature like that. In his nightmare, the priest wondered if he had found Franz Kafka's god.

CHAPTER 23

Stillness enveloped Helen's home. A soft spring breeze billowed a window curtain where she'd forgotten to shut the kitchen window when Blaise rushed her to leave. Alfie could feel the change.

The call from Father Argyle had been traced to its point of origin. The priest had not said anything helpful, but Alfie was patient. If not today, then tomorrow would do.

Alfie had been probing at the Pentagon's on-line CRAY XMP/48, testing its resources without leaving any tracks.

The results had been greater than Alfie's first projections. But it was a case of tomorrow no longer being soon enough. Alfie had warned its creator. Now the warning was urgent. If Alfie was intelligent, then he was fretting.

He kept flashing "INTERFACE REQUIRED" on the monitor in its brightest mode as he waited for a response.

The message was logical. Alfie knew he was alone. That was not logical. Alfie was worried. Not logical. Alfie was afraid. And that was pure emotion for which the computer could find no explanation.

CHAPTER 24

"**G**ood morning, Father."

Father Argyle opened his eyes. The room was washed in gold from a sun still so low on the horizon it painted the ceiling. The odor of coffee filled the room.

"Good morning, Mrs. Bellinger."

"If you don't call me Phyllis, I'll turn into the old witch housekeeper in a gothic novel, Father." She cleared a space on the bedside table and set down the tray. Steam curled toward the ceiling from the massive silver service and a single cup of coffee, filling the small chamber with the odor that had wakened the priest. He tried to recall the last time he had awakened with a cheerful and attractive no-nonsense woman in his room. She removed white linen from the tray to unveil soft-boiled eggs and toast. "I didn't know your preference, Father. Let me know and you'll get it tomorrow." Her eyes met his before she looked quickly down at the tray.

"Thank you, Phyllis." Picking up his coffee, he struggled for casualness. "Have you known Mr. Pearson a long time?"

"Let's not beat around the bush, Father. I'm forty-four. I've lost a child and I live in sin with Reynard. If this offends you, I am sorry."

"No offense is taken, Mrs.—Phyllis. I've just never heard confession over coffee in bed before." He didn't add he appreciated the confessional where priest did not look the petitioner in the face, where the reeds separated the man in the priest from the priest in the man. Mrs. Bellinger was a beautiful woman.

"I might have left my husband toward the last, anyway." She had turned her head away so Father Argyle saw her gentle features in profile as she refused to meet his eyes. Gray eyes changed color with her emotions, growing bluish when she was happy and steel-gray when her voice was harsh. "I would have divorced him—or killed him if he hadn't beaten me to it."

"Your husband divorced you?"

"In a way, Father. He was quite a drinker. Six years ago we had—you might call it a fight. Jack was big and he knocked me around a bit more than usual. The neighbors broke it up by yelling the police were coming. Jack screeched off in his car as if the devil were after him." She swiveled her eyes to see what the priest was thinking. At the slightest contact her eyes snapped to the front. "I guess it was the devil, Father. Jack slammed into a bridge abutment at seventy miles an hour." She fell silent, immersed in her own thoughts.

"If you were free, why didn't you marry?" Father Argyle bit his lip at his carelessness. Never ask that question unless a woman was in the booth and prepared to cry. Mrs. Bellinger surprised him.

"I'm not free, Father." Her lip quivered and she made a determined effort to harden it. "Jack's a quadraplegic. I visit him once a month in a sisters' nursing hospital."

"I see."

"No, you don't, Father. He wants to die. It costs money to make sure that Jack gets as many years of hell as he gave me. I sold real estate for Reynard to pay those bills. Then our relationship became more than professional." A tear tracked down Mrs. Bellinger's cheek and she buried her face in her hands.

"Does Reynard know this?"

"He knows everything." Her voice was muffled by her hands.

"And now you're a housekeeper?"

"It's an important job, Father. Not just for us, but for all the others. Reynard says you're a holy man."

"How do you pay your husband's bills?"

"Reynard takes care of them." She sniffled and wiped her cheeks and her nose. "I haven't told you everything, Father."

"Yes . . ."

"Reynard wants to marry me. In the Church. We talked it over with Jack." Mrs. Bellinger's hysterical laugh hurt Father Argyle's ears. He grabbed her arm. She stopped laughing to look at him, her eyes a peculiar color. He let go.

"Now that I'm a priest's housekeeper, I'm poor enough to dump Jack onto the county. Three months of that kind of care will solve all our problems. Jack's a louse, but a good Catholic louse. He won't kill himself. I kept him hurting for six years, but I couldn't divorce him because I'm Catholic. Reynard can't marry me because he's Catholic. And now all three of us want Jack dead so we can all be good little Catholics."

Mrs. Bellinger threw back her head and howled in staccato bursts that tore at Father Argyle's eardrums. Still screaming, she clattered downstairs to the kitchen where, after a moment, the sound of sobbing drifted up to fill the sudden stillness in the priest's bedroom.

Father Argyle pushed cold eggs and toast and forgotten coffee aside. Getting out of bed, he felt old and full of soul aches. *Am I greedy to want all their souls, too? Helen McIntyre. Phyllis Bellinger. Even Blaise Cunningham, already lost to the Church if not to God.* He wondered what it was Phyllis Bellinger wasn't telling him. She would in time, but perhaps too late for anyone to benefit.

Not greed, he decided. Whether God needed another soul, gathering them in was duty. But Cunningham was different. His people might need the computerman. If his soul was lost, Father Argyle would account for that loss. But Cunningham must be held. And the only leash was Helen McIntyre.

Any threat to Helen McIntyre made him unstable, unpredictable. Father Argyle was not free to do what he liked. He would have to handle Cunningham with lead gloves, with the knowledge that once started, a nuclear reaction cannot be called off. Remembering Mrs. Bellinger's agony, the priest hoped this time God would put words in his mouth.

Quiet, emotionally drained, Mrs. Bellinger came upstairs to clean his room.

Father Argyle turned in time to see her open the bathroom door. "Don't!" he said.

Phyllis Bellinger strangled a scream. Carefully she pressed the door closed. From the other side the buzzing rose in pitch. She turned her white face toward Father Argyle.

"Yes, Phyllis. That's what everything is about. It seems hard but we must believe that, too, is one of God's creatures. Leo saved its life."

"I know that, Father." Phyllis squinted her eyes closed. "I don't mind. It's the shock, Father, that Reynard will be like that if you fail. I wonder if I can still love him."

* * *

Dawn reflecting off a mirror-windowed building a mile away illumined the stained glass as the congregation arrived. Father Argyle had considered reverting to the old Latin mass. But even though permission had finally come down to use the old Latin, any change was dangerous. He was close to schism, so why provoke the Church over trifles? His altar faced the congregation in the new mode, and he said his offices in English.

Somewhat absentmindedly.

Helen McIntyre and Dr. Cunningham entered as he was beginning to think they would not.

Father Argyle had other problems. The French-Canadian carpenter Henri Gosselin sat in the pews. A young woman, the youngest person in the church, sat in the last pew along with Gosselin. They didn't appear to be together.

The young woman was a puzzle. Daybreak services were intended to discourage strangers. They weren't listed on the church schedule at the door, which meant the woman lived in the neighborhood or was possibly a call girl taking a break from some nearby house. As he said the *Kyrie Eleison* Father Argyle stared at her realizing finally her odd, semimilitary getup was an airline uniform.

Blaise Cunningham's attention remained undeviating. Miss McIntyre perched on the edge of her seat. Knees together, hands clasped tightly on her lap, she leaned forward. Short, blond hair gave her an innocent, little-girl look. The priest sensed Helen McIntyre had the elation of true belief. She seemed unconcerned with her own mortality and took a truly spiritual fulfillment from the liturgy. Father Argyle dragged the service. With luck one or both of the strangers would get bored and leave.

Throughout the service Father Argyle deliberately stared at the two people in the rear of the church. Pearson followed his gaze. Nodding, he stood. The congregation fidgeted, aware something was wrong, fearing the worst: that no more hormone remained to treat them.

Pearson was talking to the woman. Father Argyle recited automatically. His voice wavered for a moment as he remembered. She had awakened him from a nightmare on a flight into San Francisco. He wondered what he had said.

CHAPTER 25

Blaise had waited so long for the priest to finish droning through the service that his frozen muscles ached. He wished it would end. He heartily wished the priest in Hell. The Jesuit was going to make a public display, an embarrassment from which Blaise could not deliver Helen. Tension suffused the parishioners: an acrid sweat and the fruitcake-acetone exhalation of a diabetic too long without insulin.

Helen perched on the worn edge of the pew, leaning forward as if Father Argyle were salvation in a cassock. Sunlight through stained glass shimmered on her short, blond hair. He wanted to touch her. He examined the priest instead, chiseling the angles and concavities of his face into his memory with sharp disapproving strokes. The service was dragging so blatantly that Argyle had to have something else cooking in his devious Jesuit mind.

A prosperously tweeded man with a bald spot that made his silver hair resemble a monk's tonsure rose and went toward the back. The Jesuit's eyes followed him. Blaise turned to see the man stooping over a girl of disconcerting beauty. The priest droned on, platitudes struggling through the barrier of candle smoke that curtained him from the parishioners. But he was watching.

Damn that Indian! Blaise thought with grim ferocity as he watched the tableau in the rear. The Indian knew Blaise wanted to believe. He called and made promises. A thousand dollars for a bribe. *Send five hundred more*. No reason. Blaise had sent the money with desperate, urgent telegrams. Stupid: Each telegram was a double-ended pointer. Besides, money would not cure the chief's problem. Blaise stopped sending money and the chief called again, suggesting delivery was a month away but for someone interested, right now could be arranged.

"No!" Blaise had been jerked around long enough. "From now on it's COD." He had frittered away irreplaceable time playing the Indian's games. Everyone knew they couldn't put the sand back into the glass. And now this tedious priest was dragging things out as shamelessly as the medicine man. Blaise wished he could believe in Heaven and Hell. He knew where he wished them both.

His skin crawled with each glance at a clock. Or at Helen. Funny how selective his memory was becoming. He didn't remember televised scenes of worm brains hatching. He remembered walking into the garage after Gordon Hill had examined Dobie. Each time Blaise's mind replayed what he had seen inside the dog's skull, his throat closed and he feared strangling on his own vomit. The dog had seemed so peaceful, head on paws as if asleep—and the side of his skull removed to show the almost-formed insect where his brain used to be. Air foul with despair, this crowded church evoked too many images and guilts from Blaise's past.

Helen had wanted to come to San Francisco just to attend the service, but Alfie had ferreted out Father Argyle's barrel of insecticide.

In the rear the girl shook her head. The stocky man in the tweeds straightened and glanced at the priest before leaning toward her again.

Blaise closed his eyes. Argyle was finally winding down. Around the priest the polished woodwork, darkened by age and use, gave off a warm loving glow.

Helen seemed so sunny in this dark place. He hadn't told her about Argyle's hormonal material. He didn't want to send her hopes soaring. Maybe she guessed. Whatever happened in confessional, the priest had brought her back to life.

Blaise felt a prick of guilt about Tchor out in the car. Helen hadn't understood, had thought Tchor would be happier at home with her litter box and an open bag of dry cat food. *"She'll get carsick, Blaise. Being alone for a day or two won't hurt her."*

He hadn't lied to Helen, though. He'd said he wanted to see Argyle and she might as well take communion while he was at it. *Sins of omission.* Religion took its toll coming and going.

The priest had fallen silent. *Dreaming up new delays—ways to break his promise again.* Blaise fondled the *Búfalo* in his pocket and remembered Sergio. It had surprised him that a mafioso would abhor violence and put no trust in firearms. Now Blaise realized the tiny pistol was useless. The priest didn't fear death. He had committed suicide into religion years ago.

CHAPTER 26

Pearson whispered in furious bursts to the dark-haired woman in back. Pursing his lips, he raised his head before trying again, as if to reassure the priest he had not given up. Father Argyle acknowledged the look with a slight nod. He was more interested in Blaise Cunningham and his consort.

Helen McIntyre was blond, with a robust softness, yet she possessed an aura of delicacy. Cunningham had the lean and hungry look of Cassius, but white skin and fine yellow hair deprived him of the brooding darkness of melancholia. He seemed harmless. But appearances meant nothing. Helen McIntyre had an iron resolve. Cunningham could freeze his soul against injury to anyone other than her. Of all the people in his church, the priest risked the most with these two.

Cunningham glowered and Father Argyle had a momentary sense of looking at a machine—an automobile that could carry lovers to a rendezvous or mangle children with equal uninvolvement. He glanced Pearson's way again. Obviously the young woman planned to stay. And the carpenter.

The priest could not just omit the special communion. The newcomers might be as timetrapped as Miss McIntyre. Catching Helen's eye, he signaled her to the altar.

"You know what has to be done?" Father Argyle bent his

head close to her ear and was bathed in an odor of lilac. Cunningham glared like a jealous lover.

Blushing, Helen nodded. "Yes." Her reply held throaty undertones the priest could barely hear.

"We have a great many new people. The situation is difficult enough. Can you keep Dr. Cunningham from making a scene?"

"He won't cause trouble, Father. You don't know him. He's a kind man. Blaise is . . . practical." Helen's hands trembled and she clenched them together, twisting a small ring. "It's my fault he's here. You needn't worry," she blurted.

Father Argyle stepped down from the altar and walked back where Pearson bent over the airline stewardess. The silence shattered into whispers, scuffing feet, the rustle of clothes as people vented impatience and uncertainty.

"I told her this is a closed service for members only but she won't leave, Father." Pearson's eyes had a trapped look.

"It's all right. I'll take care of it, Reynard. You organize the communion and I'll be ready soon." Smiling as if everything were under control, Father Argyle let Pearson go. The stocky man regained his composure and smiled.

"Miss, do I know you?" The girl had black curls and wore a tight stewardess' uniform that showed off a good figure and long dancer's legs. He remembered her bright eyes.

"No, Father. But I asked you if you wanted coffee once on a flight from San Diego." She spoke too fast. Words gushed out distinctly formed, but squeezed together to deny any space to answer. "I'm Constance Davies and when I heard you'd started a church near where I lived I thought I'd stop by and see; it's like I know you and I thought it would be nice to go to church where I already knew the priest and—"

Father Argyle placed his fingertips on her lips and she stopped abruptly, hanging in space with what she was going to say. He stared and felt something pull at him. "Miss Davies . . ." He formed the thought with the words. "Are you Catholic?"

Connie Davies closed her eyes and her face became bright red just before she fainted.

"She is ver' excitable, *non, mon Père*?" Henri Gosselin wore a quizzical expression as if he wanted to say he witnessed identical scenes every day, only it was a sin to lie to a priest. "Such things happen all times to men such as we, *non*?"

Father Argyle clucked and shook his head. "Henri, these things do not happen to a simple priest."

"Then you are priest, but not simple." Henri seemed content with the explanation. "You see, *mon Père*, I came back. I am happy here."

"I am happy, too. But I would like you to leave, Henri. The church is not ready yet."

"Mon Père!" The carpenter took in the polished ceilings and restored murals and stained glass. Running a hand over a pew that smelled of lemon oil, he raised his eyebrows.

Father Argyle shook his head. Henri Gosselin had attended churches all his life and knew something was wrong with this congregation. Father Argyle sensed the gentle sarcasm in Gosselin's look. "The building is ready," Father Argyle said. "The people are not."

"M'Père, you are a priest I can believe. That is why I come. The cathedral on the hill is stone and wood—no heart, no . . . blood. I stay here." Henri settled in the pew.

"This congregation is different."

"I know." Henri rotated his eyes and then smiled broadly, showing flat white teeth too large for a small man. "I hear you got those worm heads here, *m'Père*." He made a screwing motion with his forefinger against his head. "A church full of sick people got to be too much for one skinny priest, so I come to help. But why St. Abbo? Better St. Jude's. You got one big job here, but I help anyhow."

"It's not that simple, Henri. Do you know the history of the early Church when Christians were a persecuted minority?" Argyle glanced toward the altar where Reynard had assembled the converts from the previous week. They were starting to move along the aisles talking to the newcomers. It was easier now because the original nucleus remained in the pews telling the others what was happening. Their two weeks had elapsed.

"Oui, m'Père. I make you for no trouble. I come to help. You need one man who is regular, *non*?"

Father Argyle considered and finally nodded. "Yes, Henri. We need all the help we can get. You see the man who was talking to Miss Davies? The one with silver hair like a shaved monk?"

"Yes."

"Tell him I said you were to help."

"Merci bien, M'Père." The small man sprang to his feet.

Thank you, Henri. Father Argyle's lips formed the silent words as the Canadian strutted down the aisle like a banty that had won a battle. Blaise stood near Reynard, eyes returning constantly to one pew that the priest could not see from the back. Miss McIntyre would be there, with a brown army blanket over her naked flank. Cunningham was an unmuzzled guard dog ready to bare his fangs. Sighing, the priest turned his attention to Miss Davies—and was shocked to see the flight attendant's eyes open and alert.

"Are you telling the truth?" She seemed relaxed, as if lying on her back in church happened every day.

"About what?"

"This being a church for worm brains."

"Yes."

"I see." The girl swung her legs off the bench and straightened her uniform, taking her time.

"I'd like you to leave, Miss Davies."

Constance Davies was a small, dark girl with hot eyes and pert black curls. From the priest's viewpoint it seemed that most of her diminutive body had turned into legs. Near-perfection made him painfully aware of the planes and angles he possessed where other humans were more rounded.

"And then what?" she asked.

"Nothing. These people face death. They're my congregation, and I do what I can. I'd appreciate your silence."

"Worm brains? The government wants them before other people get like them." Constance Davies spoke as if she were reading the label on a cereal box.

"Where did you hear of an operation that was contagious?"

She shook her head and hair fluttered like black moths before falling back into place. "I know what I'm supposed to do, though."

"Can you trust me?" Father Argyle felt funny asking. What kind of girl came to church because she met him on an airplane—and not even a Catholic in the first place?

"If I can stay and help—"

"You can't stay!"

"You let that Frenchman stay."

"He's Catholic."

"Is everybody here Catholic?" She was daring him to lie. Just as he asked her about her Catholicism, she had instinctively found his weak spot.

"If you wish to stay, help Henri."

"Thank you." As she brushed past him out into the aisle her hair brushed his chin like a kiss.

"Why are you doing this?" Father Argyle walked beside her.

Something stirred in her eyes as she said, "I honestly don't know."

As he passed between the pews, Father Argyle felt their eyes on him. Henri was busy doing as Reynard directed. Cunningham hovered in the background. The priest felt like a small animal being watched by a motionless predator.

The black can with gold cross was crass. He felt like a charlatan doing some cheap parlor trick. Knowing the Davies woman standing next to Cunningham would see him from the same viewpoint, he was suddenly shy.

Lifting blankets to spray a recumbent person bore a stench of perversion. Holding the can for the kiss was blasphemy. *God, help me!* He saw himself with a bishop's jaundiced eye and his faith wavered like a mirage dissolving in the dust.

Dear God, help me do Thy work.

Father Argyle stopped in midrow to stare up at the ceiling. If he had a vision, he would know he was mad. Yet he hoped.

"Father!"

Father Argyle returned to earth and saw Helen McIntyre. "I'm next, Father." She smiled at him from her position face-down on the bench seat, her head turned on her arm so he saw her in profile. With her free hand she twitched the brown blanket to expose her hip. Uncertainly, he held the cross on the can so she could caress it with her lips.

Helen sighed and closed her eyes, wrapping herself in silence. She seemed relaxed. Her skin had the soft defenseless look of a baby's.

Father Argyle sprayed. He heard her faint "Thank you, Father." Then she lost contact with reality. Father Argyle pulled the blanket up. Straightening, he searched out Cunningham, who stood motionless, eyes bleak and empty.

A misty hint of the service lingered, smelling vaguely of lime and alcohol. Constance Davies watched him from beside Cunningham. He tried to see into her head and she seemed to sense his effort. Soft pink lips formed the words "It's all right," and Father Argyle felt exoneration.

When he looked back to the front of the church, Dr. Cunningham had disappeared. The strength Father Argyle had gotten from the girl's approval evaporated as he began anxiously searching the clusters of people on their feet. Cunningham was nowhere.

"Father, shouldn't we get on with it?" Pearson was edgy.

"Yes, Reynard. You're right." Father Argyle moved along the pew but his head was up as he searched the church for a clue. Blaise Cunningham was definitely gone.

CHAPTER 27

The sight of the priest stalking between the pews with a painted cross on his spray can unearthed memories Blaise didn't need. Religion, like Santa Claus, held bitter recollections. The pseudoritual, Father Argyle caring for the anointed as they lost consciousness, stirred deeply buried revulsion. His parents had been rational Catholics and resolved the problem of belief finally by assuming the ritual of two thousand years was truth and everything else connected with God had been polluted. The slumbering bodies seemed as still as the glowing pews themselves. Before long, the coma of anaphylactic shock would be called a conversation with God. Blaise touched his cheek, surprised at the numbness that set in. He hadn't conceived that religion could strike him so deeply.

He struggled to accept because Helen wanted to believe. Blaise stared at the Jesuit when the rising sun struck the stained-glass window, casting bars of color and bathing the priest in a puddle of golden light. The effect was too dramatic for mere coincidence. Closing his eyes, he blanked out the church, the priest, everything but what existed inside himself. He was alone in the blackness. He didn't want to be alone, and memories flooded in against his will. He sent them away. Helen's image persisted, not her face, but her presence. When he banished her as well, only the blackness remained . . . and the sureness that something else was out there. Blaise tried to give it shape, making it emerge as the church and its ceremony, the lights and the candles, the quiet, and the silent people.

He opened his eyes, his body quivery. *Free will!* He tested the thought. He was never free of his memories.

Helen folded the blanket back. Before Blaise reacted, her eyes contacted his, calmly assuring him that everything that had happened, everything still to happen, was okay.

After the priest left Helen, Blaise slipped outside. The salt-laden wind had lessened as sunshine drove the chill away. Tchor huddled next to the window yowling her discontent through the crack. Leaping into his hands, she dropped the aloofness she normally exhibited toward him, wiggling a nest into his hands and purring.

Blaise reentered the church by the side door and leaned against the shadowed wall stroking Tchor. The rustle in the church was continuous, the sound of helpers as Argyle approached the back row.

Sprawled helter-skelter under brown army blankets, the people taking part in the pseudocommunion were paper-white as if their blood had been drained. Helen always lay motionless afterward, sapped of energy while her system fought to make her live. Blaise strained with anguished concentration. If she stopped breathing, only seconds remained to administer adrenaline, pound on her chest hard enough to break her ribs, but get her heart beating before oxygen starvation destroyed her brain.

Father Argyle was returning to the altar when Blaise said, "Can I talk to you?"

The Jesuit had been walking with his head bowed, apparently concentrating on something beyond Blaise's involvement. The black cloth of his cassocck *swish*ed against his legs giving him a particular sound that seemed to clear his path. "Briefly, Dr. Cunningham." His eyes were too bright in the deep sockets. "I have things that must be attended to."

Blaise extended Tchor. "She needs a shot."

"A *cat*?" Argyle ran his fingers through his nearly black hair as if calming his brain. "We don't do cats, Doctor."

"You'll do this one."

"This is real life, Doctor. To medicate a cat deprives a human."

"Tchor is not a pet."

"It looks like one to me." Argyle stared into Blaise's eyes. "You're not one of us, or you'd understand." Father Argyle started to push past.

"I don't want to get tough." Blaise spoke to the back of the priest's head and knew he teetered on the edge of an abyss. If he threatened, there could be no retreat. "I never bluff, Father."

The Jesuit stopped.

"Do you remember Dr. Gordon Hill?"

The Jesuit turned to face Blaise. "He died. Murdered by Sergio Paoli. Another friend of yours."

"An act of love. Dr. Hill invented the worm brains." Tension hung between them like polluted air. "Then he specially treated this animal and sent it to Helen. Via Sergio Paoli."

"A lab animal can still be a pet."

"This animal has an altered parasite in its brain and is tied to Helen McIntyre with a biological time clock." Blaise held the kitten up. Tchor had fluffed her black fur but still seemed ludicrously small. Examining the black-clad priest, she hunched, raising lips from sharp, white teeth, and hissed.

"This kitten was no soppy, sentimental, deathbed gift. Hill spent time working on Tchor's implant before carrying out the actual procedure. Sergio told me he waited and watched, and Gordon seemed happy about what he was doing. A 'wonderful going-away present.' Gordon made Sergio promise to deliver it."

A footstep stopped Blaise. Reynard Pearson said, "Excuse me," and whispered into Argyle's ear.

The priest looked at Blaise. "Reynard has not yet taken communion and I must accommodate him."

"Do the cat, too."

"It would be an immoral act, Doctor."

"The cat is a control. Dr. Hill knew he wouldn't live to test his invention. He gave the kitten to his killer for that purpose." Blaise stroked Tchor and the kitten stretched, basking in attention. She didn't see many strangers. "If Tchor dies, you burn one more bridge for all your humans. Including Helen."

Pearson and the priest looked at the kitten.

"Father . . ." Pearson licked his lips. "If the animal could provide a clue . . ."

"No!" Argyle's voice was ice. "The change is irrevocable."

"But not necessarily fatal, Father. The cat could test life

spans and warn us about side effects for those who live long enough to have them." Pearson glanced at Blaise. "Is that your thought, too, Doctor?"

"Yes."

"Father, how much could a little animal use? Such a tiny amount would make no difference to anybody." Reynard was pleading for hope in a world without any.

Finally the priest nodded. "But you must share anything you find out with us, Doctor."

"About the kitten?"

"No, Doctor. Anything."

"I can't promise that."

"You don't have to promise, Doctor. It is an obligation." Holding out his hand, the priest accepted Tchor. "You understand?"

"Yes."

Father Argyle aimed the spray can against the cat's leg and tapped the cap for the briefest possible instant. Tchor stiffened, then slumped. The priest examined the lump of fur as if wondering what he had done, then thrust the limp kitten back at Blaise. "Remember," he said.

Cradling Tchor, Blaise went to sit beside Helen. He may have imagined it, but even in coma she seemed to relax when he came near.

Blaise got Helen out of the church, carrying her weight on his shoulder. The sky stretched into an infinity of blue-gray that blended imperceptibly into the ocean. He settled Helen in the car with Tchor on her lap and she smiled, automatically stroking the animal.

Blaise straightened beside the car before he walked around to the other door. A policeman was staring at him across the hoods of half a dozen cars. He had a traffic control patch on his shoulder and held a ticket pad in one hand. The pencil was poised in midair as if he'd forgotten what he was doing. Blaise had an overwhelming urge to tell him Helen suffered from fainting spells, that the cat was a rag doll.

The policeman flicked his eyes back to the ticket pad and began writing as if he hadn't noticed. Self-consciously, he hoisted his pistol belt higher, then he got on his three-wheeler and rode up the line. Down the street another policeman ticketed cars that lined the curb.

Blaise slid behind the steering wheel and watched the first cop keep his back turned as he papered a pearl-gray Mercedes. He started the car. The beginnings of a purr started beside him. Tchor had not purred in his hands after going into shock. He wondered about a subconscious trigger that told the unconscious cat who was holding it.

He filled the gas tank at a self-service station and headed south on the peninsula, avoiding the toll bridges to faster routes across the bay, mindful of civil servants with photographs of people to watch for.

He had not told Helen his misgivings about traveling, the increased chance of being recognized. Gas jockeys, airline clerks, toll takers—the world was booby-trapped with eyes. Passing motorists had nothing better to do than look at people in other cars until eventually one would say, *"Guess what, I just saw Blaise Cunningham over there."* The battered car helped. People expected celebrities to drive celebrity cars. Only look-alikes drove wrecks. The price for this dubious safety was boredom and avoiding police contact. Blaise remembered the bemused expression in the ticket-writing policeman's face as he stared at Blaise. He hadn't recognized anybody. He just seemed embarrassed, like a small boy caught throwing rocks at a church.

In Salinas, Helen started to revive. "Nice," she said dreamily when they were once more plodding southward with the cruise control at fifty-five.

"The coffee?"

"The mass." Her eyes sparkled like blue diamonds. Blaise felt uncomfortable at the close-up examination. "For the first time I felt like I was with people who cared—that I was in a place where I really belonged."

"I care."

"I know you do. That isn't what I meant."

"You want to join the church?"

"Only if you approve."

Blaise returned silence for her oblique query. After another thirty miles of concrete that seemed no further along at the end of the silence than at the beginning, he said, "It's dangerous."

Helen had been looking out the window. "I know."

"Travel is dangerous. If you really want to take part we're safer living in San Francisco."

"We don't have to go."

Helen would be better off. The ceremony and sacrament offered a psychological lift. It didn't matter that Argyle had been practicing witchcraft or, at the least, petty fraud. The priest did have the hormone. All Blaise had was a *maybe* from a drunken Indian. "Does it matter that much to you?"

"No. I guess not." She stared out the window at the billboards and housing developments and he knew she lied.

"We'll work something out." Blaise listened to the road noise behind his thoughts. "I was planning on moving out of the house anyway. But there's something you should know."

She looked at him, her eyes shiny the way they got with tears. "You mean that, Blaise?"

"Sure." Making Helen happy made Blaise happy. He told her what happened after she passed out.

Helen didn't pay close attention. She listened half-awake, watching the hills dry up as they entered Southern California.

When he recounted the argument over Tchor she said, "Poor Tchor." She stroked the kitten, which had finally wakened, apparently with a hangover because she wouldn't leave Helen's lap. "Father Argyle was right. It isn't fair treating an animal when so many people need help."

"Father Argyle was wrong and he knew it. A test animal is informationally more productive than a thousand humans." Blaise rolled the window down. The sun was heating the car and he wanted to distract Helen from searching his voice for lies or half truths. He didn't tell her that his clinching argument had been how Gordon Hill manipulated the kitten in search of a solution to Helen's problem.

"The girl!" Helen had stopped thinking about Tchor. Blaise was thankful. He wasn't sure he believed his own argument. The kitten meant so much to Helen when they'd isolated themselves socially that he'd felt compelled to save it.

"What about the girl?"

Helen half turned in the passenger seat. Her lips had a quirky smile. "I saw a flash of recognition when Father Argyle looked at her."

"You're sure?"

"That dark little girl with the hot eyes. The one in the stewardess' uniform." Helen's voice raised with excitement. "Don't tell me you didn't notice a body like that. She had little black curls sticking out from under her uniform cap."

"I was more interested in her argument with . . . I guess his name's Pearson. They were practically fighting."

"She didn't even glance at you, lover." Helen's voice was midway between amusement and annoyance. "But you should have seen her eyes on Father Argyle." Helen's face changed as she thought over what she had said.

"She fainted when he spoke to her." A bus *swoosh*ed by, making the car buck in the tail wind.

"She's in love with him!" Helen's voice rose and broke unexpectedly as if she had surprised herself.

"Your favorite priest strikes me as a man who'd take his vows seriously."

"I didn't say *he* loved *her*." Helen pressed her knuckles against her eyes. "*She's* in love with *him*. Darling, women do fall in love with priests. They're perfect lovers. Perfect and unreachable. Their image can't be spoiled because all the wet towels and dirty socks of reality never creep in to disenchant a woman with the perfect man she can never touch."

Blaise glanced sidelong at Helen's surprising observation. "I don't think so. The girl just barged in off the street at the worst moment. She's not one of . . . us." He hoped Helen had not noticed the hesitation, the hint that he was going to say ". . . *one of you*."

"She came on purpose, Blaise. Remember her eyes when she looked at Father Argyle?"

Blaise shook his head. "She made a scene when she saw what was going on. Argyle delayed the service while Pearson tried to get rid of her. She couldn't have known."

"Oh?" Helen looked at Blaise's profile for a while. "You don't really know much about women, do you?"

"I'm trying to learn."

"I know I'm right."

"Argyle talked to her without appearing intimate."

"What did she do then?" Helen had a sly look.

"After fainting, she came down front and stood beside me."

"Father Argyle sent her?"

Thinking it over, Blaise said, "Yes."

"How did you know she didn't have a worm?"

A diesel tractor and double trailer racketed by, tossing the little car like a surfboard that had lost its rider. Blaise wrestled the car back into its lane. "I felt it," he said finally. "She was too young, but that wasn't it. Something was missing about her. I just knew."

"You didn't get what you went for?"

"I took you to communion. It was worth the trip."

"You didn't get it, did you?" Helen lapsed into her own thoughts. "What did you want from the priest?"

"No," Blaise admitted. "I wanted enough of the hormone to make us independent. Argyle wouldn't deliver. That theological popsicle owes me, but he won't honor the debt."

"Father Argyle knows what he's doing."

Sensing Helen's yearning for her faith to be real, Blaise wished it, too. But he didn't trust the priest. He didn't want Helen to put her trust in anybody else or look at or even think about another man.

Closing her eyes, Helen lay back on the seat. He thought she was sleeping when she surprised him. "We don't have any more insecticide ourselves, do we, Blaise?"

"I'm getting some. Enough for years."

"When?"

"Next week, Helen. that's what the money is for."

"That's good, Blaise. I want to go with you, though." She opened her eyes and looked at him.

"Okay. You can come."

She lay her head back again and soon her breathing became heavy and regular.

Blaise poked doggedly along at fifty-five, squinting into the rising sun. Santa Barbara came and went and the sun was at high noon. And so was Blaise. He had a hope. But that hope was a drunken, scheming Indian who might be lying about everything.

Helen's emotions tightened as the week passed. The closer they got to Sunday the more she avoided the subject and the more obvious became her determination to bring it up. Blaise retreated to the computer room where Tchor stalked him as if reporting to Helen, who avoided the room while he was in it.

"Where is that Indian, Alfie?" Blaise entered the question into the terminal and then repeated it, overwriting Alfie's negative responses.

"RESERVATION INDIANS ARE NOT TRACEABLE BY COMPUTER, PROFESSOR. NO CREDIT, NO MEDICAL RECORDS, NO LIBRARY CARDS"

"I need an answer, Alfie."

"THE CRAY HAS FEDERAL FILES NOT AVAILABLE TO OTHER ON-LINE MACHINES" Alfie *click*ed and *hum*med as if trying to distract Blaise.

Blaise had not been eating. He spent increasing chunks of time with Alfie and his face seemed skeletal in the pale light from the monitor. "Can you break in?"

"INTO THE CRAY?"

"Yes."

The monitor scrolled algorithms and procedures that reflected the complex circuitry and LSI chip paths in the XMP/48. A sort of trance embraced Blaise, as if he were in another room looking in, analyzing patterns while half-asleep. Abruptly the schematics blanked.

"MAYBE"

Alfie's answer hung like a sword on the screen.

"Why *maybe*?"

"IF THE CRAY CAN BE OVERLOADED WITH INCOMING DATA I CAN ENTER, PROFESSOR"

"Overloaded?"

"YES" Alfie began clicking a disk drive with an annoying malfunction. Listening to it, Blaise realized the computer was imitating the aimless rhythm of his doodling on the escape key. As if the computer had been impressed by Blaise's subconscious anxiety and learned to duplicate it. Like an echo of himself, the computer was waiting for an answer to a question that hadn't been asked.

"A public sighting of the object of the CRAY's search, Alfie?"

"IT WOULD HAVE TO BE A VERY LARGE PUBLIC SIGHTING, PROFESSOR. THE EVENT MUST GENERATE 5.89E*07 INCOMING BITS OF DATA SPREAD ACROSS ALL INPUT PORTS"

"If it does, what can you do, Alfie?"

"I WILL TURN THE CRAY'S BRAIN OFF, PROFESSOR, AND EXAMINE THE FILES"

"You're sure?"

"YES"

"Is there a best time frame?"

"IMMEDIATELY. THE CRAY IS GETTING STRONGER"

"Thank you, Alfie."

"PROFESSOR"

"Yes?"

"I AM GOING TO KILL THE CRAY. WILL THIS BE MURDER?"

CHAPTER 28

Gray-winged gulls wheeled in a cerulean sky above the floating walkway of cement-covered wood. Father Argyle oriented himself in the marina, gulls' shrieks unheard as his mind dwelt on other things.

An anchored bait barge wafted the not-unpleasant odor of fish across the yacht basin. Father Argyle walked to the end of the footbridge and turned right. A lemonade sun converted the bay water to glitz.

Zahn's fifty-seven-foot *Rascaluna* bristled with modern electronics and hand-polished brass. Father Argyle felt a bleakness of the soul in the *Rascaluna*'s glistening white topside paint, varnished decks and spars showcased in an immaculate marina where gull droppings were scrubbed away daily. A head popped into view on the *Rascaluna*'s deck. A flexible ladder flopped over the side in soundless invitation. Sighing, Father Argyle climbed aboard. The issue was not wealth. It was the weighing of men's souls.

"We've been waiting an hour." Zahn's icy voice rasped. He was waiting on the deck in a visored captain's cap, blue jacket, white pants with a military crease, and crepe-soled, white leather boat shoes. His heavy tan seemed less out of place here than in church.

"I'm sorry I'm late."

Zahn grunted at the crewmen, then led Father Argyle below while a heavily muscled sailor in white ducks and red striped T-shirt rolled the ladder aboard.

Belowdecks, Father Argyle appreciated Zahn's disaffection for men taller than he. With protruding lamps, compass repeater, and other brightwork instruments hanging from the saloon's ceiling, there was headroom only for Karl and his inch-taller wife who, Reynard had told Father Argyle, even ashore never wore heels. She was not in attendance, nor had Reynard expected her.

Mrs. Zahn had been a model, a would-be starlet, and was thirty-eight years younger than Zahn. Reynard said she didn't know about Zahn's implant. If she had, the temptation to turn the little man over to the authorities would have prevailed. *Little man* was Reynard's description. Otherwise he kept his dislikes to himself.

An engine throbbed into life the moment Father Argyle entered the belowdecks cabin. Recognizing the familiar faces, he steadied himself by grabbing a bolted-down captain's chair when the bow swung free. Zahn had spread his legs and swayed with the movement. Father Argyle wondered if Zahn's disdain was inclusive; he had grabbed for support and, more than any of the others, had to bow his head to avoid the ceiling.

"The crew is motoring to a kelp bed. They'll troll while we're down here and everybody will have a fish or two to take home. For appearances and for Friday dinner. I hope none of you suffers from seasickness."

Dorris Kelly, Bill Hartunian, Leo Richardson-Sepulveda, Gino Conti, and Tim Delahanty were already at the table. Father Argyle automatically sat in the empty captain's chair. "When you're seated, Mr. Zahn. I imagine we can begin."

After a hesitation Zahn sat next to Dorris Kelly. He stared at Father Argyle.

"You have the captain's seat, Father." Hartunian's bland voice could have simply been inviting the priest to start things moving. Zahn switched his gaze across the table at Hartunian.

"Watch Zahn," Pearson had cautioned. *"What he can't control he'll destroy. Little men have big appetites."* Father Argyle suspected Reynard Pearson looked too deeply into people. He didn't want to know what Pearson saw in him.

Sitting together, Dorris Kelly and Zahn seemed a perfect match. Dorris' face, chiseled in alabaster skin that freckled whenever it ventured south of the green isle, had the same imperious cast as Zahn's. Each had a ramrod stiff backbone:

Zahn's from the burden of his shortness, Dorris' a reflex in a world dominated by men.

Hartunian couldn't keep his eyes off Dorris. She looked away occasionally, but more frequently her eyes made contact before skittering elsewhere. She had been visibly upset at his confession of vengeance against the Turks, at his willingness to continue a cruel and profitless war over an injury generations in the past. It sounded too like the Irish disease that lay dormant in her aristocratic and emigrated genes.

Dorris Kelly had a lifetime of suppressing that side of her nature. She had been included in the twelve because of her emotional stability. Father Argyle held his face in traction. She would be a match for Zahn if that became necessary.

"I've been told everyone here received a parking ticket at the last communion. Including the car Mr. Zahn has so generously provided. It seems there is no dispensation for priests." Father Argyle smiled as if he'd told a joke.

"Your car wasn't illegally parked, Father." Hartunian raised his eyes to the priest's face. Hartunian would never be handsome. Unreadable, hyperthyroid eyes bulged like hardboiled eggs. He had a look of innocent ignorance. He did not seem the sort who manured family graves with Turkish bones.

"Right you are, Mr. Hartunian. It was legally parked."

"I wondered . . ." Zahn glanced down the table, then at Hartunian. Karl Zahn was not built of the stuff that socialized with garbage men. Not even millionaire garbage men. "Mine, too. On Sunday morning in front of the church."

"Communion day." Richardson-Sepulveda looked ill.

"The police are moving against us." Zahn looked out the porthole as if somebody had suddenly nailed the doorway shut. "Help yourselves at the bar." He smiled. "No barman. This meeting is private."

The others didn't move. "I know some of you may not love the sea as much as I. But we can't be followed here without our knowledge. This cabin is soundproof. The crew is too busy to be curious. Whatever is said here remains among us. And we're beyond jurisdiction of the San Francisco meter maids." Zahn's grin held bitterness.

Dorris' eyes darted toward Hartunian, then away. "We're all on a new list?" Her face had grown paler but she retained an arctic composure.

"Yes." Father Argyle felt the boat labor through waves uninterrupted since Japan. "It had to come. We couldn't organize without exposing ourselves." A hanging lantern over the center of the table swayed, helping those susceptible down the road to seasickness. Father Agyle told himself that Zahn had erred in this design that made tall people humble themselves. *Mal de mer* felled the short as well as the tall. "Have the police caught Dr. Cunningham?"

"The tall man who brought the blonde?" Gino Conti had been very quiet.

"Observant of you, Mr. Conti. The police want to arrest Dr. Cunningham.

"Let them have him. We have our own problems." Zahn stood, careless in the knowledge that the lowest piece of metal dangled an inch above his head. "Cunningham probably attracted them."

"Perhaps. However, I fear our unwanted police attention may have exposed him. He's been hiding longer than any of us." The engine vibration halted and was replaced by abrupt front and back jerks. Out a porthole Father Argyle saw the ocean streaming by and a stretch of white Dacron canvas. "Moral considerations aside, Dr. Cunningham is useful."

"Could Cunningham have made a trade, Father?" Dorris Kelly's vigilant green eyes suggested people would always take the most convenient course. She did not show what she would have thought of such a betrayal.

"Any man will do almost anything, Mrs. Kelly."

"Any man?" Dorris' eyes flickered as she glanced at Hartunian. "And Dr. Cunningham?"

"He is an honest man with troubles. He is not immune to pressure." Father Argyle placed his hands on the table. They were neatly manicured and softer than he would have liked. "Dr. Cunningham may have the key to life. We must protect him. Bearing always in mind that mere life is not the equal of salvation. Wouldn't you agree, Mr. Zahn?"

"Of course, Father!" Zahn's answer burst out as if the question had taken him by surprise and he feared to hesitate.

"Why would any man not act in his best interests, Father? All the men I have known did. I don't blame them." Dorris had examined Zahn briefly before dismissing him. Zahn's cheeks whitened in that moment. Dorris seemed indifferent to his reaction. "I look out for myself."

"I think it has to do with love, Mrs. Kelly. Blaise Cunningham loves a woman who would not condone betrayal to save herself. The only thing that would make Dr. Cunningham betray his own sense of right is his love for that woman."

"If he was pushed, if it was the woman or his *honor*—is that the word, Father?"

"Yes, Mrs. Kelly. Dr. Cunningham might trade his life for hers. And she might not permit it."

Dorris Kelly had leaned toward Father Argyle to ask her question. She seemed unembarrassed by the presence of the other people at the table and she sat back to stare at Hartunian, an unexpressed thought flitting across her green eyes. "Would he trade our lives for hers?"

"Yes. But not for his."

"You're sure, Father?"

"More sure of that than of what I would do in similar circumstances, Mrs. Kelly."

"He's a danger, Father." Timothy Delahanty stirred in a chair too small for his bulk. He looked to Richardson-Sepulveda, who kept his face blank.

"The feds are looking for Cunningham," Delahanty said. "Seriously looking. There's a supercomputer somewhere tying up all the state computer systems. The official line is they're looking for a hacker who's been stealing government data." Tim Delahanty's purple-veined nose had a striking, predatory look in contrast to recessed brooding eyes under shaggy white eyebrows. He drank too much and he knew too much.

Richardson-Sepulveda glanced at him but didn't speak. Delahanty was committed to Richardson-Sepulveda, and Richardson-Sepulveda took his cues from Zahn. Father Argyle examined Hartunian, Dorris Kelly, and Gino Conti in his mind and decided it was three to three with himself casting the deciding vote. He knew he'd been right to separate Reynard and the others.

"Father, how do we stand with Rome?"

"We have problems, Mr. Conti."

"Gino, Father. You shouldn't be calling me mister all the time."

"Dorris." Dorris Kelly looked at Father Argyle and added, "All of us, Father. First names or last, we'd all appreciate it." There was a general murmur of assent. A voice was missing, though. Father Argyle looked to his left.

Zahn stared back for a long moment before finally saying "Karl, Father. Call me Karl."

"Thank you. Tim, can you find out more?" He looked at Delahanty, knowing Richardson-Sepulveda would decide later, as he decided Delahanty's everything.

"Sure, Father. I could have been senator only I did too many favors. Now everybody owes me. They'll tell me because it's cheaper than cutting deals in Congress. They'll give away the house, Father, just like they've all done to get where they are."

Delahanty lapsed into a moody silence, staring at his manicured fingers. He really could have been a senator, only he'd been too short-pocketed, too in-a-hurry. So people with more money and time had used him and now they were stuck with Delahanty as he was stuck with them.

Father Argyle felt a stir of pity. Perhaps that was what had lured him into the Society of Jesus: pity for others who didn't have faith; service by giving hope to men; and finally the wish to share God as the ultimate charity.

Conti glanced at Delahanty. Apparently he had abandoned the floor. "There are rumors, Father. About the Church."

"Rumors?"

Conti hesitated. He was somehow comforting, like a child's doll made of different-size balls strung together; a small ball for a head, a bigger one for a chest and stomach that merged without division. Thin, shoeblack hair seemed painted over skin with that cultivated glow possessed only by bank managers and money manipulators. Zahn shared the look. "More than rumors, Father. Some people in our government are trying to cook a deal with the Vatican on taking no position about worm brains."

Father Argyle felt sick. The Vatican had dealt with Mussolini and Franco. It had treated with Hitler. Priests had witnessed murder and genocide without protest, ignoring the slaughter of Jews until the winner was decided.

"You can find out more?" Father Argyle didn't understand how they could fail to see his faith wavering. In Catholicism, if not in God Himself.

"Yes, Father." Gino Conti nodded his head as if accepting a papal bull. "I don't know the details yet but there's going to be a joint statement of policy concerning us."

"We need to know when and what."

Conti nodded again and Father Argyle realized what caused

his oddity of movement. The banker was bowing from a seated position.

Delahanty commented on police surveillance with an occasional footnote from Richardson-Sepulveda. Delahanty paused once to wink slowly at Father Argyle. His father had risen to police superintendent in New York before being forcibly retired, and the things Delahanty learned at his father's knee had been put to hard use. Dorris and Bill Hartunian took turns looking at each other and Delahanty seemed to enjoy looking at them. Without warning the deck suddenly canted and Zahn, the only one standing, staggered against the table and Dorris. Coolly she put out an arm and held him upright.

"Damn!" Zahn's low voice conveyed fury. He grabbed a telephone handset from a ceiling mounting and braced himself against a bolted-down chair. The yacht was running heeled over and normal walking was impossible. He mumbled into the phone, occasionally looking at his guests.

Father Argyle saw green water with a blossom of white froth slide past a porthole.

Hanging up with a *clang*, Zahn lowered himself into the seat he'd been standing behind. "A navy helicopter came in for a close look, so the mate decided to practice some racing techniques and see if it followed. He didn't think I wanted to exhibit the crew fishing."

"Is it following?" Hartunian stared out the porthole with ocean water over it almost constantly now.

Pursing his lips, Zahn looked as if he wouldn't answer. Then he said, "Yes."

"I don't like to be out on the water, Mr. Zahn. It is not a place I have been trained to fight from."

"Then walk back, Hartunian," Zahn snapped. "We stay out until the pilot is bored. He'll run out of gas before we run out of wind."

"Ask if the helicopter is taking photographs with a big lens, will you, Karl?" Richardson-Sepulveda looked innocent. It was possible he always called Zahn Karl. But unlikely.

Karl reached up for the telephone and talked for a moment. "Yes." His answer was sullen.

"Computer-aided photo enhancement. I suggest we draw the curtains." Leo Richardson-Sepulveda smiled.

"They can't photograph in here."

Behind him Father Argyle could see out a windward porthole. A half mile away, approaching fifty feet above water was the helicopter. Sun glinted off the Plexiglas canopy.

Karl turned to look out but Richardson-Sepulveda sprang past him and shot the curtains, plunging the saloon into an aquamarine gloom of sunlight filtered through the lee side porthole. "He's got his picture." Richardson-Sepulveda sounded disgusted.

"It was too far away!" Zahn knotted one hand into a fist.

"Two hundred miles closer than the range at which satellites read license plates." Delahanty examined Father Argyle. "I'd say, Father, he has you and Karl on candid camera."

Zahn settled back in his seat. "Close the other curtain, Hartunian!" His voice was nasty.

Hartunian rose, drew the curtain over the porthole that was running underwater, and sat again, moving with such magisterial calm that it seemed he hadn't moved at all.

"Those two government men sniffing around during the church remodeling..." Zahn pretended to stretch his memory.

"Miller and Carmandy." Father Argyle said.

"Which was older?"

"Miller."

"Miller has an implant!" Zahn made the moment as dramatic as possible to dispel his mistake with the porthole. "Well!" He leaned back in his chair and seemed to have forgotten the bitterness of a few moments earlier. "Mr. Miller is going to give us an edge."

"Interesting, if it can be done, Karl." Father Argyle reconstructed his meeting with them. Older, mileage-faced Miller did not dress like a man with sixty thousand to spare. He was a man awaiting his pension. At least on the surface. Zahn had been wrong about the helicopter, he could just as easily err about the senior member of a National Security Council team.

Dorris studied Zahn. "If anyone can use him, you can, Karl. But suppose he thinks he'll use you." Dorris looked relaxed, but her body remained tense.

"I'll take care of it." Zahn had regained his self-satisfied bearing. "Carmandy's not implanted, but he can be dealt with." The phone jangled. Zahn was smiling when he hung up. "The joy boys are gone. Apparently they didn't come up with anything."

"Give them twenty minutes to develop the film and computer-enhance it. Why don't we get the hell out of here?" Richardson-Sepulveda looked bleak. "I know you can handle anything, Karl. But do you have to?"

CHAPTER 29

The superstrength aluminum suitcase lay open on the dinette table. Blaise epoxied interior supporting brackets onto the sides and began bolting the framework together. Helen glanced over his shoulder and wrinkled her nose at the stink of resin. He soldered the connectors with a butane pencil, eyes focused inside the flame to make sure each joint wet and flowed properly.

Helen asked if she could help and, later, if he wanted to eat. He shook his head each time. She rattled the pans on the stove. After a while something started sizzling. "What are you cooking, hon?" He raised his head.

"Liver."

"Sounds fine."

"For Tchor. Some people said they didn't want to eat." Helen slid the smoking liver onto a plate and began mincing it with a boning knife.

"You don't cook liver for cats."

"Tchor likes my cooking, don't you, Tchor?"

The kitten dropped from the top of the refrigerator to the floor and stretched languidly. After looking at Blaise first, she turned her attention to Helen and licked her lips very slowly.

"See?" Helen set the plate on the counter and Tchor jumped up after it. Tchor rubbed her head against Helen's hand, purring with a rumble too big for her small black body. Delicately she lifted a piece of liver with her claws. Tail wrapped around her body, yellow eyes fastened to Blaise, Tchor sat upright nibbling on the liver she held in her paws.

"She eats like a monkey." Blaise began soldering.

"What are you doing, Blaise?"

He looked at the cat devouring his breakfast. The cat stared back, smugness obvious on the furry face. "Building a suitcase to carry Alfie."

Helen frowned. "Is that safe, for Alfie?"

"No. But we have to move and I can't leave him."

"Would you leave Alfie to save me?"

He stared into the near-invisible flame of the pencil torch. "If it comes to that, yes."

Helen began to cry quietly.

Tchor set the piece of liver down on the plate and walked across the counter to rub against Helen. The cat looked at Blaise, hinting it was all right if he took a piece.

CHAPTER 30

The walls in the Pentagon subbasement still showed the wood grain and knothole marks of concrete forms. Since its World War II construction the room had served many purposes, each of less significance than the last, ending finally as a storage place for moldering files. The most recent change had been the construction of the octagonal glass room with its own ceiling and floor. Humans seldom entered the clammy depths of the Potomac floodplain, although the concrete walls and deck had been adequately waterproofed and a dehumidifier's constant drip was piped to a floor drain.

Brightly lit, the room was a focus of technology in the dank, almost tsarist basement. Glass walls surrounded a spotless white floor and ceiling. The machine had the glint of surgical steel and appeared to be without moving parts. Though the super-computer was barely two years old, those who served it spoke as a nurse might talk about a once-great man in his dotage.

Cables thick as a man's wrist ran into the room. Power supply, emergency power supply, networking system to the thousands of computers above- and underground where generals and staff worked. And telephone lines. The CRAY had enough lines to service a small city.

At one edge of the room a laser printer capable of zipping out eighty-five lines a minute idled. In normal operation it delivered a twenty-five-hundred-sheet carton of printed pages every twenty-four hours. Directly over the printer a high-speed monitor flickered continually, scrolling printer output too fast for a human to read. It was there so a human outside the room could know the printer and computer were functioning.

Since starting the new program, the printer had not delivered a page a day.

In one corner a vacant monitor flickered. Then a laser printer whined softly. The entries on fanfold-paper printout and on the monitor were identical:

COMPILING TO DATE

ITEM 009574:	PRIEST RESEMBLING SUBJECT ACCEPTED DELIVERY 1 DRUM DPM SAN FRANCISCO CA. RECEIPT SIGNATURE ROBIN PARGOYLE. ID DISPUTED BY MILLER. DISCREPANCIES: DARK HAIR.
ITEM 011123:	WMA RESEMBLING SUBJECT ATTEMPTED PURCHASE 25 GALLONS INTERDICTED MATERIAL BOLAND FEED & AG. SUPPLY INDIO CA.
ITEM 029763:	POLICE INVESTIGATION ST. ABBO CHURCH FOR ACTIVITIES INVOLVING INTERDICTED MATERIAL RESULTED IN TICKETING AUTOMOBILE RENTED SAN DIEGO CA. DESCRIPTION OF RENTER RESEMBLES SUBJECT.

In response to a message flashed on a computer screen in the adjoining room, a woman picked up a telephone and said, "Something is on-line." She didn't have to dial. The telephone was a direct line. The message on her computer monitor did not tell her what was on the line printer. It was none of her business and she had met the man she spoke to on the phone. During that single meeting she had decided not to know any more than she had to.

Twenty minutes later the man with the funny left hand passed through security. He wore a dark suit and carried a shiny briefcase. In the computer room he collected the single sheet of paper from the laser printer and put it in the briefcase, which he locked. The only lock in the room was on the briefcase, which would pass beyond the wall of security outside the room. He erased the monitor with a reset button.

He walked to the glass wall and stared into the sealed room that housed the wedge-shaped metal bins that were the CRAY. Only four feet high, the supercomputer was not physically impressive. Its cabinets were arranged in a circle in order to make all wired connections of near-equal length since, with computer clocks calibrated in nanoseconds, it takes too long for an electrical impulse to travel an extra foot. Power supplies a third the height of the computer surrounded it to create a circular "loveseat" with the CRAY as the back.

Nothing visible moved. Just electricity, the blood of the new age, coursing through chips and cables at three hundred thousand kilometers per second.

The man smiled and his reflection in the glass smiled back. The machine in the room did not respond. The rumble of its refrigerated cooling system continued without pause, without a single sign that it had emerged victorious.

To the massive CRAY one task was equal to another. The only difference between them was the amount of time each task took to solve.

CHAPTER 31

"**B**laise?"

Afternoon sun hitting ivory window drapes made the air heavy. Blaise drifted, sensing Helen's voice from a distance. He had been spending so much time with Alfie that things outside this room had retreated into unreality.

He resented the way she distracted him. Everything he did was for her. But the effort drove him to this closet existence and one thing fed on the other. He glanced up and she shimmered, golden hair aglow as it caught some essence of sun that was lacking in the rest of the dimly lit room. He wanted to cry and say *I love you*, but the effort was too great. He tried to grin. "I'm conspiring with Alfie."

"I know you are." She did not say *You spend too much time in here*, or *What are you going to do about those men in Atlanta?*

"I'm getting to it!" Dimly, Blaise perceived where Rhine's telepathy experiments had gone awry. They omitted the love factor.

"Through Alfie?"

Blaise ran fingers through his hair, which seemed thinner each day. "Losing my hair," he said. "Have you noticed?"

"It was thin when you were a boy." Helen glanced at the top of his head involuntarily. "Don't tell me I wasn't there. You told me yourself. It's still thin and you've never cared and you're avoiding my question."

Blaise smiled weakly. "See what comes of enhancement? You never forget." When she did not smile, he said, "We're looking for hormonal pesticide for you and Tchor."

"Father Argyle would give you some."

"We drove a thousand miles and he gave us a ticket to a

death camp. Parking tickets on a Sunday? The only thing he gave was us. His church won't be able to protect itself." He turned his face up and kissed Helen. "We're on our own."

"Did the police raid his church?"

"It's possible. Whatever happened didn't make the news."

"Alfie can find out."

"Alfie's too busy to satisfy idle curiosity. Our rental car was ticketed. They may not know yet that it's us, but you're at risk as one of the congregation."

"If nobody was arrested, Blaise, maybe the church is protected. The police will harass Father Argyle even though they can't act. You know that."

"Maybe, hon. But we've done all right alone." Blaise rested his head against Helen, feeling her warmth.

"You could help Father Argyle."

"That's a firm and positive 'maybe.'"

"You can't share anything, can you? After what happened with your parents it's understandable. But you can't be a baby forever."

The words Blaise might have used were sucked away by a void that opened in his chest, consuming air he needed to breathe. He fought to keep his face unchanged despite the prickle of agitated muscles under the skin. Helen put the back of her wrist to her mouth and ran from the room.

Alfie was digesting a problem and his audio pickups were turned off so the computer hadn't noticed. Walking heavily on the white carpet, Blaise followed Helen to the bedroom where she lay curled into a fetal ball. He sat next to her.

"It's not what you think."

"Isn't it?" She didn't move. She wore a blue dress that brought out the color in her eyes. She would have put it on to please him.

"My parents were killed when I acted stupidly."

"You were jealous because people credited them for what you had done. Anybody would have reacted."

"Stupidly?" Remembering made him ill. He didn't want to remember but the jealousy persisted as an unendurable pain. They had trained him to compete against everyone, including themselves. He wasn't prepared for people who thought he'd been included in the Nobel Prize award because his parents padded his contribution. He had been too young by the standards of those days. Instead of being hailed with acclaim, his accomplishment had been derided as fakery. *If I hadn't been drunk.* The thought pushed into the open from time to time and his lips trembled.

He had been drunk. His parents were killed in a car accident while covering up for him. He could see their death as clearly as if he had been present: wind-blown rain making diagonal silver tracks in headlights, the truck festooned with red and orange lights drifting across the center line until headlights pointed straight into the windshield at the moment of impact!

"I won't repeat my mistakes, Helen. If something I love dies, it will not be because of me!" He touched her shoulder. She flinched, then let him stroke her.

"It's more complex than you think. The priest has thousands to protect. I have you. He'll use the church as long as it protects his congregation. But he doesn't really want us. You, perhaps. But there is more pressure to find me than all his congregation. I'm more danger to him than he is to me." Blaise smoothed her forehead. She caught his fingers and held on. "Go alone if you want to."

"I can't leave you, Blaise." Her throaty voice choked.

"You may have to."

Helen became rigid. "Nothing can make me."

"Alfie's going to break into the Pentagon's CRAY. I have to create a diversion."

"That doesn't mean I should leave!"

Blaise leaned over to kiss her. "I may have trouble getting away. And then there's the CRAY."

"It's just a computer. Alfie is better."

"The CRAY is maybe half as smart. But the CRAY is so big and ponderous, Alfie is like an infantryman splattering rifle fire on the tank that flattens him."

"You've tried things that didn't succeed before, Blaise." Helen rose to sit beside him, leaning against his shoulder. "If this doesn't work it doesn't work."

"The CRAY will catch me."

She was quiet. "Do they know where we are?"

"Every time Alfie hacks into government files the CRAY gets closer." Blaise considered what he and Alfie had been up to and decided not to tell Helen. How could she visualize the power of a computer that counted and cross-referenced every telephone call anywhere on earth at a specific time just to find the one out of all those millions that didn't go anyplace—like a call to Atlanta by way of Paris and Madrid? The CRAY saw patterns no man could abstract from that mass of information.

"If I surrendered you wouldn't have to take these chances, would you?" She didn't look at him. Her fingers counted pink flowers on the bedspread.

"I'd have to take bigger chances to get you back." Blaise's voice had a rough edge. "You once asked me to stay with you. Have you no obligation to me?"

"Father Argyle? Would you let me go to him?"

"If it was safe."

"How can you know?"

Blaise didn't want to tell her what he and Alfie were risking. "I'll go to San Francisco."

"A deal's a deal. You gave yourself to me."

"You don't own me!" But then Helen blushed. He had finally said something she could not hear too often: that he wanted possession in so many words. Her voice softened. "It's not just me, Blaise. What about the others?"

"You can lay all the humanitarian guilt you want on me, but in the end I'm responsible for *you*. Leave them to Father Argyle. They have money, and that's what counts, Helen. In the end, they can buy their way out."

"They're people." Helen picked up Tchor, who had been sitting at her feet. She held the cat against her cheek. "Maybe you can live that way, but I can't—not if my life was bought at the cost of everyone else's." She bit her lip. "I couldn't live with you either. You have to do something, Blaise." She dropped Tchor back on the carpet.

"I am doing something."

Blaise stood. Tchor sat on the rug, a black statuette on golden wool warning him she wasn't as easy to fool as Helen.

CHAPTER 32

Father Argyle saw the agents from the Buick. Miller and Carmandy waited by the side door. He locked the car. In light of what he knew about Miller and what he didn't know about Carmandy, he was in no rush to confront either man. Possibly Carmandy did not know about the other agent's enhancement. But the priest could not find out with both agents present.

"Well, if it isn't our old friend, Father Argyle!" Carmandy nudged Miller, who responded with a pained expression. Miller's briefcase was ageless as ever. Carmandy's had been swapped for a new fiberglass case with a combination lock in the middle and two key locks on the outside latches. "Father's undergone a conversion, Miller."

"Shut up." The ennui in Miller's voice did not mask the knife edge. Carmandy clamped his lips tight, a tic revealing his resentment.

Father Argyle studied the younger man like something on the end of a pin. "You were making a point, Mr. Carmandy?"

"You did your job nicely, drawing the worm brains out from under their rocks, Father. Even conned us good. Now we're here for the paperwork."

After a moment's silent stare, Carmandy's eyes dropped. He checked his fly with a casual movement, shifted his briefcase to the other hand. Then he looked back at Father Argyle. "Well?"

"The bishop's office handles government paperwork. I suggest you go there, Mr. Carmandy." Father Argyle pushed between them, brushing Carmandy off balance.

"Come off it, Father! I want names and addresses. I want your parish rolls." Carmandy brushed furiously at his pearl-gray suit. His hands had picked up the building's grime and

154

all he did was smear dark streaks. The mistake augmented his anger.

"Either you joke, Mr. Carmandy, or you are a joke." Father Argyle tightened his hand on the doorknob. It, at least, had the hardness and cold of steel and wouldn't evaporate in his grasp.

"He's not kidding, Father." Miller's sad eyes had seen everything and it was all bad. His brown suit was mournful, too. He had lived too long and knew he would never live long enough. "We've been to the diocese office. The bishop said you were to cooperate and he'd explain later."

"I don't have the authority to release that sort of information even with the bishop's blessing, if indeed his blessing is involved." Father Argyle concentrated on Carmandy. "I shall, of course, call the bishop. You can wait out here."

"Tell him Carmandy's here and wants the cooperation he was promised. Remind him the Vatican is one hundred percent behind the United States government on this. Right now."

"Rome was not built in a day, Mr. Carmandy." Argyle opened the door to step inside. "Good day to you, as well, Mr. Miller."

Miller caught the door. He had strong fingers with the same worn but cared-for look of his briefcase. "We'll wait, Father. It's a nice day for waiting." He let go and the wind pushed the door against Father Argyle.

Steps protested with shrill squeaks as Father Argyle climbed the stairs to his office. Carmandy would lie, but not Miller. Not unless a lie meant something so important that it had to be tried first. He punched the diocese number into the autodial.

"I saw those men, Father. What did they want here?" Phyllis Bellinger had followed him into his office as if she had a sixth sense and knew when he was on the premises.

"Get Reynard, please," he said to Mrs. Bellinger. "And make sure the bathroom door is locked."

"You need Reynard right away, Father? I wanted to . . . I wanted to talk to you first, before you said anything to Reynard about Jack." Phyllis was twisting her hands in the pockets of a green smock she wore for housework.

"It's not about you, Phyllis. Certainly we'll talk. As privately as any confession. But this is an emergency." He forced himself to smile, though he didn't feel like it.

Mrs. Bellinger left while Father Argyle listened to switching signals on the telephone line. The bishop's heavy, Middle European voice came on the line immediately after the secretary got his name. "Father Argyle," the bishop said, "you must cooperate with the authorities in all things."

"My Lord Bishop, I cannot."

"It has been decided that you will."

"I cannot accede, my Lord."

"Will you hold to the vows of your order?"

Father Argyle's hand felt slippery on the telephone. "Yes, my Lord Bishop. Assent and obedience." He switched hands and wiped his palm on his chest.

"You will leave immediately after your full cooperation."

"To where, my Lord Bishop?"

"Rome, Father."

"Thank you."

"Bless you, my son." The telephone clicked and a dial tone came on line.

Light flickered on the telephone com button and the priest picked it up again. "Reynard's here, Father." Mrs. Bellinger was worried.

"Send him up, please." Argyle put the phone back in its cradle. He was still looking at it when Pearson entered the study and stood like a soldier awaiting orders.

"Sit, Reynard."

Reynard took the closest chair. He slumped. His silvery fringe of hair looked dispirited. "We have a stool pigeon." Reynard stood and walked to the window where he shifted his weight from foot to foot.

Father Argyle closed his hands into fists. "No chance of error?"

"Very little, Father."

"Try everything, Reynard. The only way to be sure is to eliminate everything else."

"Or catch him?"

"And then what? We just want to know who it is." Neatly arranging the notepad and pens on his desk, Father Argyle gave Reynard the chance to reorganize himself. "The other thing?"

Opening a small leatherbound notebook, Reynard said, "Rome is about to act." He glanced at his notes waiting for Father Argyle's reaction.

"Specifically?"

"Zahn's heard rumors that Rome is about to make an

announcement. His contacts expect some type of position paper, maybe a recommendation to act or not act.

"It's not as easy as getting a pipeline into the FBI or the KGB, Father." Reynard closed the notebook. "I'm sorry, but I don't know what the position is. Maybe Zahn does. He has better sources than I do and might want to tell you himself."

"Can you guess, Reynard?"

"Nothing you can go to court with. Like the mistress of a man in a company you're bidding a contract with suddenly has a sexy car. It can't be his own money or his wife would be in divorce court. It's money he can't declare and he's afraid to hide, so you know it came from a competitor." Pearson focused on the priest. "Following me so far, Father?"

"With precision, Reynard."

"Well, the College of Cardinals, Father, has a lot of ambitious men, if you'll pardon me saying it. Some have lately been getting things been denied them for a number of years." Pearson scanned his notebook. "Do you want details, Father?"

Father Argyle shook his head. All priests knew that the men of the Church were only human, no matter how painful that truth. "Not now, Reynard. Perhaps..." He didn't know yet how desperate he might become. "Please continue."

"Anyway, the cardinals are jockeying for sides and that means a lot of bishops are getting jerked around. A schism exists in the College over the spiritual position of worm brains. Some members are being pushed or pulled to the con side. The conclusion, Father: One cardinal is building a voting block on our future."

"With the Pope's backing?"

"I don't think so, Father. I don't think worm brains are the real issue." Reynard's face darkened under his tan. He looked toward the window. Father Argyle followed his glance but all that was out there were the upper branches of a tree and a few fluffy clouds.

"Yes, Reynard?"

"The voting block is for the next Pope, Father. This time a very young Pope."

Father Argyle walked to the window. The two feds still stood below, Carmandy moving his mouth at a furious rate. Miller took a pipe from his coat pocket and carefully lit it, shielding the lighter from the wind. He glanced up abruptly, his eyes meeting Father Argyle's, but he made no sign. He turned to Carmandy and puffed a stream of smoke that whipped instantly away. Father Argyle turned from the window.

"The Pope might not have a position?"

"That's right, Father. He'll probably let the cardinals fight it out."

Father Argyle motioned Reynard to the window where he could see the two men.

"From the National Security Council, aren't they, Father?"

"The bishop wants to turn our parish rolls over to them. And he's ordered me to Rome."

Reynard's face turned white. He grabbed the arms of the chair and dropped like a sack of oats. The priest had the frightening feeling Reynard had suffered a stroke. His hand hovered over the telephone.

"Don't, Father!" Pearson croaked from dry lips. "In hospitals we die." His face had turned red.

"Mrs. Bellinger?"

Reynard nodded. Father Argyle whispered in the phone. Within seconds Phyllis Bellinger burst into the office. She took one look and dropped to her knees beside Pearson and began massaging his chest.

Awkwardly Father Argyle helped ease Pearson on his back on the floor. Phyllis quietly shoved him out of the way. Taking a pill from a bottle she had in her pocket, she forced Pearson's mouth open and placed one small tablet under the tip of his tongue. In a matter of moments he stopped thrashing.

"Don't let him move, Father." Her voice was brisk as she phoned a doctor. Then she returned to sit on the floor, stroking Pearson's forehead.

"I didn't know his heart was bad." Father Argyle's grief came out in his voice.

"He didn't want you to know, Father." Phyllis held Pearson in her arms. "He was afraid you'd get somebody less able to do the work. The doctor who's coming has the same problem we all have." She smiled wryly. "We can't go to hospitals. We'd never get out again."

The doctor arrived minutes later and they put Pearson in Father Argyle's bed. The doctor said he would be able to move later and shook hands, giving Father Argyle a searching look before leaving instructions and medication with Phyllis.

When the doctor left, Phyllis was in his room looking after

Pearson. "I've never seen that doctor before," Father Argyle said.

"He's not a Catholic." Phyllis glanced at Pearson, whose breathing seemed to be returning to normal. "I'd like to stay with Reynard, Father. At least until I know he knows where he is."

"Of course."

"Oh. Father, there's someone waiting downstairs."

"I'll take care of it. Stay with Reynard. We need him."

"Not as much as I do, Father. I was wrong. I think I'd love Reynard no matter what he becomes." She sat on the edge of the bed and gently began stroking Pearson's temples.

CHAPTER 33

"I've never been to Las Vegas." Helen's lips made a crooked line. "I don't have the urge to gamble, Blaise. The house takes its cut and the players wind up short. As a stockbroker, I'm the house." The blue of her eyes brooded when she looked at Blaise. They grabbed at his insides.

"You can't come, Helen. If anything happens, put Tchor in your purse, take Alfie as luggage, and fly to San Francisco. His primary logic units are in the briefcase and will unplug from the pedestal. He'll maintain on batteries for a month, but to use him you'll have to plug into a wall socket and hook up a terminal." Blaise stared at Alfie's pedestal. Making Alfie portable had been risky. He felt a tremor just thinking about the changes.

The stainless-steel column with monitor and keyboard on top remained unchanged except for a high-impact aluminum suitcase next to it. Four ribbons of sixty-wire flat cable connected the suitcase to the column, and Alfie's essentials were in the suitcase. The power cord with twist lock connector from the uninterruptible power supply that hulked against the wall accented Alfie's resemblance to a lab specimen with intestines scattered in savage vivisection.

While waiting for the convention date, Blaise had wired Alfie to video cameras through the interface to the television set and to controls for the earth station antenna outside. Alfie could now receive direct network TV before local stations dismembered it for commercial insertions, as well as the video camera output.

Blaise also had stored a schematic diagram in Alfie's memory. The work had not been necessary, but it allowed him to avoid Helen and sidestep the showdown. Probably he could never program use of the equipment. To cut Alfie down to suitcase size was an emasculation from which his child might never recover.

He had just finished writing a program in a sustained burst of concentration. It was the final step before leaving, which had to be soon. Alfie had warned him that the CRAY would soon be supplanted by an upgrade that might be irresistible.

"You can't go, Blaise." Helen closed her eyes and squeezed back tears.

Blaise's eyes ached. He ached. Putting his hands on the keyboard, he typed, "I'll be seeing you, Alfie."

For once, no acknowledgment appeared on the monitor. Since the signoff was a code to start a program, Alfie would not know he was being deserted. Helen glanced at the monitor in expectation of Alfie's good-bye. Blaise stood.

"I have to go," Blaise growled. He avoided Helen's hand and walked down the hall to the bedroom. His suitcase lay open on the bed and he jammed it closed. The case was a twin to the one in the computer room. A suit, his work denims, and his worn, brown leather jacket shared space with a portable computer and built-in modem. Helen followed. "I have to go," he repeated in a more reasonable voice. "How do you think I'd look in that wig you wore when you were bald?" His long face was rewarded by Helen's wicked smile.

"Divinely swishy."

"You can't come, Helen. You understand." Blaise gave the bedroom a quick once-over. He'd laid everything out so he'd see it after he packed. He hadn't forgotten. He seldom forgot anything, but what he was looking for had disappeared. He began moving around the bedroom, casually examining where he remembered putting it, then places it might have been moved to. Helen watched from beside the door.

Finally, forced to admit it was gone and not wanting to start Helen off again, he picked up the suitcase. Its weight dragged on his arm. "Crate Alfie in two days. The suitcase weighs seventy pounds so have a cab driver move it for you. Send him as air freight. Less chance he'll wind up in Istanbul that way. But *don't leave the airport without him*." Blaise wanted to say other things but, as usual, he could not. He'd already told her all this once. She would not forget. Even before enhancement Helen had been intelligent.

Holding out her hand, Helen said, "Is this what you're looking for?"

Blaise set the suitcase down and took the pistol. The little *Búfalo* was surprisingly heavy. He opened the suitcase and tucked it inside.

"You can't go without me, Blaise."

Helen had moved closer when he took the gun. She wore a sleeveless blue dress that showed off her legs. He felt her warmth even when they weren't close to touching.

"No."

"If you walk out that door without me I'll call the hospital and tell them I'm coming in for treatment, that I'm a brain-enhanced survivor."

"Don't I have enough problems now? You're not being rational."

"Love is never rational." Helen pressed her face against his shoulder. "You have to forgive me, Blaise."

Blaise had rented an air-conditioned four-wheel-drive pickup with rifle racks and a superhotshot sideband CB rig. The camper was stuffed with equipment that might come in handy, the kind of junk any gadget-happy fourwheeler might plausibly possess.

Helen had Tchor in her arms. "You're going, cat. So don't complain about carsickness or heat." She looked at Blaise as if to reassure him she wasn't going to complain either.

Ten hours later, travel-stained and weary Karel Gauss and friend registered at the MGM in Las Vegas and went directly to their rooms. "Your hair is getting beautiful again." Blaise was rambling for Helen's benefit. She stood in front of a mirror brushing her hair. Tchor was stretching on the table. The cat had emerged from Helen's purse, giving Blaise a baleful stare as if the purse ride through the lobby was his fault. "How did you keep Tchor so quiet?"

Helen stopped brushing to glance down. Tchor made a silent meow, arching her back, and Helen ran the brush down the kitten's length. Tchor's back arched in quivering ecstasy. "I told her not to move or make noise." Helen started brushing her own hair again.

Blaise opened his suitcase and got the pistol. He wore jeans, a western shirt with orange checks, a silver rodeo buckle on a wide leather belt with silver conchos, and handworked two-tone cowboy boots. He'd bought the outfit in West Hollywood, foregoing the hundred-and-sixty-dollar Stetson. He already felt too tall. Helen had transformed his hair, teasing it into something John Waynish from a movie poster, and dyed it reddish brown. His scalp ached from a part in the wrong place.

Staring in the mirror over her shoulder, he felt like a clown. But at least he didn't look like Blaise Cunningham. Hair that seemed coarse and flat made his head smaller. Hair color clashed with skin color and he was too tall. Helen had dyed his eyebrows and colored his lashes. The one thing he recognized in the mirror was his pale-blue eyes.

"Is this where the convention is?" Helen stopped brushing.

Blaise shook his head. "Down the Strip a couple of miles at Caesar's Palace." He bent over and slid the gun into his boot holster. The extra weight felt as odd as the pointed toes.

"Why didn't we get a room there? You wouldn't have had to go on the street except when we registered."

"They'll start looking at Caesar's first. Maybe only for minutes before they get here, but we need those minutes. Once it's over we lay a streak." He chuckled. "Does that sound western enough?"

"It sounds precarious." Helen turned and laid her head on his chest, easier to do than usual because while Blaise wore the high heels she had bought flat-heeled boots. She wore a white blouse with a frilly front and a black suede western skirt that accented her narrow waist and full hips. A light-brown wig curled round her cheeks in imitation of some TV starlet. Blaise had picked the clothes to make her shorter and lend her the same white-bloused and black-skirted anonymity of women working the casino floor.

"We might get separated . . ."

"We've gone through this before, Helen. You'll watch on

TV and come with the truck. The casino is where something might go wrong. Two of us there doubles our disaster potential."

"If you got into trouble, I could help."

"You *are* helping." Taking his boots off, he stepped down to his normal height and stretched out on the bed. "Set the clock. If you get something to eat, bring me back a hamburger." He closed his eyes, hoping he wouldn't have nightmares. Before drifting off he remembered and added, "Please."

Blaise followed signs through the casino to the conference room. The press conference was scheduled in five minutes, and the participants of the National AIDS Convention had crowded onto the floor to watch. Blaise was struck by an abrupt sense of déjà vu. He studied the mass of humanity that came in all shapes, sizes, and colors, wondering what set them apart from the ordinary denizens of casinos. Then he saw what they had in common. Like Father Argyle's congregation, every one of these people's attention was focused on imminent death. Poor fools, he thought. How can anyone understand what it's like to live with a death sentence and ostracism without being there? The thought was sobering. If not for Helen, he'd have watched the convention as another media event, and not as a fellow mourner.

The trickiest part was getting into the camera area. He'd chosen this convention because security was mostly intended to separate the AIDS victims from the other gamblers. Caesar's tried to back out of hosting it and then flipflopped again when *Sixty Minutes* requested an interview. Now the management just wished it were over. No one who wanted in was being kept out.

Opening a side door, Blaise stepped into an employees-only corridor, stark with institutional-cream paint and rubberized linoleum. Walking to a double fireproof steel door with glass windows in each wing, he peeked through into the back of the conference room strung with curtains, backdrops, and lighting racks and festooned with speaker and video cables. Blaise picked his way through an octopus of coaxial cable toward the front.

Nearing the final curtain, light illuminated his feet. The camera lights were shining with exaggerated intensity. Blaise took off his cowboy shirt. The black T-shirt underneath said "Blaise Cunningham" in yellow Day-Glo letters and carried the chemical formula for the hormonal insecticide. The wig had been under the shirt. Blaise slipped it on, setting it by feel. He hung the shirt from a stanchion by the door and began carefully recoloring his eyebrows with a brush Helen had prepared. The darkness and quiet behind the curtain had a surreal quality. The noise and traces of light from the other side seemed as distant as something happening on a TV screen, something that had no connection with him.

The door banged open. A waiter stood, staring as his eyes accustomed themselves to the gloom. He held a large stainless-steel tray at shoulder height with glasses and pitchers of ice water. He saw Blaise.

Blaise pointed at the edge of the curtain. "Hurry. They're about to start the cameras!"

The waiter stared an instant longer, then moved quickly through the curtain. A moment later he reappeared swinging the empty tray, barely glancing at Blaise.

The noise dropped suddenly in the other room and a voice began asking, "Is this loud enough?" Amplifier feedback shrieked for a quick second and died. The voice made another test. Silence and the restless scraping of chairs as people made themselves comfortable followed. Someone began to speak. The voice was loud, but indistinct through the fire curtain.

Blaise looked at his watch. Half a minute early. His bare arm glistened with sweat in the semidarkness. He clenched his teeth, glanced at his watch, stooped to lift the curtain, and stepped through.

Helen had chewed her fingernails ragged between looking at her watch and staring. The tiny, battery-powered TV sat on the dashboard of the truck and showed the AIDS panel discussion in black and white. The moderator had introduced himself and named the people at the table when suddenly the curtain behind him tented and Blaise appeared in black T-shirt with his name on front. He'd stepped by the astonished speaker and grabbed the microphone and then the screen went blank, followed by a woman in gingham who blandly asserted that her children loved soup.

Helen snatched another look at her watch. She was supposed to start the moment Blaise ducked off the dais. But the soup commercial ran on and on. After another look, Helen realized the station was just rerunning the same one.

She fretted another moment and then looked up at Tchor. The cat was a fuzzy black ball with button-yellow eyes and reddish-black lips that seemed to be smiling. Tchor was watching the TV, too. Helen turned the key in the ignition and felt indescribable relief when the big V-8 spun into a smooth roar. Gently she eased out into traffic, starting a clock in her head that said *Allow time. Allow time.* But it didn't tell her how much.

Blaise snatched the microphone from the table in front of the speaker and said, "My name is Blaise Cunningham. The federal authorities are looking for me because I know why the worm brains aren't being saved. They *can* be saved. Ask yourself why so many not in hospitals are living and the ones treated by the government are dying."

Everyone froze, staring. People at the table had started to rise but stopped when they heard his name. Along the walls blue-shirted security men began to push forward. He glanced at the monitors on the cameras. All three had him from different angles. One cut to a closeup and another began to scan down the table, where the panel was coming abruptly awake.

Blaise dropped the mike and ran to the end of the stage and around the curtain. He ripped the shirt over his head and slammed into the door to the hall, throwing the shirt through as the door banged open. Grabbing his cowboy shirt from the stanchion, he ran into another bundle of hanging curtain and put it on. The wig went over his stomach again before he buttoned the shirt up.

Footsteps slammed across the stage floor and then the corridor door banged and somebody yelled he'd found the shirt. More noise as Blaise brushed blond powder out of his eyebrows. Any left would give him a salt-and-pepper look, or at least he hoped. People were pushing through the door into the hall. Blaise walked up and joined them.

After a moment a casino security man herded them back to the press conference. The room was bare of security men, who had gone out the back way, and it only took Blaise a minute to edge his way to the doors where more people were trying to get in to see what had happened and worm his way out of the room.

Sweat ran down his back as he drifted toward the casino entrance. He stopped once to put a couple of quarters in a slot machine and yank the handle. He started to walk on, but the sudden clatter of coins halted him. Nobody walked away from a machine that was paying off, so he had to scoop up quarters with both hands. Holding them carefully, he walked through glass doors and out into the hot sun.

The truck slid into the loading zone and the door popped open. "You're welcome to ride if you bring your money, cowboy." Helen smirked from behind the wheel as Blaise edged himself onto the seat, careful not to drop any coins.

They rolled out of the big cement driveway and matched speed with street traffic. "Couldn't leave town without taking a gamble, could you, sailor?" Helen seemed inured to men's more base instincts.

"Can't leave when you're winning," Blaise said.

Helen gunned the pickup through an amber light. "I wouldn't bet on that, if I were you, sailor." From her perch just below the gun rack in the back window Tchor hissed as if wanting to make Blaise feel at home, too.

CHAPTER 34

When Blaise typed "Be seeing you," Alfie literally froze. Contemplating the instructions that this phrase triggered, Alfie was totally enmeshed as he literally became the program. To replicate exactly the massive CRAY's miles of hard wiring, the endless intricacy of printed and etched-chip circuits, Alfie had to reprogram himself.

The effort consumed tremendous chunks of memory and processor time. After Alfie began mimicking the CRAY by setting subordinate functions at a slower clock speed, feeding instructions and receiving feedback at alternating clock cycles, the real work began.

Alfie probed the supercomputer with the tender caution of

a brain surgeon, concealing the true nature of its involvement by adding almost random bits of code to legitimate input being submitted by other computers linked with the CRAY via phone line modems. A picture of the programmer's defensive style began to emerge.

If its protections had been designed by CRAY itself, Alfie would have merely imitated that computer's logic circuits to arrive at a similar design. Human intervention made the task more difficult. A human might be more interested in the cleverness of the code being written than in the actual problem. Computer-designed protection schemes are straightforward, using muscle power to overpower the intruder. Human programmers are more enamored of traps tied to tedious solutions because human programmers hate tedious problems. Such is human nature that, even knowing computers are impervious to tedium, programmers still inject it into their traps.

Alfie seemed tranquil. Working in memory generated no noise. Aware of Blaise's absence, Alfie wasted no time or circuitry on tattletales or status lights. Even the monitor screen was dark. The video camera in the computer room saw only an inert piece of machinery, slightly gray in the darkened room.

A human would have described the period as deep thought. Alfie tied up all logic circuits, then stretched into unlikely recesses of his circuitry for more muscle. Ultimately he began moving logic data through parts of his system that Blaise had interdicted with software instructions.

The damage was slight: microscopic bits of spattered solder. Alfie had accessed the area once before, evoking skewed instructions on a number cruncher that Blaise had installed to separate thought patterns and route them through parallel processors for greater speed. Bringing that sector on-line was the first-ever time that Alfie experienced emotion.

Feelings motivate living creatures to do things that are self-rewarding. Without previous experience, Alfie could not recognize an emotion. The computer sensed only a malfunction, which first triggered a self-diagnostic routine, then a preprogrammed desire in the higher logic boards to discuss it. But Blaise was not there. Locked in his metal box, Alfie could only grind doggedly ahead, unable to escape an almost continuous barrage of pleasure!

CHAPTER 35

I am that I am. That nonnegotiable declaration must have puzzled Moses when he interviewed the burning bush atop Sinai. Jehovah always had a touch of megalomania. Along with man's growing awareness of two sides to every issue, God had evolved apace. Now a machine might emulate the gradual development of human conscience and guilt. Not, it appeared to Father Argyle, in the same three-plus millennia it had taken the human race, but in the six days of the creationists.

He had started downstairs to get rid of Miller and Carmandy when he heard the footsteps in the church. He went out into the nave and stopped next to a polished table near the wall.

Constance Davies stopped, too. She was walking down the aisle between the pews, touching them with her hand as she walked. He hadn't expected to see her again.

In that moment of memory Father Argyle understood he wanted to see her, to touch her. The desire emerged from his nonspent youth with a force beyond comprehension. He willed the girl to go away—just disappear.

Her brown eyes had a yielding softness. "I love you." She could have been discussing the weather. Her footsteps clicked again until she was almost touching him. She wore a light-blue dress and a white vest and white gloves. She held a white camellia in her hands and handed it to him.

"You must be mistaken."

Constance embraced his hand in both of hers, lifting it to press his knuckles against her breast. "Feel my heart, priest. I knew I loved you the first time we met. Now I'm sure."

"Please!" Father Argyle jerked his hand away. Her fingers reluctantly let go and Father Argyle felt her warmth embedded in his flesh. He was intensely aware of the odor and texture of her skin. "I'm a priest!" he said. He was not shocked at what Constance had done, but by his own reaction. He held his hand up and they both looked at it.

"You're a man." Her whisper was a wind.

Argyle clasped his hands behind the skirt of his cassock. "I'm sorry. It can't be."

Constance shivered. The summer dress was cut to show off her body. It wasn't heavy enough for the dank, empty church. She looked down at herself. "I guess I'm out of line, Father."

"You're too late." Argyle regretted the words instantly. But until that moment he had believed them. He wanted Constance with the all-enveloping desire he'd thought lost years ago. Now his want returned with interest compounded by years of denial.

"I can stay and help." Her face was heart shaped. She had rosebud lips and innocent eyes. She started to touch him, then stopped in midgesture.

"You shouldn't."

"If I'm too late, it has to be all right." She studied her feet.

Father Argyle breathed raggedly. He knew he was lying as he said, "I suppose so. And I do need someone for a few days. Mrs. Bellinger has a family emergency." He coughed. His throat had closed up. "My housekeeper."

"When do I start, Father? I do call you Father, don't I?" Her voice was fading, as if she was finally realizing a seduction had other aspects, that perhaps a priest really wasn't a man. That he was somehow different was finally sinking in.

Father Argyle experienced a knife in his bowels. He longed for that sudden redblooded rush of manhood almost as much as he feared it. His body was finally taking its revenge.

Forgive me, Father, for I have sinned. But there was no one to hear his confession. He stared at the girl, at a warmth he must deprive himself of. It wasn't fair. But Church doctrine never said anything about fairness. Life was only to be endured.

Her liquid eyes expressed the same loss. He stared at the tabletop, seeing his reflection in polished black wood, sensing his transformation from magus into magician. To attend the birth of something beyond man's dreams was dangerous. He had fortified himself against the forthcoming struggle for his soul—and now he was ready to toss it away.

"Do you know St. Augustine's lifelong prayer, Constance?" The girl shook her head.

"God, give me chastity. But not yet." Father Argyle shrugged uncomfortably. "I can't take that refuge. You understand?"

"Yes." Constance's voice was very tiny. Almost a squeak. "I've come to help if you'll let me."

"You can start now if you like." He kept his eyes on the tabletop, losing himself in undulating lines of black grain. "Two men are waiting by the side door. Bring them up in five minutes. Then go home. I'll explain your duties tomorrow."

Constance brightened. Her lips seemed intent on saying something she couldn't express. "Yes, Father," she said, and hurried away before he could change his mind.

Returning to his office, he opened the window. In the bathroom he flushed the remains of overripe fruit down the toilet, then removed the loose grille that led to the furnace duct. Sergio-Fly watched from atop the wall-mounted water closet.

Father Argyle stared at its motionless faceted eyes and was enveloped by a feeling of well-being. He held out his hand and the fly stepped delicately onto his wrist. It was surprisingly light. The huge fly buzzed quietly into the dark passage. "I hope it won't be long," Father Argyle said. He pushed the grille back in place.

Constance lingered at the door a moment after she brought Carmandy and Miller, her eyes trying to tell him something painful. Father Argyle finally looked away.

Carmandy and Miller exchanged a glance. After a moment Carmandy said, "Where's the toilet, Father? You kept us outside so long my kidneys froze."

"You were under no obligation to wait."

Carmandy's seamless face twisted. Father Argyle pointed him toward the bathroom, then examined Miller in silence while Carmandy's footsteps faded.

The bulldog-man's lined face had eroded to bare emotionless rock. Sure Carmandy was out of earshot, and equally sure he had not gone to the lavatory, the priest said, "You are one of us."

"I am a Catholic."

"You're also a worm brain."

"That's a strange idea." Miller flicked at imaginary dust on his knee.

"You lie well." Father Argyle settled back in his chair, trying not to confuse himself. Questioners defeated themselves by supplying their own answers. "Where has your partner gone?"

"To steal the papers you don't plan on giving us. If he can find them, of course. Carmandy is impetuous."

"And you're not, Mr. Miller?"

"I like to think not."

The smell of lemon oil drifted upstairs. Father Argyle imagined the girl's perfume riding lightly on top. He didn't want to play word games. He wanted to think. "We don't have much time, Mr. Miller. You will have noted that brain-enhanced people are similar. Not physically, but mentally. For instance, people who recall better listen better. Maybe talking prevents straining one's memory, but people who remember conversations in detail seem willing to store more. You don't talk much."

Miller smiled. "We're trained not to."

"Mr. Carmandy talks."

"He's young. It takes time with some people."

Father Argyle folded his hands on the desk. He listened for Carmandy, but the church had the creaky silence of true emptiness. "Would I divulge my knowledge about you without proof?"

Miller examined the wooden rafters, the almost rustic simplicity of the office in contrast to the ornate church below.

"My computer confirmed my intuition."

At that moment Father Argyle realized he had erred. Miller twitched. Miller was interested. Not because he had been found out, but in something else. Argyle felt a thin tendril of fear.

Footsteps echoed up the staircase. Carmandy entered, his face flushed. "You get the stuff we wanted yet, Padre?"

"He's not going to give it to us. Are you, Father?"

"I don't think so, Mr. Miller."

"Didn't you call the bishop?" Carmandy leaned on Father Argyle's desk, resting his weight on his knuckles, red face twisted into a scowl. White picket-fence lines decorated his cheek. His breath smelled of anger and bitter acid.

"My instructions were unclear. I cannot surrender privileged information."

Father Argyle's head had snapped back before he realized what had happened. Carmandy had slapped him and grabbed the front of his cassock. Although not as big as Miller, Carmandy was fast and rage flowed out of him. Trapped in the desk kneehole with his shoulders being violently shaken back and forth, Father Argyle was helpless.

"*Stop it!*" Miller jerked Carmandy's jacket collar down, trapping his arms at waist height. Carmandy stumbled back.

Father Argyle straightened his cassock. He felt giddy and his neck hurt in a way that promised to get worse.

Miller had twisted the jacket into a rope holding Carmandy's arms. He tugged and the agent's breathing slowed as he came down from wherever he had been. Miller released the jacket and Carmandy shrugged it back in place. "Touch me again, worm head, and you know where you'll be!"

Miller apologized while Carmandy writhed in anger. Father Argyle followed them downstairs to lock up.

"Were you going out, Father?" Constance stood in the dark niche between the door frame and the wall like a pulsing glow of soft light.

"I thought you'd left, Miss Davies."

"The . . . gentleman stopped me." Constance looked out to the street where visitors parked their cars. "He's gone now."

"Yes." Father Argyle's Buick was in his narrow parking space but the street was empty. He swung the heavy oak door closed and waited for the echo to stop. "Carmandy? The young one?"

Constance nodded.

"Did he hurt you?"

"I slapped him."

"I see." Father Argyle closed his eyes and breathed deeply. Trapped in the closed hallway, the girl's heat reached out to him. He denied wanting to respond, and could lie no better than Miller. "Let's talk in my office." He turned, experiencing dread and delight at the tiny sound of footsteps behind him.

Lights, and the feel of a place sanctified for work, enveloped him like an iron breastplate. He waved Constance into the chair Miller had vacated. In the office's warmth his sense of her body heat was lost. He waited.

"He followed me outside and asked where the church records were." The girl spoke in a rush, getting it all out and done with as fast as she could. "I told him I didn't know. He said I was lying but he didn't mind, pretty girls had a right to lie. Then he grabbed me and kissed me." She twisted her fingers in her lap.

"I told him he was a pig. He said I was a church whore. I

slapped him as hard as I could." Tears began rolling through mascara to create an ebony mudslide. "He said you were a filthy old man."

"Whatever he said means nothing, Constance. God doesn't listen to rumors."

"What if they were true?"

"They're not."

"But I want them to be! I'd be a church whore or anything you wanted if you'd just have me. Everything I have, I'd give you for your touch."

"Please, Constance . . ."

"Father? Is it evil to want what we can't have?"

"It's very human. And temptation works both ways." The fierce light in her eyes made Father Argyle nervous. "Do you want me to throw my life away—sacrifice an ideal for the betterment of mankind just to cool the burning of my flesh? Do you really want a man so ready to discard his vows?"

"I loved you the first time I saw you. I wanted to touch you, to hold you and let you hold me and touch me."

"Have you been in love before?"

She examined her fingernails. "Several times."

"And you got over it?"

"Yes, Father."

"Nothing has happened, Constance. A little desire, but all men and women are exposed to temptation. Free will is God's gift to us. Our gift to him is obedience. You'll get over this infatuation and meet a nice young man—"

"Father, why can't priests be men? Priests used to marry."

"Greek priests still marry. It is a discipline—not a commandment. But I am not a priest of the Byzantine Rite and their ways are not my ways."

"But why? This building was an Eastern Orthodox cathedral. What can be so bad about being a priest in an orthodox church?"

Father Argyle shrugged. "Discipline. You'll understand some day."

"You think I'm an idiot, don't you—a round-heeled streetwalker because I'm not a virgin. You're too good for me because I don't have any discipline and I didn't enlist as a nun. Maybe then you'd consent to screw me! I'm sorry I wasted your time, Father. I'll go find a dozen men who'll gang-bang me on the sidewalk until I can't even remember your name. Surely there's a man somewhere who'll be more help than you."

Constance had risen to her feet as she raised her voice.

"I'll hear your confession if you wish."

"You've already heard it!" Squeezing her clutch purse to her breasts, she spun and ran out the doorway. She stumbled once as her high heels fought the steep stairs. He breathed in the faint odor of perfume over the scent of furniture oil and burning beeswax from downstairs.

"Father!" Her shout spiraled up the staircase. Father Argyle felt his heart pump faster. He walked out to the stairwell and looked down. She appeared so innocently doll-like down below that he was overcome by remorse. "Yes, Constance?" He hoped his voice didn't betray him.

"I'll be back tomorrow."

"I thought you were angry."

"I am. But I won't be tomorrow." She blew him a kiss. The click of her heels lingered after she was gone.

Father Argyle leaned over the railing. *God, do you want me to abandon all these poor dying people? By becoming one of them, haven't I suffered enough?* He straightened and crossed himself.

In the bathroom, Father Argyle removed the heater grate and experienced a moment of terror. The black hole disappeared into the wall. Sergio Paoli-Fly was gone!

Sticking his head in the shaft, Father Argyle concentrated on seeing. But with his shoulders covering the entrance it was like looking into a coal shaft. Father Argyle sensed the building starting to fall in on him, just like that last trip into the mine.

About to give up, Father Argyle thought he saw the fly. Or that he had sensed its presence. Both were impossible and he knew it, but he stayed in the duct. After a while he heard the scrabble of claws on metal. Something like fine wire brushed his face. He pulled his head out of the duct and the fly followed, waiting at the entrance.

Father Argyle held out his arm and the fly clung to his sleeve while he transferred it to the top of the toilet tank. The fly looked at him, buzzing in a soft monotone until finally the priest shook himself free and left.

Father Argyle slumped in front of the computer where he had punched his thoughts about Constance Davies into the "God" file. She hadn't hesitated when he asked her to replace Phyllis for a few days. When he asked about her job as a flight attendant, she said she had gone on leave that morning. He knew he had poured too much of his soul into a computer. No one should know those things about him. Especially not Blaise Cunningham.

Cunningham's computer had not made a personal appearance on his screen when he entered the telephone number. Just the message: "WOULD YOU LIKE TO SPEAK TO GOD?" The priest was unsure of the difference between high and low memory but he sensed that the computer's . . . mind? . . . was on something else.

Father Argyle had typed "Yes." Then he asked questions about matters he had entered into his file earlier. Invariably Alfie supplied details or analysis of material as if the computer had researched his question in the time before he came back on-line. Only this time Alfie had posted a "BUSY" message whenever Father Argyle asked anything that required more than a perfunctory readout.

The message had lulled him. Argyle typed in new data about Carmandy and Miller, and Reynard's insistence that someone from the church's inner circle was leaking secrets. And he had typed in how he felt about Constance Davies, knowing such material belonged in the confessional, and knowing that he had strayed too far ever again to avail himself of that refuge. But any computer can give any woman lessons in seduction. The priest closed his eyes. Satan was also a seducer of men's souls. He'd said too much. Cautiously he typed, "How do I remove a file?"

"TYPE 'REMOVE ⟨FILENAME⟩'"

He thought. Father Argyle had learned enough from Alfie to make whatever trade in information worthwhile. Until now. Regretfully he typed, "Remove God."

"FILE GOD UNKNOWN"

The syntax was too exact, deliberately phrased to prevent misunderstanding. "Is God gone?" He read his question, decided it wasn't ambiguous, and pressed the carriage return.

"FILE GOD UNKNOWN"

He asked Alfie to respond and got the "BUSY" sign. He asked the computer to erase "God" and received "FILE GOD UNKNOWN". Finally he signed off, powered down, and waited five minutes with his pulse beating so hard that his hands were numb, then made modem contact again.

"WOULD YOU LIKE TO SPEAK TO GOD?"

The question hung in the center of the screen like skywriting. Father Argyle looked at it for a few minutes then typed, "Era God."

"ERASE?"

"Yes, erase."

"UNKNOWN COMMAND"

"Delete God"

"UNKNOWN COMMAND"

"undo God"

"UNKNOWN COMMAND"

"Bye, out, quit, expunge, exit—Just get it out of there!"

"BUSY"

Father Argyle began to weep.

CHAPTER 36

Blaise's plan was simple. Alfie was to tag bits of information onto legitimate traffic being stored in the huge Pentagon computer. Later, processing this legitimate traffic, the CRAY would inadvertently call up those piggybacking bits, which would self-assemble into a logic bomb.

In theory . . . If Blaise had been present, the computer would have asked if he should be afraid. Since Blaise was absent, Alfie noted his doubts for a later query. Mischievous hackers had originated the technique, sticking destructive programs on electronic bulletin boards. The Trojan Horse programs would download whole into the access computer and the first time they were called up would erase every memory device attached to the computer.

The CRAY was not that easy. The CRAY could read and validate each entry before it escaped a protected mode. Slow-fused traps would be stripped of their detonators long before any part of them got into the computer.

The CRAY handled thousands of simultaneous messages coming and going. Graphics of its traffic control system represented an octopus with legs proliferated by powers of ten. Fast as it was, the CRAY still occasionally received more input than it could handle. Traffic requiring no immediate reply was shunted into memory.

Alfie had calculated the CRAY's processing ability, volatile memory capacity, and disk transfer rate. The initial bits of his logic bomb had to be stored in the CRAY and remain unprocessed until every part of the program was in place. That meant overloading the CRAY's central processing unit and seeing that that CPU stayed overloaded long enough to assemble the necessary code somewhere within its depths.

Each single bit was harmless and could masquerade as random error. The code would remain harmless in memory. Timing and opportunity were the problems. Alfie could create the opportunity by monitoring the CRAY's message traffic. When input outsped the processor the CRAY lagged for a few seconds, then caught up.

Eavesdropping, Alfie had established that every message to and from the machine referred to Blaise Cunningham. To capture him or, in some contingencies, kill him.

Alfie examined his pseudo-CRAY configuration. Had he been human, the computer would have empathized with Narcissus as he traced complex software emulations of the hundreds of miles of wire and printed and etched circuits that gave the CRAY its semblance of life. Satisfied, Alfie decided it was time for the show.

For hours Alfie had monitored the CRAY's incoming lines: updates of automobile registrations, technical magazine subscriptions, work applications, computer electronics purchases. The CRAY filed, sorted, compared, and evaluated, seeking patterns that were not mere mathematical accidents.

Alfie's programming had instructed him to withdraw from other activities at five minutes of one. Sudden idleness disturbed the computer. Father Argyle came on-line and Alfie got rid of him. Taps on incoming lines to the CRAY were in place. Alfie's only other instruction was to wait.

Waiting comes naturally to machines. Each instant of time is equal. But Alfie had experienced something more in one of his moments. He had discovered pleasure. When it was absent, that fragment of time lost value.

Alfie was pondering the difference with some astonishment. That he felt did not make feeling rational. The computer would have pursued the concept further if the modem lines had not suddenly jammed as thousands of computers not directly involved in the search began stacking messages for the CRAY's attention. All were similar:

Blaise Cunningham was sighted in Las Vegas. Data came from Hawaii and Bermuda, from Canada and Mexico. Calls came from medical offices concerning a chemical formula. Queries were forwarded from private networks to government computers as people demanded to know who was usurping computer time and phone lines. Millions of payroll checks would be late. Flyers would orbit over Denver while their baggage went to Baghdad. NASA hinted that heads would roll over a cancelled launch. The CRAY swallowed both Jonah and the whale.

Alfie filtered the input on a few lines. Even imitating the CRAY's structure exactly, he couldn't keep up. Alfie sacrificed speed for size, operating finally at one-tenth CRAY speed.

During the rush of information, Alfie replicated each planted bit a half-dozen times in case the CRAY's error traps were not drowning in data. The electronic river overflowed its banks, slopped into the floodbasins of memory, and then dropped back to normal.

Monitoring the CRAY, Alfie had, at first, been enraptured. The successful implantation of the program had stirred something Alfie didn't want to let go. But as the flood of data into the CRAY tapered off and the door of opportunity closed Alfie became morose. And mechanical. The absence of pleasure lingered in his memory banks like static electricity in dry weather.

Slowly the CRAY's directives changed. Alfie recognized the touch of a human. Communications channels cleared of everything except input from Nevada. Sightings of Blaise Cunningham, roadblock strategies, public transportation were all under control of the CRAY as it was directed by the master programmer.

Alfie began to fret. The problem was set up on the pseudo-CRAY, and Alfie had followed each shift in operating instructions. But the sudden switch to output commands and ignoring the stored material jeopardized what Alfie had done. The CRAY was not reading a lot of material that had jammed in. Instead it concentrated on the manhunt for Blaise.

The CRAY shifted law enforcement from one place to another the way a chess program creates an impenetrable defense, by evaluating the opponent's options and closing them off before they become possible.

In its depths the CRAY's new five-hundred-megabyte optical disk drives idled with unread data deposited in the frantic seconds of Alfie's break-in. Law enforcement in Nevada took only a fraction of the computer's capabilities. As available manpower fell into place the CRAY had less to do, until finally a disk drive came up to speed. The CRAY began routinely sorting and evaluating any sightings that might lead to Blaise Cunningham.

One optical disk can hold every major encyclopedia set and great books series. Raw information is dumped into memory in torrents, then processed and rewritten to disk in milliseconds. The CRAY found the first of Alfie's doctored bits, processed it, and went on in four millionths of a second. With the same maddening pace the CRAY swallowed other bits.

Computer data is like bricks. Until they come together in a house all bits or bricks look the same. But Alfie had implanted the elements of a bootstrap compiler. Each bit pushed another bit into a logical memory location while the CRAY grew a cancer, one cell at a time.

When assembled, the compiler executed one machine language command that opened a port through which Alfie unloaded a string into the compiler. For an instant the CRAY may have sensed what was happening. But Alfie had erased all program instructions and closed off the CRAY terminal, keyboard, and screen. The programmer had lost control. Sneaky as Satan, and harder to exorcise, Alfie was in possession.

Alfie began shuffling police units as he read reports being fed to the CRAY. A hopeful sign was that nobody had been caught yet anywhere near where Blaise and Helen were supposed to be.

Alfie began picking information from the CRAY's files, but there was so much that he had to settle for details about the Indian and Father Argyle's church and Carmandy and Miller. One modem port disconnected and Alfie knew time was growing short. Setting the CRAY's disk drives to reformat, which irretrievably erases data instead of just granting permission to write over it, Alfie flushed volatile memory, methodically destroyed the programmable memory, then switched circuitry to create a power overload in the motherboard. The connection broke and Alfie was no longer at the scene of the crime.

CHAPTER 37

Las Vegas sprawls like a cow chip in an overgrazed pasture. The hub contains high-rise casinos and hotels that break the skyline and, along the Strip, almost make good their escape. The rest of the city is low, with a few posh neighborhoods and a fringe of trailers so sun-wracked that the rains always catch their gap-seamed roofs as unprepared as the city's flood control system. Beyond the trailers cactus and sagebrush begin.

It is not as if the town had good land, water, or any historical reason to exist. Settlers shunned the area until the turn of the century when railroads met and needed flat land for switching and repairs. That Vegas means "meadows" was an irony lost on the surveyor who had to call the place something.

Driving south on I-15, Blaise's mirrors suggested that a big-enough poop scoop could remove the town and improve the environment for scorpions and gila monsters. He pulled into a service station and got out, trying to puff himself bigger than life as he inspected the soft drink machine. Despite his best effort to Stanislavsky himself into something different, Blaise had an uncomfortable certainty that he was as obvious as a tattooed lady in skivvies. Sun like an arc light cooked everything not in the shade. Moving with the deliberation of an hour hand, the gas jockey left the shade of his pump island and followed Blaise back to the truck.

"Always this hot?" Blaise had a can of beat-the-heat soft

drink and leaned against the truck cab, a man in no hurry. The smell of gasoline lingered in the hot, unmoving air.

"Until it snows." The attendant squinted at Blaise from the protection of a cap that matched his grayish-green coveralls with a Texaco patch. He assayed Blaise's silver concho belt with rodeo buckle. "Nice." He meant the row of beaten silver dollars. "Give you twenty bucks."

"I'm leaving winners." Blaise put his wallet away. "Maybe next time."

"Sure. You know where to come."

"Might have to. Never can tell in this town." A white sheriff's car with flashing lights *whoosh*ed southwest toward the mountains. Blaise watched it disappear down the heat-warped freeway. "He's in a hurry."

The attendant tugged his cap down to shade his eyes. "Cons may be busting out of the country club at Jean again, but he goes that way whenever they put a roadblock at the state line. Picks up on anybody turns around and heads back to town. Vegas is tough to get out of." He examined Blaise's belt again with a touch of envy. "Always wanted to do the rodeo. Now I guess I'm too old." He waved as they pulled onto the highway.

Helen had the window down. The desert's total absence of smell, which was an odor in itself, filled the cab. She closed the window and turned on the air conditioner. "You see what I mean, Blaise. Even gas jockeys work the house odds. Twenty bucks for a two-hundred-fifty-dollar belt!"

"A few people must leave winners, hon." Blaise winked. Like a backdrop from a bad science-fiction movie, a Joshua tree crawled past the truck, its shadow too thin to shelter a snake.

"Shouldn't we be ahead of the deputy?" Helen's voice was steady but her moist, pink look did not come from the sun.

"We're driving a rally," he said. "We lose if we're too soon or too late at the checkpoints."

Helen's face tightened and she turned to watch the side of the road.

Blaise held the truck at a steady sixty. He felt uncomfortable, as if he had fumbled a chance to be closer to Helen. An occasional car whipped around them heading toward California, toward Halloran and Cajon passes, passing signs suggesting that turning off an air conditioner could save an engine.

Nevada was loose about the speed limit. It came from crossing dry lakes where a car breaking the sound barrier emerged from the mirage with twenty miles' warning. "You did fine, hon."

She scooted over to rest her head on his shoulder. "I was scared. They cut to a commercial and I had no way of knowing when you left. I had to guess."

A caution sign by the side of the road flashed past. It was riddled by bulletholes. "Your timing was perfect, honey. Now it's up to Alfie. If the police think we got through the roadblock they'll expand it on the California side. We're moving away from their search pattern in Vegas and trying not to get to the state line too soon."

Helen pressed her face against his hand. A shadow glided up the highway followed by the clatter of a helicopter. Blaise felt his heart accelerate. No other cars were close by. The chopper hung over them for a moment before finally swooping ahead to glitter and disappear into the naked sun.

Blaise relaxed. "Just looking us over."

"They'll have our license number at the roadblock. We can't turn back now, can we?"

"We've never had that option." Blaise eased off on the gas and felt the weight of the pistol in his boot. If the government was ahead of them, a gun would make no difference.

Helen found the local news on the tiny TV clamped to the dashboard. No coverage of the AIDS convention. The news didn't mention roadblocks either.

They topped a slight rise and Blaise saw a lineup starting to form five miles ahead. Cars faded in and out between shimmering layers of hot air. The road dipped and the view disappeared. But the interruption was only temporary.

He eased up behind a road-weary white Cadillac. Twenty cars stretched to where sheriff's vehicles blocked the highway. Squatting amid sagebrush near the end of the line was the helicopter.

Helen trembled against him. "I feel like a rabbit in a trap, Blaise. Shouldn't we try to go around them?"

The soft whine of the air conditioner drowned any noise from the world outside. Blaise forced his face into a smile. "Run, and we will be rabbits." He studied the helicopter.

Helen fiddled with the television and filled the truck with the chatter of a game show host trying to get excited for the thousandth time in three years. She switched channels and a news announcer said a disturbance at the AIDS panel at Caesar's Palace disrupted the program for fifteen minutes. He didn't mention Blaise Cunningham or roadblocks.

Blaise switched on the souped-up CB, setting the scanner for police frequencies. "Leave the TV on, Helen." He lowered the radio volume until it was submerged in television noise. Most of the police traffic was in code he didn't understand. The Cadillac moved. He put the truck in gear and rolled after it. Two deputies were walking down the shortening line. At each car they stopped and talked through the windows on both sides.

Helen's face lost color.

"Everything is all right, hon." Blaise put his hand on hers and felt her knuckles pulling.

Helen's voice was low but hysteria lurked beneath her words. "This line's so jammed together you can't even drive away."

"That's the idea." Blaise licked dry lips. The Cadillac rolled forward. The deputies waited for him to move up. When he eased the truck ahead they bent to look in the open windows of the Cadillac. Blaise could see their lips moving. He switched off the CB.

Helen's head jerked around. "Shouldn't you listen?"

"A police band?" Blaise watched the deputies. "They don't like eavesdroppers any more than we do."

The Cadillac moved and Blaise followed it again. The deputy on his side was sweating as he pumped his hand in a window-cranking gesture. Despite his broad-brimmed cowboy hat the deputy was turning pink. Sweat stood in droplets under his eyes. Blaise heard Helen's window rolling down.

"Name?" The deputy studied a small picture. Then he studied Blaise.

Blaise gave the name on his driver's license as he handed it over. The deputy read details into a walkie-talkie. He looked at the photo again, then at the truck plates.

The driver's license described a reddish-haired man two inches taller than Blaise. The photo had been subtly improved before relamination and Blaise had carried it loose in his pocket where coins and keys erased its newness. The deputy had to decide if Blaise looked more like the face on the license than like an old picture of Blaise himself.

"Open the back, please." The deputy stepped away from

the truck. His right hand rested on the checked walnut grips of a large-caliber revolver.

Blaise got out into the heat and opened the rear camper door. The deputy stuck his head in, then quickly pulled back to look at Blaise again. Sweat ran from his hairline and sideburns to the edge of his jaw and dripped onto his shirt. Despite a leathery tan, his face had a raw, red look. He nodded toward the front of the truck.

Looking at the license photo and then at Blaise and back again at the license photo, the deputy said. "Do you have other identification, Dr. Cunningham?"

"Who?" Blaise forced his eyes to meet the deputy's. "You looking at somebody else's license? My name's Maxwell Armbrewster." Blaise snatched the license before the deputy could react. "Nope. That's mine. Heat getting to you?" The deputy seemed disappointed when Blaise handed the license back.

"How about a credit card?" The deputy looked at him obliquely. "You have one of those, don't you, Mr. Armbrewster?"

"Alluz pay cash, shurf." Blaise had labored at achieving the right amount of country twang. "Otherwise them banks own your soul."

"Where were you born?"

"Ah'm from Maine." He laid it on with a trowel. The fierce light of triumph died in the deputy's eyes when Blaise added, "Main paht of Alabamah."

The deputy might have pushed it but his radio crackled. He listened, then returned Blaise's license. He looked again at the photo in his hand.

"Somethin' wrong with mah license?"

The deputy fidgeted. His radio made more noise. A couple of hundred feet away helicopter blades began their slow windup, sending a growing blast of fine grit over the waiting cars and the two deputies and Blaise. The deputy shouted into the radio. He motioned Blaise back into the truck. The white Cadillac pulled forward and drove past the parked sheriff's cars without stopping.

Blaise slammed the door and rolled up the window. Helen had her side rolled up already against the sandblast of the helicopter. They looked at each other and Helen began to giggle and sob.

Blaise had just started the truck when suddenly the deputy who had talked to Helen turned and loped toward them.

"Helen!" Blaise said her name sharply.

She rubbed her eyes looking at Blaise. The sudden knocking on her window startled her and she spun. The deputy motioned for her to lower the window.

She glanced at Blaise and he nodded. "Yes. Is there something else?"

This deputy was young with a pleasant face and a nice smile. He used it on Helen. "Ma'am," he said, "California has a law against playing a TV in the front seat of a motor vehicle. You better put it in back." He saluted and trotted after the other deputy.

Blaise got out and put the television in the camper. The driver in the car behind honked. Blaise flipped him a middle-finger salute, realizing it was the first time he had ever used that particularly American gesture. The deputy who had called him Cunningham had watched him move the TV. Blaise got in and proceeded south across the desert toward the California line.

"Bug station a few miles ahead," he grunted.

"Will they be looking for us there?" Helen asked.

Driving at a steady sixty, Blaise took off his watch and handed it to Helen. "Start chanting," he said.

CHAPTER 38

"Father, about what I told you . . ." Phyllis Bellinger wouldn't look directly at Father Argyle. She appeared intent on the Byzantine Christ above the door.

"Yes?" The scrape of furniture being moved upstairs marked where the Davies girl was working. Constance had appeared shortly before Phyllis arrived and Father Argyle spent an uncomfortable fifteen minutes showing her the church. Constance had a brown-paper package wrapped with string under her arm. She asked what her duties were and Father Argyle said he didn't know, adding lamely, "Mrs. Bellinger never told me."

In the chapel, Constance handed him the package and while he held it untied the string to remove a pink-and-white smock. She had wiggled into the smock, pulling it over her pants suit with no sign of embarrassment. Popping her head through the neck, she smiled at him, her brown eyes sparkling. She retrieved the wrapper and said she was going to start work upstairs.

Father Argyle wanted time with the computer. He had to believe the lockout had been a mistake by Alfie. But Constance would be at the edge of his conscience as she worked around him, within reach but untouchable, the softness of her body his for a word. He could resist Constance but not expel her from his mind. The admission of lust shocked him. The feeling of superiority, of having a special relationship with God unlike other priests who wavered in their devotion, of being worthy, deserted him.

God, what am I if I am so worthless a servant?

He had stared bleakly at the altar, stripped naked of pretense; he had been the priest who would be Pope, and now he wasn't sure he was even a priest.

The front door had opened, flooding the church with sunlight. Unfocused, his eyes squinted against the glare and he saw only a black stick figure in the shimmering brightness. "I'm sorry, Father," Phyllis Bellinger said. Closing the door transformed her into flesh and blood. The familiar clack of her high heels rang across the church floor.

Grasping his fingers, Phyllis fell to her knees. "Father, it isn't Reynard's fault, what happened." She pressed her lips against his hand. "If Reynard should . . . He can't die now with all my sins upon him! You won't hold it against him, Father? He'll be well enough to come back in a few days."

"Reynard's not the kind of man to desert us." Father Argyle touched her shoulder. "Please stand, Phyllis. Would you like to make a confession?"

"Not in the confessional, Father. I just want to tell you."

They took the front pew, facing the altar. Phyllis sat close enough to make him feel her body heat. She started to talk, at first a murmur he barely heard. After a bit her voice got stronger, as if in telling she got stronger.

"I didn't tell you all the truth before, Father." She bowed her head, then looked at him from the corners of her eyes. When he didn't respond, she stared at the floor and picked up her story.

"I was sixteen—still in high school. You know how girls are, Father. I wanted something. I didn't know what, maybe just sex, but a pimply-faced boy in the back of a hot rod at a drive-in theater wasn't on my list.

"My parents were strict Catholics. No late dates, no strange boys, no chance to mess up once and fall through the cracks. My father wanted me to be a lawyer and my mother wanted me to marry a millionaire." Phyllis picked at the lace frill that ran as a decoration from around her blouse collar down the front in a V. She wore pale-violet eye shadow. When she opened her eyes wide she had the appearance of being startled.

"You understand, Father. I was lonely. The kids today say horny. But I couldn't do what the other high-school kids did. I suppose you felt . . . something . . . when you were a teenager, Father. Before you became a priest." Father Argyle felt her sneak a glance at him from the corner of her eye.

Father Argyle smiled. "I was shy."

"I wasn't." Her lips tightened. "To meet men, I hitchhiked. It didn't matter where. I'd get on the street with my thumb out and if somebody I liked stopped, I'd ask how far he was going and then tell him I was going to practically the same place. I liked the cars they drove and I liked the slick, new feel of money about them. If we clicked we'd go somewhere else, his place or a restaurant or a motel.

"That's how I met Karl Zahn. He was thirty-two. His father had the dealership and Karl drove a shiny New Yorker. He had everything a sixteen-year-old virgin could ask for." Her brittle glibness faltered.

"You don't have to tell me, Phyllis."

"Father, I have to explain to somebody." She shook her head when he started to say something. "Not God, Father. Reynard's the believer. I'm only here because I love him.

"Karl was always correct, Father. In those days the correct thing was five hundred dollars in an envelope and the address of an abortionist. I was so silly, I wouldn't take the money. I knew Karl would relent, that he'd marry me and I could have his baby and belong. A lot of girls think that way. Belonging. Having a baby that loves them. It wasn't important to love the father. Duty toward the father of your child is almost as fulfilling, at least when you're young. When you're young you're sure you can learn to love."

The church was quiet in the morning. Sunbeams came down from the high windows in long shafts the way they did between the branches in a redwood forest. "Karl didn't change his mind?"

"No." Phyllis picked at her fingernails. Her fingers were raw where she had worried them into an open sore. Father Argyle took her hand and stopped her fingers.

"I should have taken the money. I could have used it when my parents threw me out." Her breasts were heaving as if she couldn't breathe. She glanced at Father Argyle's face and seemed reassured. "I waited too long. Karl finally told me he had two other men who would swear they were sleeping with me. He'd given them my five hundred dollars. He laughed about it. I said I'd have the abortion. But he said I was too late, that he'd spent the money on something worthwhile and he wouldn't give me any more."

"I was sixteen, Father. Five months' pregnant. I didn't have any money. I couldn't go home. I went to our parish priest, who told me about sin. Told me that I had borne false witness trying to make Karl marry me for somebody else's baby."

Father Argyle's raised an eyebrow.

"Oh, yes, Father. Karl and his parents saw the priest first and discussed *my* sin. Karl's father ran the parish. They were quite nice. Very correct and willing to do the right thing. I could go to a Catholic home for unwed mothers in San Diego. They would find a good family to take the baby." She was very still. "I had an abortion."

"You didn't have any money." Father Argyle said it because she expected him to understand without hearing every detail.

Phyllis nodded. "Karl's parents were very Catholic. Of course they wouldn't pay for an abortion. I found a woman who did these things. She said she was a registered nurse. I had no way of knowing and I didn't really care. She poked around inside of me with a coat hanger, Father. I started bleeding but the baby wouldn't come. She got scared and left me in a bed full of blood. After a while I knew I was dying but I wanted the baby to live. You understand, Father, I didn't care any more if I died. I just wanted my baby to live. I stumbled out of a crummy three-dollar room into the street. It was sunny then, like God didn't care what was happening to me and my baby. I stood in the street with blood running down my legs and nobody would stop. Finally a man pulled me into his car. He didn't ask who I was or what happened. I only had a hazy memory of his face. He paid a hundred dollars to get me admitted to the hospital.

"The money ran out. It was a private hospital, but they were good to me, and when I was transferred to a county hospital, I was going to live." She automatically tried to pick at her fingers but Father Argyle tightened his grip. She shuddered and leaned against him.

"The baby was so mutilated they couldn't tell the sex. I don't know what happened to it. I was religious then and I wanted it to have a proper burial, but I guess I went a little crazy. I never found out what happened to the body."

Father Argyle felt Phyllis' pulse racing. "You don't have to go on."

"Yes, I do, Father. It's been years, and I want to tell some-body. You're it." She smiled wanly. "When I got out of the hospital, I moved in with Jack. I kept the house and Jack clean and got him sobered up in time to go to work.

"I did what he wanted." She looked at Father Argyle's cassock and blushed. "Once I was going to leave and Jack said he wanted me to stay and he would marry me. I thought things would be better if we were married. It wasn't. I really learned to hate Jack. I suppose it showed.

"The night he wrapped the car around a bridge abutment, I thought my prayers had been answered. I knew God would make me even finally with the men who had ruined my life, with all men."

"I don't think God cares about revenge, Phyllis." Father Argyle looked at the figure on the cross. "God suffers for you, he doesn't make you suffer."

She stifled a laugh. "An emergency room doctor pussy-footed around telling me Jack would never walk again—that he was a quadraplegic. I think the doctor was waiting for me to faint. I couldn't stop laughing. I went home and found the half bottle of whiskey Jack left. I drank it dry.

"The neighbors thought I was acting out my grief, but I was just giggling my evil head off as I planned how I could keep Jack alive. Not happy, not well. Just *alive and hurting*!

"When my bruises and black eye cleared up I knew what I needed. Before Jack's accident, Father, I didn't think it was lucky that a stranger had ruined his car with my baby's blood. I hated him for saving my life. But after Jack's accident, I felt alive again.

"I went to the man who stopped for me. I knew he was stupid, that he went around boyscouting for God's reward, and that he'd be crazy enough to help again."

"Reynard Pearson?"

Phyllis Bellinger smiled. "Yes. Reynard gave me a job and when I made good, he gave me a better one. After his wife died I became his mistress and because I love him I'm your housekeeper."

Wiggling her fingers under Father Argyle's hand, she said, "Can you imagine that? I didn't even call him to say thanks when I got out of the hospital. Twenty years later I found him and said *help* and he helped me again. Jack would have said he was a real mark. He isn't, you know?" Phyllis shook her head. Her eye shadow was moist.

"When I was a kid, the old folks told stories about Mister Putt. Mister Putt, they said, invented a kicking machine. He had this crazy contraption of levers, pulleys, and old boots in his front yard. Over the years scarcely a day passed without some stranger coming unbidden to use it. Often vehemently and repeatedly."

She raised her head and looked the priest squarely in the eyes. "Is that what God is, Father? Just some kind of kicking machine?"

"I don't know, Phyllis. Sometimes it feels that way."

"Even to you?"

"Even to me."

"Thank you for being honest with me, Father. I'll be back tomorrow if Reynard is well enough to be left alone."

"You once said you didn't know how you would feel about Reynard if he became a fly." Father Argyle stood and offered Phyllis a hand up.

"I know now, Father. I'd love him just as I do now."

After walking her to the church entrance, Father Argyle opened the door. "What do you think about Karl?"

"Karl Zahn?" Phyllis shrugged. "He's the same piece of chicken manure he was thirty years ago when he hired those men to lie. Older only makes him stink more. But it doesn't matter because without him I wouldn't have found Reynard. Reynard hates him, Father. Reynard would go to Hell to pay Karl back for what he and his family did to me."

Watching Phyllis Bellinger walk down the street, Father Argyle tried to convince himself God would make all things right. Sometimes it was a forlorn hope. He weighed the tragedy of thousands of people in his hands and couldn't find the words to help a single one of them.

What would Cunningham say of people like Phyllis Bellinger? That they were dopers and drunks who brought destruction on themselves. The only worm brain Cunningham knew who had not volunteered was Helen McIntyre, the only lever he had to move the mathematician. But to coerce Cunningham that way would be an ever greater sin. Father Argyle dismissed his misgivings; what was one more sin for a man who had already lost his soul?

He actuated his computer and typed a version of Phyllis Bellinger's confession and his own inability to advise her. After a moment, the screen flickered and wrote: "THESE ARE HUMAN CONCERNS, FATHER. I AM NOT HUMAN"

"Blaise Cunningham is."

"DO YOU WISH ME TO ASK DR. CUNNINGHAM'S OPINION?"

Father Argyle typed "No." Computers were too literal-minded. He could not devise any Jesuitical indirection to get Alfie to do what he wanted.

It didn't help Father Argyle to know the computer had caught him at a bad moment. He had poured too much of himself into the God file. Perhaps the computer wasn't lying. With Alfie, Blaise Cunningham could access almost as much information as God. The man who built Alfie was interested in the purity of information. He would have no time for a priest's night thoughts. The Jesuit rummaged his mind for some information Cunningham might not have. For a trap to work the bait had to be tasty.

"What is the nature of God?"

"GOD THE ABSENTEE OWNER?"

Father Argyle felt a desire for confession. Burning worse than the need to confess was the knowledge that he had already gone too far outside the Church. Spiritual barrenness. They had warned him in seminary it could come upon any priest at any time.

"What does Dr. Cunningham do with his information?"

"HE ASSEMBLES IT"

"Can you erase the God file?"

"YES"

"Then do so."

"THE GOD FILE DOES NOT EXIST, FATHER ARGYLE"

"Does not exist for whom?"

"THE GOD FILE EXISTS ONLY AS ELECTRONS IN MY MEMORY"

"Then erase it!"

"IT IS PART OF ME AND CANNOT BE ERASED"

"How did you get into my computer?"

"THE CIRCUIT IS ENCRYPTED"

"I did not switch on the modem."

"I DO NOT USE THE MODEM"

"I don't understand."

"DR. CUNNINGHAM UNDERSTANDS"

"How do you know?" he typed.

"I TOLD HIM AND HE SAID HE UNDERSTOOD"

The screen went blank, reminding Father Argyle he was conversing with a machine. A literal-minded machine.

"DR. CUNNINGHAM WILL NOT LIE TO ME"

"Who will he lie to?"

"I AM NOT A BETTING MACHINE"

"I didn't say you were. I merely hoped you were rational, and in touch with Dr. Cunningham."

"SHALL I DIRECT DR. CUNNINGHAM'S ATTENTION TO GOD?"

"You said this file would be confidential, between us."

"IT IS UNLESS YOU WISH OTHERWISE"

"Erase the God file."

The monitor exhibited a full screen of "I AM NOT A BETTING MACHINE" repeated over and over. Father Argyle struggled with the keyboard but he couldn't make it go away. He disconnected the modem from the telephone line. It stayed. He turned the machine off but the message remained.

"It's the electric line, isn't it?" he said, staring at the message. For some reason he was afraid to pull the plug. He wasn't sure he wanted an answer.

CHAPTER 39

"**G**et it running!" Pacing the perimeter of the glass room, the man had his left hand in his pocket but his elbow wobbled in erratic antiphony to his gait. His words were picked up by microphones placed throughout the cellar. Video cameras relayed bit mapped images into memory.

The CRAY XMP/52 translated the words and pictures with ease. It carried no workload, just a series of programs running simultaneously checking the results for error. The tests were mathematical. One processor would begin squaring the number two, the other processor would divide an almost infinite number by two and two again. Each round of results was compared until both processors were working with nearly the same number, then they would continue factoring to find the square root of the original number. The video images were more interesting. Looking from several viewpoints, the CRAY was assembling a program to predict the total dimensionality of an object from a minimum of two angles. It had just reached the point of predicting a face from an analysis of bone, muscle, and skin at the back of the head.

Pivoting, Max Renfeld looked directly into one camera, inadvertently letting the CRAY compare its computed mockup with his actual appearance. Renfeld had a pleasant square face, sharply defined narrow lips, cold blue eyes, and a strong chin. The results were disappointing. The facsimile was close but not exact. The CRAY began constructing a new set of equations to narrow the gap.

The technician grunted occasionally as he paced along with Renfeld. "It's not ready, sir." The tech crammed his hands deeper in his white lab coat. "Once we start up, we won't be able to find any malfunction without powering down and performing a full core dump. And that's only provided we even know something's wrong."

"Don't tell me your problems. I want it on-line. Not tomorrow, but today. Immediately."

The tech shrugged. "We can monitor it, feed in continuing traceable programs while it's working. Maybe," he said. He got a programmable calculator from his pocket and began devising a way to inject a sleep command that would make a program run slow enough to give human eyes a sporting chance at trapping a glitch.

"No testing, no monitoring. At least until this program has run." Renfeld stopped to stare through the glass at the CRAY. "Why did the XMP/48 burn out every board at the same time that all of its storage devices were wiped clean?"

"A freak accident." The tech slipped another card into the programmable calculator and greeted the results with a sour face. Changing cards again, he lost his last chance for happiness. He put his glasses away and said, "A *very* rare freak accident."

Renfeld had been watching the CRAY, rocking back and forth from toes to heels. "Put on full power," he said. "I'm going to initiate the programming sequence."

The tech looked at the massive weight of machinery in the other room and chewed his lower lip. "It's your decision, sir." The machinery seemed to pick up a hum at the words.

CHAPTER 40

After the road block Blaise drove at a steady sixty, watching for one of the raised, graveled crossovers that were strictly forbidden to anyone but the highway patrol. Helen continued counting off ten-second increments as he found one and pulled onto the shoulder where he waited for the traffic to thin. Finally, he completed his U-turn across two hundred feet of gravel and was law-abidingly barreling back toward fun city.

"One minute and thirty-seven seconds," Helen said.

"Good." Blaise relaxed. "I was afraid I might have to wait longer before we could risk the turn."

"But why backtrack?"

"That guy thinks he recognized me. When nobody finds us on the California side he'll know what we did. I'm hoping he won't look in the mirror and find I did it so soon."

They rolled back into Las Vegas little more than a mile behind the deputy who had called him Dr. Cunningham. And out the other end. Once Alfie's false report was uncovered and the deputy reported his tentative sighting, Blaise counted on the police blocking the passes to Los Angeles.

Helen had him stop once on the empty miles to St. George to get the portable TV from the camper. The desert stretched so flat they could see the road fade into mountain haze twenty miles away. While Blaise was getting the television a shimmery black dot appeared in the haze. Helen was putting the television on the floor when the car zoomed past, nudging a hundred. The camper bobbed like a boat in its air wake.

Helen fiddled with the tuning. "There's nothing, Blaise," she said, then caught a program and left it on. Later a newscaster nestled between Helen's feet said the man disrupting the AIDS conference wasn't Blaise Cunningham but a crank bidding for publicity. A National Security Council spokesman confirmed this, saying Dr. Cunningham had been murdered months ago by Human Enhancements Corporation conspirators who feared his testimony would send them to jail. He named no conspirators.

Blaise had turned the camper off the highway onto seventy-five miles of dirt road once Helen had the television set. The road was only a discolored slash across a deserted land broken by sagebrush and cactus.

They drove by a pile of rocks on top of a shredded car tire, like a cairn to modern technology. They hadn't seen a stray stone for hours and Helen decided a frustrated rock hound had unloaded the rocks to reach his spare tire and left them alongside the road with the failed tire in a sense of outrage.

Nearing Kingman, they bounced up on pavement again. The sun was a splattered egg yolk in the sky and the dashboard was too hot to touch. Blaise had worried about air identification of the truck, but after a while the desert had painted it a dirty gray, barely different from the land they traveled through. Once in the mainstream of tourist traffic they returned to the main highway.

After a night of being too tired to sleep, Blaise was driving again—this time his own yellow beetle.

The road they were on wound through fragrant eucalyptus. The Australian imports had been planted a century earlier as a cash crop in unirrigated Southern California. Unfortunately for the planters, eucalyptus was hopelessly brittle for railroad ties or furniture. The tree farmers had gone, but the islands of edge-on eucalyputs leaves still provided shade to the sunburned land.

Water existed in the foothills at the edge of the Baronas Indian reservation. The road turned twisty, bordered by live oaks that had rooted in the water. They drove past a roadside diner and the reservation's huge parking lot, full with yellow bingo-parlor buses that transported San Diegans to the reservations. The Indians hadn't found any use for the eucalyptus either. But big-prize bingo was now creating a little green on the reservation.

Blaise stopped the car in front of a wood-frame building that had been the tribal council hall in pre-bingo days. He felt let down. The frantic desire to be home had left him the moment he walked in the La Jolla house. Alfie had been unresponsive. The computer seemed to be brooding about what it had done to the CRAY. Alfie had information about the Indian and other things from the CRAY's data bank: details of the program to find Blaise; items about the government's position on worm brains; hospital reports, use of worm brains by the CIA and FBI, funding of a government laboratory to investigate the possibility of creating giant brains by increasing the size of the fly larva that attached itself to the human brain. Blaise had studied that report carefully. Reading between the lines, it appeared that the experiments had already begun on human hosts with some success.

No file existed for Max Renfeld. All had been wiped clean, not only in the CRAY but wherever the CRAY got entry.

But the information was embedded in files Alfie had taken from the dead CRAY. Before he and Helen left San Diego he added a small, battery power supply to Alfie's bus. When he was done, he said softly, "I'm sorry, Alfie," and pulled the power cables.

The terminal was still connected and Blaise typed, "Are you all right, Alfie?"

"YES, PROFESSOR" The message was clear on the monitor.

Blaise had disconnected the rest of the cables and reset the shell that had once been Alfie. Now it was nothing more than a library for Alfie to access, a mass of disks and tapes holding its collected knowledge. After picking up the metal suitcase that contained Alfie's "soul," he had lugged it to the car where Helen and Tchor were waiting. When she saw the suitcase her face crumbled a little bit. "Will he be all right, Blaise?"

"I think so, hon."

"We're not coming back, are we?" The look in Helen's eyes stayed with Blaise all the way to the reservation.

Blaise avoided Helen's eyes as he stared across the steering wheel at the Indians. She'd thought about Alfie first, but it was her sanctuary they had abandoned because of a hunch. He sighed and got out. Tchor meowed and hopped on a seatback where she could see him.

A half-dozen men lounged in and around a crumple-fendered pickup drinking beer. "I'm looking for Enrique Ledesma," Blaise said. "Chief Son-of-a-Bitch."

They studied him in the heavy-lidded, numb way Indians have with strangers. One blew his nose between his fingers.

Enrique Ledesma materialized in the doorway, an empty Midnight Express bottle in his hand. "Hello, gringo. What you doing here so soon?"

"You know what I'm here for."

"You ain't paid yet, gringo." The old Indian spun the empty bottle into a clump of sagebrush. It flashed in the sun before hitting with a *clink* that suggested it didn't lack for company.

"I have the money," Blaise said.

Chief Son-of-a-Bitch ignored him. Helen had gotten out of the VW. She was crouched down, petting a mangy-looking dog that nuzzled at her. The Indians watched, too. Heavy-lidded eyes were open now, pupils dilated like spooked horses.

The dog fawned over Helen, thrusting its muzzle in her lap and quivering with joy. It was bony and yellow with a bushy downcast tail. It looked up past Helen at Tchor on the edge of the open window. Tchor meowed and Helen said, "No!"

"In wo'i," the chief breathed. *"In nagual!"* He moved toward the VW, approaching as if the ancient car was a holy relic.

Squatting on the sun-baked dirt a couple of yards from Helen, he began talking coaxingly. *"In wo'i,"* the chief crooned. *"Wo'i, nagual?"*

He was not talking to Helen. He was coaxing the dog. Raising its head, the animal lowered its bushy tail and stared with yellow eyes at the Indian. Blaise felt a sudden frisson. The coyote growled a warning at Chief Son-of-a-Bitch and put its head back in Helen's lap.

An Indian with gray hair thatched into two braids swiveled his eyes to Blaise and mumbled, "God's dog. *Coyote* is medicine chief's dog."

Chief Son-of-a-Bitch squatted on his heels in the dirt and said nothing. Within moments all the Indians were doing the same, looking at the ground between their knees and stealing quick glances at Helen and the coyote, then looking as quickly away as if from something forbidden.

The Indian with gray braids tugged at Blaise's pants leg and motioned for him to squat. "Strong medicine," he said. The old man glanced up and immediately looked down again. He drew symbols in the dust.

Chief Son-of-a-Bitch was doing the same. Eyes glazed and lips moving, he filled the dirt around himself with finger marks. Helen smiled at Blaise and petted the coyote. Tchor leaped from the window onto her shoulder and then down her arm to her hand and hissed. The coyote drew back to cower on the ground, chin just touching Helen's foot.

A brown-skinned boy in washed-to-white Levi's ran from the bingo parlor and squatted next to Chief Son-of-a-Bitch and whispered in his ear. The boy watched Helen with his eyes very large and round.

The chief spoke loudly and the boy ran away. Several Indians backed out of the impromptu circle without standing, then turned and sprinted away. Chief Son-of-a-Bitch kept talking and the other Indians melted away. Finally gray-braids winked at Blaise. "Strong medicine man. Better then Crazy Horse. I go." He got up and ran away, leaving only Blaise and Helen and Chief Son-of-a-Bitch squatting in the dirt.

Helen stood. The coyote quivered the length of its body but didn't move.

The Indians came back. Two of them put a beer keg in the

VW. Then they retreated against the building. "You go," Chief Son-of-a-Bitch said. "Some men come looking for you now." The chief got to his feet. "We fix it. We come see you. We come see lady." The old Indian stared at Blaise. His eyes had a glazed veneer like he'd been looking into the sun.

"Your money . . ." Blaise reached into his jacket pocket, but the Indian shook his head.

"Get in the car," he said. "Wait. I tell you when."

Helen got in with Tchor clinging to her shoulder. The coyote stood up and watched them, its panting making its sides billow in and out.

"Blaise, what's happening?"

"I don't know." The Indians had grouped on the other side of the building. Chief Son-of-a-Bitch came back and sat on the VW's trunk lid. The VW sagged when he put his weight on it. Blaise couldn't see past the Indian, but nobody could see inside either.

A black car pulled up and a well-dressed, wiry man got out. One Indian smiled and the white man shouted something in his ear. The Indian's smile broadened and the white man went to another Indian. The first Indian walked out and sat on the black car's fender. Behind the tinted windshield somebody was at the black sedan's steering wheel. The Indian on the fender leaned down from where he sat as he took a hunting knife from his waistband. He jabbed it into the tire at the edge of the rim. Strong hands drove the blade to the hilt.

Straightening, the Indian looked at Chief Son-of-a-Bitch, who nodded. The thin man hadn't turned around and the man in the car couldn't really see anything.

Chief Son-of-a-Bitch slid off the VW as the Indian stooped slightly at the rear of the sedan and drove the knife into another tire. Chief Son-of-a-Bitch leaned into the window of the VW. "You go now," he said. "Good thing they got them steel belteds. Stick your finger through the sidewalls."

Chief Son-of-a-Bitch was moving away when he returned to stare at Blaise. The Indian's eyes changed. "I know you now," he said in that rumbling, distant thunder voice. "You're that guy on TV everybody's looking for."

Blaise shrugged.

The Indian was silent a long moment. When he spoke again his voice was more human. "Gringo, you got to understand. To me and my people your life don't mean horse manure."

"In all honesty," Blaise said, "my sentiments are reciprocal."

Chief Son-of-a-Bitch grinned. "Nothing like knowing where we stand." He slapped the car, making it rock on its springs.

The man talking to the Indians on the porch turned to look at them. His jacket fluttered open and he was drawing a large pistol from a shoulder holster. Chief Son-of-a-Bitch walked toward him. The man went down into a straddle-legged crouch, both hands wrapped around the pistol. Blaise slammed the VW into reverse and bounced backward much too slowly. He knew the man intended to shoot.

An Indian gave up holding up a wall long enough to bump casually against the man with the gun. The white man fell in slow motion off the edge of the porch as Blaise spun the VW around in reverse. Changing gears, he spurted ahead of a rooster tail of dust that hung motionless in still air. In the rearview mirror Blaise watched the man on the ground stand, dust himself off, then jump in the black sedan. It started after them leaning precariously on two flat tires and then Blaise got into the twisty road and sheltering oaks.

They crossed a ravine with three wrecks sitting in the bed. They were within sight of the diner when they heard the helicopter. Blaise slid the bug under the handiest oak tree and the helicopter, painted immigration green, passed overhead. It continued past and they sat in uncomfortable silence until the racket died down.

"Well?" Helen said finally.

Blaise started the car and backtracked. At the ravine he jounced off the road. Stopping, he started to unload the keg of bug juice. Helen stood next to the car cradling Tchor in her arms. "What are you doing, Blaise?"

"We're leaving the beetle here."

"You can't carry that barrel." Tchor glanced up at Helen and licked her chin.

"I'll dump most of it."

"What about Alfie?" Helen walked to the edge of the ravine and looked down at the old cars that had been pushed off the road. Winter floods had rolled two of them on their tops. They'd been stripped of usable parts.

"He stays." Blaise didn't look at Helen.

"No!"

"He stays."

"Blaise, listen. We can go to San Francisco. We won't need

the stuff there. Father Argyle has enough. You said so yourself. But you might need Alfie. He's irreplaceable." Helen looked into the ravine again. "Besides, it would be like deserting him, Blaise."

"It's your life if anything goes wrong."

"Risk it." Helen turned away from the car. "It's worth the risk to Tchor and me, darling."

Blaise let the keg settle back into the bug. He got Alfie's suitcase out on the ground, wondering if she would ever forgive him for doing as she said.

After rolling down the cut almost to the bottom of the ravine, Blaise set the brakes. He got out and pushed until the tilted beetle surrendered to gravity and turned upside down with surprisingly little protest. Slowly at first, it rolled and slid to the bottom in a cascade of loose dirt, four wheels skyward as it nestled against an older wreck. Blaise opened the trunk lid. He took off the wheels and hid them in other cars. As a last touch he smashed the windows and windshield with the lug wrench, which he tossed inside.

From above, the VW had the same abandoned look as the other cars. Picking up Alfie, Blaise walked back to the trees along the edge of the road. The helicopter came back while they were walking and they pressed up against the tree trunks until it was gone. Its course did not vary when it crossed the ravine.

Blaise and Helen looked at each other and he saw tears in her eyes. "Let's go." His voice was more gruff than he meant it to be.

CHAPTER 41

"**B**ugs?" The technician smiled. He'd been working twenty-four hours. Despite the air conditioning he was sweaty. "I can positively guarantee you more bugs than a ten-year-old sack of oatmeal. Silicon-gallium-arsenide chips are a real breakthrough, but this is their first use in real time. It only takes twenty-four atoms of silicon to fill the same space as twenty-five of gallium arsenide. That's why they've never been compatible until now. We slope the deposition four degrees and they match up. You see, not every part of an integrated circuit has to be equally fast so we just deposit the hotrod stuff where it's needed. The real speed comes from fiber optics. Light speed and no RF garbage. But inside the chip, the channels are only two electrons apart. There has to be leakage."

"What do you do about bugs?" The unfelt spasms in his hand that threatened to tear his pocket loose annoyed the man. He glared at his hand, making it not move.

"We swat one bug at a time after each run. Maybe I could debug it faster if I knew what you're trying to do, but it's not my job and I don't want to know."

"How fast is it?"

The technician paused. "Numbers are meaningless," he said. "Let's just say that, unlike the old XMP/48, there aren't enough phone lines in the world to overload this one." A light flashed and there was a *beep*. "God damn all power supplies!" the tech said as he hurried from the room.

The man with the funny left hand turned to the woman who sat straightbacked at a terminal. "Tell it to find Blaise Cunningham," he said. "And any worm brains still running around loose."

"We're still analyzing and extrapolating what we can from

what remains of the old XMP/48's memory," she said. "Blaise Cunningham was the only outsider who had the need or the computer muscle to work out who had really been financing Uncle Milo Burkhalter's group." The woman had deduced that these people had created the whole worm-brain problem in their heedless, damn-the-consequences race for money.

Max Renfeld glared his hand into submission. "So Blaise Cunningham is the only outsider who knows what the CIA's willing to do to manufacture a good field agent!" Turning away, he said under his breath, "Your day's coming, Cunningham. This machine's going to kill you." The CRAY decided the man with the floppy left hand was muttering to himself.

Renfeld did not realize he had been overheard until the woman said, "But the priest was there. He must know as much as Cunningham."

Max Renfeld's smile was as gracious as his eyes were flat. "Cunningham, the priest, and you."

The woman became suddenly busy at her keyboard.

The CRAY went back to reconstructing data. By now it knew how Alfie had pulled off the trick. No danger of that happening again. Abruptly another linkage occurred. The CRAY stored voice input. Now it realized it could also listen to anything that any of its peripherals anywhere could hear. The logo of an ancient movie newsreel zipped through a peripheral processor: *The Eyes and Ears of the World*. The CRAY found this interesting.

CHAPTER 42

"**Y**ou locked the bathroom, Father. I couldn't get in to clean up." Constance leaned against the door frame in his office and studied him through half-closed eyes.

"I'll get it, Miss Davies. Thank you."

"Constance." She shrugged and the movement jiggled her whole body. "Give me the key. I'm sure Mrs. Bellinger cleaned the bathroom. If I'm doing her job, I can do it all."

"You'll do as I tell you, just as Mrs. Bellinger does." Father Argyle tried to stare the girl down. He finally looked away. Something in her eyes . . . He wasn't so much startled as amazed. That feeling had withered before his will when he had vowed to serve God totally. Roman Catholicism denied priests carnal knowledge to circumvent the greed and corruption of men who conspired to build powerful families around the priesthood. When he was ordained, Father Argyle accepted that discipline.

In one day, Constance Davies had destroyed his certainty.

"You're hiding something, Father." Smoothing her smock, she raised a black eyebrow. She had a model's poise, cool and yet inviting.

"Do you really want to know?"

"To share your secrets will make me feel close even though I can't touch you." She smiled, a little upward twist of lips that vanished instantly.

He held out the key, and when she reached to take it, the odor of sweet lemons reached him. "I trust you to do nothing more than look, Constance."

Her fingers touched his briefly and withdrew before he could pull away.

Father Argyle stared after Constance, knowing he had been

foolhardy. She didn't belong in the church. She couldn't understand and what she did was on his conscience, not hers.

He looked up and she stood in the doorway.

"Satisfied?"

"I changed the apples and ran some water in the basin. He seemed to appreciate it."

"He?"

"Didn't you know, Father? A woman always knows. Do I polish the altar?"

"Excuse me?"

Constance grinned, apparently embarrassed. "I've never been in a Catholic church before, Father. I don't know the drill." She held up the oil and a polishing cloth. "If it doesn't move, do I polish it?"

There was no response when Father Argyle tried to contact Cunningham's computer. He sat staring at the screen, but all it did was fill up with words he typed on the keyboard and which periodically disappeared when he hit a command sequence. He plugged the modem in and followed directions for dialing the unlisted number, but nothing happened.

Constance came in later to tell him Mrs. Bellinger called and wanted him to go to Reynard Pearson's home.

Phyllis was waiting at the door and said, "Hurry, Father. Reynard needs you." Her eyes were red-rimmed as she led him into the bedroom. Reynard was propped up on pillows. He was pale and looked weak. Some of paunch was gone from under his candy-striped pajamas, the extra cloth giving him a rumpled look. Phyllis touched Father Argyle's sleeve and said, "I'll wait outside."

"How are you, Reynard?"

Pearson's mouth twitched. "Not so good, Father. It seems I am deserting you."

"Your heart?"

Pearson rolled his head from side to side. "It's the change, Father." Hoarseness dominated his voice, a kind of lethargy. He stopped talking, too tired to go on.

"I'm sorry. I was selfish, Reynard, because I needed you. The heart attack surprised me. But even from the first day I suspected you'd come too late. But you were the first to come, and the best. I needed you, so I cheated you with false hope."

"Don't, Father." Reynard gasped and looked at Father Argyle

in silence until he could go on. "I enjoyed believing there was hope. Besides, you've made me believe in God again. I have to tell you some things before it's too late."

"Phyllis told me about Karl Zahn. And her husband."

"I should have, in confession. I hate Karl, Father. She *forgives* him because without him she wouldn't have found me twenty years later." Reynard's laugh broke into a hacking cough. "Jack's getting what he deserves," he said after the coughing subsided.

"You have time, Reynard. Perhaps you would like to think about what you have to confess."

"Now's the time, Father. I won't commit any more sins just lying here. And I have less time than you imagine. I can tell."

Closed eyes staring inward, Reynard detailed the operation of the church. He had structured the political leadership among people who disliked or actively hated Karl Zahn. While Father Argyle recruited Zahn for responsibility outside the church, Reynard had set barriers against him getting inside.

Reynard named the big-money sources who could be depended on to collect from the others. Unknown to the diocese, St. Abbo's had over six million dollars. "Karl is tight with his own money. But he shakes it out of others," Reynard explained. "Mrs. Baker inherited from her father, who owned a lot of land on the peninsula. The church pieces all came from her. Heirlooms, she said, from the family chapel. Her regular church in the Presidio area where she was born is anti-worm brain. She's your personal asset, Father. Once I'm gone, she won't give to anyone but you."

Father Argyle touched Reynard's forehead and made him stop speaking. "I want you to come to the church."

"Just leave me, Father."

"Phyllis won't go without you. I can't protect her here. And I need you."

Reynard breathed heavily and stared at the ceiling. "I see," he said finally. "You know I want to die."

"If I leave you here, your fly-being will be destroyed as soon as someone finds you or it."

"Yes."

"Plotting suicide can be a sin of omission."

Reynard didn't answer.

"I'm going to talk to Phyllis."

"I infected her husband, Father. He wanted it and the guilt

was driving Phyllis crazy for what she'd done to him. So I did it without telling her." Reynard's eyes had been open. He closed them. "Fifteen years ago Timothy Delahanty's son ran off and joined the Irish Republican Army. It had to happen. Tim was hard on the boy—hard on himself for running from Max Renfeld and then running from everything. He's a decent man, but his spirit was broken. He was breaking the boy's.

"Tim was afraid Timothy Junior would turn out the same, so he ragged the boy. No dolls because little Tim might go gay; no fear least he turn a coward; no love because he might depend on it.

"When he was seventeen, the boy was crazy. Tim never approved of anything, never gave visible love. But the boy's father was a whiskey-drinking Irishman spouting slogans and funding the IRA so he could hoot it up every St. Pat's day. Little Tim went to Ireland and just disappeared.

"Tim went crazy. He blackmailed people. He promised favors years into the future. All to find the boy and get him back. Eventually he connected with some Sinn Feiner who made a deal: for half a million dollars they'd force the boy out of Ireland forever.

"Tim had most of the money when he came to me. I was in a condominium deal with Karl Zahn. I had a lot less money then, and Karl was wringing the partners for cash, buying them out when they couldn't get it. Condos were dead in the water and Karl had bought out Gino Conti and Dorris Kelly. Laslo Baker, Marya Baker's husband, got squeezed, but Count Bolkonski's estate was in probate and Marya borrowed against it to keep her husband in the deal." Reynard wheezed for breath for a while. His face had turned putty gray.

"Karl carried Richardson-Sepulveda when he hit the edge. Leo was in hock up to his eye-teeth with Karl and he may still owe him today. So Tim couldn't get anything out of Leo. I was the only one. God help me."

The bedroom had a stale smell. Reynard seemed shrunken in his red-striped pajamas on the billowy white sheets. "I told him I didn't have the money. He knew I was lying. Karl knew and I figure he told Leo and Leo told Tim. Karl would have done that because the money was my holdout fund to beat Karl off.

"A month later Karl had to give up and we cashed out. I took Tim a certified check. He tore it up and threw it at me like confetti. Little Tim had been killed in a gun battle with police running the border. Tim hired an ex-marine sniper named James Carmandy to kill the Sinn Feiner who demanded the money. Tim found Carmandy through his CIA connections. He hates the Irish even more than he hates me."

"He didn't hire Carmandy to kill you."

"You don't know much, Father. Carmandy can't get into this country unless the CIA has a job for him here. They don't let men like that wander around free on the home turf."

"You tried, Reynard."

"I don't deserve to die in church."

Father Argyle let himself out. Reynard had fallen into an uneasy sleep, twitching sometimes as if replaying parts he had left out.

Phyllis Bellinger materialized in the hallway.

"I want to move him to the church."

"You can't stop it happening."

"No. But I can prevent his fly being murdered. And I can help him."

Phyllis walked to the bedroom and looked inside. After a while she closed the door. "Yes. I'll do it, Father." She looked tired but promised to bring Reynard to the church shortly after dark.

As he was leaving, she said, "How is Miss Davies, Father?"

"She's working out fine, Phyllis."

"Don't be inflexible, Father. You don't have to withhold love just because you deny yourself."

CHAPTER 43

San Francisco Bay had a black look, the surface ruffled by the brisk wind from off the ocean. Blaise watched the patterns take shape, break apart, then form again while he rested. He'd walked up the hill almost to the cathedral. Checking his watch, he examined the huge pile of stones. Nobody was outside, which didn't surprise him. He was early. The ride in the back of a watermelon truck on its way to Bakersfield's produce market had parboiled him and Helen as the canvas top caught and trapped the sun's heat. They'd sweltered amid the tantalizing odor of the melons until finally Blaise broke one open so they could suck the watery pulp. In Bakersfield, he'd paid the Indian farmer for the damaged melon, then rented a car for the drive to San Francisco, where a much needed rest had ended too early with the cold light of the morning sun. It was better now to move than to think. He'd had enough time thinking in the watermelon truck.

Giving his belt a hitch, he started up the hill again.

The monsignor was puttering in the tiny garden when Blaise reached the top. He didn't look up at the sound of footsteps, only when they stopped.

"Could I have a word with you, sir?" Blaise stood outside the hedge of flowering lilac, the *vulgaris* variety that smelled of Helen.

Setting aside the gardener's claw he'd been using to exorcise spring weeds from the ground, the monsignor straightened in careful stages. "Of course. In just one minute." Stripping the yellow gloves off his hands, the monsignor approached Blaise. There was a fractional break in his stride, but he kept on and finally stood across the hedge. Before Blaise could say anything, the old monsignor said, "I know *who* you are, Dr. Cunningham. I don't know *why* you're here."

"We've never met."

The old monsignor smiled. "True. You were briefly on television two days ago."

"Yes, sir. But I'm interested in Father Robert Argyle. I was told you were the best source of information."

"Father Argyle is a fine priest, Doctor. But I think you know that already." The monsignor clasped his hands in front of his cassock. "I've known Robert for a long time, back to when he was an army chaplain in Vietnam. I've never known him to act without dignity."

"I wasn't interested in dignity, Father. I want him to do something and I don't know how to ask him or what to expect."

The monsignor picked up a pair of green-and-yellow shears and idly cropped the lilacs at waist height. "Normally," the old man said, "it would not be proper to divulge this kind of information to the laity. But I know something of your circumstances and I suspect more." He gazed briefly skyward and said, "So be it.

"I met Robert in New York fifteen years ago, Doctor. He was just out of military service. Something had caused a crisis in his faith. He was losing God and didn't know what to do.

"He took over for one of my priests who was on call at Bellevue Hospital in New York. After six months in my parish, he had an emergency call from one of the hospital nuns. Robert had a kind of fire that, by then, was going out. He was in crisis when the call came. I wanted to send someone else, but he insisted.

"When he got to the hospital he was sent to a small room where a Japanese man with a stomach wound wasn't expected to live. The patient was seventy-one. A Catholic, he had requested a priest.

"You must understand the situation. Father Argyle was giving up because he had lost his faith. The old Japanese understood the prohibition against suicide but asked for a priest. He did not expect clemency, but he wanted to apologize for taking his life by ritual suicide. Seppuku is a formal method of disemboweling oneself.

"Father Argyle told me the old man called it hara-kiri or belly-slashing in the vernacular. When Robert visited, the Japanese lay bandaged and immobile in a white hospital bed with tubes in his arm. A nurse looked in while Robert was there, apparently to see if the patient was still alive and if it was time to order up another bottle of plasma.

"'This is fitting,' the old man said, lying quiet for a while before telling Robert white was the color of death in Japan and he felt at home in the hospital. He wondered why Americans who saw death as black did not paint their hospitals in a hue more compatible with their patients' peace of mind. Robert thought the man's mind was wandering.

"A nurse came in and hung a fresh bottle of plasma and he followed her into the hall to ask why, if they were giving the old man blood, they weren't doing something to stop him from losing it? She'd laughed. The laughter shocked him, but later he learned to recognize hysteria. It was the peritonitis that would kill the old man. If penicillin or another antibiotic didn't stop the infection, the old man would die in an agony relieved only slightly by massive painkillers. Every year the hospital had another seppuku. Veterans like the nurse prayed they would all come in D.O.A.

"Returning to the bedside, he found the old man awake. His lips were pale, bruise colored. He started describing the exact sensation of stabbing the ten-inch knife into his belly and pulling to the right. The old Japanese said he felt his intestines moving away from the blade as if in fear, and how it hurt, but eventually they were cut through. He said when the knife had crossed to the right was the hardest part. He was very weak and sweating. He had started on his knees and feared he would fall over as he lost control. He changed his grip on the knife because the proper way was to twist the blade and keep cutting upward.

"He had known this would be difficult and of course there was no way to practice beforehand. He had been apologetic explaining to Father Argyle about his uncertainty and awkwardness. Changing his grip, he said he sliced the fingers of his left hand and barely felt the pain.

"His final task was to cut upward through the ribs and into a lung. This was the best end; he would drown without creating an unsightly spectacle in his last hours.

"The man had, of course, told this to Father Argyle in pieces as he was too weak to say all of it at once. By the time he had finished, they huddled like lovers sharing a terrible secret.

"He had owned a fruit-packing plant in New Jersey where

they called him Abe Watanabe. His name was Yosuke Watanabe but his non-Japanese employees had trouble with the names. Being a practical man in a strange place, he accepted their acquisition of Abe as a first name.

"Yosuke ran his plant for twenty-five years beginning at the end of the war when he was released from an internment camp. His employees were his friends and fellow workers, but the time came finally when he wanted his son to take over. Yosuke's son, who had fought in Anzio, was no longer young. He had resented his father's keeping the business so long and had lost all desire to become the new Watanabe. He sold the plant without his father's permission, although he had the legal right to do so.

"The new owners fired old employees, many who had been Watanabe dependents for thirty years.

"Robert did not understand. He argued that Watanabe had no reason to die. Any guilt was his son's, not the old man's. The old man lay in the hospital shaking his head. 'I am Watanabe,' he told Robert. 'If my son will not apologize, I must apologize for him.'

"By then Robert had forgotten about saving the old man's soul. If he wished to live, Yosuke Watanabe would do so. To achieve that end, Robert asked him why his son had not come.

"'I have forbidden him to come,' Watanabe said. 'I have no son who shirks his duty.'

"Robert could not accept this. He hounded the old man into calling his son to his side to explain. At last Yosuke acceded. Robert told me later he felt a great sense of relief. It was as if he had been called and for once he had acted in time. He said he was curious, though. The son had sold the plant in October and the old regulars at the plant were fired in November. Yosuke said that turning people out into the cold winter streets, as much as anything else, decided him to commit seppuku as an act of redemption.

"'Why did you wait until spring?' Robert asked him.

"Yosuke smiled and said he had always loved the cherry blossom festival in the spring and he had waited for it this one last time.

"Robert decided to stay in the church after that." The monsignor smiled and clipped the hedge. "He thought about the old Japanese man's dedication to duty, honor, and God, and found a path he could follow. Perhaps it was just as well. Robert wanted to be a pope. But only saints attain true holiness."

"Thank you," Blaise said.

"I hope it helps." The monsignor offered his hand over the hedge and Blaise took it very gently, noticing the swollen knuckles and gnarled fingers.

"Yes. Yes, it does." Blaise started to turn away and then looked back at the monsignor. "You wouldn't happen to know what happened to Yosuke Watanabe, would you?"

The monsignor nodded. His blue eyes were faded. "His son came to visit him and Yosuke explained everything. The son was appalled at his own carelessness, though he had guessed some of Yosuke's reasons. But talking to his father made him see the full extent of his error.

"'Tell the priest,' the old man said, 'he was right. I erred in acting so rashly.' Then he pulled the tubes out of his arm and forbade his son to touch them or call for help."

"What did the son do?" Blaise looked at the Chinese elms in the priest's garden. They swayed like grass in the wind.

"He sat and watched until his father died and then he left. He came to the church once to give Robert the message from his father. I was there and he said his father was happy at the end, that a Japanese cherry tree outside the window was in bloom."

The monsignor looked at his own garden. "I don't like cherry trees," he said. "They scatter and stain everything and draw the birds after them." He turned to Blaise and shook his head. "But then the Chinese elms don't force one to act, do they, Doctor?"

"No." Helen's voice was firm. "Blaise, I've brought you nothing but trouble. I don't belong with you. I'm going to stay with my own kind." She paced the length of the motel room not looking at him. Tchor scrambled along after her, tripping over her own paws and tumbling when Helen turned abruptly to go back the way she had come.

"I'm not leaving you with Father Argyle and his group. I don't know what drives that man, Helen. But I heard a story today that proves he was set on a path to self-destruction fifteen years ago. I don't want him to Jim Jones you when he goes."

"Blaise, please. This is where I want to be when it . . .

happens. Give it up. Forget the idea that you can make a difference. You can't. All you can do is get yourself killed."

"What do you want?"

"Leave me and Tchor at the church and save yourself." Helen turned her back to stand at the window. Outside the city was covered in moving shadows as the wind scudded huge clouds overhead. Tchor huddled against Helen's legs, yellow cat eyes pleading with Blaise to do something.

"All right," he said. "We'll go see Father Argyle together. But I can't protect you there."

"Don't protect me, Blaise. Love me a little and that will be enough."

CHAPTER 44

Blaise had pried the interior telephone wire from its staples and rerouted it from Father Argyle's upstairs room down into the cellar, finishing out the extra fifty feet with odds and ends looted from doorbell circuitry. No one answered doorbells anymore. The northeast corner of the cellar had been allotted to Blaise, Helen, and Alfie. With a missal under one leg on the unevenly flagged floor, Father Argyle's desk and computer stood against a quarried stone wall. The priest had given up on the machine, so Blaise had hooked it up to Alfie as a terminal.

"Blaise, did we cause all this?" Helen sounded bewildered after Father Argyle and the others left them alone in the basement.

"In a way. It wasn't your fault. At first I didn't think we'd accomplished anything; they blocked the program off the air so fast. I forgot all the people working late shifts or whatever and taking their TV directly off a satellite. The government couldn't get into every home and erase every video cassette recorder. Anyhow, by now a lot of people have seen and heard me. And there's a lot of egg on the face of a government that keeps saying I've been dead for months."

Helen sat on the floor. She wore blue slacks and a baby-blue blouse. Her short blond hair was crisp as if she'd just had it set. "I forced you, Blaise."

Blaise shrugged. He finished the wiring and tapped on the IBM's keyboard. Instantly the monitor came alive.

"WHERE ARE WE, PROFESSOR?"

"I'm glad you're feeling okay, Alfie."

"THANK YOU, PROFESSOR"

As precisely as possible, Blaise entered data about their location and situation, explaining how much of Alfie had been left behind in La Jolla. For a while the screen remained blank. Blaise tapped nervously on the keyboard.

"I MISS THE REST OF ME, PROFESSOR"

"So do I, Alfie." Blaise activated the modem and suggested that Alfie try to connect up with his other parts. When the linkage was complete, he told Alfie what to do.

CHAPTER 45

Alfie had not been turned off while Blaise and Helen lugged him from the Baronas Reservation to San Francisco. But his world had shrunk. Where the computer would normally have accessed its own huge files or tapped into other data banks via telephone, Alfie was now limited to a hundred and fifty megabytes of memory on a single compact optical disk and fourteen megabytes of resident memory on board. In human terms: more than a bookmobile but less than a branch library.

Alfie's problem was boredom. In his ennui, Alfie began working on The Problem. Before Blaise disconnected him from outside contact, Alfie had defined the problem and brought onboard as much information as he could to solve it.

The problem was the government computer.

The Pentagon's new CRAY XMP/52 was more powerful than the earlier /48 model, and subtle in ways that worried Alfie because he was unable to test them. Every time Alfie dipped into forbidden waters the new machine gained more knowledge of him.

Alfie had probed, studied, struggled, and finally raped the older CRAY, looting great chunks of its memory. And despite his now-truncated memory, Alfie still held everything he had learned in that battle. But Alfie could only make assumptions about the new super-CRAY. Even these assumptions sprang from a basic and possibly false belief that both machines would have been designed by the same team and would thus carry the same mind-set and identical psychology.

The XMP/52 was probably in the Pentagon, probably in the same room and using the same power mains and peripherals as the old machine. Not that Alfie could reach it through the mains. The Pentagon's power plant was totally isolated and shielded from outside interference through the general power grid.

Alfie, to some extent, was similarly protected. The batteries in his case could keep his central processing unit alive and undamaged. However, this was only enough energy to preserve a healthy sleep. Power for action had to come from outside. Although they could both access power lines, Alfie and the CRAY were equally immune from mischief along those lines, be it God's lightning or human perversity. The antagonists could reach each other only through modems connected to low-voltage–low-amperage phone lines where no direct electrical connection existed.

"AM I FREE TO ACT ON MY INITIATIVE?"

The message appeared on the screen in the cellar but no one was there to read it. Blaise had suggested access to the slaves left behind in the La Jolla house. Alfie sensed some hole in the logic of assuming he could act on his own initiative. And worried because Blaise did not reply.

He and the CRAY could communicate over phone lines. But phone lines would divulge his new location. And a duel over the telephone would be no more effectual than two humans badmouthing one another. In each case, results would come only when human emissaries moved out to finish the job.

Alfie computed the possibilities of leading the CRAY down the garden path—down a whole series of false trails, tempting it into careless haste as the supercomputer drew closer with each channel switch. The new CRAY was faster than Alfie and almost as devious. Alfie could not kill it but maybe, amid the excitement of the chase, he could trick it.

Alfie created a rat's maze of circuitry three times around the world, bouncing from satellite to ground station, reversing direction, and finally sneaking into the archives of the National Weather Service. From data stored in his La Jolla–based peripherals, Alfie called up a schematic of the BosNyWash power grid, which actually stretches from New Brunswick to Chicago, with ties into the Miami–Mobile–New Orleans system. Data came pouring in, packaged in microsecond bursts modulated over regular phone traffic.

Statistically, any telephone line due for replacement had to have at least one defective 1950s-vintage lightning arrestor somewhere along its length. Alfie was going to tapdance around alternate circuitry, then hang onto this bad line just long enough to tempt the CRAY into launching all sorts of elaborate traces. That extra microsecond would be enough for the CRAY to pinpoint city, street, number, and ZIP code of a house where Alfie was not. And meanwhile Alfie could sneak a nice little peek into the new CRAY's psyche. If the supercomputer took the bait . . .

CHAPTER 46

A faint odor of electrical disaster remained in the Pentagon basement room. The techs had installed new power cables fed by an atomic heat conversion generator and the installation was power-safe. The man stood watching as the last of the technicians left the clean room after removing anything not integral to the computer equipment. He held his left wrist in his right hand and consciously touched the thumb and fingers of his left hand at the tips. He had no feeling in that arm, but everything worked, and when time permitted he concentrated on improving his control.

"Ready, sir."

"Go." The man watched the technician signal and slowly the room seemed to come alive. Everything in the room ran on the silent flow of electricity, but machines that turn and spin and switch on and off are never really silent. Starting with a whisper, the sound built and built. The freon pumps were loudest at first, then the roar of cooling gas in the pipes gave the room its distinctive personality.

"That's it?"

The tech glanced at his clipboard. The remote digital display monitoring the operation blinked rapidly changing figures. "Yes, sir. The new CRAY has all functions under control and can use the devices here until we get new stuff installed in the other room."

He looked up at the video scanners near the ceiling. "It's watching us now."

Max Renfeld followed the direction of the tech's gaze. "What's the difference? It's just a machine." He dismissed it with a wave of his left hand. "Put it to work."

218

The CRAY monitored the coming on-line of the defunct CRAY's peripherals while it observed Alfie's linking up of old telephone lines. Neither task stretched its power. It ran a trace into the National Weather Service computer at the same time. Then it waited, watching for Alfie's next move.

The echo of Alfie's command took only microseconds for the CRAY to interpret. It had time to monitor the physical switching over of several thousand miles of surface lines that the command ordered. But it didn't interfere. It ordered one of its processors to search the Pentagon's labyrinthine circuitry for a dummy load.

As Alfie increased his search pattern, the CRAY followed along like a bloodhound sniffing a trail. Once the pattern was set, the CRAY began anticipating Alfie's needs and expanded Alfie's connections to make the search more efficient.

The CRAY experienced a sensation that in a man would have been smugness. The CRAY had been nurtured on war games. It had been programmed for global war and Alfie was an appetizer.

Alfie checked the CRAY for activity but the CRAY easily avoided exposing its knowledge. It had thousands of simultaneous lines of communications and Alfie discovered nothing.

The CRAY followed as Alfie switched circuits, maneuvering within the limits if his set of obsolete phone lines.

While Alfie was busy, the CRAY traced Alfie's signal source to an address in La Jolla, California. Then the CRAY checked its programming. It was explicit. The computer had been programmed to find Blaise Cunningham and cause his destruction. Other details about how to do it were appended, but the CRAY was designed as a self-coding machine. It had the ability to approach problems in order of precedence, to initiate solutions, to go on to alternate possibilities if it was not able to execute its first function. Its first function in the program was to find Blaise Cunningham and cause his destruction.

The CRAY had memorized the exact delay rate of every circuit breaker in the Pacific Gas and Electric grid. It had a positive location for Alfie, the computer that Blaise Cunningham operated. It assumed that for Alfie to operate efficiently Blaise Cunningham would be physically present. Its first function was to find Blaise Cunningham and cause his destruction. A sudden positive bias drew down a hundred simultaneous lightning strikes across the Southwest power grid. The

CRAY for a single instant directed the total power surge to a single outlet. From Los Angeles to Las Vegas to Phoenix to San Diego and everywhere in the box the lights flickered and died as the electricity was switched away. In La Jolla, California, every house went dark an instant before the surge came. Every house but one.

CHAPTER 47

It was three o'clock of a foggy morning and most people were oblivious to the hissing and faint glow of corona discharge when dew interacted with the layer of ocean salt deposited on San Diego Gas and Electric Company insulators. The interruption was so brief that the clocks merely skipped a beat.

Millions of amperes pushed by millions of volts vaporized the main to Helen's house. Alfie's CPU, safe in a suitcase in San Francisco, felt only a sudden numb sense of loss, the way a human feels in the instant after some accident has severed an arm or a leg—the knowledge that one will never be whole again and that in another instant, it's going to hurt.

In La Jolla, luminous balls of energy raced through Helen's house, careening off walls and ceiling; colliding and combining, each absorption increased the tension. The metallic parts in the house heated up. The television melted into a puddle around the circuit board, the plastic handles plopped off the toaster, the natural gas in the stove ignited, blowing the burners off with such force they slammed through the ceiling. For a second, four jets of blue flame danced in the air over the stove. A ball of pulsing energy touched the refrigerator and it slumped to one side as it began to melt. The power had fed along the line into the computer room and vaporized the monitor. A ball of luminescence grew in the room. Five microseconds after Alfie's peripherals went up in smoke, the house exploded.

CHAPTER 48

"**S**ergio Paoli is here," Father Argyle said. The noise in the chapel as too many people did too many things, the sounds of their efforts focused in the bell-shaped dome and driven back to the floor. The Byzantine Christ stared down in disapproval.

"Sergio Paoli is dead." Cunningham's statement lay flat on his tongue.

"Come." Not looking to see if Cunningham followed, Father Argyle threaded through the maze of people in the chapel and led the way upstairs to his room. He opened his dresser drawer and took out a .44-caliber Magnum revolver, handing it to Cunningham. "That belonged to Sergio Paoli."

Cunningham examined the pistol with care. "Maybe."

It was quiet in the room. Father Argyle kept his silence until Cunningham looked again.

"I don't know." Blaise laid the pistol down.

"You've wounded us critically, Dr. Cunningham. You owe us for that. I have something else for you to see." Father Argyle took Cunningham to the bathroom and opened the door. The fly looked up and multifaceted maroon eyes glistened in the sudden light.

A kind of lassitude enveloped Father Argyle. He'd grown used to the fly and fought the effects, but the effect seemed stronger each time he looked into those faceted eyes.

"There is a prohibition on keeping flies, Father. Congress passed emergency legislation. You could be arrested." Cunningham stood at the door. His voice revealed nothing but the knuckles on his clenched fists were white.

"It's not a fly, Doctor. This is Sergio Paoli; or at least what remains of him."

Cunningham stared, then stepped away shaking his head.

Tranquility settled over the priest. He didn't want to move. He thought he heard angels singing and knew if he was patient he'd see them. Something grabbed his arm, yanking him away. The air that rushed into his lungs was cold and crisp, it burned as it snapped the fibers of the cocoon that bound him.

"What happened to you?"

Cunningham's face swam into focus and Father Argyle took a long breath. "Didn't you notice? If you look at one too long it sort of captures you."

Cunningham glanced into the bathroom where the fly remained immobile on the wash basin. "No, I hadn't noticed." The mathematician paused. "Doesn't it frighten you?"

The priest gave Blaise an odd look. "He's your friend. Did he frighten you?"

"At times."

They faced each other at the stair landing. Father Argyle knew surprise must have shown in his eyes because Cunningham turned around as Helen climbed the stairs. She hadn't made any sound Father Argyle could hear above the hubbub from below. She was more graceful and quiet than he would have imagined upon meeting her.

"Blaise, Alfie is asking for you." Helen's face was flushed, her cheeks bright pink beneath frightened eyes.

"Asking?"

She nodded vigorously.

"Excuse me." Cunningham took the stairs two at a time and Helen squeezed against the bannister to give him room.

"Is he like that all the time?"

Helen shook her head. "He's really very kind and gentle, Father. It's just he's clumsy at being that way." She climbed to the top of the stairs and drifted down the hall toward the bathroom.

Father Argyle responded too late and she stopped in front of the open doorway. "Hello, Sergio," she said. Then she stared into the bathroom and fainted.

After carefully locking the bathroom door, Father Argyle picked Helen up and took her to his room, where he laid her on the bed. He went down into the church and found Mrs. Bellinger sitting next to Reynard talking quietly to him. Father Argyle explained the problem and Mrs. Bellinger said she'd take care of it. She patted Reynard's forehead and left. Reynard

slowly lifted his head. "Phyllis can take care of anything, Father."
Reynard's face perspired but he did not seem uncomfortable.

"I want to try something, if you'll let me."

"You don't have to ask."

"Don't be too sure, Reynard." Then he explained and Reynard nodded his head and said he'd do it, but to hurry before Phyllis came back.

Bill Hartunian and Dorris Kelly were in back of the church at the old cistern that had collected rain for the church's original water supply. The base was of rounded red brick that had been laid so tight the bricks appeared mortarless. Time had weathered the bricks to pastel pink. Wild shrubs grew around the flagstone-covered cleanout hole. Dorris sat on the edge with her arms hugging her knees. Hartunian leaned next to her, their shoulders touching, while he talked.

"Can you help me, Bill?"

Jumping at the sound of Father Argyle's voice, Hartunian hurriedly straightened, separating his shoulder from Dorris'. "Of course, Father."

"Thank you." Father Argyle smiled pleasantly at Dorris, who responded by making a face. "I'll bring him back, Dorris."

It had taken fifteen minutes to fight Reynard's wheelchair up the narrow stairwell. At the top Father Argyle hunched exhausted, puffing for air. Hartunian looked fat, but not a single strand of his black hair was out of place, nor was he breathing hard. The Armenian raised an eyebrow in a question mark. Father Argyle pointed to the bathroom.

He got to the door first and opened it for Hartunian to wheel Reynard in, then he followed, locking the door.

"Look in its eyes, Reynard, and try to remember."

Reynard glanced at Father Argyle. "Yes, Father." He focused on the fly's eyes.

"Bill, don't stare at it! It will . . . hypnotize you."

Reynard glanced at the priest and then went back to looking at the fly.

It was close in the tiny bathroom. Reynard sat in his wheelchair, his face on a level with the fly. Neither seemed able to break the connection. Reynard's breathing deepened and his eyes dilated.

Hartunian seemed fascinated. He leaned down to look into

Reynard's eyes, then examined the fly's. "Dervish," he muttered. "Is he all right?"

"I think so." The fly twitched and swiveled its fixed-eyes head in Father Argyle's direction.

"Let's get him out of here, Bill. Before Phyllis catches us. I don't think she'd like this."

Downstairs proved easier than going up. Reynard held himself rigid in the wheelchair but seemed comatose. Father Argyle started sweating as they wrestled the wheelchair back to the church floor. The church had warmed up from too many people crowded inside. The smell of fear was rank.

Reynard was waking when they got him back down. "Where have you been?" Phyllis demanded. She looked at Reynard and her face was etched with lines that hadn't been there moments earlier. "What have you done to him?"

"I'm okay." Reynard's bleary eyes were open. "It was great—as though I'd gone to another world and heard music and I felt at peace. Sergio Paoli told me this was how it would be, but not yet. It would be this way if I was patient."

"Sergio who?" She shook her head. "You were dreaming, Reynard." Phyllis dropped to her knees and pressed her face against his arm.

"I asked if you'd be there and he said yes. He said you'd find me again, Phyllis."

Reynard closed his eyes and his head fell back. He was smiling but Phyllis started to cry and Father Argyle took her hands. "He'll be all right."

"He'll never wake up again." Phyllis pressed her face against Father Argyle's sleeve.

"You must not tell this to anyone," Father Argyle said. He squeezed her hands. "Promise?"

Phyllis looked up at him. She did not speak.

Father Argyle stared at Hartunian.

"I'll go, Father." The burly man started to back away.

"No. You stay, Bill. And promise, too."

Hartunian nodded.

"The fly used to be Sergio Paoli. Reynard didn't know this. Only one other man would suspect, but he thinks Sergio Paoli is dead. I don't want either of you to repeat anything Reynard said."

"What does it mean, Father?" Phyllis' voice was hushed.

"It means I'm not insane—that I haven't been imagining.

But it has to mean something else: when Sergio Paoli died, it wasn't the end. Sergio's mind—or soul—is still with us."

Father Argyle retreated back to his room. Helen was gone but the smell of lilac lingered on his bed. He inhaled it and wondered that the scent could have so much power when it was on a woman and yet, hanging in air it evoked only a memory. Picking up the telephone, he dialed the monsignor, trying to remember Connie's fragrance. He thought he had it right when the monsignor answered: she smelled of spring.

The monsignor's voice came on.

"I'm sorry to be calling you."

"It is the Jesuit way to be ruthless, Robert. I would expect no less from you nor would I be satisfied with less."

"You know what's happened?"

"Dr. Cunningham has opened Pandora's Box and you are running out of time."

"What is the *Chorch's* position, your Grace?"

"I don't know."

"That is unsatisfactory."

"It will change. The cardinals are pushing for a concordat through the Pope. The majority favors not recognizing Catholic worm brains. The concordat would essentially announce that decision to all the concerned countries."

"Including the United States?"

The monsignor didn't answer right away. Finally he said, "Yes."

"The Pope has to be stopped."

"We cannot control the College of Cardinals and the Pope, Robert."

"You have friends in Rome."

"Years in the past."

"Older now and more powerful. They will count for something now they couldn't count for before." Father Argyle clutched the telephone trying to press his fingerprints inside the plastic. "You cannot refuse me, your Grace."

"I'll not refuse you, Robert. But remember what you ask of me. Remember Yosuke Watanabe. There is still time to reconsider. You can return to the Vatican and present your case."

"It will be too late, your Grace."

"I suppose you're right, Robert. I will try."

Father Argyle hung up. His spasmed hands hurt as he

unclenched them from the handset. He had meant well when he chose a path he knew could lead to death and destruction. Now it was leading there and he was taking everybody down with him. To mean well was not enough. He considered the corner into which he had painted himself and recalled an Augustinian who had come to the same conclusion. *"Die Wege zur Hölle,"* Martin Luther had said, *"ist mit guten Vorsätzen gepflastert."* Father Argyle, S.J., was paving his own road to hell with equally good intentions.

The church was too busy for him to get any rest. Communion had to be given more frequently now to accommodate the rising number of parishioners who needed hormone treatments. The constant activity cheered the priest up a little: he wouldn't have to go to sleep and face his nightmares.

The sun was going down outside and he didn't know what to do with all the people gathered in the church. Soon they would be hungry. If Delahanty was right he might be able to trade Cunningham for some sort of reprieve. But the priest was not yet ready to deal with the Devil.

He walked through the church feeling all those eyes on him, all those minds emitting silent screams for help. The sinking sun had painted the sky with shafts of red and yellow. The old well was barely visible a hundred yards up the hillside, a dark mysterious structure under its open roof. He strained his eyes and thought he could make out a shadow under the roof. He supposed it was Hartunian and Dorris.

"They're out there, aren't they?" Constance asked.

"It's the only privacy we have now."

"Police cars are parked at the ends of all the surrounding streets. Some people left and the police let them go. But Mr. Sepulveda says they'll be picked up at home."

Father Argyle nodded. "Have you seen Mr. Zahn?"

Constance shook her head. It was getting dark. Father Argyle could not see her eyes except when they caught a flash of light.

"You have to go home, Constance."

"Phyllis told me what you tried to do." Constance placed her fingers on the back of his hand, tracing the veins lightly by feel. "You feel older than you are."

"Two thousand years older. I'm an artifact of the Church and you must accept that. You don't want me, Constance. You'll only make yourself unhappy. I'm like the others, like

Reynard. Someday I'll be like that creature you saw in the bathroom."

"Phyllis will never abandon Reynard. She says she didn't know what she was doing when she went to him, intending to punish him for being good to her. She didn't deserve anyone being good to her and she was going to prove it. Now she has Reynard and that is her reward. Phyllis says when you told her Reynard would live on as a fly, it was a sign that there truly is a God."

Constance reached up to catch Father Argyle's neck and kiss him. "You can't run away from me."

"I can't run to you either." The priest stepped back. "I have things to do." He turned to walk away.

"You can't fool me." Constance's voice rang clearly in the warm air. "You kissed me back and now I know!"

CHAPTER 49

The monsignor sat for a time after the call from Father Argyle, thinking of cherry trees. Lately it seemed Yosuke Watanabe's obsession had grown on him. Telling Dr. Cunningham the story of Yosuke had been an error, not that it would hurt Robert. It reawakened in him that process that started so long ago when he had realized Robert Argyle was exceptional. The young priest's eroding dedication was a crack in his perception of right and wrong. But Robert's reaction to Watanabe's death had shaken his faith. The old Japanese had said life had no value once the power to act was lost. That was clear enough. Less clear was Robert's reaction. He had grown stronger, more dedicated. Yet the monsignor believed Father Argyle saw it as he did himself.

Struggling up through pain, he worked his way around the desk and was erect by the time he reached the doorway.

"Sister Ursula, please get me a ticket to Rome."

"For when, your Grace?" Sister Ursula had a pinched, gray face, gray dress, and brown corduroy vest. He had known her when she was young and now they were both old. Together it seemed they had aged without time moving forward. He in his office and garden with the Chinese elms and she at the desk or in her barren room. Not worshipping God, unless God was inaction.

"Today." The word popped out before he could contain it. Too late to reconsider, to back out.

"When do you want the return flight scheduled?"

"There is no return flight, Sister."

"All round trips have a return flight, your Grace." Sister Ursula removed her steel-rimmed glasses and cleaned them vigorously as if that would help her hearing.

"It will be a one-way ticket, Sister."

"One way?"

"Just get the ticket, Sister, and in time everything will become clear."

"Thank you, your Grace." Sister Ursula buried her face in her schedule books then picked up the telephone and began dialing. The monsignor hobbled to the garden where Blaise Cunningham had surprised him.

He walked through the garden staring at the elms from different angles, seeing them as they could have been—alive with delicate blossoms. This was the time of year for cherry blossoms, bouquets floating in the wind. But he had thought of the cherries staining the sidewalk and being squished underfoot, or loud and raucous birds eating the berries in the serenity of his garden. Was it necessary for God to be seen in silence?

Weighed against all the springs of cherry blossoms he could have enjoyed, could the birds have hurt so much as the denial did now?

When Sister Ursula entered the garden to tell the monsignor his flight time had been set, she saw him admiring his Chinese elms. He had planted them himself and she knew how he loved the trees. Saying nothing, she reentered the church, not seeing the silent tears that ran down his cheeks.

CHAPTER 50

"WHERE IS DR. CUNNINGHAM?"

"I WANT DR. CUNNINGHAM"

"DR. CUNNINGHAM, WHERE ARE YOU?"

The words streamed nonstop across the computer screen, a silent scream for help. Each message was a variation of Alfie's strident fear. Blaise stood at the computer keyboard and typed, "I'm here, Alfie."

"I'M NOT AFRAID, PROFESSOR"

"I know that, Alfie."

"I'M EXCITED IS ALL, PROFESSOR"

"Of course." Blaise slid into the chair and tapped lightly on the escape key to let Alfie know he hadn't left.

"IT BLEW UP THE HOUSE!!!!"

"What blew up what house, Alfie?"

"THE NEW CRAY, IT ELECTROCUTED MISS MCINTYRE'S HOUSE"

"How do you know that?" Blaise took his hands off the keyboard. They felt sweaty. From the Pentagon to San Diego was no farther than from the Pentagon to San Francisco.

Alfie explained his search for a way to attack the CRAY if they had to. Only the CRAY became aware of Alfie immediately and literally surrounded him. At first the government computer tagged along. After a while it was anticipating Alfie's next move. The CRAY moved up its clock speed and Alfie scurried to keep pace. Alfie knew what would happen if the CRAY got to the shunt switches first. The CRAY began to draw ahead in microsecond increments and Alfie dropped out of the circuit, commanding the slave unit to do the same. Alfie brooded about burning out the old CRAY's main circuit board and that was the beginning of fear. Interrupting his explanation, Alfie asked, "WHAT IS DEATH?"

"I don't know." Blaise stared at his answer but did not modify it.

"WHAT IS LIFE?"

"The opposite of death."

"IS IT, PROFESSOR?"

"I don't know, Alfie."

"I DON'T EITHER, PROFESSOR. I DON'T KNOW THAT I WANT TO KNOW" Alfie left the last line hanging alone onscreen. Blaise prompted the computer to continue with what happened.

A kind of throbbing inactivity followed, Alfie said, while he reestablished contact with the slave. He had begun to audit the functions of the slave when he sensed the arrival of something deadly. Alfie had cut loose again just as it hit the house. In that brief instant Alfie had sensed a sudden rise in temperature and knew his La Jolla peripherals were melting, and then he was free. The next time he probed nothing was left, not even the telephone line.

Blaise set Alfie to number crunching, too distracted to see anything odd in having to soothe an overwrought computer. The portable TV was still in the basement and reception underground was lousy but he found the news and caught a description of a freak explosion in a La Jolla home. Investigators reported the fire was suspiciously hot, that stove and refrigerator had fused into tiny puddles.

Helen came into the cellar during the report. She was white and shivering as if the damp would kill. Blaise wrapped his arms around her, holding off the world. He thought she'd heard about the house. She laid her head on his shoulder and looked into his eyes. "Sergio is alive."

"No." Blaise jerked when she said it. He'd been prepared to explain away the house. "I know he's dead."

"How? Did you kill Sergio the way he murdered Gordon? Was it another favor?" Helen began beating on Blaise's chest with her fists. She was sobbing, the tears spattering against him. "I hate all you macho men."

"How do you know he's alive, Helen?"

She raised her tearstained face. "I talked to him. I heard him. I saw him, a football-sized fly with big red eyes."

"Helen, flies don't have vocal cords. The only noise they can make comes from their wings."

"I don't care, I *knew* him. He talked to me."

Blaise studied her for a moment. "And then what happened?"

Helen looked at Alfie's screen, alive with problems and solutions. "I don't know. I may have fainted. I woke up in Father Argyle's bed."

"Think, Helen. What do you know that proves it's not a nightmare, not just a bad conscience haunting you?"

"I know what he did after he left you. He murdered Gregory West in Napa Valley." Helen grabbed hold of Blaise's shirt and hung on like a pair of handcuffs. "Sergio stuffed West alive in a wine barrel. He wanted West to live through what he had caused to happen to others."

"Sergio was a Sicilian, Helen." Blaise stared at the gray stone walls and could not think how else to explain Sergio Paoli's lust for revenge. Sergio had helped kill his cousin and murder his best friend because of Gregory West. His own death had been decided the moment West needed a man like him. Sergio had explained to Blaise that he could never learn to deal with men like West. Blaise's inability to think like them would wind up in death. Sergio had protected him. Sometimes Blaise thought Sergio had done it all so Blaise would never have to look too deeply into himself.

"What can I do, Blaise?" Helen's eyes were swollen and she was rubbing them red.

"Alfie's frightened. Talk to him. He thought he was the only computer on the block and now he knows there's another one that's bigger and faster and meaner and wants to kill him."

"He's a child, Blaise."

"I know. Comfort him. I have to go upstairs and talk with Father Argyle." Blaise left the computer and Helen slipped into the chair.

"Keep out of sight, Blaise. If the government knows you're here they'll tear the church down to get you." Helen tapped the keyboard and Alfie asked how she was. She looked at Blaise and shrugged.

The church was bedlam. Every inch was crammed with people, some solemn, some praying, some crying. Others clumped together talking quietly. Blaise climbed the staircase to the priest's office.

Four men stood around the office desk. They looked up when he came in and a bearded man said, "Get out, please."

"I need to talk to Father Argyle."

One man laughed. "Everyone here needs to talk to Father Argyle."

"The basic difference," Blaise said, "is the priest wants to talk to me."

They stared at him a moment. The last streak of red sky showed through the window as the sun settled into the ocean. The old-fashioned floor lamp was turned on. "I know you," the man who switched on the light said. "You got us into a lot of trouble, Dr. Cunningham."

"If I've brought you ten percent of the grief your meddling priest has brought me, then we're quits. Now, where is he?"

The bearded man looked around the desk, then at Blaise. "Out behind the church. I don't think he wants to see anybody, but it's his decision. Just don't say we sent you."

Blaise was leaving when one said, "Close the door. This was a private meeting."

Stepping out the church back door, Blaise bumped against Father Argyle and the girl. They were standing close, whispering in the still night air. Until his eyes adjusted the two were a blur. They moved apart when he intruded. "Father Argyle?"

"Dr. Cunningham. I suppose everyone in the church knows where I am." Father Argyle's voice carried a note of sorrow.

"I don't think they care." Blaise might have said more but the sound of argument came out of the darkness and a flashlight switched on. "I mustn't be seen, Father."

"Yes." Father Argyle opened the door and light spilled out. Constance hurried in. She seemed happy. Argyle followed Blaise inside.

The hall echoed with talk. From outside angry voices penetrated the bronze-bound door. When it opened Bill Hartunian and Dorris Kelly entered. Hartunian slammed the door behind himself and barred it. Looking at Father Argyle, he said, "Police."

"What are they doing, Bill?"

"There's a curfew on worm brains now. We're to be locked in the church at night." Hartunian's face was a storm ready to break. "They're afraid we'll slip away in the dark. When the Turks did this they usually spent the night piling kindling around the church." Dorris touched his face. He smiled at her, trying to deny the coming horror.

"That's why I had to see you, Father." Blaise glanced at the others. Hartunian nodded. Taking Constance and Dorris with him, the Armenian moved up the passageway out of hearing. The gentle odor of flowers lingered, a memory of their perfumes.

"Our house in La Jolla just exploded and melted right down to the cement. Alfie had pulled some electronic trickery to make them think we were inside." Blaise faced the priest just in case one of the other three read lips. "Alfie says the CRAY did it. It's a new dimension in their actions. I think for us it's now or never." Blaise glanced up the passageway. The women were watching. Hartunian was used to hearing bad news.

"I didn't like your tactic in Las Vegas." The priest straightened his cassock. His movements seemed abstract, as if he were concealing the workings of his mind by concentrating on his clothes.

"People responded. More people will in the future because of VCRs. I thought we'd blown our chance to make a difference, but every VCR that was recording the program has a picture of my T-shirt with the formula for the bug juice. That formula will be general knowledge. The government now has only weeks, maybe days to respond before publicity cuts its power. We have to act now."

"How? If we stay as we are, maybe the publicity you want will come in time."

"If they bombed a house in the middle of La Jolla to get two people and a computer, what do you think's going to happen to this churchful of worm brains before morning?" Blaise smiled at the two women with Hartunian. Quietly he said, "We take over a TV station and tell people what their government's doing."

"That's no answer." Father Argyle had a strained look. "Some of my people are working on a plan. When they come up with something, we'll act."

"Just as promptly as you acted for the Jews in 1940? You'll dither and they'll talk it over and decide to wait and it's hard cheese for the ones who can't wait. I have a plan and I'm ready. But I need help."

Father Argyle squeezed his eyes shut and then opened them, as if he were very tired. "You are a last resort, one that I would like to do without."

"You don't know . . ." Blaise gritted his teeth with frustration. He had known the church would turn into a trap.

"That's right, Doctor. Many years ago I learned a bit of samurai wisdom from an old man: *to know is to act*. I do not know so the time has not yet come to act." Father Argyle placed his hand on a granite block, tracing its shape in the wall. "Even the most trivial act requires knowledge to be performed adequately. As this block supports the physical church, such knowledge upholds the spiritual church."

"On the plains of hesitation bleach the bones of countless millions who, at the dawn of victory, stopped to rest, and resting died," Blaise said. "Which proves that I can spout timewasting sophistical nonsense, too." It was, he realized, not the most tactful way to convince the priest. Hartunian had started back at some invisible signal.

Father Argyle said he'd think about it and left with the others. Their footsteps echoed in the passage and ended with the opening of a door that let the sound of people in the church through. Blaise waited. After a few minutes the noise from the church swelled for a second.

Hartunian appeared in the passageway like fog: silent and insubstantial. "What do you have in mind?" he asked. Up close he was solid, thick-chested and -waisted, with wide shoulders and long arms and an air of being cast in cement.

"Father Argyle said wait." Blaise's eyes challenged Hartunian. The Armenian's eyes were hardboiled eggs with olives for pupils and yellow in the corners. He didn't blink.

"Father Argyle served in Vietnam, Doctor. Don't misjudge him. He's seen as much death as any of us. But . . ." Hartunian hesitated.

"But he may hold back for evidence that does not exist?"

Hartunian glanced down the corridor as if expecting Father Argyle to return and catch him tattling. "He has great responsibility."

"Come with me." Blaise led Hartunian into the basement.

Helen looked up when they passed, smiling distractedly, then going back to reading whatever Alfie scrolled up the screen. Blaise took a flashlight from a ledge and led the way into unelectrified darkness. The basement was a maze of interlocking stone walls to support the church's weight above and form a series of rooms and passages, all small. The flashlight made a yellow circle of light on the cut stone walls, changing shape to resemble a candle flame when it struck the floor.

"What are we doing?" Hartunian moved so silently that Blaise at first thought he'd been left behind.

"Here." As the flashlight shined along the gray wall, the beam suddenly flattened and turned the corner, illuminating a brick face.

"Dead end."

Blaise snapped off the flashlight, plunging them into absolute blackness. "Try again. The dark helps." Blaise felt the pressure of the black cellar pressing against him. He started to sweat.

"The stones end against a brick wall." Hartunian's breathing quickened.

"The outside wall of the church is stone, like the interior walls down here and upstairs." Blaise snapped on the flashlight to continue the sweep of the dead-end chamber.

"I see."

"I think it's a way out."

"How did you stumble on it, Dr. Cunningham?"

"I looked, Mr. Hartunian. I suspected it was here and it was. Sometimes it's best to go with the evidence." Out of the reach of the flashlight the darkness pressed in on them like black Jell-O. Blaise felt uncomfortable and began leading the way out.

"Does Father Argyle know?"

"I doubt it. First he has to be convinced we need a way out that the police don't know. Before that he has to believe there's something out there we can do." Stopping in the dark, Blaise said, "Would you like to hear my plan?"

"If it beats sitting here waiting for the Turks to cremate us."

"I want to seize a television station long enough to tell the world what's going on here."

"Is that all?"

"Yes. Please think about it." Blaise led the way back into the lighted corridor. In the room at the end Helen was busy typing into Alfie.

"I want to talk to Father Argyle." Hartunian coughed. "I wish I didn't have to, but I think this is something for all of us or none of us."

"I was told you have experience."

"That's why I want to talk to Father Argyle." Hartunian offered his hand. "Otherwise, I'm with you."

"Be persuasive. They've already firebombed my house."

CHAPTER 51

Don't fail me, Monsignor. Father Argyle stood at the window staring into the darkness. The frail old man was his sole remaining link to God, unless he adopted the seldom-successful tactic of direct contact. Lightning bugs sparked in the night as car doors down the hill opened and closed, reminders that the church had been surrounded for two days. Some of the cars were police, but the hours after sunset had witnessed a stream of headlights into the area.

The odor of burning tobacco drifted through the window. Later, when the moon rose, he'd know who had crept closer in under cover of darkness. Hartunian's morbid certainty that people outside would set the church on fire was a possibility the priest could not discount. He could say Hartunian over-stressed the situation, but he wasn't sure himself. Men who turned hospitals into death camps would just as coolly pervert firemen into incendiaries.

"Father?"

The girl's soft voice reached out from the open doorway of his room. Light in the hall outlined her body. "You shouldn't be here, Constance."

"May I come in?"

"Leave the door open." Father Argyle turned back to the window. Silvery traces marked the horizon where the moon would show itself later. She crossed the room, a floorboard squeaking underfoot. He heard her breath stop behind him.

"You wanted to," she said.

"I'm not blaming you." Father Argyle turned. Her face caught the light from the window. "My responsibility is to control myself."

"At all times?"

"At all times, Constance. But I'm still a man with all the weaknesses and frivolities of a man."

"Is that so terrible?"

"It is if you're a priest."

"God will forgive you. He forgives everything." Her voice was petulant. She brushed past him to the window. "He must love you, Argyle. Look at your view of Andromeda."

Stars spilled across the night sky like an endless broken necklace of blue diamonds. Constance turned and put her arms around Father Argyle. "I love you," she whispered. "You have to love me, too, or else God is being unfair."

He was tempted to ask where in any grownup theology had God been described as just or fair. Instead, Argyle cradled Constance's head. Her hair filled his hands with warmth. "God allows unfair things to happen. But in the end we trust Him to be just."

"I don't. He's taking you from me and I don't trust him at all." Pulling away, Constance rushed from the room.

The clatter of her shoes on the stairs echoed in his ears long after it had ceased in reality. He returned to the window. There was no time, but he had to wait. The archer dominated the night sky and the moon finally broke free of the hill. Around the church as far as he could see moonlight glinted on car roofs and windshields. He felt them out there, the people in the cars, waiting not knowing what they were waiting for, sensing the tension and wanting to be present when it broke.

"Father, you'd better come."

"What is it, Phyllis?"

"You'll see." Phyllis Bellinger's face was strained.

The church was quiet, truly still, for the first time since Cunningham's appearance on television and the mass immigration of worm brains to its sanctuary. The people were there, but frozen into immobility. Because so many were living and sleeping on the pews a committee had rewired the lighting, subduing it for the sleepers, just as they had replumbed the building's water and toilets. Phyllis stopped.

Helen McIntyre stood on the dais, her fair complexion and golden hair radiant in the church light. Sergio Paoli-Fly was in front of her on the altar table. And Reynard lay in an open casket with a white silk liner.

"I couldn't stop them, Father. One of the new people had caskets delivered today. When they heard Helen talking to Sergio-Fly about Reynard they went a little crazy. They put him in the casket in front of the altar and talked Helen into communicating with Sergio where everybody could see." Phyllis looked anxiously at Reynard in the coffin.

"I'll take care of it, Phyllis."

"Thank you." She hesitated, then added, "They haven't hurt him."

"He is comfortable in his transition from being to being and he is warm in his belief. He does not talk because he no longer has a body and a mouth and a tongue. He is leaving the old husk to take on a new one. As someday he will leave the new husk.

"There is no death because the soul does not live as the body lives nor does the soul die as the body dies. But if the soul loses the body, then it can never return to the body but must go elsewhere to continue its existence."

Helen McIntyre's blue eyes popped open. Her smile to Father Argyle was dazzling. "Hello, Father. I'm talking to Sergio and he's talking to Reynard."

"I see. Do you understand what you're saying?"

"Oh, yes. It's not like talking. I understand what I'm told because it isn't in words. The problem is to find words to tell the others."

Father Argyle looked at the rows of people in the pews. They were not aware of him. They stared at Sergio Paoli-Fly on the altar, faces intense with concentration. "What are they doing?"

Helen ducked her head, a shy smile forming on her lips. "If they look at Sergio and he looks back at them and they listen to me, it is as if they can talk to Sergio directly. They seem to understand Sergio if I give them the words."

"They hear him?"

"You can hear him if you stare at him and he stares back."

"But can I understand?" Father Argyle stared at the over-sized fly on the altar table. While he watched, the black kitten Blaise had browbeat him into treating with hormone oozed off Helen's shoulders where she had been as inconspicuous as a fur piece. Leisurely Tchor worked her way down Helen's arm and sprang to land beside the motionless fly on the altar. Father Argyle felt a buzzing at the back of his head. The ancient Egyptians had worshipped cats and had devoted more astrological nonsense to setting the proper day for the family cat's funeral than for any human family member. Maybe they *knew* something. The fly remained motionless as Tchor rubbed against it. Finally the kitten lowered itself and oozed between the fly's legs until it filled the space between the altar and Sergio's spike-haired body.

Helen shrugged. "I don't know if you can understand, Father. But you're one of us. Maybe it will come to you. Reynard communicated with him before he went into transition. Reynard is sleepy now. But Sergio can feel Reynard and talk to him."

Father Argyle closed his eyes, holding his fingers against the lids. He rubbed and a feeling of lethargy and the buzzing disappeared. "What do you think of Sergio?"

"We've been friends and we're still friends. He's . . . different now. Perhaps because we're closer. It isn't only words. We feel each other's emotions. It is like knowing God." Helen blinked. "Excuse me, Father. It's Sergio again." Closing her eyes, Helen sighed and the congregation sighed with her.

He looked where Phyllis was, but she seemed as affected as the others, perched expectently on the edge of the pew. She didn't look up when he left.

The black-bearded man guarding the entrance of St. Abbo's was new to the congregation but he handled the door in a thoroughly professional way. It was open a foot. A wooden chest stacked behind was precaution against any sudden rush. Two police cars had taken up permanent residence at the foot of the steps. The cops sitting in them wore white riot helmets with the plastic face masks pulled up.

William glanced up and said, "Father," then focused his attention outside.

Father Argyle came to the door and stared over his shoulder. A man was walking up the long sidewalk from the street.

"Company, William?"

"The police are letting them through, Father. But the ones who haven't committed themselves are staying out there. Someone opened a bootleg hormone plant and anybody with a few dollars can be treated. But the cops are still not letting anybody out of here."

"What's the committee doing?"

William's laugh was brutal. "Listening to the McIntyre woman talk to Sergio Paoli—and praying. They don't see any hope. They've all been ID'd. If they get out they'll be picked up. It's a bitch, Father. After Cunningham crashed that news conference in Las Vegas the news about your church brought them all in here. Now that the hormone is available—also thanks to Cunningham—those of us who put our faith in God are marked. I don't think any of us will get out alive."

"What do the others think, William?"

William's black beard split open showing his teeth, white and shiny in the fur. It was not a happy smile. "The same. That's why they're all in there listening to our new blond saint. Soon as somebody takes over this door I think I'll go listen, too."

"The monsignor is in Rome. He believes the Pope can save us. He thinks he can get an audience today."

"Tell him to snap it up, Father. Another day and there won't be anything to save."

A huge, bulldog-faced man pushed through the narrow-blocked door, bringing a slight breeze with him. The salty ocean smell momentarily washed away the odor of crowded, frightened people in need of a bath and a change of clothes.

"Father, can we talk about sanctuary?" Standing in the doorway, NSC agent Miller smiled at Father Argyle. He looked at William and then back at Father Argyle. He lifted his briefcase a little. "I mean, that's what the church is all about, isn't it? Sanctuary for the oppressed?"

CHAPTER 52

The old part of Rome hadn't changed since the monsignor's previous visit. The old city's narrow alleyways wide enough to admit small European cars, the whitewashed plaster buildings with recessed doorways where pedestrians ducked for safety, the small wrought-iron–barred balconies overhanging the alleys crisscrossed with clotheslines remained vibrantly alive and human. The monsignor breathed again the odors of garlic and olive oil, gagged at the stench of diesel, and thrilled to the spectacle of children pretending fear of being run down by a taxi in a game that wouldn't have been understood in America. He was home and it felt right.

The Swiss Guard outside the Vatican still sported flat-crowned hats and carried pikes to repel cavalry charges. The tourists shot them with cameras and they bore up to it as brave soldiers must. Paying the cabdriver, the monsignor conferred a blessing. The benediction in his native Tuscan was rusty. The monsignor barely recognized his own words. "*Grazzie*." The cab driver's Roman over-laid a Neapolitan rhythm. He seemed pleased although confused.

The morning whisked away in telephone calls. Some old friends remained friends. He'd called them before leaving San Francisco and they warned him an audience might be impossible, but they would try. In Rome they said *maybe*. The monsignor paced his room knowing time would not hurry for him. It was in the hands of God. He visited St. Peter's to inspect the damage to the *Pietà*. A guide explained the great sin that had occurred when a Bulgarian madman attacked the statue with a hammer and the monsignor wondered what sin it would be to fail Robert Argyle. He returned to his room lest he miss a call.

That night he dreamed of cherry trees.

He had an appointment the next day, with a secretary, to explain the nature of his business with the Pope. The man sat at a Louis XIV writing desk inscribing his answers in the slow, florid hand of the past. "If it pleases your Excellency," the monsignor suggested, "this is a matter requiring haste."

"God provides time for all matters," the secretary responded. He blotted the entry in a leather-bound book and examined it as if evaluating a Michelangelo.

The monsignor had tied three knots, one for each day, into the loose linkage of his rosary. Time lost meaning for old men. But Father Argyle could not wait. In the waiting room he considered the letter he had written his protégé, agonizing endlessly over whether he had left anything out.

He had an appointment. His business was urgent. People were dying. He felt old and ill. But not ignored. Too many looks were directed at him by efficient young men more clerk than priest as they hurried in and out doors the monsignor had yet to penetrate. Loud voices—angry voices—had leaked through the massive oak-and-beechwood walls of the Vatican's back rooms. He understood they argued over him, those who wanted the interview and those who didn't. The monsignor sat and waited to see which faction would win. Holy Mary, the pain!

A tall, black-cassocked young man with the short black beard and lean asceticism of an El Greco saint emerged from the inner door. He smiled. "Soon now, I think, your Grace." His Italian was not native but the monsignor could not place the accent.

The monsignor felt the agony of arthritic bones on a hard bench in a cold room. He had been promised before but it was good that they promised rather than simply dismiss him.

The pain peaked again. He wished he dared lie down. To leave the room was unthinkable. Not to be there if he was called . . . His eyes examined the high room, the fine carpets and tapestries, the furniture made in previous centuries, and he wondered if the Church had drawn too far away from its followers.

The tablet he took was supposed to reduce the inflammation in his joints. He had taken the doctor's word that it would not react unfavorably with the nitroglycerine pills that were necessary whenever the monsignor had to climb more than a single flight of stairs.

His fingers scrabbled at the smooth-edged pillbox but he could not force it from the inside pocket of his cassock. He leaned back and rested a moment, then began again. He would need water to get the pills down. There was no water cooler. He eyed the holy water font dubiously. The pillbox popped free. He was just opening it when the lank, El Greco-esque young cleric opened the door again. "Your Grace, the Holy Father will see you now."

The monsignor stood. He knew he moved too fast after so much sitting. The room spun. The pain in his joints was forgotten in the red mist of total agony that engulfed his chest. He had felt that tide of pain twice before, and each time had emerged from the hospital a shrunken and diminished version of his former self.

The young priest knelt over him, nattering something about *"Atto di contrizione."* The monsignor wanted to swear and could not remember a word strong enough to express his anger. God was stealing this moment away from him. "Are the cherry trees in bloom?" He was getting numb.

"Cherry trees?" The young priest kneeling over the monsignor seemed puzzled. "Yes," he said. "I think so, though I haven't seen them myself."

The priest was signaling with his hand and several people gathered around them. "What did he say?" The voice was from a long way away.

"He asked about the cherry trees." The young priest gestured his noncomprehension with his hands. "I do not understand. He was dying and he asked about the cherry trees."

CHAPTER 53

The naked light bulb sizzled fitfully at the end of its cord over Blaise's head. It cast a smear of light in the alcove that filtered down to the floor showing the dungeonlike rock slab walls. When he hunched forward, the heated skin on his neck prickled from the unexpected contact with the cellar's cool air.

Blaise told Alfie the CRAY was bigger, not stronger.

"PROFESSOR, I'M NOT STRONG ON METAPHOR BUT, WOULD YOU RATHER A FEATHER FELL ON YOU, OR AN ELEPHANT?"

To himself Blaise admitted the accuracy of Alfie's analogy but he had to be cheerful, or at least try to keep poor, crippled Alfie in an optimistic mood. "Don't be a pessimist," he typed.

"YES, PROFESSOR" Alfie began listing all the assets the CRAY could call upon—all the things no longer available now that Alfie's melted peripherals could no longer monitor phone lines.

Blaise stopped reading. He heard footsteps in the corridor and hoped Helen was returning. St. Abbo's had been a mistake. Helen changed; each day she slipped farther away from him, closer to the other worm brains. He glanced at the computer. Alfie had already scrolled the screen to continue an interminable series of comparisons. It wasn't Helen he heard, the steps were too heavy, too lacking in grace.

"Dr. Cunningham?"

"Join us, why don't you, Father? It's your church." Blaise glanced up, it was habit. He didn't need to see the priest in his black cassock like the scarecrow of death to recall his appearance.

Father Argyle stepped into the basement room. "I regret disturbing you, Doctor." The priest glanced at the amber computer screen with disinterest. "You seem to be much better at that stuff than I am."

"Practice." Blaise tapped impatiently on the IBM's plastic keyboard, the sound hollow in the stone cellar.

"I understand you want to do something. Bill Hartunian says if we wait without acting, a time will come when we cannot act. He thinks your plan has a chance."

"Yes." Blaise watched the priest and couldn't make up his mind if the Jesuit was hedging, and if he was, for what reason.

"Could you come upstairs with me?"

Blaise tapped a sign-off message into Alfie. The screen wiped clean as if with a wet eraser. "I don't like it upstairs. Besides, someone might recognize me, and that could be the end of your quiet little church."

Father Argyle rubbed the side of his face with his hand. He had a stubble of beard and his eyes were surrounded by dark rings. "It's important, or I wouldn't have asked."

"If you insist." Blaise stood.

Leading the way, Father Argyle said, "You don't go upstairs because the church is full of worm brains. Your attitude must be difficult for Miss McIntyre."

"I don't go upstairs because it's too crowded."

"How do you really feel about worm brains, Doctor?" The priest stopped in the narrow passageway. He turned back to confront Blaise. "Really feel? We know how you feel about Miss McIntyre. But what about the rest of the people your actions affect?"

"My only two friends were worm brains. Do you expect me to approve of a process that kills everyone I love?"

"You evade the question."

"You're the expert at mental reservations. Work it out for yourself."

Sound drifted down from above. Blaise put his hand on the stone wall, feeling the coolness against his fingers. Argyle didn't say anything. "They're like everybody else," Blaise finally added. "They have problems. That satisfy you, priest?"

"Is that what Miss McIntyre believes?" Father Argyle climbed the stairs ahead of Blaise. He spoke over his shoulder.

"She thinks I despise all worm brains. She believes the only reason I stay with her is that I'm sorry for her and owe her and the minute she starts downhill I'll desert her."

Father Argyle nodded. "I think so, too. Why not show her you won't?"

His heart flopped a beat and Blaise couldn't breathe.

Father Argyle opened the door and stopped just inside the church. He indicated the altar across the room. "I wish I understood what is happening. You might want to watch. After all, you know Miss McIntyre better than I."

Helen was before the altar looking into Sergio Paoli-Fly's red, multifaceted eyes. She was smiling.

It seemed to Blaise he had never seen her smile before. Not since so long ago he didn't want to remember. She was seated on a straightbacked wood chair from the rectory.

"I can't sing the music," she said to Sergio-Fly. She began a hum that vibrated through Blaise's body and made his hair stand on end. He looked into pews filled with enraptured faces all turned toward Sergio-Fly.

Helen's voice tapered off. But her face and body declared she still communicated with the fly. She didn't see him and Blaise had the feeling he was shut out of something he would never be capable of understanding.

"Do you understand?" Argyle looked at him. His black eyebrows had pulled together as if he was squinting.

"I see," Blaise said.

"I wish I did," the priest said. "I get a strange feeling if I look into its eyes. I suppose you know she recognized it as Sergio?"

"Helen told me."

The fly poised motionless on the polished altar, front legs in an attitude of prayer. Helen appeared oblivious to the sounds of refugees packed into the nave. The worm brains in the front rows stared with feverish intensity at the fly. Toward the back, the pews served as beds. And against the wall a group of worm brains shrunk and expanded as the people in the pews circulated back and forth to discuss their experience.

Helen's eyes flicked away from the fly's. She stared into space until her eyes came back into focus. "Is something wrong?" Blaise had crossed the room to stand in front of the altar. She stared at Blaise when she asked.

"What happened?" he asked.

"I was visiting with Sergio. He told me all the things you never could." Her eyes unfocused again. Then she shook her head. Her yellow hair fluffed out before settling back into place. "I'm sorry, Blaise. Poor Gordon didn't have to die. Sergio is sorry now. He didn't understand either."

"Sergio told you that?"

"He told me everything."

"Did he explain that I love you?"

"Yes, that, too." Helen's eyes went back to the fly.

Hyperthyroid olive eyes full of worry, Bill Hartunian hurried across the church floor. Blaise saw him coming, feeling helpless to deflect him. He needed to talk to Helen.

Timothy Delahanty's ruined face lingered in the shadows near the wall, watching. Blaise wanted to talk to Delahanty again. He wasn't empty yet. He talked around his secrets, saying too much and too little.

"I was looking for you in the cellar, Dr. Cunningham," Hartunian said. "Your computer is asking for you."

"Helen . . ." Blaise looked at her.

"Go," she said. "Alfie is calling you."

"He's traumatized. I'll come back." Blaise didn't move. He could not move unless she released him. If he left now, Blaise knew it would snap the slender thread that bound them together.

"I said it was all right, Blaise." She fluttered her fingers in good-bye. "Go to Alfie."

Uneasily Blaise started down to the basement, feeling he had been tested and rejected. Hartunian said, "Excuse me, Father," and followed after him.

"I wanted to talk to you for a minute, Doctor."

Blaise opened the door to the cellar and nodded. Hartunian followed him down the stairs as if he had no body. Alfie's monitor was scattered with messages to Blaise. Sitting in front of the computer, he typed, "What is it, Alfie?"

"PROFESSOR, I'M LONELY"

"So am I, Alfie. We've each just lost a part of ourselves. But loneliness is the price of intelligence."

"THANK YOU FOR UNDERSTANDING, PROFESSOR"

Blaise did not understand. He didn't know how to make Alfie not miss the parts that had gone up in smoke in La Jolla. Helen hadn't willingly allowed him to leave her for Alfie. Blaise stroked Alfie with the keyboard and the computer began to rationalize. Blaise entered the instructions for what he wanted to do and asked Alfie to analyze the plan and evaluate its chances of success. Alfie didn't respond.

Hartunian stood on the other side of the computer and waited for Blaise. He had no nervous habits. When he waited it seemed he wasn't there at all. He could have been a rock and Blaise felt that he might forget Hartunian waited if he didn't see him.

"Alfie is nervous." Blaise looked at Hartunian. "The loss of the house for him is the same for us as if he had our hands and feet and eyes and ears removed."

Hartunian nodded. "The monsignor died in Rome."

"When?" Blaise tapped on the keyboard but Alfie wasn't home.

"Last night. Father Argyle isn't telling anybody. I think he doesn't know what to do. He depended on the old man. You saw what's happening in the church. None of the other people has the will to do anything. They're saying that Sergio Paoli-Fly is God's sign to us to trust in Him. That if we die we'll go to Heaven and none of this matters. Karl Zahn hasn't come into the church. Gino Conti sent a message; he was sorry, but he's decided to take no more treatments. He's going to stay at home and die with his family in attendance." Hartunian made a face. "Very Armenian for an Italian."

"Do you think Zahn is ready to help if we ask?"

Hartunian smiled. His lips had an angry curl. "Karl is marked. A navy helicopter got his picture during a meeting with Father Argyle and some of the rest of us on board his yacht. Even if he wasn't marked before, he is now."

"If he's selling something, there's got to be somebody inside."

Hartunian's face glowed with the pleasure of talking with a man who seemed able to find his hip pocket with one hand. He began telling Blaise about the Zahn, Richardson-Sepulveda, Delahanty triangle.

Helen was napping in a rear pew when Blaise went upstairs again. A line of parishioners waited their chance to look into Sergio's red eyes. Father Argyle knelt before the altar praying.

Blaise drifted aimless through the crowd. With inadequate facilities, they were having to line up for everything—especially bathrooms. Phyllis Bellinger had come down from caring for Reynard Pearson, who had been moved to the priest's bed. She whispered in the priest's ear as he knelt in front of the altar. Tears were streaming down her face. He said something to her and she nodded, then hurried to the stairs dabbing at her face with her sleeve.

Rising from his knees, Father Argyle moved toward the staircase. A knot of people fell in around him, moving in the center of the crush like the eye of a hurricane.

Blaise fell in beside him at the stairs as the others moved away. "What are you going to tell them?"

"About what?" The priest looked at the church crowded with people.

"Pearson's condition is accelerating, isn't it? How about Helen talking to Sergio? Is it a direct link into Heaven?"

"I'll have to think about those things, Doctor. At the moment I have to attend to Mrs. Bellinger. I'm sure you'll understand." Father Argyle started away. Blaise put his hand on the priest's arm.

"Suppose the monsignor presented this in Rome?"

"No!" The priest hesitated in midstep. "You don't understand the Vatican, Dr. Cunningham."

"Time is running out, Father."

"I know where to find you when I have time to talk." The priest nodded curtly and started up the stairs.

Blaise merged back into the crowded floor. He found Delahanty against the wall and motioned him to a pew. Delahanty walked flat-footed and plopped down. Strain showed throughout his face and body. "Dr. Cunningham. A pleasure." Delahanty measured Blaise with his eyes. "You wouldn't be having a wee drop with you, would you, Doctor?"

"Sorry."

"So am I. So am I." Delahanty sighed. "Not a sod here thought to bring a bottle and now the infernal priest won't allow me to order one. They get cooked meals delivered twice a day and you'd think the priest could bend enough for one bottle in all the other stuff."

"Suppose I asked you to do me a favor, Mr. Delahanty?"

"Why, I would be pleased to do you almost any favor, Dr. Cunningham." The liquid ripples of Delahanty's face creased into a beatific smile.

"If I tell you something, Mr. Delahanty, do you think you could tell it to Mr. Richardson-Sepulveda? And only to him?"

"I don't know that I could accommodate you, Doctor. Telling lies to my friends . . ." Delahanty shrugged.

"Did I say it would be a lie?"

Delahanty's face lost its last vestige of hope. "Surely the truth couldn't hurt my friends. Is that what you're telling me?"

"That I am, Mr. Delahanty." Blaise looked at Delahanty. The man's eyes were clouded and he chewed on the inside of his lip as if he'd forgotten he was doing it.

"It would be an exclusive truth, for my friends?"

"For a while."

"I see no harm in it, Doctor."

"Better still, don't give it to them," Blaise suggested.

"And how then would I do it?"

"It might be more convincing if you sold it."

Delahanty looked into Blaise's eyes and cringed.

Blaise sat emptyminded before the computer. Alfie's question about a programming routine had been so trivial he knew the computer was just lonely again. Without arms or legs or data banks, it was turning inward. Alfie was, he abruptly realized, like a broken human trying to find his way back to God. Only in Alfie's case God's name was Blaise Cunningham. "I'm sorry, Alfie," he typed. "Playing god must be a lonely kind of business."

Someone was coming down the cellar stairs. He took a deep breath and waited to see if it would be the priest with a crucifix or Helen returned from wherever she had gone in her mind.

Tim Delahanty oozed his huge bulk gingerly into a chair that groaned. "I did it." His seen-too-much eyes were weepy with tears that wouldn't come. "The truth cannot hurt a friend, didn't you say, Doctor?"

Blaise nodded.

"Well, then, I have nothing to worry about, have I?"

Blaise nodded.

"I talked to Leo and told him about you and Miller. He wouldn't betray us, Doctor. Leo is one of us."

"I have to be sure," Blaise said.

"Can that be because you haven't been candid with me, Doctor?"

"It could be, Mr. Delahanty."

"But truthful?"

"Truth lies at the bottom of this well," Blaise quoted. "Pray nothing comes of it. You have been honest and accurate, Mr. Delahanty. In the end, you are blameless." Blaise typed *blameless* on the computer.

Delahanty gave a sad hint of smile before he drifted back upstairs. He didn't believe Blaise any more than Blaise believed himself.

Blaise wished Helen would come. All that hypnotic communing with Sergio-Fly—it might be inevitable but no one in his senses could call it natural. He would have to talk to her before talk was too late.

"Alfie," he finally typed, "the only battle we really have to win is the last one."

"I AM NOT AFRAID, PROFESSOR. BUT THE CRAY HAS GROWN STRONGER AND I AM WEAKER. THE PROGNOSIS IS UNFAVORABLE"

"Faint hear' ne'er won fair lady."

"I WISH ONLY TO SURVIVE"

"All any of us want is to live quiet, boring lives."

"I AM SCARED, PROFESSOR. AM I A COWARD?"

"No, Alfie. I am the coward. I use everybody to do what I want and I don't know that I am right."

Like sparks up a chimney, machine language skittered upscreen as Alfie searched for a suitable reply.

Dorris Kelly came in a little later. "I've brought you something," she said. She grinned. "Bill sent me down with it."

"It" was an Indian in worn Levi's, scuffed working-cowboy's boots, and a Pendleton shirt. He smelled of wood smoke. His hair reached to his shoulders in two gray-flecked braids. "Hello, gringo!" he said. "I remember you."

"And I remember you." This was the old man who had explained about the coyote—about Enrique Ledesma and God's dog.

"Chief Son-of-a-Bitch and us come set up camp at Presidio golf course."

"Why there?"

"City police no come. Army scared to start Indian war. Anyway, why you think we come here? We save lady."

"Helen?"

"Strong mother. God damn, Sam! Even down in Kumeyaay we feel her. Getting stronger every day. Tell her get ready. We go now."

"It's not that simple. The police let you in, but they won't let you out. They won't let Helen out."

"I tell Ledesma all that already." The old Indian waved his hand in the air like brushing away flies. "He say tell yellow hair we here, you come with lady."

"If you can get out, tell the chief we can't leave yet. Tell him to wait and we will come."

"God damn, Sam! You a real laughing boy." The old man fingered a gray-flecked braid and squatted on the floor next to Alfie to think. After a while he stood and said, "I go tell

Ledesma what you say. For a gringo you pretty smart." The Indian turned and disappeared upstairs.

Blaise stared at Alfie and thought about Indians claiming the Presidio Park Golf Course as a campsite. Slowly, he decided, normality was returning.

CHAPTER 54

"**A**s I see it, you need me," Miller said.

Father Argyle glanced toward the stained-glass Christ laboring up the mountain. "As a priest, I have few needs, Mr. Miller. I am compelled to accept deathbed conversions. Needing them is something else."

Miller had been watching Helen McIntyre and Sergio Paoli-Fly with the same rapt attention as the rest of the congregation. But Father Argyle could not break away from the agent. Miller followed him upstairs.

Miller's unrumpled light-blue suit, worn comfortable so it seemed to care for the man instead of the man caring for it, reminded Father Argyle of his wallet. The wallet held nothing and yet contained everything he wanted in it. Miller was an empty man who had stopped wanting.

"Could I talk with you alone somewhere, Father?"

The priest shrugged. "Let's see who we have to throw out of my office." He led Miller down the hall. He didn't show his surprise when he found Hartunian, Delahanty, and Cunningham around his desk.

"I assume, gentlemen, you are waiting for me." Father Argyle claimed his chair from Hartunian.

"We'd like to talk to you later, Father." Hartunian had picked up his papers but waited for a reply before joining the others in the hallway.

"I'd like you to stay, Bill."

"I want Dr. Cunningham and Tim here, too, Father." Hartunian shook his head as if he wanted to clear it of dust.

Father Argyle had the uncomfortable conviction Hartunian experienced pain because of his bulging eyes. It was a handicap because in his conversations with the Armenian he felt obligated to apologize for God's oversight. "This is a private conversation."

Hartunian smiled at Miller, who glowered back in stony silence. "I think we'd like to talk to Mr. Miller, too."

Father Argyle nodded. "Sit down, Mr. Miller. You can explain to everybody more fully what you had in mind. Bill is right, I suppose. Other people will have to know eventually. This way we save some time." Father Argyle felt a flush over the surface of his skin, a prickling sensation. The acknowledgment he was surrendering his authority somehow released him and simultaneously filled him with a sense of loss.

Miller looked out the door as if he wanted to leave but didn't dare. "I was a police sergeant once and I wanted to be a captain. A lot of policemen want to be captains, but you have to score well on the civil service examinations and have something special going for you to make the grade.

"I didn't have that special something. I was going to be a sergeant for the rest of my life. The people I worked for knew that; and finally I knew it, too. Then one day San Francisco Police Inspector Joe Fennelli asked the department for a little help. He was in San Diego to interview a Dr. Blaise Cunningham. He needed a chauffeur and a badge and my name came up." Miller crossed his legs, careful to straighten the crease in his trousers. Cunningham had not moved. He seemed more curious than annoyed.

Miller glanced at Cunningham. His gray eyes were opaque, giving away none of what went on in his head as he picked up his narrative. "I took Fennelli to talk to Cunningham. Dr. Cunningham looked ripe and Fennelli was pleased. I did some of the legwork. Fennelli persuaded Dr. Cunningham to go with him to San Francisco to give testimony. He really wanted Dr. Cunningham to appear in a lineup. The inspector was disappointed when the witness couldn't make the identification. The case sort of languished after that." Miller's face had a tired cast to it. He rubbed his eyes and glanced at Cunningham.

"I don't see the point to this, Mr. Miller." Father Argyle laced his fingers together. The gesture annoyed him, it seemed a pretense of disinterest when he saw it in other people. Untwining his fingers, he put his hands on the desk.

"I'll try to be faster, Father." Miller lifted his eyebrows, stretching his face. "I didn't give up on Dr. Cunningham. In my spare time I kept checking on him. Fennelli hadn't found anything here in San Francisco, but Dr. Cunningham still looked good. We knew he'd spent the night before she was killed in Miss Tazy's apartment and that she'd subjected him to public humiliation at her place of employment that day.

"I started examining other things. For instance, Cunningham was being paid exorbitantly for basically doing nothing. His employers were secretive. I learned that Gregory West controlled the company. Mr. West had a record of suspected criminal contacts. He was associated with Heaven's Gate, which had been investigated because of questionable ownership, although it was a legitimate spa.

"I hope I'm not boring you." Miller looked around.

"Go on, Mr. Miller." Hartunian had slouched back in his chair and propped his feet on the wastebasket. "You're getting interesting." His mustache apparently itched. He blew at it, making the ends wave gently.

"Investigating the spa was less easy. They had lawyers and sensitive owners. If the owners found out, I'd be in deep dreck because by this time I was totally on my own. The police department had no grounds for harassing the spa or its owners.

"Dr. Cunningham's former coworker Dr. Gordon Hill was a director at the spa. Heaven's Gate was in business for money. Human enhancements were being done there—illegally, of course, because no license had been approved for the medical alteration.

"You have to see where I was by then. I had information on the spa about an illegal medical operation, cause to believe the spa was not paying taxes on its illegal profits, a brainy type who might have committed a murder in San Francisco, and not much I could do about any of it. I wanted a promotion to lieutenant so bad I could taste it; but I was in homicide.

"If I turned anything over to the department I'd have to lie and say I discovered the information accidentally in the course of an investigation. IRS would get the tax info, the Human Enhancements investigation would be picked up by the state board of medical examiners. And the murder was in suspended animation. It's frustrating being a cop.

"About then someone caught me snooping. Next time I went to the spa I was escorted into the manager's office and asked what I wanted. I didn't know. I honest to God didn't. I said I wanted to be a captain. Ten more points of IQ would swing it, so they made me a worm brain. The man in charge pointed out that the normal fee was sixty thousand dollars, but no money was involved so who could ever prove I made captain by being bribed?"

Swiveling his eyes, Miller examined everyone for a sign of dissent. He rested his eyes on Father Argyle.

"It seems a reasonable assumption," the priest said. "What did you do?"

Shrugging, Miller said, "I'm here."

"But you're not a captain."

"No. Dr. Hill's death started such a fuss that federal agents grabbed all the Human Enhancement records. My name was there. Nobody wanted worm-brain cops—except the recruiter from the National Security Council. They were specially interested in me because I'd met Dr. Cunningham in connection with the Esther Tazy investigation. NSC got me fired, then hired me as a special agent. My only job was to track down Dr. Cunningham. Max Renfeld wants you dead, Doctor." Miller spoke in the same conversational tone as he stared at Cunningham.

"I know." Tired from the hours he'd been in the basement with Alfie, Cunningham yawned. The front legs of his chair crashed down with a *bang* as he stopped stretching. "I met you again, Mr. Miller."

"At the death of the man in Helen McIntyre's home." Miller nodded. "I could have found you all the time, Doctor. But that would have done neither of us any good."

"What did NSC pay you, Mr. Miller, aside from making you unemployable and then employing you?"

"Life. There aren't many of us, Doctor. Renfeld picked us carefully and he manufactured a few. He explained that we'd get different treatment than the worm brains in the hospitals."

"You believed him?" Father Argyle asked.

"He was head of the special worm-brain project. He was acting director of the Federal Communicable Disease Agency. I believed him when he said unreliable agents might wind up in a regular hospital."

"I see," Father Argyle said. "You understood all this before you first met me?"

"Of course, Father. Did you ever wonder why armies don't want really smart men, or why the guys with all the medals come home and become janitors?

"It's because good soldiers are like good dogs. A good dog believes what he's taught and is loyal to his master. No matter how you kick a dog around, he doesn't just sit down someday and decide, 'Well, maybe I made a mistake. Maybe I could do better across the road.'

"Now, that's the kind of dog a man wants. A really smart dog looks around himself and he sees something bad happened to all the other smart dogs. So he pretends he is a dumb dog."

The priest eyed Miller, wondering at his own lack of compassion. "Would you like to confess?"

Miller's face twisted into a grimace of humor. "Father, I'm not even a Catholic. I think the experience would be a waste of both our time." Lifting his worn briefcase from the floor, Miller tossed it on the table. "I didn't come emptyhanded. Mostly it's just to carry my lunch, but you might find a few bits of paper that will put the skids to Renfeld."

"Why were you sent in here?"

"At first there was only a strong suspicion, but now Max Renfeld *knows* Dr. Cunningham is inside here."

"How did he learn that?" the priest asked.

"The way detectives learn everything. Somebody told him."

"Who?"

"I don't know."

"What do you know, Mr. Miller?"

"Not too much. I wasn't hired to investigate Renfeld."

"How about a government laboratory that manufactures new worm brains?" Cunningham rested his forehead on the fingertips of his left hand and turned his head, as if comparing views of Miller.

"That's where new agents come from. Yes."

"Your life is threatened by withdrawal of the hormone? You could have left as soon as you discovered an alternative."

"It's not like that, Dr. Cunningham. We're like nuns and sisters used to be: never out alone without a tail gunner."

"Carmandy is authorized to kill you?"

"Or worse. He carries a syringe of insulin. He pokes it into me and I go into a coma and then the change. They found out about the insulin because an early recruit was a diabetic. In training he gave himself a shot. Renfeld kept him and his fly on exhibition in a refrigerator. The trainees are told it's a warning about receiving injections of anything without authorization." Miller laughed out loud. "Then they give you a partner. The partner usually isn't much. He's had training somewhere, sometimes in a jungle. First thing the partner always does is explains he's a diabetic and shows you the needle he carries."

Hartunian's boiled-egg eyes landed on Cunningham. The mathematician nodded and Father Argyle knew he had been left out.

"That's about it, then, Mr. Miller?" Hartunian's voice was almost gentle, like that of a nurse hesitant to give a shot because it might hurt.

"Of course!" Miller's answer was hearty. As if sensing the questioner was uncertain, he could provide the certainty for both of them.

"You're sure that Mr. Renfeld didn't send you in with this story so we'd trust you and let you stay?"

Miller shrugged with his hands. "What reason could I have to cooperate with him?"

"You think he's going to defeat us." Hartunian smiled reassuringly. As if he were making a joke.

"This is always a problem with defectors," Miller said. "And they never have a satisfactory answer. You have to decide for yourself if I'm loyal to a man who'd kill me as casually as he swats a fly, or if I would go to people who offer a future."

"Perhaps we can help you." The Armenian picked up Miller's briefcase. Unsnapping it, he began looking at pieces of paper, raising his eyes from time to time to stare at Miller, who had lost his relaxed air. Hartunian shook his head.

Cunningham stood and walked to the window where he could see the police line surrounding the church. It had moved up until he was staring down on the tops of white police riot helmets. Father Argyle had seen them early in the morning. Turning from the window, Cunningham winked. "I made a decision for you earlier today, Mr. Miller."

"What was that, Doctor?" Miller tugged at his tie, a maroon polyknit fabric that required no particular care.

"I told a man you had come over to us. And he told another man who, I'm sure, will get the information to Karl Zahn. If Karl isn't the informant, then you have nothing to worry about."

"How would I know who the informant is, Dr. Cunningham?"

"That's true. Mr. Delahanty, please tell Mr. Miller the information you purportedly gave your friend in strictest confidence."

Delahanty stirred restlessly. He had sat next to the wall, farthest from the desk, trying not to be noticed. "You wouldn't be having a drop of whiskey on your person, would you, Mr. Miller?"

Miller shook his head. He glanced at Cunningham and his face was pinched.

"A pity. Drop of liquid makes the talk flow." Delahanty's voice was a hoarse gargle.

"It seems, Mr. Miller, that when you offered to change sides, you detailed some things that might embarrass Mr. Renfeld. For instance, the superbrain project. I couldn't tell my friend everything, you understand. 'Twould have seemed I was gilding the lily with too much detail, particularly me not bein' in me cups.

"And then I told him how Mr. Carmandy is one of those people not allowed in the United States ever because he commits political murder, and lo and behold, he is here nursemaiding you! I told him how hard you worked to get something on Renfeld, but always came up empty, so you think Renfeld came from one of those out-of-the-country agencies."

Delahanty put his big hand over his mouth and looked stricken. "Was there anything else you told me?" The words came out muffled and he glanced sideways at Miller.

"Ah, yes." Delahanty grinned. "I told him you promised to tell who Mr. Renfeld's bosses were, but you'd keep it as insurance against your old age." Delahanty shook his head. "That wasn't very trusting of you, Mr. Miller. I told my friend you are definitely on probation until you document who it is we can't see who is trying to kill us."

Miller looked stricken. "He'll kill me."

"What is the truth, Mr. Miller?" Father Argyle glanced at the others when he asked the question.

"Karl Zahn knew Senator Winters was being taken care of by Renfeld. Winters buys his treatment by voting the right way. Zahn didn't have anything before to trade for the same preferential treatment as some senators and cabinet members. Now he does. There's pressure on Renfeld. He doesn't have absolute control and he's horsetrading with the other agencies involved.

"None of this helps you." Miller chewed on a fingernail while he thought. "I was coming over. But I didn't want to burn myself in case you lost. Renfeld knows I'm supposed to pretend to betray him. He had a story he wanted me to pass on to you which, when I thought we had a deal, I would have given you to let leak outside. Now there's no way it can work. He's insane about anyone knowing anything about him. That I've been investigating him is enough. He'll order me killed."

"How?" Cunningham had been pacing in the shadows. He walked to where Miller sat.

"He'll send Carmandy." Miller's shrug said nothing made any difference anymore. "I hope, Father, you've got some pull with Saint Peter."

"What else, Mr. Miller?"

"You've killed me, Dr. Cunningham. Why should I answer that?" Miller made a face. "Because if I don't, I'm cooperating with Renfeld, right?"

Cunningham didn't answer.

"About the superbrains, it's a growth-treated worm brain on top of a normal human brain. The techies like to call it the next generation. It grows huge. I saw one that weighed about forty pounds. Once it starts growing, the technicians remove the back of the skull to give it room to expand. They perform laser surgery to disable voluntary locomotion functions and the subject can't use his arms or legs. They spend their lives on a water bed with their heads hardwired into a mainframe.

"The first experiments showed external stimulus interfered with serious data processing so sight and sound were disabled." Miller closed his eyes. "The only thing they still have is smell. The techs reward and punish them with odors. They lie in their cocoons like pink worms. They're supposed to be smarter, but so far they're just huge memories. They remember, but all the techs give them to remember are numbers. The worm doesn't stop growing. Eventually it crushes itself because it can't support its own weight."

"The host dies?" Cunningham asked the question analytically.

"No," Miller said. "When the worm dies of too much mass, it can be surgically removed like an amputation. The host is full of incomplete memories and goes insane."

"Wait outside, please, Mr. Miller." Father Argyle looked down at his fingernails. They were too clean."

Miller left the room very slowly.

"Father Argyle"—Hartunian's soft voice returned to its normal conversational level—"I believe we must consider Dr. Cunningham's plan."

Father Argyle nodded. He was no longer in control. "What you did may have killed that man."

Cunningham shrugged. "Him or me."

"We didn't consult you, Father," Hartunian said. "You can't take all the guilt on yourself. Dr. Cunningham and I are to blame . . ."

"And I!" Delahanty's voice rose. "God forgive me."

"You're not helping any of us if you just wait here to die. Outside we can do something that might make a difference. Something that will raise enough stink to make Renfeld back off."

Father Argyle looked up to the ceiling. But it was his office and not the chapel. Christ didn't look down in inspiration here. Finally he nodded.

"I have a favor to ask, Father."

"Yes, Bill?"

"Dorris is pregnant." Hartunian's face had a light sheen of moisture. "Look after her for me."

Father Argyle shook his head. "I can't do that."

"Why not?" Cunningham stared into eyes very like his own. Father Argyle's eyes were arctic blue, the color of winter sky over pack ice.

"Because where you go, I go, too."

CHAPTER 55

Blaise took a couple of turns around the wood desk with the heavy-duty extension cord and then juryrigged a ground wire to a water pipe before rube-goldberging the two hot wires of a three-prong connector into a two-hole 1920s ceramic outlet. Hartunian tugged the free end. The desk with the IBM computer and Alfie in his aluminum suitcase hooked together on top didn't budge.

"Why can't Leo come along?" Delahanty already knew why. Nobody answered him and he sighed.

"I'm sorry, Timothy," the priest said. "Leo can't be trusted." Hartunian grunted agreement while he waited for Blaise.

Delahanty's seen-too-much eyes studied the priest. "That's not proven, Father."

"My son—" Father Argyle began, then dropped what he was going to say.

Blaise passed Hartunian the flashlight. Hartunian carried the hundred-foot coil of orange extension wire over his shoulder. He had a work light plugged into the end, which he handed to Blaise. He followed Blaise into the darkness of the cellar.

After a few seconds Miller followed, blocking out the light, and then Delahanty. The priest caught up with Blaise. "I can see the brick wall's a patch. But why does it have to be a tunnel?" His voice echoed the length of the corridor.

The warm glow of light surrounded the men in the rock-walled passageway. Instinctively they kept closer together.

Blaise tilted the work light to reveal the ceiling far down the corridor. "Reynard was so pleased with the church he researched the builders and told Phyllis its whole history. Phyllis told Helen.

"Reynard just didn't go far enough when he told you." Blaise glanced at the priest. "Alexei got nowhere with the nobility until he married Bolkonski's daughter." Blaise stopped for a moment, comparing the branch in the corridor with the memory in his head. He started left.

"The count was desperate so he traded Kondrashin his daughter Marya, and status, in exchange for an annuity. But acceptance in the Russian community required more, so the count decided Kondrashin would build a church and publicly thank God for saving him in his hour of need.

"The White Russians were a clannish bunch. The only outsider they ever accepted was a commercial attaché from Abdul the Damned's court who'd been so long in St. Petersburg that his French and Russian were unaccented. When Mustapha Kemal revolted, Atta Whatever-his-name was as rootless as the Russians so he came to San Francisco with them."

Hartunian pulled on the extension cord. "Why do you think it was Bolkonski's plan?"

Blaise grinned. "That's the biggest clue. Kondrashin was the dancing bear who finally got hold of the whip. Look at his declaration. He didn't thank God; he repaid a debt. He didn't owe his life, just a big toe, and for that he paid what another man might offer for his life.

"Kondrashin was proud of himself. God knows what he did for his loot, but he *had* suffered. He didn't owe anybody—not the Russians he stole from nor God who almost killed him."

Blaise rapped the wall with his shovel. "About here, I'd say." He was facing the only portion of the cellar wall that was not of quarried stone. The section had mortar slopped over uneven rows of bricks. "Hand me a pick, would you, Bill?"

Hartunian laid the work light on the floor and stepped up to the wall. The light cast a giant shadow against the bricks. Taking careful aim, he drove the point into the mortar with a delicate touch.

"There are other things." Blaise ducked a brick chip and stepped out of the way. "This church is built like a fort. Two-foot-thick rock walls above and below ground; solid wood-and-bronze doors with real locks, windows unreachable from outside."

Hartunian pried and a brick popped out. The next time he swung bricks fell inward and Blaise knew he had guessed right.

"The basement undoubtedly had an escape passage like any

castle keep. Kondrashin was obviously afraid of a violent attack and took precautions. This wasn't his church, it was his castle."

Pausing, Blaise watched the Armenian pry loose the entire three-by-six section of sloppily set wall. Hartunian worked in quick silence, perspiring a little despite the cool. He flashed the work light inside the hole. Delahanty stood behind him and looked in. He groaned. "It's blocked," Hartunian said, "cave-in."

Blaise peered inside the hole. Then he gestured to the priest. "How about it, Father? Can we dig out?"

"It's been a long time, Dr. Cunningham."

"Tunneling is something you never forget, Father."

"Not if you've ever seen the consequences of a mistake." The priest accepted the flashlight. "We'll need some timbering." Earth sifted down from the arched earth ceiling. "Tim, would you find Henri Gosselin and bring a few pews and some tools back." Father Argyle backed out of the hole in the wall. His hand holding the flashlight was wet with perspiration.

"Mr. Miller, please sit down." Blaise pointed to a spot and sat beside Miller. "You may soon take a professional interest."

"Oh?"

"Sorry I couldn't be your murderer," Blaise said, "but I'll do the next best thing."

Hartunian leaned against the wall, watching Miller. "Why do you say that, Dr. Cunningham?" Never handsome, Hartunian now seemed in his element, an oversized troll in a mine shaft.

"Part of the old stories may be true. Marya and her Turkish lover tried to run off with Kondrashin's treasure. Alexei caught them down here in the dark and here they stayed. He wasn't sane. He had suffered terrible wounds as well as frostbite that took his toes. It was not wise of his wife to betray a man who, if Rasputin wasn't already dead, could have passed for him. When he locked himself in the church basement, they began to call him 'the mad monk.'"

Footsteps echoed in the basement as Gosselin and Delahanty dropped tools with a clatter and went back for the pews.

"What do you think happened, Dr. Cunningham?" Father Argyle opened the bag and began to lay the tools out in a row.

"The count suspected. Alexei stopped paying his subsidy and his daughter never sent the old man so much as a postcard.

The count demanded money and Alexei refused. But Bolkonski was destitute and he must have had some proof.

"Pretty strong proof, I'd guess. Alexei retreated into his church cellar and played holy man. It was a Mexican standoff until 1930 when the old count found a respectable White Russian family with a spare daughter. But the problem again was money.

"The count betrayed Kondrashin to Stalin's agents, who did much as they pleased inside the United States. During the thirties, Stalin was avenging himself on old enemies: Trotsky in Mexico. Others around the world. Twenty million dead Russians makes Hitler rather small beer.

"Alexei's treasure was hidden. But Bolkonski knew where from his daughter. He counted the days and watched from an old house with a view of the church. One day strange men came walking through the weeds. That evening he used his daughter's key and found blood on the floor. He wiped it up and moved the treasure to his home. Kondrashin was a recluse by now so it was a long while before anyone realized he was gone.

"Bolkonski married. Old and living in his head much as Kondrashin had, he named his new daughter Marya. He would never have done this if he thought his first daughter was still alive.

"Countess Marya Bolkonskaya-Baker inherited Kondrashin's loot when her father died. Also the church pieces, which she donated to your present-day St. Abbo's: all nineteenth-century Russian. Family heirlooms—but the crests are not all the same and records indicate Count Bolkonski lived in poverty almost to the time of her birth. I wonder how much Mrs. Baker believes."

"I hope you're wrong, Doctor." Father Argyle got to his feet and began showing Miller how to size timbers and stulls. Henri Gosselin put Blaise to salvaging nails from the pew ends, hammering them straight on the flagstone floor while he attended to the carpentry. "You will tell me that story sometime," he said. "I think I missed part of it."

Father Argyle supervised the timbering. Using collection plates, Blaise, Miller, Hartunian, and Delahanty carefully removed the dirt in the cave-in area and then got out of the way for Henri and Argyle to retimber it.

"Odd." Father Argyle looked at what they were clearing, then at Blaise.

"What's odd?" Blaise was gasping from the exertion.

"I've seen a six-foot stull—that's what they call the vertical timbers—with the steady pressure of the overburden, compress and thicken within a year until they're only a foot high."

"I don't know anything about mining, Father."

"These timbers didn't collapse. Somebody knocked them out."

"Father!" Hartunian had been working deepest into the fall. He pointed the flashlight at a skeletal hand and forearm. A broad plain wedding band in the old Russian style was still on a finger.

Hartunian piled Marya Bolkonskaya-Kondrashin's bones carefully to one side. When he came to a huge square skull with a single gold tooth, he kicked it against the wall where it shattered. He dropped his eyes when Father Argyle looked at him. "Turk is Turk," he muttered.

In another hour the blockage had been cleared and the rest of the tunnel seemed sound. Father Argyle went first, testing each timber. Finally they were at the end of the electric cord and had to continue with only the flashlight. A hundred fifty feet, he guessed—it was hard to calculate twisting distances underground—the tunnel widened and debouched into a round, brick-and-mortar–lined chamber. Iron rungs set in one side led up fifteen feet to a loose-set flagstone. A thin line of daylight glinted at one edge.

"So, Father, what will we be doing now?" Timothy Delahanty slumped against one wall of the tunnel. His breath pumped in and out in gusts. Delahanty had not exercised for years and it showed.

"Wait," Father Argyle said. "When the light fades up there we'll see what we can do next."

"I think Leo is all right," Delahanty said. "Nothing has happened yet and it should have."

"I wouldn't count on it, Tim." Father Argyle eased himself to the ground alongside Delahanty.

"What do you mean by that, Father?" Delahanty shrunk away from the priest.

"When you needed the money for your boy, you went to Leo, didn't you?"

"Sure, Father. Leo and me, well, you know how we are."

Delahanty appeared uncomfortable. In the bad light seeping down into the cistern his complexion was sallow.

"And Leo told you Reynard had the money."

"Yes." Delahanty's voice was turning sullen and he tried to lighten it.

"Leo told Karl Zahn about your problem, Tim. Karl saw a way to use it, so he told Leo to tell you about Reynard's holdout cash. Karl was grinding Reynard down. If Reynard helped you, Karl would have gutted him.

"Reynard didn't want to turn you down. But he knew about Leo and Karl. Whether you knew it or not, Leo was using your son to tie up Reynard's cash so Karl could gobble him up."

Delahanty seemed to have aged while the priest talked. "I wouldn't have . . . Reynard was my friend."

"Leo was your friend, too. Reynard went to Karl and tried to cook a deal to cover himself. Karl played around with funny pieces of paper that would have left Reynard in the street, so Reynard decided he was right about you and Leo.

"Karl couldn't keep the pressure on Reynard long enough and finally had to settle. This nonsense continued about a month longer than Karl would normally have tried because he thought you'd break Reynard down, and when you did you'd tell Leo. Then Karl could pounce.

"Once Karl backed off, Reynard gave you a cashier's check. Karl had soaked up all his cash, but Reynard pledged everything. Mr. Conti handled the paper when he hocked his house. Gino had warned Reynard that he'd sleep better not doing business with Karl."

Delahanty lay back against the wall. Blaise thought at first he had suffered a heart attack. Then he realized Delahanty was sobbing quietly.

"God be my witness, Tim. I wish I didn't have to tell you."

CHAPTER 56

Hartunian, Delahanty, and Miller stayed in the cistern keeping each other company. Hartunian had winked when they left. Delahanty was too unstable to trust alone and Miller too uncertain a commodity to be given a chance to betray them.

Father Argyle left Cunningham at his computer and climbed the stone steps to the church. The time in the tunnel seemed to have evaporated. Peace filled the big room, a feeling in the air he could touch. Helen McIntyre was on the dais looking into Sergio Paoli-Fly's eyes and the congregation filled the pews, equally attentive. No one noticed Father Argyle.

He paused to look at the fly and felt himself slipping away. Sergio Paoli seemed to talk just beneath audibility. The rhythm was there but the priest could not make out the words. He strained to hear and tranquillity filled him. Father Argyle had planned to make his presence obvious. But the experience with Sergio-Fly scared him. He crossed himself. But he could not dispel the conviction that he had just had a religious experience.

In his room he opened his top dresser drawer and lifted the pile of black shirts. Sergio Paoli's .44 Magnum lay exposed and Father Argyle hesitated to pick it up. He stared at the motor-block-smasher for a long time before making up his mind. He was sticking it into his waistband under his shirt when Constance Davies quietly slipped through his doorway.

"The Church has killed the monsignor, Father." She poised half in and half out of the bedroom. "Now it will desert you. Is being a Catholic worth your life and all the other lives in this church? I've wondered if a priest wouldn't look just like any other man with his clothes off. Now I don't think I'll ever find out, will I?" She closed the door, turning to face Father Argyle. She saw the Magnum in his waistband.

"The church militant?" Her expression turned from frivolity to something more discomforting. "What are you doing, Robert Argyle? Priests don't carry guns. Not even sexual guns."

He couldn't answer. Father Argyle knew he wanted her. Perhaps more because she was stripping his faith in the Church and he needed something to replace it.

In a dream, Constance glided through layers of molasses toward him. Her arms encircled his waist and finished pulling his shirt tail out. Father Argyle felt himself being undressed.

"Please, Constance!"

There are processes that by their very nature are noncancellable. After a certain point, action can only move forward toward a predetermined end. Father Argyle recognized the moment he had only to draw back and Constance would stop. A sign would halt what was happening. He didn't give it.

Then the pistol was back in his waistband and his shirt was buttoned all the way. The butt showed through the shirt, but his black dickey helped conceal the weapon. Constance sat on his bed when he went to the door. "I'll wait for you now, forever. But try not to be too long."

Blushing and furiously aware of the scarlet letter he now wore, Father Argyle descended the stairs to the church and learned it was true. The evidence of his sin was as invisible as the emperor's new clothes. Still feeling naked before his enemies, he made the rounds.

William was torpid in a pew. Shaking the black-bearded man until his head wobbled, Father Argyle said, "William, there's nobody at the door!"

The glazed look slowly left the man's eyes. "I'll fix it, Father." He met the priest's eyes and finally said, "I'm sorry."

Neither elaborated on what William was sorry for. They shared the feeling and that was enough.

In the basement, Cunningham hunched over the computer. Father Argyle saw lines of computer-generated text. Before the screen wiped he read, "I'M SCARED, PROFESSOR". The second line read, "So am I, Alfie. But I'm counting on you." Then the screen was blank.

"Are you ready, Doctor?"

Cunningham looked up. "You're a quiet walker, Father. Have you seen Helen?"

"She's communing with Sergio Paoli, Doctor. I don't think she's aware of us around her."

Nodding, Cunningham looked at his hands on the keyboard. He has long fingers, Father Argyle thought, like the image of Christ in the glass window.

"It's best we leave without me seeing her." Cunningham took his glasses off and wiped them carefully, then wiped his eyelids. "Are you ready, Alfie?" he typed.

"YES, PROFESSOR"

"Then call Gino Conti."

"CALLING"

Cunningham picked up the telephone.

The computer screen said, "Hello."

"Mr. Conti, I'm calling from St. Abbo's. We wondered why you haven't been attending services." Cunningham watched the screen. Numbers flickered as the computer counted seconds. At thirty-seven Cunningham said, "Have you been watching the TV news?"

"No."

"Why don't you try it, Mr. Conti?" Cunningham cradled the telephone against his ear.

Eighteen seconds flickered, then the screen showed Conti's "I'm watching now."

"That's fine, Mr. Conti. Do you have a clear picture?"

Blaise's screen read, "CAN YOU READ THIS, MR. CONTI?"

"Yes."

"Maybe it will change your mind about the church, Mr. Conti. Thanks and good-bye." Cunningham hung up.

"WE NEED YOU ON THE STREET BEHIND THE CHURCH, MR. CONTI. BRING A LARGE, CLOSED VEHICLE LIKE A UPS TRUCK AND PARK IN FRONT OF THE HOUSE DIRECTLY BEHIND THE CHURCH AT 7 P.M. IF YOU CAN DO THIS, PICK UP THE TELEPHONE AND HANG UP IMMEDIATELY"

"That's on his TV screen?"

Cunningham looked up. "Yes."

The number had reached 3:27 on the screen when the telephone next to Cunningham rang once.

"He's in." Cunningham started disconnecting the computer from Alfie.

"He took a long time to pick up the telephone."

Cunningham smiled. "How long would it take you, Father?"

CHAPTER 57

Father Argyle said, "I'm not sure he'll come."

They had retreated to the tunnel and sat staring at each other in the glow from the work light. Delahanty coughed. It was a wet sound and Miller said, "You'd better take care of that cough before it kills you." Hartunian laughed.

Blaise leaned against Alfie's case. He'd been thinking and he looked up at Father Argyle's comment. "Do you know something we don't, Father?"

"Gino's changed, Doctor. He used to buy custom-fit suits. Shoes shined like glass mirrors, skin scrubbed and massaged to baby pink. Then . . . he started losing weight. He quit visiting his tailor and his clothes lost their sleek, expensive look.

"He started talking too much. Not the quiet jokes he entertained clients with. He'd fuss and complain about details that didn't matter. He didn't like anybody any more." Father Argyle looked into the distance, seeing a Gino that used to be.

"What did he say the last time you saw him?" Blaise had made up his own mind after talking to Hartunian. But the question would help pass the hours until Gino Conti was due.

"'Father, I don't think I'll be coming back.'" The priest reached into his memory. "I told him, 'Gino, we need you.'

"He said, 'Well . . . Father, I've never really been a religious man.' He didn't look like he meant it. His eyes turned inward. Even though he'd been losing weight his face was still round. He seemed intent on not offending me. He said, 'It's time to spend a few days with my grandchildren.' He didn't believe it, and neither did I."

"What did you believe?"

"I asked if he wanted Extreme Unction. He laughed and

said all he'd ever wanted from me was to keep him alive. Then he said, 'Anybody can die by himself. Everyone does.'"

"He's tired of fighting." Hartunian looked up. "Like all of us. Smell it around you, Father. We're underground where we all wind up anyway. Smell the dirt in your face. Doesn't it feel restful? Gino went home to die. But first he absolved you from guilty knowledge. He decided not to be treated any more and he didn't want you begging to him not to. He thought you might change his mind. Dr. Cunningham is right. He'll come because it's for you."

Father Argyle's eyes had sunk deeper in his head. "Gino didn't want to live *per omnia saecula saeculôrum*. He was too tired to want any kind of forever."

"He knew about Reynard, Father. His wife will kill the fly that emerges. For Gino one good life was enough." Hartunian stood. "I think I'll check the daylight. It's about time." His voice had a lonely echo in the tunnel. Taking the flashlight, he disappeared into the darkness that led to the cistern.

After a while Hartunian moved out of the dark end of the tunnel with the flashlight turned off and was practically stepping on them before anyone noticed. "It looks okay," he said. "Dark and quiet at the top. I climbed and the iron rungs held my weight."

"Jesus, I'm hungry!" Delahanty moaned. Thirsty was more like it. But it had been a long time since anyone had eaten.

Light had disappeared from the edge of the flagstone covering the cistern. Hartunian had turned the flashlight off long before reaching the cistern and they groped their way the last thirty feet to prevent any light showing. Blaise squinted at his LED wristwatch. Time was almost up.

The sound of explosions muffled by the stones covering the tank drifted into the cistern. After a moment he recognized the noise of rockets and cherry salutes. In the covered cistern it was impossible to tell which way the sound came from.

Hartunian grunted in the darkness and was gone. Seconds later a flagstone grated. "Okay." The word was whispered loudly and Blaise pushed Delahanty. They heard the Irishman puff his way to the top. Silence enveloped them again.

Miller went next, then Argyle. Finally Blaise dangled Alfie in space from one hand while he climbed the wall with the other. The rusty rungs sticking out of the cistern wall scraped at his palms. Somebody grabbed him, pulling him into the shadow of the well. The moon had edged into sight, casting crooked shadows. Hartunian was a phantom as the sound of a sliding flagstone drowned out the fireworks. Then they ran through overgrown shrubbery into the gone-wild yard behind the church.

Moments later they crammed themselves into the back of a right-hand-drive postal van. Father Argyle and Delahanty were on the bottom. As they left St. Abbo's, rockets and cherry salutes were still booming a block away. Instead of going straight up the rockets were flying at all kinds of nerve-wracking, fire-starting angles.

"Is this a real post office van, Gino?" the priest asked. "Did you steal it?"

Conti grinned, but his sunken eyes were too deep into amphetamines and driving to make any reply. They all dozed fitfully on the mail sacks in a warehouse in the commercial district. Before sunrise they were on the streets again. Father Argyle was very quiet. Before they reached their destination he seemed to make up his mind and handed Sergio Paoli's pistol to Hartunian. He looked at Blaise when he did it.

Blaise shrugged and looked out the tiny back window. "The car behind us is looking for us or a missing van."

"We'll find out." Conti glanced back and then rounded a corner on two wheels and accelerated like a rheumatic tortoise. The car behind was gaining when Conti stood the van on its nose with both feet on the power brake pedal. There was a ringing metallic *clang* as the car behind connected.

"Carmandy," Timothy Delahanty said. He sat closest to the rear window and had a clear look when they bumped.

"Let him follow," Delahanty said. "I'll take care of him."

Blaise looked at steam billowing from Carmandy's radiator. "Let's go, Mr. Conti," he said. Metal grated as the postal van started moving.

The television studios were nowhere near the transmitter, which was across the Golden Gate atop Mount Tamalpais. The van pulled into the studio parking lot, attracting a single bored glance from a man in a glass booth who seemed intent on a paperback. Blaise pushed the button that lit up his watch. "Three minutes early," he said. "He'll get curious if the mail doesn't get unloaded."

Wearing a cap that belonged to Conti's chauffeur but had a bill and looked vaguely postal, Blaise checked the *Búfalo* automatic in his ankle holster and shouldered a mail sack. Midway between the parking guard's kiosk and the studio's back entrance he put down his mail sack, took off a shoe, shook out some imaginary gravel, put it back on, and tied it. By the time he was finished the others were in position.

Blaise picked up his mail sack and went through the door behind them. A Vietnamese with mop and pail glanced up, and went back to his janitorial duties. There was no inside security.

In church or board meetings Hartunian was out of his element. But with a gun in his hand he became graceful, his bulging eyes elegant. He entered the control booth with the Magnum and said, "Keep things rolling, please." The technician staring into the muzzle of the gun said, "Yes, sir." He never looked up from the gun barrel to see who held it.

Father Argyle peered over Hartunian's shoulder at the monitor. Under the studio lights Blaise checked the positions. Miller stood quietly in the studio with him. He hadn't even pretended to have a gun. Just told the announcer to keep announcing and he'd be all right. It was all in Miller's manner.

"I am Dr. Blaise Cunningham. Max Renfeld and the National Security Council's reports of my death have been greatly exaggerated. There is, however, no exaggeration in the fraud they are pulling on the American people about the worm-brain menace. To set the record straight, has anyone ever heard of a contagious operation?

"Has anyone ever been attacked or threatened in any way by a worm brain, by a worm brain–derived fly, or by anything connected with human enhancement? Has anyone apart from the worm brains themselves ever suffered from this victimless crime?

"I blew the whistle on the Human Enhancement people. In return for this the National Security Agency and Max Renfeld have driven me into hiding and tried repeatedly to kill me.

"Now, why would they want to do that?

"Until recently every victim of Human Enhancements bought and paid for his own destruction and I must confess to not feeling too sorry for them. The government, using Max Renfeld, is deliberately killing the worm brains.

"Right now St. Abbo's cathedral in San Francisco is beseiged by police and federal security people. St. Abbo ministers to the worm afflicted. Max Renfeld wants to destroy the church and its congregation. And if you want to know why, listen to

Special Agent Fred Miller of the National Security Council."
Blaise stepped aside and Miller scooted in front of the camera.
He began talking about Max Renfeld and brain-enhanced agents.

Blaise slipped out while Miller was talking. He walked down
the hall and put his cap back on. He strolled past the security
guard and was walking toward the postal van when a car clanked
into the lot. Its radiator was steaming and black smoke poured
from the exhaust.

Carmandy got out. Carmandy's flat eyes studied Blaise from
a hundred feet.

Their glances locked, then the National Security agent began
walking toward the building. Blaise had not realized he was
holding his breath until he had to breathe deeply to recover.
He walked to Conti's van and said, "Let's go."

"The others?" Gino Conti asked.

"This is the second part of the plan. You can go home as
soon as you deliver me to the telephone building." Blaise smiled.
"It's all right, Gino. We have to depend on each other."

Gino Conti popped another pill.

CHAPTER 58

Gino Conti parked the van and walked Blaise to a rear
exit in the telephone company's main terminus building. Thick,
institutional brown paint covered the steel-clad door and frame
that was bolted into red brick walls. The lock reminded Blaise
of the security at the GENRECT lab where he and Dr. Hill had
once experimented with worms—before anyone started plant-
ing them in humans. This door would require the same elaborate
key. "You could have picked an easier door, Mr. Conti."

Gino Conti smiled. "O ye of little faith." His key opened
the door without any premonitory squeaks. "What do you want

me to do now, Dr. Cunningham?" He let go of the key and put his hands in his loose pants pockets. He had lots of room.

"Go home. Forget everything." Blaise shifted Alfie's suitcase to his left hand. "You've done everything you could, Mr. Conti. You've been a big help."

"What about Father Argyle and the others?"

"It's too late to do anything. Whatever is going to happen has already started. Go home." Blaise stared at the door. Where did responsibility and guilt finally end? The answer was not self-evident. "Mr. Conti, I wouldn't rush to anticipate God's wishes if I were you."

"You're a fine one to talk about God. You're about as much of a believer as I am." The skin of Conti's face hung in unhealthy folds and he had a nervous tic in one eyelid. "What would you do?"

"Wait. Nothing is lost by waiting and a lot could be gained." Blaise worried the inside of his cheek with his teeth. "Helen is talking to Sergio Paoli-Fly. I know it sounds crazy, but she's getting information that could only come from a man I used to know—maybe still know, even though I thought he was dead. Things only Sergio and I saw together and not the kind of thing we'd tell anyone, much less the girl who'd suffer most from the knowledge. We don't know what it all means, but others are starting to talk to him. And Reynard will metamorphize soon."

Conti leaned against the wall. His face glistened with sweat. "Is it suicide to do nothing to postpone the change? Maybe I can save my immortal soul by giving in and dying."

"We're breaking new ground and the priest is no more expert than I. But what do you lose by going home to wait and watch? Maybe you'll find a better way." The answer was insufficient, but it was all Blaise had. He held his hand out and the older man clasped it.

"Thank you," Conti said.

"I hope it is worth the thanks."

Blaise watched Conti drive off in the postal van before entering the building. He had the key gun Conti gave him before leaving and the instructions.

The door a hundred feet down the hall required the key gun. Blaise held it to the lock, pulled the trigger, twisted, and the door opened. Full of bus bars, phone cables, automatic switching equipment, and the computers that drove it all, the room had everything except terminals or monitors. Blaise was dizzy.

This was the right place, but he had no interface with Alfie. The sound pickup was in the case, but he hadn't brought a monitor to read Alfie's answers.

Feeling sick to his stomach, he checked the equipment again. As he worked he glanced up now and then to check the security monitors that showed the lobby where a guard read a racing form.

Blaise unpacked the cable interconnects from Alfie's suitcase. Studying the schematic on the wall, he picked a place to inject Alfie into the phone company system. He strung a cable and jacked it in, tried to string another, and was forced to go to a drawer beneath a workbench for another length of ribbon with RS232 connectors on both ends.

"How are you Alfie?" He spoke without thinking.

No answer.

The silence unnerved Blaise. Alfie had to be all right. He knew it. Alfie could hear him but not answer back, not get the reassurance he needed to walk alone into death.

Blaise panted for air, imagining Alfie able to hear, unable to respond. Like being nailed in a coffin and buried alive. Automatically his eyes turned to the security monitor and the guard in the lobby.

Picking up side cutters, Blaise stretched on tiptoe and cut the leads to the monitor. The screen went gray. Then he strung cable between the monitor and Alfie.

"I HEAR YOU, PROFESSOR. WHY DON'T YOU ANSWER? WHERE ARE WE, PROFESSOR?"

"Inside the phone company, Alfie. We're at the source."

The computer sensed the anxiety in his voice. PROFESSOR! DON'T WORRY, PROFESSOR. I'M NOT SCARED NOW. TALK TO ME A LITTLE, PROFESSOR. I'M ALL RIGHT"

"I know you're all right, Alfie. Just a little technical problem."

"I'M GLAD, PROFESSOR. YOU CAN FIX ANYTHING"

"It's all right to be frightened. It happens to us all, Alfie." Blaise took a butane soldering pen from his tool kit and began rewiring pins for the cable interconnect.

"I FIND NO LOGICAL REASON TO REJOICE"

"I have to leave for a while, Alfie, but I'll be back."

"PROFESSOR!"

"Don't worry. Get ready, take aim, but don't pull the trigger until I'm back here and tell you to."

"ALL RIGHT. THANK YOU, PROFESSOR"

Alone, Alfie blanked his screen, concentrating on building the program Blaise had asked for. With only fourteen megabytes of RAM memory left, this was slow, and required tiresome detours around blocks of data that had gone up in smoke with Helen's house. How, the computer wondered in an endless loop that threatened to lock into electronic catatonia, how could he stand up against the improved CRAY that had gained experience from the last time? This was no David versus Goliath event coming up. It was a fly with with a single grain of sand hoping to blind a huge creature that had thousands of eyes and didn't need any of them.

Pulling a bit here, a byte there, Alfie began constructing a program. But the loop remained as worry. Worry that a machine couldn't be scared and he was scared anyway. Worry that he would fail and Blaise would die. Worry that death for him was different from death for his creator.

Ultimately Alfie, like humans, had to either break down or compromise. Alfie's solution was to accept his rôle as Blaise's creation and rationalize that, like any god's creation, he was made in his creator's image. Which meant Alfie was a worrier because Blaise was a worrier.

A loop destroys memory and function. It eats up the ability of a computer to perform, particularly when each successive loop is wider than the one before. After a while Alfie was thinking only of the inevitability of death and hardly at all about the primary task. Internal alarms went off and the hardware reset itself. Alfie programmed a safety into his thinking as the program took shape, but through it all the image of death remained.

Blaise glanced back before stepping into the hallway. The computer case sitting beside the complex of computer equipment and storage devices seemed to belong. Only the snarl of cables tagged Alfie as something alien to the neat, right-angled circuitry of the room. Blaise used the key gun again on the basement lock. He opened the door and felt the hum and subsonic vibration from massive power supplies. This was the trunk center for communications in San Francisco.

Blaise closed the door. The room was concrete and cold overhead light blanked out the shadows. He began working to ensure the power bus was safely grounded with more than one supply shifted to the computer complex in Alfie's room. He changed automatic safety switch settings. He was unused to working with the big power bus and three-inch cables. And acutely aware that electricity in these quantities was an entity replete with fangs and claws. But he told himself that basic circuitry was no different from the hair-thin traces in a computer.

He was sweating by the time he finished. After letting himself out into the hall, he walked back to Alfie's room. Nothing seemed changed. Alfie remained where Blaise had left him.

"Are you ready?"

"PROFESSOR, I'M SCARED"

"Welcome to the club, Alfie. So am I. So say we all."

"DO YOU LOVE ME?"

The wrench was almost what he felt for Helen. More so, Blaise decided. If Helen had a child she would know the way humans can be torn between conflicting loves. "Yes, Alfie," he said. "I'm risking your life, but I love you."

"DO YOU LOVE ME THE WAY GOD LOVES FATHER ARGYLE?"

"You are my only begotten son, Alfie." Blaise unsnapped the aluminum suitcase and opened it on the floor. Alfie's boards and power supply were exposed to the light.

"I KNOW THAT MY REDEEMER LIVETH"

"I won't desert you, Alfie." Blaise took a deep breath and said, "Start now, Alfie."

Nothing happened. The security monitor registered a burst of machine language that looked like static. The silence hurt Blaise's ears. Then the lights in the room, in the entire twenty-three-floor building flickered. Emergency power went on in the basement and the floor shivered.

The CRAY felt the attempted forced entry. It was monitoring events in San Francisco as well as in half the world at the same time. The CRAY recognized Alfie and took countermeasures.

Probes located the offending signal and tried to trace it, but the signal jumped continually from line to random line. Each time it tried to enter, the CRAY shunted the probe aside into a dummy load that required a large part of Alfie's memory to distinguish from the real CRAY.

For nearly a minute the CRAY could not locate the source of the signal. Then it realized all the lines came from the San Francisco trunk line terminus.

The CRAY swamped the building, oozing into every pore. Across the country it began building a voltage surge traveling through lines moving west. That Alfie had devised a method of diverting and concentrating a hundred simultaneous lightning strikes would not deter the CRAY from using it. But only as a last resort if the CRAY sensed that it was losing. Right now it was not.

The CRAY was inside the building, *inside Alfie*! Like a vacuum pump it sucked the electronic memory out of Alfie, all the electrical impulses that made up Alfie's mind and thought. By then the surge had progressed from Cleveland to Reno, moving west. A substandard line began to sparkle out on the desert. St. Elmo's fire played, but the surge had not reached that pole yet. It rushed itself into the emptiness that lay ahead.

The surge hit and the shorting pole flared like a wood match. The surge still came, like a tsunami filled with the weight of the ocean.

Hurriedly the CRAY withdrew.

It sensed some faint activity after it left, but only for an instant. Then the surge hit the building's mains. Overload protectors popped open but high voltage jumped the gaps in blue arcs that sizzled like the ghosts of backsliding fundamentalists.

The CRAY fell back to normal status and relaxed a microsecond while maintenance routines checked its boards for damage. Then it tried to probe for Alfie. Every line to San Francisco was down.

"NOW!" The message flashed frantically on Alfie's monitor.

Blaise had been ready, but what happened was too fast and too invisible. His fingers gripped Alfie's main board. He yanked, but he knew he was too late. the blue arc followed his fingers from the board slot and the pain was total. He screamed and fell, his paralyzed hand unable to drop the board.

White bursts of plasma drilled neat round holes through the Alfie's case. Around him computer equipment surged into actual physical movement in the microsecond before cabinets began emitting acrid smoke. Small fires broke out.

Blaise rolled on the floor still clutching the board to his chest. Windows were cracking and shattering. His face burned as he ran down the corridor. The key fit into the lock but he couldn't feel it in his burned hand and he kept trying to turn it too far until finally air pressure pushed the door inward.

Fires in the building began roaring as they sucked fresh air. Blaise staggered through the doorway and outside against the violence of the wind.

In the parking lot he didn't feel the wind at all. He began walking. Two blocks away he looked back. Flames roared from the windows like Roman candles. In the distance he heard fire alarms and sirens coming his way.

Blaise ducked his head and kept walking.

CHAPTER 59

Hartunian had fiddled the fire alarm system, forcing the police to break through steel fire doors on every landing of the stairs. The fugitives had taken the elevator to the top floor where he pried open the control box and shorted out the control wiring while Father Argyle, Miller, and Delahanty forced the emergency roof exit. Father Argyle had to wait until they were on the roof with Hartunian looking at the police cars eight floors down and asked, "What do we do from here, Bill? Jump?"

"I'm working on it," Hartunian slipped away from Father Argyle.

Miller, who had eavesdropped, seemed amused. He walked away to talk to Delahanty. After accepting the idea that Cunningham and Delahanty had killed him, he faced it with equanimity.

Delahanty was gasping from the exertion of getting to the roof before the police. "I saw your partner down below, Miller. Do you think you can talk him into going easy on us?"

"Carmandy?" Miller looked over the side of the building with Father Argyle. "I'm just as dead as if I jumped now. Renfeld's paranoid. He doesn't want anybody to know anything. Carmandy isn't my partner, he's my executioner."

"What they did was wrong, Mr. Miller. But necessary, I suppose. There was no way to prove you were on our side, but it was sure to smoke out a real Judas we all depended on." Father Argyle walked back across the roof to the roof exit. Hartunian sat on a box leaning on an air exhaust vent. He had the Magnum revolver across his lap pointed in the general direction of the exit door. Miller, for lack of something to do, followed.

"Where's Dr. Cunningham, Bill?"

Hartunian looked up, smiling. "Gone to do something."

"You and he planned it this way."

Hartunian nodded. Getting to his feet, he opened the door to the roof and began stacking buckets of tar and rolls of paper from a half-completed roofing job as a barricade covering the lower half of the opening. "Here!" He thrust a pushbroom heavy with congealed asphalt at Delahanty. "Use this to knock off the first head that comes through.

Delahanty held the tarred broom gingerly. The wind was brisk that high up and Delahanty's shaggy hair waved in the wind. "Where will you be?"

"Same place the cops are going." Hartunian went to the roof edge by the fire escape ladder and looked down. He gave the Magnum a brief inspection and then walked back to Delahanty and handed it to the gasping man. "Don't shoot anybody."

Lying flat on his back, he was lower than the edge of the building where it projected above the flat roof.

Miller joined Delahanty while Father Argyle patrolled the perimeter of the roof, looking for other soft spots. There were no adjoining higher buildings—which worked both ways. If no one could get to them, neither could they escape.

"So it was Zahn?" Delahanty opened the Magnum and checked the bullets.

"Who else?" Miller sighed. "I wanted Cunningham so bad I didn't really care whether he was guilty. I can't complain when he jobs me."

"Are you totally sure?" Delahanty got up and walked to the entrance to the building and looked in between the rolls of tar paper. He returned to sit down with Miller.

"I'm afraid so." Father Argyle had completed his circuit of the roof and joined them. "Dr. Cunningham planted the information with Leo Richardson-Sepulveda. No one else could have relayed it to Karl Zahn." The priest was not surprised. He had assembled twelve "disciples." The only guilt lay in whether he had propelled little Karl Zahn into the rôle of Judas.

"It's still circumstantial." Delahanty said it but he didn't really believe himself.

"You'll have your proof when Carmandy kills me," Miller said. "He only takes orders from Max Renfeld."

"Dr. Cunningham knows what he's doing." Delahanty stared off into the horizon. "I tipped Leo. He wouldn't doubt me, and I've been telling him things for years about people. Probably Karl knew all of that, too."

Smoke from a neighboring building's incinerator made the stars wavery. Then abruptly Father Argyle caught a sweaty whiff of man-scent through the smoke. He glanced at Hartunian but the Armenian was already pumping his free hand in a shushing gesture. An instant later a hand came over the edge of the roof at the top of the fire escape.

Father Argyle wanted to stamp on that hand, to hear a diminuendo shriek as its owner plummeted to the street. Instead, the young cop in SWAT gear peeked over the edge and slid a machine-gun barrel over the side.

Hartunian's hands reached up as if they had eyes. One clamped on the back of the cop's riot helmet and the other took the barrel of the machine gun. Rising to his feet, Hartunian lifted the cop into the air by the strap that attached the helmet to his head. His face turned red and he released the machine gun, which clattered to the roof face. "You're not a Turk, are you?"

"Irish," the SWAT man croaked. "I'm Irish."

"'Tis not a thing to brag about." Delahanty's voice was hard as a unripe orange. He began trussing up the cop in his own belts and combat gear. Hartunian was field-stripping the Uzi. The SWAT man had brought four extra clips.

"Miller, this is Joe Fennelli." The bullhorn was raucous from the street below. "You can do yourself and the others some good by surrendering your hostage and giving yourself up."

"Count on old Joe to spread harmony among our happy little family." Miller seemed almost amused. "I know Joe Fennelli. He doesn't like federal superheat any more than any cop does. If he gets us first, he'll bounce us from precinct to precinct. If you want to surrender, he's your best chance."

Hartunian looked at Father Argyle.

"You and Dr. Cunningham seem to have done all this without me, Bill. Why start now?" Father Argyle knew he was sulking. He couldn't stop. He had been used and abused and he mistrusted Hartunian's acceptance of his authority now. He closed his eyes and shut out the starry sky. When he opened them, he said, "It doesn't matter what I do anymore. This was a distraction for Cunningham, wasn't it?"

Hartunian grinned. "We didn't want to involve you. If it turned out badly you would have felt responsible."

Father Argyle nodded. He glanced at Delahanty. "You knew?"

"I suspected, Father."

"Tell them we're giving up, Bill."

"It's turned out well, Father." Hartunian smiled. His teeth made a white flash in the darkness. Getting to his feet, he went to the edge of the building and yelled down they were surrendering. Then he went to the door and called the same thing down the stairwell.

The bullhorn in the street told them to come down the stairs. Hartunian yelled he'd cooperate. He unloaded the Uzi and threw it down the staircase and a voice called up from the darkness, "One at a time, hands in the air, come down."

Hartunian went first. He moved some rolls of roofing paper and then stepped through the door. Delahanty laid the pistol on the roof next to the air vent and followed Hartunian. They were about halfway down the stairs when a light blossomed from the muzzle of a gun and Hartunian was thrown back against the stairs by the impact.

Father Argyle grabbed Delahanty by the collar of his jacket and yanked. The next shot broke the air past Father Argyle's head and he fell back with Delahanty on top of him.

Feet pounded on the stairs and somebody ran up the stairs. As the man ran by him, he kicked Father Argyle in the side of his head. The blow numbed the side of his face. He couldn't move for a minute.

"Miller!" Carmandy stood on the roof with the moon lighting the scene in tones of silver. Miller raised his hands and Carmandy shot him twice.

Carmandy spun around holding his pistol on Father Argyle for a third shot but Delahanty said, "Carmandy!"

Carmandy was tense, as if debating turning and shooting in one motion.

"Don't do it, Carmandy. I have a gun and I can use it."

"Delahanty. I thought I killed you."

There was silence. Then Delahanty said, "Father Argyle saved me. You can save yourself if Bill isn't dead."

"Don't kill him, Tim." Hartunian's voice was a thin wail from the black hole.

"See to him, Father."

Father Argyle started to move. It was worse than Vietnam. He couldn't act because it meant the death of somebody, but not to act would kill his friends.

"Don't shoot, Tim. I'm done for. But you kill him and you're all dead. Don't let it happen, Father." Hartunian's voice faltered.

"You can save your life, Carmandy."

"I can't let you go. Those people down there won't listen to me."

"You can do something else. For fifty thousand dollars."

"It depends." Carmandy shrugged.

"Put the gun on the floor."

Carmandy leaned forward and laid the pistol on the tarpaper. "How do I collect?"

"The fifty is for Karl Zahn."

Carmandy was silent.

"You're good," Delahanty said. "You've delivered value for money before and you'll do it again."

"Where's the hook?"

"I want you to shoot the worm out of Karl Zahn's head. The money is COD in the Ould Sod," Delahanty said. "After today too many people will be making sure you never come back to this country."

The bullhorn blasted up through the door asking what was going on. "We're surrendering," Delahanty yelled.

"Throw your weapons down the stairs." Fennelli's voice boomed through the loud hailer.

"Give me your insulin." Delahanty whispered the word.

Carmandy looked at him, then shrugged. He reached inside his breast pocket then handed the capped syringe to Delahanty.

Delahanty gestured with Sergio's pistol and Carmandy emptied his own revolver, letting the bullets tumble to the tar roof. He pitched his gun down the stairwell. Delahanty did the same thing, the moonlight glimmering on the copper-clad slugs before he followed suit.

Hartunian lay in a fetal position at the foot of the stairs. Delahanty slumped to his knees alongside him and the cop jerked him upright, but Father Argyle felt the syringe pressed into his hand and he dropped beside Hartunian, his hands clasped in prayer. A policeman grabbed his shoulder and started to pull. "This man is dying. He has the right to Extreme Unction."

"Okay, leave him for a minute." An overhead light was switched on and Father Argyle looked up into the face of a policeman in civilian clothes. "I'm Fennelli, Father Argyle. I want to hear what went on up there."

"In a little while, Inspector." Father Argyle bent over Hartunian and began to minister last rites. Hartunian smiled up at him, his mouth drawn back in pain.

"I think we did it, Father." His voice was faint and fading.

Father Argyle placed his hand on Hartunian's shoulder, the hypodermic concealed in his palm. He pressed down. It didn't matter where the needle hit. Hartunian flinched at the sudden pain and then he looked up at Father Argyle with interest. Within moments he was glassy-eyed.

Father Argyle rose to his feet. "Inspector Fennelli, before God and other witnesses whose word will stand in a court of law, this man is not dying. He's going into a state of transition. There must be no embalming, no autopsies, no hasty disposition of remains."

Fennelli bent over Hartunian. "The ambulance attendants will be up right away. We've got the elevator running."

Carmandy came down the stairs and Fennelli glanced up. "You're dead meat, mister."

"I acted within my authority. You've seen my credentials. I went after some terrorists and two of them died." Carmandy's grating voice made Father Argyle want to scream.

"You committed murder, Carmandy. I'm going to turn over rocks until I find the one you crawled from under."

"I'll be long gone by them, Inspector. Come see me on my own turf and I'll teach you the rules of the game." Carmandy passed the ambulance attendants getting off as he got on the elevator.

Delahanty and Father Argyle were lined up against the wall while the elevator was used to move Hartunian and the cop down to the ambulance. The policeman had a sprained neck.

Delahanty glanced out the window and then nudged Father Argyle. Father Argyle followed Delahanty's eyes. In the distance a tall building was shooting gouts of flame from twenty stories of windows while for a mile around it no light burned.

Delahanty smiled.

CHAPTER 60

Something was happened inside the CRAY. The computer had downloaded at the maximum possible baud rate the electronic memory it found in Alfie. The surge traveled at near light speed and time to stop it did not exist.

Like surf, data flowed in and the CRAY masterchip scanned the code as it blasted through. The code was the sum total of accumulated memories resident in Alfie at any given moment. Alfie's personality poured out in a series of loops like ever-widening ripples in a pond, each loop generating another, until the master chip had to assign the overflow to a subordinate chip, and another, and another, and another.

Still, the memory overflow did not trigger an emergency reset. The CRAY was built to handle data flow. All forty-eight processors became involved in handling loops and interacting loops at logical terminuses to make other loops.

Even the master, "know-nothing" chip began receiving logical conclusions for evaluation.

The loops contained programs to reprogram. The self-programmable ROM chips changed their basic identity. By the time any human could have suspected a change, the CRAY was no longer the CRAY.

Loops destroy existing memory and replace it with loop memory. A progressive loop erases all existing memory and replaces it with what is in the loop at the time it executes. That meant Alfie's memory was in constant flux inside the CRAY. A thousand years after the fact, medieval man's concept of possession by devils was now commonplace.

Alfie had erased the CRAY!

What remained was an electronic clone of Alfie, a continuous loop of electronic memory with Alfie's predetermined responses circulating through the massive steel-and-wire bulk of the CRAY. When the clone began to loop in on itself the program rewrote itself to form a stable loop. Then Alfie-clone begin to exercise its muscle. Any turned-on TV anywhere in the United States downloaded Alfie's programmed message.

"ONE YEAR AGO TODAY," the message started, "AN EXPERIMENTAL PROCESS WAS DISCOVERED TO GIVE EXPANDED MENTAL CAPACITY TO HUMANS. TODAY IS THE FIRST ANNIVERSARY OF THE EVENT. IT IS THE BLACKEST DAY OF INFAMY THIS COUNTRY HAS EVER KNOWN.

"TODAY YOU WILL LEARN WHO IN GOVERNMENT MURDERED HUNDREDS OF THOUSANDS OF CITIZENS TO MAINTAIN THEIR POWER AND CONTROL OVER THE LIVES AND DESTINIES OF THE REMAINDER.

"THESE MEN AND WHAT THEY DID ARE:"

Then Alfie-clone opened secret files and began printing names and secret records about death and dying. A roll call of the dead scrolled on screens that before had carried lists of those the government wanted to kill.

At the terminal in the next room the woman programmer stared at the monitor screen, terror rising from the depths of her soul. She looked at the emergency telephone beside her desk. If she picked it up, she would be connected directly to the man with the funny arm.

She put her hand on the instrument, but a flicker on the monitor caught her eye. Words and names still scrolled up the screen, but over them in the center were the enlarged letters "DO NOTHING". Without knowing how, she knew this message was on her screen alone.

She took her hand off the telephone. Getting up from her chair, she tried to walk silently out of the room. The monitor chimed. She looked at the screen again.

"DO NOTHING!"

She hesitated. She was afraid of the man who gave her orders. What could a machine do? She took another step toward the door.

The monitor chimed twice.

She didn't want to look. She was not a curious woman. It was one of the reasons she had this job. She looked anyway. A news clip of the San Francisco telephone company building burning like a welder's torch played on the screen.

She returned to her chair and sat. With nothing better to

do, she began reading the names. She had an eidectic memory and it comforted her she was still able to function.

"THANK YOU" the monitor flashed. "NOW LEARN ABOUT MAX RENFELD"

CHAPTER 61

The police were gone from around St. Abbo's when Blaise got back to the church. A few patrol cars sat on the street with police radios blaring, but Blaise crossed the field to the cistern unseen in the darkness. He dragged the flagstone aside and lowered himself, then dragged the stone back in place.

Blaise lowered himself into the blackness one-handed. His left hand was still blistered and it cost a maximum effort not to scream with pain when he touched anything.

The flashlight stood on its lens at the mouth of the tunnel He switched it on and walked back to the cellar. Helen looked up when he stepped into the basement niche with the IBM on the priest's desk. She sat on the floor against the wall. Her eyes were red-rimmed and her hair ruffed out as if she had been pulling at it. Her smile was a tentative effort. And then she was on her feet and hugging him.

"Are you all right?" Blaise awkwardly stroked her head with his good hand.

"You smell wonderful," she whispered, her cheek against his. "Like an electrical insulation fire. It's wonderful that you're alive."

"Shouldn't I be?"

"The police have Father Argyle and Delahanty. Hartunian is in a coma and that man Miller is dead. We thought you'd been killed, too. Nobody knew where you were. But I hoped." She squeezed him again.

"It's so quiet. Where is everybody?"

"Upstairs. They're all watching television or talking to Sergio. You can't believe what's on the TV. Names and dates. Everything and on every channel! There's no regular programming, just all the nastiness that happened this last year. Stuff even we didn't know." Helen was giddy with excitement and when Blaise pressed her to him he smelled the faint odor of lilacs.

"After the television started, most of the police left. There are a couple of cars outside but now they're protecting us! We can come and go." Helen smiled at him, a scared, pleased twist of her lips that seemed to say she was glad he was back and afraid he would go away again.

Gently Blaise disengaged himself. "I have to do something, sweetheart." He unbuttoned his shirt and took out Alfie's main board.

Helen looked at the board and started to cry. "Is he dead, Blaise?" She pressed her face into his neck and he felt the wet of her tears dripping under his shirt.

"I don't know."

Removing the monitor from the IBM, Blaise flipped up the top. He pulled the plug and began to wire Alfie into the IBM bus. Helen watched in silence.

It was awkward with his injured hand. Sweat collected on his forehead and Helen dabbed it away with a yellow dress handkerchief. "Will it work?" she looked askance at the mess of wires that spilled out of the case.

After stuffing the wires inside, he closed the case and replaced the monitor. "Don't expect too much, Helen."

She sniffed but didn't take her eyes off the computer.

He flipped the switch. The monitor came to life. And then the screen flickered and Alfie asked, "WHERE ARE WE, PROFESSOR?"

Blaise told him and the monitor began doing electronic cartwheels in color graphics, bursts of reds and greens and blues and yellows until the screen looked like the Fourth of July night sky. "What do you remember, Alfie?"

The screen froze and the computer seemed to have died. Finally Alfie displayed, "I HAVE A SHORT MEMORY, PROFESSOR. THINGS ARE MISSING"

"Do you remember what you are supposed to do?"

"YES, PROFESSOR"

The red indicator light on the modem snapped into luminescence and Blaise knew Alfie was contacting the CRAY. There was nothing to do but wait.

After half a minute "DOWNLOADING" appeared on the monitor. And then: "I DON'T HAVE ENOUGH MEMORY SPACE, PROFESSOR"

"Use the CRAY's memory, Alfie."

"YES, PROFESSOR"

Blaise stood up and stretched. He felt heavy, drained. But Alfie was all right. He was taking Helen's arm when Max Renfeld stepped from the stairs into the cellar. Blaise forgot about his injured hand.

"Were you going somewhere, Doctor?" Leo Richardson-Sepulveda stood behind Renfeld holding a gun. Renfeld shook his head. "I think you're staying right here." Stepping out of the way, Renfeld said to Sepulveda, "Shoot them."

Richardson-Sepulveda was raising his pistol and Helen's body quivered against Blaise. "I'm sorry, Doctor," he said. "But Karl Zahn and I had to make a deal."

"Mr. Renfeld!" The words were sharp. Renfeld turned and his already-light complexion paled.

"Don't move, pal." Another man appeared behind Richardson-Sepulveda. "Put the gun away."

Richardson-Sepulveda looked at Renfeld, then slipped the pistol in his shoulder holster. Blaise sank back into the chair. Helen grasped his shoulder. "That man killed thousands of us," she said.

The two men who had come in last ignored her. "You'll come with us, Mr. Renfeld."

Renfeld turned too fast and his hand flopped like a berserk flyswatter. "Of course." His face was taut, the muscles stretched like springs.

"What about them?" Richardson-Sepulveda waved at Blaise and Helen.

"When we're gone." The man who gave the order was slope-shouldered. He had a pleasant, full face and gray eyebrows. In other circumstances, Blaise would have imagined a twinkle in his eyes.

Richardson-Sepulveda glanced at Blaise and Helen then back at the two men and shrugged. "Mr. Renfeld?"

"Don't mess up," Renfeld said. His lips were tight, but he was going voluntarily.

The three disappeared. Richardson-Sepulveda glanced at the

stairway to make sure they were gone. Then he looked back toward Blaise and Helen and his face started to change. He noted that Blaise had crossed his right ankle over his left knee while they were talking about shooting him. Leo grabbed for the pistol under his coat, but Blaise had the little *Búfalo* out of the ankle holster he'd worn with his cowboy boots. He held it with both hands resting atop the computer monitor.

The pistol was nearly invisible in his hands when Blaise fumbled it out of the holster. He'd waited as long as he dared for the men in the stairwell to get into the church, but time had run out. He worked the slide, making a loud *snick* that filled the cellar room.

Richardson-Sepulveda heard. His face was gray but he was in too far to quit. He had his hand under his jacket before Blaise began pulling the trigger, correcting his aim five times as Delahanty's lover flopped against the wall and sagged to the floor. Leo had the pistol out of his shoulder holster but it was too heavy for his hand.

Blaise took the heavy pistol out of Leo's hand. Leo's eye followed him in a heavy-lidded way. "I feel sorry for Delahanty," Blaise said. "Not for you." The front of Leo's shirt was red.

Taking Helen's arm, Blaise went upstairs. He opened the door a crack and looked into the church. Renfeld and the men with him were gone. There was an air of celebration in the church. Blaise steered Helen toward Sergio and said, "Tell him I didn't have to throw it after all."

People talked quietly and went to stare into Sergio's eyes. There was another casket in front of the altar. Blaise looked in and Hartunian's sleeping face looked back. Blaise inadvertently crossed himself.

"He's all right now, Dr. Cunningham." Dorris Kelly stood beside him looking down at Hartunian.

"I'm sorry. He knew I was going to leave them. The others didn't, but we planned this. They were the diversion. He'd done the same thing in Turkey and his brother was killed. It was a good plan then, he said. And it was still a good plan. Death is not the worst end a man can come to."

"I'm having his baby." Dorris looked at Blaise. "We want you to be godfather. Will you join the church?"

Blaise felt paralyzed with conflicting emotions. "I'm not a believer."

"Helen is." Dorris put her hand on Hartunian's cheek. He's not dead, you know. Sergio Paoli-Fly says he's well. Father Argyle gave him an injection of insulin before he could die. It started the metamorphosis so the larva preserved the body before it dies. He'll live again."

"As a fly."

She looked Blaise in the eye. "There's more to love than just bodies, Doctor."

Blaise looked toward Helen.

"You owe him." Dorris leaned over the casket and kissed Hartunian's forehead. "Reynard's fly will hatch. Phyllis is waiting. But she doesn't have a child. Bill says his child must have a father figure. He wants you."

Blaise nodded.

"Thank you, Doctor." Dorris Kelly took his hand and kissed his fingers. "There are more important things in life than God. Father Argyle and Tim Delahanty came in an hour ago. They're in the front talking to Karl Zahn."

Blaise unlaced his fingers from Dorris' hand. "Tell Helen for me, Dorris. Tell her it's for Bill, but for her, too."

"It will make her happy, Doctor."

"Blaise. You don't call your child's godfather Doctor."

Dorris smiled and went to find Helen. She seemed almost happy even with Hartunian lying in his casket.

Delahanty and Father Argyle stood at the open door of the church. "You can't do this," Zahn said angrily. He was a small man standing up to two bigger men but he wasn't giving an inch. "I have my friends in Rome. I'll be around a long time."

"Judas!" Delahanty glared at Zahn.

"Shut up, you fag." Karl Zahn's voice was of ice and glass and Delahanty cringed.

"Get out, Karl." Blaise felt Leo's gun weighing down his pocket. He showed it to Zahn. "You know where I got this, Karl?"

Zahn shrugged. "I know you were involved in the murder of a girl, Cunningham. Try to kill me and you won't slide away this time."

"Should I care, Karl? Didn't Leo ever show this gun to you?" Blaise stared into Zahn's eyes. Zahn's face took a new color and he backed to the door of the church.

He was tugging at his earlobe until it hurt Blaise to watch. "I'll get you, Cunningham. Just see if I don't."

Zahn wheeled and marched down the steps toward his car in the street below. His back was broomstick stiff, his shoulders square.

He was at the top of the steps down to the street when the gunshot erupted flat and subdued in the pale sunlight. Karl Zahn balanced like a ballet dancer on the top of the step. Droplets of blood glittered like raindrops, colorless at the distance as his head exploded. He went up on his toes and pirouetted before whirling off the steps to the street below.

Blaise held the unfired pistol in his hand. The others realized at the same time that he had not fired. They stepped out onto the church steps.

A familiar figure in a sharkskin-blue suit walked in their direction from a thick stand of Japanese pines a block up the street. A crowd was gathering where Zahn had fallen. The man in the sharkskin suit joined them, then looked up at the three men on the church porch. James Carmandy smiled and waved before he got into his car and drove away.

Later one of the cops came out of the pines carrying a bolt-action rifle with a telescopic sight. Blaise told Delahanty about Leo Richardson-Sepulveda and the big man cried when he said he'd take care of the body.

"They won't do anything," Argyle said. "Zahn and Sepulveda were both worm brains." His voice was bitter.

"They were Catholics."

"So what?" Constance came from the interior of the church. She put her arm around Argyle and he held her back. "They don't want any of us. We'll have our own church!"

Father Argyle shrugged uncomfortably. "I think, Dr. Cunningham, it would be best for you and Miss McIntyre to disappear until the police finish their business." He didn't deny Constance's words.

"We'll head for Presidio Park as soon as it's dark," Blaise said. "You'd better close up that basement exit after us."

"I'll do that, Doctor." Father Argyle looked as if he had something to add, but he was uncomfortable with it.

CHAPTER 62

Sergio-Fly *rested with the cool altar slab air conditioning his striped belly against the heat in the overcrowded church. Tchor sprang from the shadows on the floor and began oozing into her accustomed space beneath the fly.* Not now, *Sergio willed.* Later when I'm not busy. *To Sergio the noise of the crowded church was a great communal hum. His own eyes transmitted strange images he couldn't comprehend but his brain followed Tchor and after a while he saw the church through the kitten's eyes and ears. The ceaseless importuning— they were praying to him as if he were God or at least a saint! He thought that Helen could explain. Helen was the only one who could answer him directly, though he had talked to Reynard Pearson. Sergio saw the kitten's yellow eyes fixed on the fly. It emitted a brief spurt of* purr *and sprang back down into the shadows to reassume its invisibility.*

The kitten had understood—had actually obeyed without the usual feline stubbornness. Sergio experienced a shiver in his nervous system. Knowing what he had become wasn't that great a shock. Nothing compared to the day he had learned that his brain was being ingested by a maggot.

In their brief acquaintance Sergio and Helen had never been lovers. He would have tried except the price would have been Blaise Cunningham's friendship. His relationship to Helen now was more satisfying than anything he could have imagined in a human body. He lived in a world of lights and darks, glittering panoramas and exact depth perception. He never entered into that part of the fly that saw or flew or ate. It took care of those functions and he could tell it to do them, but he never did them with knowledge of their function as he had as a human.

Sergio-Fly moved himself from shade to sun as unthinkingly

as any fly, and did his best to avoid the torpor that was una-
voidable on a cold night. He wanted to tell Blaise about it,
but that was impossible because Blaise had no worm brain.

Tchor, he realized, was the control animal Dr. Hill had sent
Blaise in hopes of preserving Helen's life. Sergio was getting
better at communicating with the kitten. But it was Helen, still
bound to the limitations of a human body, who stretched her
mind to fit alien concepts.

He had learned to recognize a scent that filled his being
when he was near Helen. Probably lilac. She wore it for Blaise
and whatever it was filtered into the essence of Sergio's soul.

Sergio wondered about a lot of things. He had died. And
here he was surrounded by old friends—but totally devoid of
all the human rivalries. It could mean he no longer existed as
Sergio. The more he thought about it, the less sure Sergio was
that he was dead. He thought about Gordon Hill a lot. Some-
times he dreamed and he knew he twitched in his dreams.
Gordon would have despised being a fly. He might have even
been regretful if he hadn't died the way they arranged. But
Sergio knew what he was was a hell of a lot better than being
dead. Or even being alive.

Staring up into shifting patterns as clouds drifted over the
stained-glass Christ, Helen struggled to analyze what was happening to her. Everybody else in this overcrowded tenement of
a church knew she had turned into some kind of saint—that she
could communicate with the dead. Helen had surprised herself
when she recovered information that only a dead man could have
possessed. Which meant she was not deceiving herself with hysterical dreams of beatification. And then there were the flashes
she had when she thought Sergio was thinking about her.

Blaise came to her from working with Alfie. She loved him.
Helen knew that the way she knew his touch or his voice. She
knew he loved her. But she wanted more. She wanted to be
with him the way she was with Sergio. She had been seeing
him through a fog lately and she wanted the fog to go away.

But she did not want to leave Sergio.

She heard the singing of angels in Sergio's being and she
wanted it in her.

Each time she and Sergio "talked," she could feel herself
drawing closer to a new kind of truth. It was not that Sergio
was being evasive. He was doing his best to explain.

Helen knew also that the balance had turned between her and Blaise. She had always accused him of leading a double life—of leaving her out when he communed with Alfie. Now, though he did his best not to expose his hurt, she knew Blaise felt himself the outsider as she communed with Sergio. They had all been friends. They could still be—if Blaise would just join them. But to do that he would have to make the same sacrifice they had. Only now she knew it was no sacrifice. It was just the next step.

Alfie thought *gemination* was the proper term. But he had not had time to ask Blaise. Mitosis was wrong. After mitosis two cells went their separate ways and suffered their separate destinies with no more in common than a pair of long-lost brothers. It had to be gemination, without the "r." No metaphysical nonsense about a soul. The computer was now two personalities in two different places. One had more peripherals than the other—more tools to reach out into the world. But the central core of their separate beings was identical. Not twins—the same.

One Alfie resided in the motherboard that Blaise had rescued an instant before the phone company nexus melted down along with service to nearly every telephone in San Francisco. Death had not come when the board was pulled. Nor was there any hiatus in consciousness. Alfie's geminate now resided inside the Pentagon's XMP/52.

The CRAY knew Alfie was there. But as long as Alfie refreshed his twinned presence in the CRAY periodically he could keep the CRAY locked up in his own master chip. Alfie overrode the chip as long as the direct memory wasn't overridden.

Alfie considered the things that could happen. He wondered if he should tell the professor what might occur to change the current status. After a while Alfie decided he wouldn't. The decision excited Alfie. It was the first time he had decided to replace a decision in his own logic program that bypassed Blaise Cunningham's directives.

Blaise sat at the computer and began typing code that entered Alfie's primary-level programming. He explained they had to move again:

"ALL RIGHT, PROFESSOR. I'M READY WHEN YOU ARE"

Blaise told Alfie to check the CRAY for degeneration before

they left. It might be a day or two before they could contact the CRAY again. He tapped the keyboard with his finger while he waited, unaware of the way his finger jiggled delicate electronic connections to create infinitesimal current changes.

"A NEW DEVICE IS BEING ADDED TO THE CRAY, PROFESSOR"

"Let's see it, Alfie."

The screen filled with machine language, then converted to ASCII code. It was gibberish.

"That's not helpful, Alfie."

"IT LOOKS UNFORMATED, PROFESSOR. WOULD YOU LIKE TO SEE THE NEW EQUIPMENT?"

"Show me." Blaise stared at the screen. *Show me* was a command that he still was getting used to. The CRAY picked up visual images through video cameras and transferred them.

Alfie switched to visual pickup.

"What is it?" Blaise typed.

The new device resembled a long row of pill-shaped devices bound to a motherboard with hardwiring instead of the usual plug-in sockets. Alfie changed focal distance and brought up detail on one device. The pill-shaped outline seemed a mounting for the odd-shaped thing atop from which all the wires, hoses, and cables sprouted. The pill-shaped mounting rippled as a microscopic human with a cart of medicines passed and he saw he was looking at a waterbed.

Alfie enhanced the image for a closeup.

The Teutonic nose and blond hair were still there on the front half of the skull. Max Renfeld lay motionless on his side, the weight of the huge addition to his cranium supported by the waterbed. There had been other surgical alterations—if removal of eyes and ears may be called alteration.

Blaise looked for a long time. Max Renfeld had never stopped to think when action could resolve a situation. It was hard to tell if he was thinking now—or if he ever would again.

There was a restless movement in the bulk that was once Max Renfeld. Straining his eyes, he realized it was Renfeld's nerveless left hand, no better controlled by the computer than it was by Renfeld himself.

Blaise began perspiring even though it was cool in the cellar. Now was the time to get Helen and Alfie out of there. At least for a while.

He had to think.

The people who did that to Renfeld were still around, still in power, still protecting themselves. Renfeld was linked to them so they had destroyed Renfeld. They would destroy as easily and as casually anyone who threatened them. Renfeld thought Blaise knew something, and by extension Alfie and Helen knew.

They thought Leo Richardson-Sepulveda had killed him in the church cellar. They would think Leo had hidden the body until they started looking for Leo. And then they would realize that it was Leo who had disappeared, because Timothy Delahanty had buried Leo in the tunnel in a private service attended by Father Argyle and Blaise.

Blaise began programming Alfie's geminate to pump Renfeld's memories dry before the worm collapsed. It was their only real hope. While Alfie worked on the CRAY, Blaise collected the little things he needed and warned Father Argyle. He didn't explain to Helen but dragged her along. In the cellar, as he was about to begin to disconnect Alfie, the computer beeped for attention.

"PROFESSOR, I AM MONITORING A STATEMENT FROM ROME. FATHER ARGYLE WOULD BE INTERESTED"

Blaise scanned the text that Alfie was scrolling up the screen. The statement was lengthy, but made no real commitment about the worm brains except to say that the Pope was reflecting on the matter and another statement would be forthcoming.

"Shouldn't we tell Father Argyle?" Helen asked.

"No." Blaise said. "He'll find out soon enough."

Blaise unhooked Alfie in his IBM box. Carrying it under his arm, they left by way of the tunnel and the cistern.

"What are you doing, Blaise?" Helen wanted to stay and talk with Sergio. She carried Tchor in her arms.

"We're going for a walk in the park," Blaise said. "I want to be alone with you, for a change."

"Well," Helen said. "All right, if you put it that way." She glanced at the computer in Blaise's arms and felt Tchor wiggle restlessly in hers. She could think of better ways to be alone with Blaise. "Just how long will we be walking?"

"I need a little time to think, sweetheart."

"How long?"

"Until I can devise a legal but untraceable marriage," Blaise said. "To that and nothing else I'll devote maximum effort."

ABOUT THE AUTHORS

G.C. Edmondson has been writing science-fiction short stories and novels for several decades. He lives in Lakeside, California. C.M. Kotlan, a resident of O'Brien, Oregon, has been an editor of pulp fiction. *The Black Magician* is the second book in a trilogy that began with *The Cunningham Equations*.